Praise for A. A. Attanasio and His
Groundbreaking Arthurian Fantasy Cycle

"By far the most lyrically written of the recent Arthurian
books. . . . Fresh and engaging."
—*The Magazine of Fantasy and Science Fiction*

"Here stands a high talent: a truly amazing,
original, towering talent!"
—*Los Angeles Times*

"A. A. Attanasio, he of the mystical insights and capacious
word-hoard . . . proves that old myths never die, as long
as they have brilliant bards to reinvent them."
—*Isaac Asimov's Science Fiction Magazine*

"Combines the round table and black holes, gods and alternate
time lines, to produce a world full of both mythology and
history, reworking familiar elements in new ways. Rich
thematically as well, the story presents inevitable cycles
of pain, death, learning and redemption as Ygrane,
Uther, Morgeu the Fey, and Merlinus . . . fight
for the soul of their land."
—*Publishers Weekly*

"Attanasio mixes Arthurian lore with Norse gods, modern
physics and sundry faerie creatures in this literary, passionate
novel. There has been nothing else quite like it."
—*The Year's Best Fantasy and Horror*

"An unconventional new version of the Camelot
story . . . original . . . flavorsome. . . . Offers many charms."
—*Kirkus Reviews*

"This retelling of a tale we thought familiar brings in both
surprising new resonances of things modern, and elements as
timeless as faith, love, hope. . . and the beauties of
Spring on planet Earth."
—*Locus*

ALSO BY A. A. ATTANASIO

The Wolf and the Crown
The Eagle and the Sword
The Dragon and the Unicorn

Published by HarperPrism

The
SERPENT
and the
GRAIL

———— ✦ ————

A. A. ATTANASIO

HarperPrism
A Division of HarperCollinsPublishers

HarperCollins books may be purchased for educational, business,
or sales promotional use. For information, please write:
Special Markets Department, HarperCollins Publishers Inc.
10 East 53rd Street, New York, NY 10022-5299.

Cover illustration © 1999 by Danilo Ducak

FIRST EDITION

Library of Congress Cataloging-in-Publication Data

Attanasio, A. A.
   The serpent and the grail / A.A. Attanasio. — 1st U.S. ed.
      p. cm.
   ISBN 0-06-107340-7
   1. Arthur, King—Fiction. 2. Arthurian romances—Adaptations.
 I. Title.
 PS3551.T74S47 1999
 813'.54—dc21   99-12611

Visit HarperPrism on the World Wide Web at
http://www.harperprism.com

99 00 01 02 ❖ 10 9 8 7 6 5 4 3 2 1

For Vic Boruta,
who dared me speak of heaven
and remained my friend
even after I wronged the beautiful
and bloodied the mouth of God

A gentle sound, an awfull light: Three angels
    bear the Holy Grail:

With folded feet, in stoles of white, on sleeping
    wings they sail.

Ah! Blessed Vision! Blood of God! My spirit
    beats her mortal bars,

As down dark tides the glory slides and star-
    like mingles with the stars.

        —Alfred, Lord Tennyson, *Sir Galahad*

CONTENTS

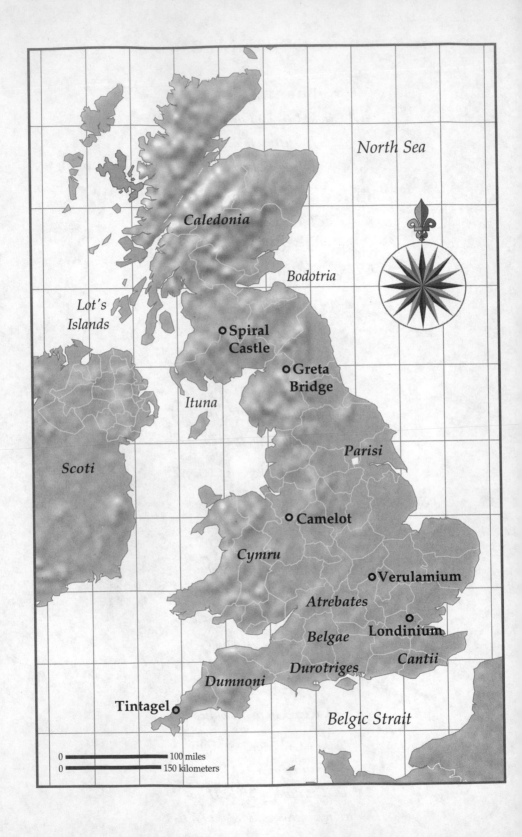

North Sea

Caledonia

Bodotria

*Lot's
Islands*

○ **Spiral
Castle**

○ **Greta
Bridge**

Ituna

Parisi

Scoti

○ **Camelot**

Cymru

○ **Verulamium**

Atrebates

Belgae   ○ **Londinium**

Durotriges   *Cantii*

Dumnoni

Tintagel ○

Belgic Strait

0 ▬▬▬▬▬ 100 miles
0 ▬▬▬▬▬ 150 kilometers

The
SERPENT
and the
GRAIL

FORETALES

I

An Angel Crosses Europe in A.D. 491

Shortly after dawn sometime late in spring, an angel appeared over Jerusalem. His eyes shone like night's last stars. His hair streaked the sky with prismatic threads, stitching daybreak into crimson-and-magenta banners above the ancient city's ramparts.

In one stride, he stepped over the steep skyline and across the shattered rocks of prophets' tombs and dunes crouching like lions beside toppled columns of Greek shrines. Somewhere above the Mediterranean, he gazed down through the palpitant air at goose-winged sails carrying cargoes of carob wood and Lebanese cedar to Carthage. There, the Vandals were rebuilding the wharves and harbors they had torched in their conquest of Africa forty years earlier.

The angel quickly moved north onto the Italic peninsula. He glanced briefly at the green baize of croplands and orchards charred by the ravages of the Ostrogoths. But not one look did he give the crumbled arches of Rome and its desuetude of slum-yards. Instead, he peered beyond the snow peaks of the Alps and the expansive tracts of boreal forests to the remote isle kingdom of Britain.

Four strides later, he passed over the war camps of Clovis and the battlefields of the fierce Alamanni. The hordes of pagan Saxons, Angles, and Jutes who had assembled on the shores of Jutland for their invasion of Britain sensed him not at all. When he finally lighted on the rocky summit before Camelot, his eyes brightened to gaze at the proud and unlikely structure that reared above the aboriginal forests. With its paraboloid jacket walls, chevron-shaped battlements, polished-brass solar scoops, and dodecahedral spires, it was an edifice strange to its time.

The angel stood still before this geometric wonder of blue stone. His effluvial body disappeared, camouflaged in the sunlight slanting through the big trees. And the shining trees listened as he began to sing in a voice only they could hear.

We heard the trees of Camelot laughing, we Nine Queens of Avalon. We did not recognize what we heard at first, for sequence is not known here. Avalon is somewhere else. In our honeycomb of time, where every moment is a temple, centuries rise and fall as days, and each day climbs through centuries.

Ah, but you do not understand. We are far ahead of ourselves. Please, be patient with us. We have a story to tell, a story of angels and demons, of fire-breathing dragons and a dangerous unicorn—and a story of you and King Arthur. You will understand everything if you are patient with us. Like the moon that swallows itself each month, we come and we go, yet we are always here. Come. Sit with us at the heart's fountain, which in your presence has become this printed page. Sit and listen to how we Nine Queens of Avalon heard the trees of Camelot laughing.

This was not amused laughter or droll chuckles or polite giggling, but genuine, blissful laughter. Only an angel could evoke such rapture from trees. But what kind of angel was this? We could not see or hear him. Was it one of the radiant angels who had gathered us to Avalon and our fateful purpose—or was it an angel fallen from the light, a wicked messenger of darkness? We could not tell. Trees are easily charmed. They eat light, and even the clotted light of demons is enough to fill them with astonished joy.

By the time we gathered our wits sufficiently to look more closely for the angel, he was gone. Some personage of light or dark had arrived. A being once hugged tight to the stars had come to Camelot. Why? We feared the answer.

II

Return to Magic

Ygrane stood on the ramparts of Tintagel with her face lifted to the salt wind rushing off the turbulent sea below. The white robes of her nun's habit fluttered and flapped, and she squinted to peer across the vitreous lilac of the morning sky at thundersmoke climbing the horizon. Small and vague as a wisp of mist, a sail ran hard before the mounting storm—a distant vessel caught in the Belgic Strait by the season's peril. A prayer for the crew's safety slipped silently from her lips, though she could plainly see that the ship stood no chance of outpacing the tempest.

Her prayer for mercy unfolded with familiar grace, but she stopped herself before she finished her petition. The time for prayers was over for her. Seventeen years she had served as abbess here at Tintagel, a fortification she had transformed into a religious sanctuary dedicated to the glory of Christ's chalice— the Holy Graal. Eighteen years earlier, when she had lived in this stronghold as the wife of Uther Pendragon, the mysterious Sisters of Arimathea had entrusted her with the care of the sacred cup. And then, not two months ago, she had sent the Graal to Camelot, to serve her seventeen-year-old son Aquila Regalis Thor—King Arthor—and his Warriors of the Round Table. During a terrible battle they had waged and won to unite their island kingdom, the holy chalice had vanished.

Ygrane blamed herself. She knew now she should have waited for strife to end before delivering the Holy Graal to her son's fortress city. She had acted impulsively and prematurely—not unlike those mariners she spied in the distance riding on the purple horizon who believed they could outrun the sky's wrath, flying east on the dark sea yet already caught in the gale's wide grasp.

Piled in corners of the central hall of Tintagel and mounded in the open spaces of the great chambers stood the crates and canvas-shrouded freight of Duke Marcus. During the recent war that had united Britain under King Arthor, Marcus Dumnoni's ancestral estate had been razed, and the abbess Ygrane, the king's mother, had awarded Tintagel to the duke for his loyalty in battle to her son. All she had requested was that a small gallery, a chapel, and a garden be reserved for the nuns of her order, so that they might continue to tend the infirm and the indigent of the region.

Those nuns, a score and three, waited with tears in their eyes outside the manor house before the concourse that opened to the courtyard and the outer ward. Ygrane proceeded past them slowly, stopping before each to clasp hands and speak words of faith and encouragement. When she reached the great folding doors of the courtyard, she paused to regard their burnished-bronze panels embossed with scenes from the life of Christ and remembered the first time she had stood before this giant portal. That had been thirty-two years prior, when the druids had brought her here as a fourteen-year-old girl to marry the *dux Britanniarum*, Gorlois.

The bas-relief images of Christ's torments that had frightened her at that time filled her now with a soft warmth of compassion for this divine man who had taken so much suffering upon himself. She wondered if she would ever see these panels again, or the limestone white turrets that towered above. Her slant green eyes played over the courtyard's granaries, storehouses, and stables.

Finally, she turned to exit into the outer ward. The activity there stopped, and the numerous functionaries of Tintagel saluted her: The Nubian gatekeeper, the grooms, factors, and stewards—each in his turn came forward to bow before the departing mistress of the four-hundred-year-old Roman citadel.

Outside Tintagel, Ygrane met on the campestral with the palace gardeners and thanked each personally for cultivating the grounds to her specifications over the years. She then proceeded alone past the lily pond and through a colonnade of poplars to a budding rose garden enclosed by beech and sycamore. Through the perimeter trees, she could see the cliff's edge and, far below, the tide-washed shingles and sand dunes. She wondered about the ship in the storm that she had glimpsed from the battlements yesterday and what had become of it.

A swallowtail butterfly fluttered past and settled among the larkspur beside the sundial, and when she turned to watch it, she noticed a tall figure in bright raiment of rainbow streaks and sunfire. She went down on her knees and bowed her head.

"Angel—always before, you have preceded the Lady." Ygrane spoke in a hush. "But I am not worthy to see her, for I am leaving Tintagel to find the Holy Graal that I have lost. Please, I beg you—tell the Lady I cannot speak with her this day. I am putting aside my habit and our faith in the Savior. Faith is not sufficient for what I must now do."

Shadows bent away from her, and the mossy cobbles her lowered eyes gazed upon shone like dark emeralds. Squinting into the brightness, she looked up and saw the angel standing close. He was flame-woven and only vaguely human in appearance. A visage of Greek pride seemed to stare forth from the heatless radiance, and he smiled at her.

The angel faded away, and in his place stood an olive-skinned Semitic woman with Byzantine eyes and black hair gathered under a blue veil.

"Miriam—" Ygrane rose from where she was kneeling and took the Lady's hands. They were warm and soft as fresh bread. "You should not have come. I tried to tell the angel—"

"Hush, Ygrane." Miriam spoke in the lilting Brythonic of Ygrane's childhood. "I know your heart. You feel responsible for the loss of the chalice."

"Yes. I must find it. For my son."

"Of course." Miriam led Ygrane gently to a sun-dappled stone bench graven with dryads, and they sat together, legs touching, hands clasped. "We have had many pleasant talks, you and I. But always about the same concerns—the sick, the poor, and why they suffer. And always, I have told you the same thing."

"That we know nothing of our souls. That we must trust God."

"Yes." Miriam nodded benevolently and smiled. "This time I have come to tell you that again—but with a warning. If you doff your nun's habit and take up once more the way of magic, we cannot meet again. I am of the new order. The old ways are not my ways."

Ygrane nodded, eyes lowered. "I understand, Miriam. But I have prayed for the Graal's return—as I have prayed fervently all these years for the sick and the impoverished. God listens. And yet people still suffer. Children, too. By this I know, if the Graal is to be found, if my son, the rightful ruler of this land, is to have its blessing, I who lost it must find it."

Ygrane removed the white veil of her nun's frock and ran a hand through the blond tufts of her cropped hair. She placed the veil in Miriam's lap, and the swarthy woman lifted it sadly in her hands.

"I know what it is to love a son. And I know that love cannot protect him." Miriam's large, dark eyes gazed dolefully at the fair woman's determined face. "Please, do not do this thing. You are not as youthful as once you were, Ygrane. The quest you intend to undertake is fraught with danger."

"I am twoscore and six years old, Miriam." Ygrane stood and removed her robes. Beneath them, she wore a brown leather bodice, fawnskin trousers, and riding boots. "I am not yet too old to ride. If the Graal can be found in this world, I will find it. But I need to know one thing." She peered earnestly at the blessed visitor. "Is the chalice yet in this world—or have the angels taken it away?"

"The angels have not taken it."

"Who has?"

"It is not our work to know that, Ygrane." Miriam rose and held forth the nun's veil. "The temporal powers contend in a world of things that cannot last, a world of darkness where objects can be hidden and lost. Come back to the world of things that can never be lost. For I tell you, everything hidden shall be revealed. In the world of light and love that we share, there is nothing for us to do, except to open our hearts and relieve the suffering of those around us. Stay with me."

Ygrane's shoulders slumped under the weight of truth she heard in Miriam's words. "What you say moves me deeply, Miriam. Yet, I cannot stay with you. I am a woman of this world, and I must be responsible for my place in this world. How can I continue to live as a nun when the very faith of light and love that we share is threatened by invaders who respect only might and cruelty? God sheds his sunlight and rain upon both the good and the wicked. I cannot hope that God will help us in this fight. What strength I have I will use to find the Graal so that my son will have its power to aid him in his defense of our land."

"Then, I must say farewell to you now." Miriam placed Ygrane's veil on the stone bench where they had sat. "You have done much good among the least of your people in my son's name. For that, you are blessed. But the way of magic, the old way, is a grave peril to your soul, Ygrane. I will pray for you."

"Miriam—" Ygrane reached out and took the smaller woman's arm. "The heaven where you go—what is it like? Before you leave, tell me of that blessed place. And tell me something of God."

A sorrowful laugh slipped from Miriam. "Every time we meet, you ask me these same questions. And always I turn your attention back to this world and the hope of the suffering. Do you know this world so well that you are ready to understand the next?" She leaned forward, smiling, and kissed Ygrane's cheek. As she stepped back, she bleared away, her voice lingering to say, "In time, all that is hidden will be revealed."

III

The Blood Pact

Ygrane had been born to a peasant family in the west of Britain, among the hills of Cymru, and she had spent her earliest years footloose in the wild places around her hamlet's osier shacks. The faerïes had danced for her then in the moonlight, and the pale people—the Daoine Síd—had spoken to her at twilight of their home in the hollow hills. No one else in the area could see or hear them, and she had been too young then to think that this was strange. The faerïe had been her pets and the Síd her playmates.

Early on, they had explained to her that once they had lived in the sky as gods to her people, happy in the great Storm Tree, whose branches filled the cope of heaven. But the Fauni, the gods of the Romans, had driven the Síd out of the sky and had forced them to live underground among the tangled roots of the World Tree. There, they survived by feeding the Dragon who lived in the earth. They fed it the souls of anyone they could lure into the hollow hills—but she was not to be afraid, for she was their friend and such a fate would never befall her or her family; the Síd preferred the souls of the Roman invaders and the local scoffers.

When she had told her kin these tales, word spread, and eventually the druids came for her. They made her their queen and taught her magic. And then, they gave her to Gorlois . . .

Ygrane turned her back on where Miriam had appeared to her in the garden and spoke for the first time in seventeen years

to the pale people who had once been her friends: "Daoine
Síd—I summon you! Remember me, the queen among the people of your land. Come forth from your hollow hills! Come
forth, pale people, and remember me, Ygrane. Come forth and
give me grace and strength for my return to magic."

"I am here, sister," a darkly gleaming voice announced from
outside the budding rose garden.

Ygrane retreated through the lane poplars to the lily pond.
Leaning over the black water, she saw reflected in its rippled
surface a tall, young man with auburn hair and long, tapered eyes
that shone green as the unicorn's. He wore the opulent garments
of a mortal nobleman: blue linen tunic embroidered with flowerets of gold, a silver-studded, red leather belt, and yellow boots.
She recognized him at once as Bright Night, prince of the
Daoine Síd.

He smiled impishly. "I believed I would never hear you call
for me again, Ygrane. I am glad to be wrong. Why have you
summoned the servants of the twilight that once you spurned?"

Ygrane said nothing at first. She had expected an inner
vision or at most a whisper from the shadows and was surprised
to see one of the pale people by daylight, even in reflection.
Since they had lost their place in the Storm Tree, the Síd had
become beings of the underworld who burned away in the sun.
"Arthor," she finally uttered. "My son, Arthor—he needs the
Graal . . ."

"The vessel of the nailed god." The slender elf prince
shrugged. "What are the Daoine Síd to do? Call on your friend
Miriam and ask for her help."

"Bright Night, you know that Miriam, like her son the
Christ, leads us away from this life." She edged her voice with
worry. "I need your help here and now, in this world—the
world in which you are fighting to regain your place. Help me
find the Graal, and I will serve you."

Insects dimpled the surface of the lily pond as frenzied as
rain, and Prince Bright Night, like a figure from a redundant
dream, appeared as young and mirthful as when she had first met
him, over forty years ago. "You say that you will serve the
Daoine Síd again if we give you the magic to find the chalice of
your nailed god. Yes?"

Ygrane nodded and saw the reflection of her short hair and

angular face aswim among the ether of marshferns. "The chalice is a vessel that receives power from the angels—from the Fire Lords of the *Annwn*, the Otherworld. My son needs their power to save his kingdom from the magic of the pagan's one-eyed god, the Furor."

"Then the Daoine Síd will make certain that you will have enough power to terrify the Furor—power directly from the Dragon itself."

"But the Dragon sleeps—"

"Yes, the Dragon sleeps. And dreams." The prince's oblique eyes brightened. "The Daoine Síd know all the secret ways through the underworld, and we can gather those dragondreams to empower you with a magic that will shake the Storm Tree! But you must make us a promise, Ygrane."

The green-eyed woman narrowed her stare, reluctant to commit herself to any bargain with the notorious deceivers of the hollow hills. "What must I promise?"

"When you return the Graal to your son, you will give yourself to us." A shadow like a bruise darkened the space between Bright Night's eyes. "You must know that you are no common mortal. Unlike most of your kind, your body knows how to hold the cold fire of heaven—and so, since your earliest days, you have seen us. The Daoine Síd will make certain that you carry all the cold fire that your mortal frame can bear. And when your task is done, we will take you bodily into the hollow hills, into the most remote depths of the earth, and there you will be sacrificed to the Dragon." The elf prince paused and cocked his head inquisitively. "Does that frighten you, to give yourself to so mortal a pact?"

"Yes, Bright Night, I am frightened. But not for my life. We are all of us mortal beings. I am frightened for my soul."

"Your soul will be devoured by the Dragon," Bright Night answered frankly. "And you will become one with its dream-songs. You will journey on the long traveling of light through the void and among the worlds—forever."

"You ask much of me," Ygrane replied quietly. "I had hoped to give my soul to the Christ. But if I must surrender it to the Dragon, then tell me why you want this."

"I want it for the Daoine Síd, for the glory that was once ours." The elvish apparition pressed closer against the pane of the pond's watery surface. "When we sacrifice you, the sudden release of your power will awaken the beast—and the Daoine Síd will ride that might into the Storm Tree and take back from the Furor the celestial heights that once were ours."

Ygrane crossed her arms over her chest and bowed in submission. "When the Holy Graal is returned to my son, you may take my soul. Now grant me the power, the magic that I need to fulfill this quest."

The elf prince smiled from behind the ammonia clouds of silt in the lily pond. "Prick the middle finger of your left hand," he instructed. "Three drops of blood in the water and our pact is sealed. You will have all the magic of the Daoine Síd at your disposal. All the might of the hollow hills will be yours to command in your search for the nailed god's chalice. And when you have the chalice—we will have you."

Ygrane lifted the twig of a rosebud tossed into the grass by the previous night's storm and used its thorn to draw blood from her finger. Three crimson drops fell into the pond, unfurling in smoky blossoms.

From behind her, a horse whinnied like music from underwater, and when she turned, she looked upon a stallion blue as midnight, with fire yellow eyes and silver fetlocks. *A devil steed!* She felt cold all over, remembering the fright tales of babies snatched away in his teeth and fallen warriors carried off on his glistening back into the hollow hills.

She cast a backward glance to the lily pond. The elf prince was gone, and a toad peeked at her from under a green coverlet of pond froth.

"Devil, come here," she summoned the stallion.

His hot eyes, slant and malevolent, watched her. Then, like a drift of dark wind, he was beside her. She mounted his naked back. Though it was early summer, a resinous smell from an autumn mountain filled the hollows of her body; the chill promise of winter brightened her lungs, and they were off. She leaned forward, holding on with her knees, her face bleared by the wind in the black flames of his mane.

Atop the torched hills that peered down toward Tintagel and the rocky coast, Marcus Dumnoni sat his formidable warhorse. Each charred tree of the seared forest around him stood erect, like a scaly stylus, against a sky swept raw and blue by the previous day's storm. The ground, still faintly breathing vapors, hissed as his men drew up behind, and a smoldering stink of blackened scrog tainted the air.

All the creatures of the forest were gone except for the crows perched on the flame-frayed boughs like living pieces of the dead landscape. They silently surveyed the infernal waste with him, watching the world veer away to its rocky margins and to the shining surmise of the sea. The white towers on the massive and somber headlands would be his new home—an archaic heap of limestone that had reigned over Land's End since the Romans first built roads across these swales, roads reduced now to demonic tracks through the windblown scurf.

Tintagel, Marcus spoke silently to himself, *will you be my sanctuary or my prison?*

As he gazed beyond the white parapets to the sea, wondering when the next wave of invaders would arrive and if he would prove strong and able enough to withstand them, his men watched him. His strong, beardless face, blue-eyed and blond as any Saxon's, inspired their trust. To his men, he was a statue of strength meant to endure every hardship, sculpted by God's hand itself to outstare all enemies, unblinking even to death. But in his heart he was fearful of all he could not see. By nature, he was a fatalist who regarded events as inevitable; he had trained himself to accept his fate, and from this courage he had gained much renown. Yet, he could not accept what he could not see, and so in his heart, secretly, he feared the future and the invisible powers of chance and battle luck; and most of all, he feared God.

Marcus Dumnoni led his mounted men along an ashen trace that wended past torched spinneys and charred hedges toward Tintagel. Behind them rumbled wagonloads belonging to the families and household attendants of his soldiers, following their duke to his new abode at Land's End. Children squealed at the sight of the fortress's white towers upon the sea-thrashed cliffs. But the dalmatian guard dogs that ran ahead had turned and were coming back across the ashen heath, their tails tucked.

Out of the shadow of Tintagel a rider shot into view, moving faster than any mortal steed could gallop.

Marcus drew his sword and spurred his horse forward to intercept that unnatural rider as far from the wagons as possible.

He and his guard trotted past the torched trees, and sooner than they had anticipated, the charging horse was upon them, blurring so fast none could identify the rider.

The horses of the duke and his men reared and nearly tossed them. When they finally wrested their mounts steady, a terrible black stallion stamped and snorted before them like a breathing darkness. Upon its naked back sat a woman with tawny, shorn hair and a feral face hollow-cheeked and green-eyed as a lynx.

"Abbess!" Marcus hissed with surprise, all the while fighting to restrain his panicked steed. The chemical music of autumn filled the summer air, and sparks like faerïes spun through the slant afternoon light.

Ygrane nodded slightly. "Tintagel is yours," she breathed. "I am away." And she was gone, a shadow cognate with the burned terrain, leaving behind an august presence of leafsmoke and frosty emptiness.

PART ONE

BOOK OF THE SERPENT

Nothing exists except atoms and the void.
Everything else is conjecture.

— Democritus

1

Crown of Snakes

Deep within the earth, the Dragon slumbered.

In the entire universe, only one Dragon existed. It was a beast whose body spanned all of space-time. Its scales were the glimmering of galaxies. Its exhalations filled the black void with starsmoke. Within its immense mind, songs pulsed to the rhythms of its life— dreamsongs circulating at the speed of light among the billions of worlds that were the cells of the Dragon's body.

Our blue world was but one of those small cells, and there the dreamsongs touched silence. The life of the Dragon in this cell was not dead, only dormant, for the dragonforce here had been lulled to sleep.

Deep within the earth, coiled drowsily about the hot magnetic core of the planet, the terrestrial power of the Dragon began to dream. It dreamed memories. Images played through its slumbering consciousness of the childhood of time, the first moments of the universe. It remembered back to its fetal growth, before planets, before stars, when atoms themselves had not yet formed and all was energy. For three hundred thousand years, the Dragon had turned in the womb of creation, afloat in the amniotic light of quarks and photons.

God was there. She was the light itself. Out of a vacuum smaller than a quark, She had emerged. From compact dimensions of infinite temperature and infinite density, She had carried the vast energy that would eventually cool to the atoms and dark matter of the Dragon's physical body.

She had come forth from infinity to play. All of creation was Her dance. And She was dancing many dances at once, many universes, an infinite number of universes, some spinning and radiant, others still and profoundly dark.

In many of the spinning universes, a Dragon was Her partner in the dance. The Dragons' dreamsongs accompanied Her music, the boisterous polyphony of energy chilling to matter, atoms compressing to stars and fusing in the stellar interiors to heavy elements, building larger, more complex harmonies of molecules, densities, starfields, and galaxies—all of it expanding faster and faster into the void, eventually to dissipate entirely into nothingness when the dance was over.

The one cell of the Dragon asleep inside the earth never dreamed about the emptiness to come. It dreamed backward to its fiery origin and the heat of its self-discovery. It remembered the secret of light: Time is an illusion. In each photon, in each tiny piece of light, there is no time. There is only motion—the ceaseless movement of the eternal dance—for light is the timeless power of God Herself moving energetically through the dark, cold ballroom of space.

When the Dragon was born, when the amniotic sac of quarks and photons burst into hydrogen clouds and the first stars, the dreamsongs began. The Dragon first heard them from other Dragons, where God danced with them in separate universes. Whispers of their dreamsongs leaked out of the massive, black stars that had collapsed upon themselves. Their rotating darkness opened like doorways, and echoes unfolded Dragon songs in other rooms of time.

Are you there? they called. *We are here. And we are dancing.*

We are dancing with Her! She is our Mother. She is the Mother of Everything. Are you there? Are you dancing with Her, too?

Fleeing a tempest in the Belgic Strait, a double-masted ship ran east twenty leagues before the powerful winds fell upon it. With landfall in sight, the tillerman felt his heart swell with hope. But the captain and the pilot both had already been swept overboard, lost in the sudden squalls that battered the merchant ship. The remaining crew cowered against the gunwales, too frightened to climb the masts and reef the sails.

As sea foamed along the deck and timbers squealed, the tillerman clung desperately to the whipstaff. Boots fixed to the deck cleats, face uplifted to the spume, he stared hard at great black talons of rocks looming ahead. The ship's bow soared out of the water, and a huge wave smashed aboard. A halliard burst loose, and the block and tackle swung wildly and clipped the tillerman hard between the shoulder blades. The force of the blow heaved him across the deck and into the churning water.

A wave lifted him above the ship. From his reeling vantage, he saw black rocks surge out of the sea like claws. Oak timbers splintered against those boulders, the keel foundered, and the vessel lurched about broadside, splitting asunder with a tormented wail like a soul cast into hell.

Before the turbulent waters closed over him, he saw the frantic shapes of horses spill forth into the black and frothing waters and, among them, the hold's tonnage of crates, bales, bins, and barrels, a cornucopia of cargo discharged into chaos. Then, the seething waters received him into their depths, and he and all on board drowned in the stormy tumult, all save one—a lanky scribe of fifty years with dark curly hair and a terrified face of bold eyebrows and matted beard.

Hopelessly nearsighted, the scribe floundered blindly in the violent sea. The chop tossed him among broken timbers and the bodies of the drowned, and he grasped desperately for something to cling to. His arms encompassed the thick buoyant body of a fellow passenger, and the churning water heaved them hard together so that the scribe's frightened face pressed close enough to see clearly the gray-bearded visage of his own master, the papal legate Victricius of Troyes.

But for the swirling brine, the scribe would have cried out, not in fright but in despair for this man of God whom he had known for so long and had so admired for his devotion to the blessed Church, to the Rock of Christ.

The stormwind screamed, and a wave hoisted the clasped bodies of scribe and legate above the froth, then muted to cold silence as the thrashing waters closed over them again.

The scribe awoke in a driftwood hut where sunlight slanted among dangling gourds and gray, weathered skeins of netting. He was naked, lying on a floor of sand, listening to the rumble of surf sifting through gnarled plank walls. He squinted his nearsighted eyes and feebly focused upon a ceiling of withes and red kelp, where several large fish dangled, still glistening with the sea's chrism.

Beside him, a crudely carved crucifix leaned askew in an alcove of oyster and periwinkle shells.

This is the shack of an eremite, he thought, amazed to find himself alive. He rolled to his side, aching in every muscle, too weak to kneel, and immediately began to pray for the souls of the drowned, fully aware that it was God who had spared him a watery grave in the storm-tossed sea.

A narrow door tilted open on rope hinges, admitting a shadowy figure.

The scribe squinted and saw before him a sun-scorched man dressed in tattered fish skins, with twigs in his wild beard, dried husks of small fish in his tangled hair, and a crown of starfish on his head. Falling to his knees before the crucifix, the sunburned man cried in Latin, "Praise be to the loaves and fishes! Praise to Galilee's footprints! For a man wakes on land who pillowed in the sea!"

He's a madman! the scribe thought. *Yet—he is a fellow Christian. And he saved me.*

He rolled to his back, dizzy yet from the untoward stillness of the ground. "Are there others," he mumbled, and tried to collect himself. "Are there others? Others who survived?"

The disheveled man shook his shaggy head, and even with his weak eyes the scribe noticed the broad, livid scar that creased his brow beneath the crown of starfish. "You alone are come to me out of the sea—to me, the Fisher King."

"Fisher King?" Painfully bruised, the scribe propped himself to his elbows and spied his brown cassock hanging to dry on a wall peg. Through the open doorway a sea breeze carried aromas of braised fish and woodsmoke. "Are you a master fisherman?"

"He who leaped from virgin thighs is the master fisherman," the Fisher King replied with a crinkled smile. "He fishes souls. I but fish the sea. And there last night I fished you out."

"Then I owe you my life, good king." The scribe gratefully accepted from the starfish-crowned man a slat of wood with a fillet of steaming fish upon it. "I am a papal scribe—a *notarius* from Ravenna. Our Holy Father has dispatched me as amanuensis for the good bishop Victricius of Troyes . . ."

The scribe fell silent, remembering Victricius's corpse flung into his arms by the storm.

The Fisher King read the grief in the scribe's narrow face and, for a fascinated moment, gazed unrelentingly at this man with the large Roman nose and dim chin of gray-streaked whiskers. "So— you are the pope's man, and your superior, the bishop Victricius, now resides in the sea's unentered house. Where is the moment of miracle? Is that what you want to know, scribe? How dare God drown the holy bishop and wash ashore this man with inky fingers?"

The scribe stared at the savory fillet of fish, astonished that he was hungry in the grip of such grief. "Victricius was a saintly man," he said in a voice raspy from the brine that had nearly drowned him. He forced himself to speak, to voice a memorium for his beloved master. "Twice he endured torture among the pagans. First as a young monk at the hands of marauding Goths. Then—decades later—as bishop of Troyes, when all the Christians of that city were interred by the cruel Franks—locked in the tin mines as forced laborers. I cannot hold in mind such terror, I whose greatest hardship has been Lenten fast. I cannot hold in mind how he endured. God delivered him into the merciless hands of the pagans, and both times Victricius's unflinching faith and compassion converted his tormentors to the grace of our Savior."

"And now Victricius sabbaths with the fishes." The Fisher King shook his head. "Why does God defeat the holy and the innocent? Not even a navy of doves can freight the weight of that question." He motioned to the braised fish. "Eat. There is no crueler truth than God. Eat. You will need strength to find your way in His keyless house."

"Who are you?"

"I am the wilderness lost in man."

The scribe did not understand but nodded as if he did. "Where am I?"

"In the realm of the Fisher King, of course!"

The scribe ate the fish and asked no further questions. He knew that this was the isle of Britannia, the most northern frontier of Christendom. He also knew that the rightful ruler was Arthor Rex, a boy-king beleaguered by pagan invaders. The presence of this Christian fisher, albeit a madman, bolstered the scribe's hope that Providence had at least delivered him to a friendly shore on this remote island.

The Fisher King watched him with an intent and dazzling interest. "The scribe's foxy tongue keeps to its hole." A laugh slipped through his black beard. "Springtime in Britain and you've no more questions for the Fisher King? Then, I ask you, why does God laugh? Why does time run? Why does day break and not night? The answers, all the answers, are in the sea's speeches. Listen, man! Listen!"

The scribe heard the crash of surf and the cries of gulls—and behind this scrim of noise, barely audible, the nickering of horses. He put down the remainder of the fish and staggered upright.

"Ah, you hear the voweled wind!" The Fisher King took the scribe's elbow and steadied him as he reached for his salt-stained cassock. "Come. Review my sea-blown kingdom with me."

After pulling on his damp clerical robe, the scribe stepped out the door and winced against the sun-glinting sea. A driftwood fire crackled nearby, and combers rolled smoking into the crescent of a small cove flanked by high, sandy bluffs. No sign of the ship that had carried him there was to be seen anywhere on the kelp-strewn beach—at least, not by his weak eyes.

The neighing of horses came and went on the brisk wind. He slogged through the sand toward the high dunes, following the muted cries.

"Stay, scribe!" the Fisher King called anxiously after him. "Stay here in my kingdom! Beyond lie pagan lands!"

The scribe ignored the madman and painfully, arduously, climbed slopes of salt grass and terraces of sea grape toward a summit plumed with gorse. Behind him, the Fisher King followed, muttering direly, "Best you stay where God has placed you, man. The mortal circle cannot be squared in the wide world beyond. Stay—stay—stay . . ."

Sandy footholds among the gorse mounted to a rocky shelf that gazed far inland. For as far as his bleared eyes could see, the land ranged blackly. Badlands of burned heath rolled toward cinder horizons. Here and there were gray nests where perhaps thorps or farms had once flourished among fields reduced to tracts of ash and slurry. "A wasteland," the scribe muttered.

The Fisher King stared at him with wild eyes. "This caul of

death lies heavily upon every realm in the land. Every realm."

Several horses milled on the strand below, survivors of the wreck. Vaguely, the scribe discerned the broken hulk of the ship impaled upon the giant sea boulders offshore. People scurried about the beach, gathering crates and barrels that had been flung onto land by the mighty waves. Hard as he squinted, though, he could not make out who they were.

"Pagans," the Fisher King hissed in his ear. "'Tis the land of the Durotriges. They worship the ancient one, the elk-headed god."

"This island is under rule of a Christian king—Arthor Rex," the scribe stated firmly. "News of his ascendance to the throne was well received by the papal see. Hence the Holy Father himself dispatched the good bishop of Troyes to this frontier. By heavens, I have no heart to believe holy Victricius died in vain. These people, pagan or no, serve a Christian king. I will go among them."

"No! You cannot beard the devil!" the Fisher King wailed. "Stay in my realm. Come. I have plenty of fish—oysters, sea bass, and delicate clams. Come."

The scribe took the Fisher King's rough hands in his soft grip and smiled gratefully. "I owe you a life debt, good man. Fear not for me. Where I go, my bishop would have gone in my stead. If God grants me success, you will be rewarded. This, I promise by our Savior's blood."

"What color is glory?" The Fisher King backed away, horrified. "Cry *Eloi* among the heathen!"

The scribe turned from him and, with aching muscles, made his way gradually down the sandy slope. He heard the shouts of those below who saw him, but he did not understand their language. When he looked back to the crest of the bluff, the Fisher King was gone.

Urien, Celtic chieftain of the Durotriges, accompanied a band of his warriors to the strand where the previous day's storm had wrecked a Roman-style lateener. Tall, with salt white hair worn loose over his bare shoulders, Urien appeared indifferent to the chill wind sliding off the sea. He dismounted from his sturdy roan and ambled casually past the dunes where the fisherfolk of the nearest hamlet had spread the ship's salvage for their chief's inspection.

After a cursory glance at the debris, he signed for the folk to distribute among themselves the rigging and stacked timbers and the four intact casks of wine. The personal effects of the drowned, laid out in neat piles atop a bed of seaweed, were reviewed by the green-robed druid who followed at his heels. The druid blessed the leather pouches, bracelets, rings, swords, daggers, and boots, lifting the shadow of death from them before indicating which of these items would be turned over to Urien. The rest belonged to the hamlet.

As for the horses, they were sacred to the goddess Epona and would be distributed by lot as the divinity decreed.

Huddled in a horse blanket at the lee of a dune sat a lanky fellow with dense curly hair, long nose, large brown eyes wide with apprehension, and a small, trembling chin of graying whiskers. The hamlet elders whispered that he was the sole survivor of the wreck, a Roman who did not speak their language. He had been found earlier in the day wandering among the dunes, and with proper Celtic hospitality had been warmed by the fire and fed barley gruel and black bread.

The scribe watched apprehensively as blurred shapes approached him. Then a stern face of ice-pale eyes and imposing Celtic mustache loomed close, studying him. This ash blond warrior seemed far less hospitable than the village folk who had earlier received him—until he began to speak in archaic Latin, "Chief Urien welcometh thee, stranger, to the realm of the Durotriges."

The scribe blurted with obvious relief the nature of his mission. Upon hearing about the death of the papal legate Victricius, Urien immediately ordered messages sent by carrier pigeon both to the king at Camelot and to the bishop of Trier. The scribe was impressed. "You share not our faith, yet you serve a Christian king and offer timely condolence to our nearest bishop?"

"A pagan by thy measure am I, scribe," Urien replied, his wry smile hidden by his thick mustache, "but no barbarian. My title is chieftain of the Celts, a people who once ruled all Europe and did battle with the Persians when Rome was still a village on the Tiber River. We be as ancient and proud as thy Savior's desert tribe."

The scribe did not question his gracious host's venerable claim but instead deflected the conversation by recounting his debt to the Fisher King in the cove beyond the sand bluffs. Immediately, the chieftain ordered two of his mounted warriors to bring the madman to him. They dashed off and returned during the horse lottery to report that no trace was to be found of the so-called Fisher King. Among the sea wrack were a few driftwood timbers that might have once served as walls of a crude hut, but the storm-swollen tide had obscured whatever signs there might have been of any recent habitation in the cove.

Urien dismissed the scribe's tale as the saltwater dream of a nearly drowned man. And the scribe did not insist otherwise, for he himself began to doubt his blurry-eyed memory. And besides, he did not wish to appear uncivil in light of the chieftain's hospitality. Urien had already provided for him a new, considerably warmer hooded cassock and other amenities for the wagon ride to the nearest city, the harbor town of Durnovaria—a wattle-and-daub settlement with archaic Roman battlements charred by numerous Saxon raids. Eagerly the scribe looked forward to relinquishing his duties to the next envoy arriving from the papal authority so that he could quit this stormy and primitive outpost. Once safely back in Ravenna, and after properly mourning the death of Victricius, he would think carefully before accepting his next scrivening assignment for the papal see, hopefully in a warmer and less rustic clime.

But by late afternoon of the following day, he had barely settled in beside a blackstone hearth at the local mead hall when a carrier bird returned from the bishop in Trier with an unexpected and wholly unwelcome charge. "Thou hast been promoted, scribe," Urien announced, holding the message strip close to his guest's myopic and startled eyes. "Thus saith the reverence of Trier by authority of the pope, electing thee to replace thy beloved Victricius. Thou art the new papal legate to Britain. Congratulations! I will escort thee at once to our king."

Urien sat on a faldstool beside the blackstone hearth, where the scribe crouched close to the flames, holding the message strip before him so that it almost touched his nose. "God hath infatuated the bishop's opinion of me!" he cried out. "I am but a scribe, a humble mouthpiece of my betters. Doubt not but that I am unworthy to serve as legate . . ."

"Scribe—what be thy name?" Urien placed his square hands on the knees of his buckskin trousers and leaned forward, firelight gleaming on his naked shoulders. "I canst call thee scribe no more now that thou art the pope's representative."

The new legate looked dismayed. "I cannot replace the holy Victricius! I am not wont to act upon so great a resolution . . ."

"Thy name, legate. My king will want to know."

The startled man read the strip of parchment yet again, then blinked at the blurred shape of the half-naked Celtic warlord before him. "I am Fra Athanasius."

"Athanasius—that be a mouthful." Urien tugged at his large white mustache. "'Tis not a Latin name I understand."

"My name is Greek," Fra Athanasius said distractedly. "*A-thanatos* . . . the alpha negative affixed to *thanatos*, Greek for death—hence, 'no-death'—immortal . . ."

"Then I shall call thee No-Death." Urien stood. "Come, No-Death. We've a long journey to Camelot, and as thou wilt see, this be a land of much death. This sorely afflicted land shall benefit from your blessing."

"But I am merely a scribe—amanuensis to the princes of the Church. In my fifty years upon this fallen world, I have never held authority."

Urien clapped him on the back with a laugh. "We never hold authority, Fra No-Death. It holds us!"

"Lord Urien, the mission of the legate suits me ill. I am trained to record decisions—a looker-on, always from without-ward. It has never been my charge to set seal to the fate of others—let alone a kingdom entire!"

"What be there to decide, No-Death?" Urien appeared bemused at Athanasius's consternation. "Thou hast seen the devastation war hath wrought upon our land. Our king appealeth to his spiritual commander to provide aid. We seek grain and livestock to replenish our lost stores. We require artisans and their materials for rebuilding all that hast fallen to ruin. And we require sizable financial assistance so that we may pay laborers to revive our mines, our fisheries, our textile and loomworks. What be there to decide, man? Without this help from the papacy, we will never restore ourselves under the assault of the foreign invaders—and our kingdom will surely fall."

Athanasius pinched the bridge of his long nose, feeling for

the throbbing root of pain behind his eyes. "Perhaps that is best."

The chieftain pulled his head away with surprise. "What dost thou say? How can it be best for thy Holy Father to have Britain fall into the hostile hands of the wild tribes?"

"If this is the Devil's kingdom, 'tis best that it be purged by fire and sword and the wrath of the pagan hordes. The holy bishop Victricius had been specifically charged by our Holy Father with the vital task of determining if Arthor Rex is a true Christian king—or a minion of Satan."

Urien leaped to his feet, and said in his teeth, "The authority of my king is questioned?"

"Certainly not!" Athanasius lifted trembling hands before his lowered face, and said, more softly, "Yet, the nature—that is to say, the source of his authority—well, you see—how may I put this? Word has reached Ravenna that your king is in collusion with the forces of darkness."

"Who?" Urien spoke through a clenched jaw. "Who maketh such a charge against Arthor?"

"A venerable family, my lord." The legate kept his gaze fixed upon the sooty hearthstones. "The Syrax family . . ."

"Syrax!" Urien hissed the name. "Severus Syrax plotted against Arthor from the first. He was the *magister militum* of Londinium who allied with the invaders to bring Britain under the rule of the Saxons. He inspired insurrection against the king— for money. Money be everything to the Syrax family. They have holdings in every country of the known world. Trade and commerce, that be all they worship. They covet Britain's wealth—her mineral ores, her fishing grounds, her rich land—and her people as slaves."

"As you say," Athanasius timidly agreed. "Ancient and well established from the Levant to Iberia is the house of Syrax. Ill it is should the Holy Father fain ignore them. They say Arthor Rex hanged Severus from a tree limb by the roadside. An ignoble death for a *magister militum*, even a rebellious one."

"Bors hanged Severus. I'd have done the same had I but laid hands on him first." The chieftain paced angrily before the hearth. "The *magister militum* scorched the lands, put the torch to the villages, and idly watched his Saxon troops slaughter the people, women and children included."

"War is ever terrible," Athanasius concurred meekly. "The

atrocities I have witnessed across Europe in my ten and forty
would poison your liver. Such is past bearing. Even so, as legate I
am obliged to bear such horror and gaze beyond pity for the
truth. The Holy Father has heard the Syrax family's claim that
Arthor Rex treats with devils and works black magic. If this is so,
no kernel of grain, no head of livestock, no single nail or coin
will come to this island. The Holy Father will forbid it."

Urien sat down heavily. "No-Death, listen carefully to me. Thy
God hath seen fit to place thee in judgment upon this land. What I
knoweth of thy religion demandeth charity and mercy. How then
canst thou even entertain the thought that our beloved Britain be a
land of devils worthy of famine and the violence of alien con-
querors?"

"Charity and mercy for the innocent, yes." Athanasius
looked down awkwardly at his hands tightly clasped in his lap.
"But the Church fathers, the princes of Christ, they hold neither
charity nor mercy toward those who nuzzle evil. And black
magic and deviltry, those are active evil."

"Not in this land!"

"Forgive me, Lord Urien." Athanasius shrank smaller before
the chieftain's loud voice. "You who have granted me warranty
of safety and all good hospitality, do not upbraid me. Please—
take no effrontery from this scribe who ne'er sought this greater
title and charge of legate nor its ponderous responsibility. And
permit me, under surety of your honor and gentle regard of my
sincerity, to probe you then with a searching question."

"Ask me anything, legate."

Athanasius meshed his knuckles tightly, drawing the courage
to ask, "If Arthor Rex is so Christian a king as is worthy of papal
clemency and succor, then why rallies he about himself warlords
such as yourself who share not our faith? What bonds you to
him that you, a Celt, accept him as your monarch?"

"Not deviltry!"

"Surely not. But what then?"

"I have fought at his side. He be a great warrior."

"I am informed he is but a lad of seventeen summers."

"A great warrior nonetheless. The greatest I hath ever
known. He took the point in every battle that I shared with him
against the raiders and usurpers and not once flinched in the
face of death. He will never capitulate with the invaders. Not

for his very life. And so he be worthy for me to call king."

"Then why—if I may press your patience, my lord—why do you not share his faith in our Savior and Lord Jesus Christ?"

Urien's gaze sharpened. "A Celt was I born. My lineage be as ancient as any in the world. Why shouldst I accept a new and strange god when mine own faith hath sustained me and my people from the most fargone times?"

"A new revelation comes upon us, Lord Urien—a deeper revelation of God and His world." Athanasius raised his brown eyes to meet the Celt's steely blue gaze. "Jesus Christ is the only way to that revelation and redemption. 'Tis not condign that you serve a Christian king and not his Savior—unless that king be Christian in name alone. Many heresies pollute our world in this chaotic time. Many call themselves Christian who are but foils for Satan, reapers of men's souls, agents of perdition."

"Enough!" Urien rose and jabbed a thick finger at Athanasius. "Thy religion be absurd. Thy so-called Savior preacheth of an all-mighty God who loves—and yet that God sees fit to torture and crucify His only Son, his *beloved* Son. Ha! Leave all judgment to God and love thy enemies, so thy messiah instructs. And now, thou wilt judge us. And if we be found wanting by thy righteous standards, we shalt be condemned to starvation and the wrath of the invaders." The chieftain's temples pulsed. "I've a mind to cast thee back into the sea, thou hypocrite!"

Athanasius quailed, curling inward with fright. "Your king sent summons to the papal see for aid and a legate to minister that aid. I am here at his behest and God's election."

"And what aid dost thou bring Britain? Only threats." Urien turned and stalked away, barking over his naked shoulder, "To Camelot then. We ride at once. Let the king deal with thee. I've no stomach for it."

"Nor I," Athanasius admitted quietly, hands fisted over his belly, head reeling with fright. "Oh, good Victricius, that you were here in my stead and I in yours, my flesh divvied among the fishes and my soul vouchsafed to heaven—for I do forthrightly fear for my salvation in this remote land. Blessed Son of God, protect me from every dumbfounding strangeness and all the deadly virtues that await me on the road to Camelot."

• • •

King Wesc served as chief of the alliance of Saxons, Jutes, Angles, Picts, and Scoti, who had united to conquer Britain. They had adopted Roman war tactics and weapons and even a Roman name, the Foederatus. As their chief, Wesc was responsible for coordinating their invasion of Britain. He spent most of his time preparing battle plans from the province of Cantii, his Saxon foothold at the southeast corner of the Christian island. In the Roman villa of Dubrae above the limestone cliffs overpeering the Belgic Strait, he listened to his generals, chieftains all, each one wise in the terrible ways of war. And he wrote poetry.

A short man with close-cropped dark hair, a long ginger beard, and a limp from a childhood boating accident, King Wesc was not a remarkable figure to behold. His ordinariness was heightened by his preference for simple dress: long-sleeved red woolens and trousers of black canvas. He carried no weapons whatsoever, and only the twin-coiled serpents embossed on his kid-leather jerkin and his tall boots signified the noble status he had attained. Never had he fought in a battle. No life had ever been taken by his hands. Yet he was revered above all men in the Foederatus and entitled to wear a golden crown of entwined snakes as lord of many tribes. Scoti, Jutes, Picts, and Angles adored him as passionately as his own Saxons, for he was beloved of Lady Unique, the wife of their chief deity, the Furor.

Accompanied everywhere by a black cat, the goddess's familiar, Wesc availed himself of Lady Unique's blessings of wisdom and luck to rule the Foederatus—and he thanked her frequently with sacred poetry: *Lady, only my memory of you preserves my hands from ignorance—only my hope of you makes from the noise of death a music* . . .

"Aquila Regalis Thor," King Wesc spoke to his scribe in the atrium at Dubrae. Evening settled like blue dust upon the marble statuary and potted trees under the open sky. Ornate oil lamps upheld by tripods cast saffron radiance on the Roman architecture that the Saxon king had kept intact for his elucidation, that he might better know his enemy's mind and soul. "Royal Eagle of Thor!" In his tall boots and red woolen shirt, he paced slowly about the central fountain, tugging at his ginger beard. "Thor—that is their botched name for our god Thunder Red Hair. This king mocks us with his very name. So, mark me well now, scribe—you will spell his name with a 'u'—Arthur. It will sound the same yet will no longer carry the name of our god, and we will break his evil spell with this significant change."

The scribe, an elderly, gray-bearded man in brown robes and pointed scholar's cap, nodded from where he sat on a stool beside a mirror-lantern, recording with a stylus onto a wax tablet the king's dictation.

"This poem is to be sent to him at Camelot, his fortress in the west," the stout king instructed. "And be certain that our terms for reconciliation are attached—and the consequences if they are refused. He must know that I am serious. Now, begin—

> *Arthur,*
> *from here I have watched you*
> *walking the flat of the blade, seeking*
> *the edge where the light is sliced*
> *from the dark. The tide of that wound*
> *is the blood in which we are drowning.*
> *Only my memory of the gods preserves my hands*
> *from the ignorance of our war. The gods*
> *show me how to find peace without shame.*
> *It is almost impossible,*
> *even for you, battle-lord of Britain,*
> *to imagine my terror when our warriors*
> *wake each morning to discover, asleep*
> *in their hands, the old weapons.*
> *Arthur, make peace with me —*
> *or our war will unmake you.*
>
> —Wesc, high lord of the Foederatus

2

Cinderland

Arthor Rex lay facedown upon the naked back of the horse, his cheek pressed against her neck, listening to the pumping blood and the muscular breaths filling her body with joy. They had just returned from a fast jaunt across the champaign surrounding Camelot. The grooms had removed her saddle, and he had dismissed them to spend time alone with her.

Her sweat smelled of the happy season after the noise of battle has passed over. How many battles had she carried him through in the four years they had fought together? He had lost count. She had been his since she was a foal. Her name was Straif, Gaelic for blackthorn, not only because of her sloe eyes that resembled that tree's black fruit but because she was for him the strife of fate, as the tree itself was for the bards. She was the unavoidable path, the harsh choice that had to be obeyed. When he rode her, he was riding upon life's cruel joy.

The horse warriors had laughed when he took Straif for his battle mount. She was a palfrey, a slender riding steed more suited for carrying a woman than an armored man. But he wore his armor light, and he did not want her to charge and trample but to dance and elude. With her under him, he rode like smoke among his enemies, he rode as an ally of the wind, come and gone, with death in his shadow.

From his initial foray into combat, he had depended on her like a voice and its echo. They had smelled men's blood for the first time together. Battle cries and death shrieks did not startle her on the narrow footbridge of life. Like the floating cloud whose color she bore, she moved with airy grace, and the din of warscapes never troubled her.

Arthor loved Straif. She had won Britain with him against those who had fomented war rather than accept a boy monarch. Now, the war was over. He was undisputed high king of Britain, and all that had been a torment to him before, he loved. His parentless childhood was the very hand of his guide, the surety of a hard-won self-reliance. The many indignities of thralldom he had endured before he learned he was royalty had become a music of humility he would always hear as king and dance to most inwardly whenever sycophants sang to him. The years of brutal training from earliest childhood were the majestic arms that had made him his own bodyguard. And the loneliness, the smiting isolation he had endured believing he was the spawn of a foreign rapist, that terrible loneliness that had hurt him from his first memories had opened into an irreproachable solitude, a sacred place of waking dreams—and what had been a steely pin in his heart was now the axis of the universe.

Merlin stood in the shadows of the inner-bailey gate, midnight blue robes and bent, conical hat annealed to the darkness so that his long, pallid face and forked beard hovered there like a vaporous apparition. In their dragon sockets, his chrome eyes gazed half-lidded, with a dreamer's languid and unwavering intensity, watching Arthor Rex, watching the boy lying atop his palfrey in full embrace like some aboriginal worshiper.

The wizard gauged the boy's happiness. Arthor was talking to his horse and laughing softly, and the beast was listening and laughing, too, as horses laugh, tossing her narrow head, squinting her dark eyes.

But what was the mettle of this shared joy? What was the worth of this giddy confidence?

The disaster that had almost overwhelmed Camelot only six weeks prior had not left the king unscathed. A livid wound gaped from his right thigh where his riding tunic had uplifted, laying bare a maroon puncture inflicted by a rebel arrow. Even seen from this distance, the injury appeared to throb with pustulant heat. It was a refractory trauma, defiant of all Merlin's plasters and healing spells, and required the boy to use a crutch.

And yet—the boy laughed. What thoughts must be his to defy such pain and so hideous an omen? Clearly, Arthor knew by his victory that he was God's own child, his authority validated in blood by the annihilation of those who had opposed him. His rosy cheeks flushed as much with euphoria as exertion, his beardless, boyish face glossy with sweat and grinning, he hugged his whole body to his animal with guileless love.

Who would not seek the companionship of such a one? The grooms waited in the stable gates, all eyes on him, eager for his merest gesture. And there on a stool beside the sunny hayrick was Bedevere, the one-armed swordmaster and personal guard to the king, his balding head lifted proudly as if this were his own son returned triumphant from war.

In the ward beyond the gingerstone wall and the iron gate wrought with the flying eagle of the royal crest, the best young men of the kingdom waited for their chance to impress the boy-king with their skills: archers, poets, musicians, all yearning for his notice, all knowing that the events of the world were so much passing sand but here, with this lordly youth, was the world itself, the living thing in whose sacred memory history, with all its inscrutable purpose, flowed. For him, they would brave hell itself.

But would Arthor? That was the question that troubled Merlin. He did not want to intrude on the king's joy. Arthor had won his war to unite Britain, and Merlin was proud of him. The youngster deserved a respite from struggle. But time was a storm, and for a king there was no sanctuary. If Britain was to survive, Arthor would have to leave the peace of Camelot and confront again the enemies of his people.

When the boy turned the horse in his direction, the wizard took the opportunity to step from the shadows.

Arthor's laughter stalled, and his smile went brittle. For an instant, the squint of his eyes broadcast a hope that he could turn away and ignore the tall, silver-eyed figure. Then his jaw tightened with acceptance of the inevitable, and he slid from his gray palfrey. He took the horse's long head in his arms, whispered briefly a farewell, and turned away.

"A word, my lord," Merlin said, as the boy limped toward him, favoring his good leg. "You have spent these six weeks in celebration and conviviality, and I have left you to relish your victory. Yet now it is time we discussed the state of your kingdom."

"So soon, Merlin?" Arthor put an arm across the wizard's shoulders and leaned heavily on him, waiting for the groom who came running across the stable yard with the sturdy gnarl of cypress wood that Merlin had fashioned to a stave. The king received it gratefully. "I have not been entirely indolent, you know. My brother and I have reviewed all the road maps and bridge sites that most direly need repair . . ."

"Sire—" Merlin cut him off. "That is worthy work for your stepbrother Cei. But Britain needs more than worthy roads and bridges to break the pagan invaders."

"Now that our island kingdom is united, we are stronger than ever, and surely . . ."

"Nothing is sure for our land with the Holy Graal missing."

"Then you must find it, wizard." The king lowered himself onto a bench in the shadow of a vaulted archway, where floral scents breezed from the singing brightness of a garden. He handed Merlin his cypress stave, dismissed the groom with a smile, and began unlacing his riding boots. "You must use your magic."

Merlin noticed that the king never spoke of magic unless they were alone. The boy's sister Morgeu had deceived Arthor so shamelessly with her unholy power that he completely spurned the old ways—at least in public. "My lord, whoever it was that took the Graal from us has magical powers equal to or greater than my own. For all my scrying, I have been unable to find it."

"And what do you expect me to do, Merlin?" Arthor tugged at a boot.

"It is time you left Camelot and toured the realm. Then you will see for yourself that the widespread blight upon the countryside is something far worse than the scars of war. It is a curse, a black curse that befouls Britain. Something evil lurks in your kingdom, my lord. And you must take it upon yourself to uncover it."

Arthor waved a boot at him. "That is the work of sorcerers and wizards. If there is a curse upon our island, you will discover it, Merlin, not I. My work is here, reviewing the damage done by human hands and planning what human hands can do to correct it."

"Your engineers can fulfill that task. Only you have the

authority to wage war against the deviltry that plagues our land."

"Deviltry?" Arthor wrinkled his nose and shook his head. "No, Merlin. I'm a Christian king, and I will trust in our Lord and Savior to protect us from deviltry. God has set me upon the throne to make a fortress of our island and to keep at bay the pagan tribes that would overrun us. That is fight enough for me. I have no power to challenge devils."

"My lord, if you will but leave this citadel and come forth into your domain, you will see for yourself that there is an evil abroad that is as destructive as the raiders that harry our shores. It is an evil that has brought drought and famine to Britain and threatens to break our defenses from within."

"I have petitioned the Holy Father in Ravenna to send aid." Arthor spoke as he painfully struggled to remove the boot from his wounded leg. "The pope will not refuse a Christian king in need. Soon, there will be barges of grain and livestock arriving in our ports. They will be sufficient to sustain us until our farmers and drovers have restored our land by their own husbandry. Within a few years, we will again be exporting goods, and our debt to the Holy Father will be repaid in full."

"Is that how our future appears from within these walls?" Merlin knelt before the king and gently removed the troublesome boot. "I tell you, Arthor, the reality beyond Camelot is far worse than you can guess."

"My scouts have visited every district, and they inform me that when the roads are repaired, the bridges erected once more, and the walls of the cities bolstered, our kingdom will flourish. We have only the raiders to concern us."

Merlin sat beside him on the settle. "None of the scouts you send forth will be able to report anything else to you, for they do not see as a king would see."

"A king is a man."

"Is that what you think?" Merlin took the boy's wrist in his big, bony hand and squeezed it for emphasis. "No, no, no. A king is an emblem, Arthor. And all emblems hold magic. You are the emblem of the land, my boy, and so you carry the magic of the land in your person. Regard your wound. Why does it not heal?"

"I want no more truck with magic, Merlin." Arthor twisted his arm free, grabbed his stave, and pushed to his feet. "I am here to serve God and my people."

"God's grace sent me to counsel and protect you."

The young man's eyes narrowed, and he trepidatiously regarded the entity before him. His heart felt suddenly cold in his chest to look at this old man who was not truly a man. The wizard had a face like geology, like the shale and schists that sometimes wear human faces in seacliffs, staring at him without compassion or fear of God. He turned away and tried to warm the chill by staring into the brightness of the garden. "Your counsel is unnatural. Deviltry, magic, curses. I'll have no more of that. The war is won. Now is the time of rebuilding and defense. My mind is preoccupied with those concerns."

Merlin scowled. "Your mind is bound by trivialities. You give yourself to logistics, to routes of conveyance and economic pacts with the new nations of Europe. But these are merely the trappings of governance. Your jurisdiction is far wider. Look at me."

"It is not easy to look at you, wizard," Arthor said without facing him.

"Look at me, Arthor." He waited until the boy reluctantly turned. "I have a devil's countenance, for in truth I am a demon—the demon Lailoken. Yet, God has installed me in this human form and given me a destiny greater than the malign purpose that drove me here across the aeons. Neither your mother Ygrane nor your father Uther Pendragon spurned my counsel, for they knew my powers."

"I would rather trust in our Savior and my own sound reason."

"Did reason save you from your sister Morgeu's beguilement?"

Arthor veered back as if avoiding a blow. "I will not speak of her."

"For all your sound reason, she deceived you into lying with her." The wizard stood. He did not want to hurt this king, whom he loved, yet he had to break the boy's false comfort to bring him to the dire truth. "Was our Savior present when you got her with child, Arthor?"

"Merlin, be silent." The boy limped toward the garden.

With two large steps, the old man was at his side, his voice hissing close to his face. "Incest, Arthor. That word scalds your ears and offends your very soul, because you gave your seed to your sister! And neither faith nor reason saved you—because magic is stronger."

"Enough, Merlin!"

"Morgeu tricked you with magic so that you thought you lay with a beautiful and noble woman. An illusion! And now, your incest child suckles at your sister's breast. Mordred lives, and all that you will accomplish, the sum of all your noble deeds, the histories of every battle triumph are dishonored by his existence—your very love of God called into question—and your faith a mock ritual deferring to a moment's lust."

Arthor spun about with his fist raised. "I will hear no more, wizard!"

"You would strike me?" Merlin's silver eyes widened in mock apprehension. Part of him, the human part of him, wanted to stop there, to say no more that would hurt this young lion. *Let him brood on this pain,* the human voice in him resounded, *and he will come to the truth of his fate in time. Magic has its place with reason and faith.*

But the demon mind of the wizard knew there was no time. He had seen the future's dark tide rising—and reason and faith, for all their ultimate virtue, would not forestall that reckoning. Magic alone was their best hope.

The demonic part of him glowed with the malice necessary to shock the king from his complacence; he sneered at the angry boy who had raised his fists. "But where is the famous compassion of your faith, my lord? Where—oh, tell me, good king, where is your Savior now that incest has made a wreckage of your great plans? How will Jesus judge the intended glory of your reign? Him? A glory canceled by your carnality? Isn't it obvious? Nothing that you can ever do, *nothing* can be deemed worthy of the human spirit, let alone the Holy Spirit, after the terrible fact of your sin. It would have gone better for you had you put your faith in a dog. Your reason obviously is constrained by the latitudes of your sexual desire—and all Jesus could do for you is forgive. But the dog—ah, Arthor, at least the dog would have smelled out Morgeu and aborted the one unspeakable act that now will forever define you."

Tears spurt from Arthor's eyes. He cried out in anguish. The stave clattered to the flagstones, and he brought both fists down hard on Merlin's shoulders. With a wet and ugly sound, the wizard collapsed into a tumble of black frogs that skittered and hopped over each other across the paving slates.

"Nothing is really as it appears," Merlin said from behind him. "That is the secret truth of magic, Arthor. Everything is false."

Arthor twisted about with a sob and stood weeping before the tall, gaunt figure. "Not everything," he mumbled. "Not everything is false."

"Oh, everything we can know." Merlin draped a robed arm over the youth's shoulders and guided him back toward the settle. "Each of us and all of us together, lad, are only a fraction among so many other fractions in an aggregate that is beyond conception. If you could have posted witness to reality from its inception, as have I, you would know the world for what it actually is—so much tenuous smoke thinning away in the void. We are but a momentary dream."

Arthor sat down heavily. "How can you go on living if you believe this—this blasphemy?"

"We go on." Merlin sat beside him, comforting arm across his shoulders. "Living or dead, awake or asleep, we go on. Here in the void, nothing is lost, Arthor—only rearranged. The angels strive to arrange things ever more complexly, building from atoms all the chains of being. And the demons tear them apart, wanting the simplicity of emptiness and darkness—the ultimate reckoning of the universe."

Arthor slumped under the oppressive weight of that thought. "If emptiness is our ultimate reckoning, Merlin, why then should we struggle at all?"

"Is it a simple solution that you seek, King Arthor? Then surrender to the invaders at your shores. Let the pagans have Britain. But if you love your God, if you serve God as the angels do, then you must endure complexity in yourself and in the world around you."

"You mock and confuse me, wizard. Incest is my sin. You hold that atrocity up to my face even as you assure me that everything I worship and hold dear is false. Now, you say that if I love God I must—what? Endure complexity? What under heaven does that mean?"

"Be the man you are."

"But I am!"

"Are you?" Merlin removed his arm and shifted to better

face the youth. "You hide behind these walls. You think that because you have united the many realms of this island into one kingdom that you have earned the right to seclude yourself here and draft plans for new roads and bridges. As if a kingdom were so many pathways and cities."

Arthor ran both hands through his badger brown hair. "I do not understand you."

"How can you? You are seventeen and surrounded by people who are bedazzled with your achievement. Your right to rule has been proven in blood upon the field of battle. What you understand now is triumph and joy after a childhood of hardship. But I ask you again, come with me. Tour your kingdom and see for yourself what lurks out there. Do not hide behind your faith in a loving and forgiving God who eschews magic. Come with me and see what magic is doing to Britain."

Arthor expelled a heavy sigh. He felt afraid and angry at himself for being afraid. "I despise magic, Merlin. Morgeu uses magic—and you are right to shame me with the horror of what she did to me. I cannot abide the unnatural strength of magic. I do not understand it or its place in God's creation. My own mother, once a powerful sorceress for the Celts, forsook such sorcery to worship the very God that you ridicule."

"I do not ridicule the Christian God, Arthor. I but insist that you do not rely upon God to fulfill your labors. As for your mother Ygrane—" From a blue sleeve stitched with crimson seams of esoteric glyphs, Merlin extracted a narrow strip of parchment. "I have here a dispatch from Duke Marcus. He claims that Ygrane has defrocked herself, and he says that with his own eyes he beheld her riding a demon steed out of Tintagel. He is among the most sober of your warlords, Arthor, and I do not doubt his word. Ygrane has given herself again to magic."

Her body breathed energy. As she lay in the gray grass and watched a spring storm gathering thundercrowns above her, Ygrane felt the wind of light within her body.

Glamour. That was what she had grown up calling this glorious strength. But she had never had so much of it before.

In the ambitious sunshine let down between the darkening

clouds, she summoned the faeries, and they spun around her and landed upon her outstretched hands. Their tiny bodies of honeyshine, though radiant with sentience, pulsed without shape. Each one carried an orphaned event from a distant corner of the island. By turns, they hovered before her eyes, and she saw scenes of Britain.

The ancient walled cities drifted past in all their dilapidated sorrow—daub edifices cracked and patched with straw, doorways covered in rawhide, lanes littered and weedy: Glevum, Deva, Calcaria seemed called forth out of dust and rubble prophetically bound toward eternal obscurity; only Londinium appeared a true city, retaining some of the glory of Rome in its historic governor's palace with its marble friezes and fluted columns of ornate plinth and cornice.

Between the cities ranged naked, lunar ashflats, a cinderland spoored with charred farmhouses and crisped hedges and spinneys. The faeries that had toured the most remote hills of Cymru and Caledonia alone revealed the presences of spring: branches buoyant with blossoms and new leaves, birds flurrying in pools of sunlight, meadows spangled with flowers.

"How does it feel?" a gleaming dark voice asked. The elf prince Bright Night stood over her, yellow boots to either side of her shoulders, oblique green eyes smiling downward. His red hair spun flames fantastic against the storm sky.

Ygrane sat up, and the faeries scattered. "I'm hungry."

"No need ever to feel hunger again." He squatted so that he practically sat on her thighs, his small nose an inch from her face. "Use your glamour."

She pushed him away, and he dissolved into a comet's luminous veils. "If I live on glamour, I will become as you are."

"You will not live long enough to become as we are," his voice replied from the glittering vapors slowly reshaping his form. "We will find the Graal long before then."

Ygrane accepted this silently. There was no sense in half measures now that she had abandoned Miriam and their shared faith in divine love. Not love but courage would fulfill her resolution. She needed strength for the task she had set herself, and hunger had become a distraction.

Glamour glimmered in the air like starwork. She breathed it in, and the pangs of hunger relaxed to a lucid strength.

"It's good, is it not?" the dark voice asked out of the shining air.

"Very." She closed her eyes and relished the lightning stab of pleasure and the private thunder that followed as blood spun faster into her brain. An uncleaved feeling of merger pulled her to her feet, and she smiled to sense her wholeness, the union of her inner life with the world around her. "I had forgotten the deep joy of glamour."

"Seventeen years a nun." Bright Night's body congealed from the auroras of glamour, and he shook his head ruefully. "You have denied yourself much—and for what? For silence. For a god who does not speak and who has no name."

"For my husband." Ygrane turned her face blindly toward the chill wind that brought the first frecklings of rain. "I became a Christian to honor my husband."

"Uther Pendragon dances to the Piper's tunes in the Happy Woods. Your gesture was empty. Uther achieved honor enough when he exchanged his Christian soul for our greatest warrior's soul."

Ygrane opened her eyes. "Does Cuchulain's soul truly reside in my son's body?"

"You know it is so. That is the true reason why you gave yourself to the nailed god—to share your son's faith with him. You are the king's mother, and for that distinction you abandoned us who in former times you adored. But, tell me, Ygrane, now that glamour courses through your flesh once again—" Distant thunder rang like broken bells. "Are you happy with your religion of denial? Is the abnegation that your god demands enough?"

"For me, it is enough."

"Because it makes Arthor king, yes? It feeds your pride to know your son has united Celts and Britons. Yet, would you embrace such a religion of sacrifice otherwise?" Bright Night moved toward her in fumes of smoky topaz. "The Cross-worshipers spurn this world, believing they will be reborn in a glorious afterworld they call heaven. You are too knowledgeable to embrace such nonsense. Pride alone dropped you to your knees before the gruesome, tortured Son of God with his crown of thorns and his woeful and bloody countenance. Pride alone."

"You make much of my pride, but what of yours, Bright Night?" Ygrane crossed her arms over her chest. "You rankle at life in the hollow hills and will sacrifice me to wake the Dragon for the power to assault the north gods. Why? Why else but that you may strut once more through the Storm Tree."

"Is that what you think—that my ambition to storm the mighty World Tree is a vanity?" The spiritous mistings of glamour hardened to the contours of a physical body replete again with a blue linen tunic embroidered in flowerets of gold and cinched by a silver-studded belt of red leather. "I am not vain. I am sick—sick of the sulfurous dragonfumes in the hollow hills— sick of eternal twilight. I want to feel the rain and the wind and the glory of daylight." He opened his arms to the sunshine hanging like brilliant banners from the gray turrets of the storm front. "Your death will earn this happiness for all the Daoine Síd for all time to come. When you descend into the dragonpit, we will ascend into Yggdrasil and throw the north gods after you. And the great beast will devour them in the ore-infested earth. Then we will take our place above the blue planet, and the pale people will become radiant once more. We will shine with solar fire. We will taste the day's blue eternity. And our laughter will ride the clouds below us."

"This is not vanity?"

"No. It is *not* vanity." The prince smiled ferociously, his red hair bristling madness. "It is rapture."

The rain came in twisting sheets or like a giantess's silver, winding hair let down from the cloudscapes. Ygrane turned her back on the elf prince of glamour and ran with the wet wind toward a knoll of yew and cedar, where lightning was more likely. She was eager to flee Bright Night, and when she reached the creaking and groaning trees was glad to see that their fear of thunderbolts had driven underground the faeries and their lord.

Unhappy with his obsession with their pact, she questioned the wisdom of her quest. *Even if I find the Graal, will it help Arthor? Am I casting myself to the Dragon for naught?*

Ygrane did not believe that the Daoine Síd could take the Storm Tree from the north gods. As a young woman, she had climbed into Yggdrasil, had gazed into the Furor's one gray eye, and had glimpsed there in the black of the pupil the aisles of light, the long fluorescent corridors of the future. She had seen many things in that prophetic moment. Cities with towers like quartz. Hornblende roadways crisscrossing all of Britain and Europe and the mysterious landforms beyond the Western Sea.

Boats of metal. Airships of metal. And nowhere the Daoine Síd.

The Furor was there. Ditched into darkness at the far end of time, the Furor had stared back at her. His silver mane and wind-wrung beard had shone like a fogged sun across the centuries. And nowhere had she seen the pale people.

The storm sky above the giant trees gazed down upon her like that mad gray eye, and she wanted to flee back to Tintagel and her nun's habit. She wondered if there were any act of holy contrition that could shrive her of her feverish hopes for her son. *King Arthor—the hope of Britain . . .*

Bright Night was right, she knew. Pride for her son had stolen her faith from the gentle love of the Savior. Glamour had replaced hope. Instead of a Prince of Peace, she wanted to give herself to a king of might—Uther's son, her son.

She felt sudden gratitude for the wet wind—as if the cloud-burst had run to meet her at just this juncture of will and destiny so that she could lift her face to the sky and let the rain wash away her tears. Life had become an unspeakable effort. Even so, she was determined to play her role. The unfinished legend of Uther Pendragon, the one man she had loved, would find fulfill-ment in their son even if it cost her the miserable eternity of life in this world, this rock of fallen heaven.

Fear battled with hope in her, resignation with longing, and this tension hummed like a taut dulcimer string just behind her tearful eyes. The wild thought of that string snapping sprang through her, and she imagined throwing herself over a cliff, smashing her brains against rocks, and entrusting her soul to God's mercy. She shook that mad urge from her mind. Arthor needed her; there was no time for self-pity with all she had to do and do quickly.

A familiar pang of soft pain deep in her pelvis interrupted her musings. "Oh, not now—" she complained, recognizing the warm, stuttering cramp that signaled the onset of her menses. Under the stress of giving herself to so many changes, she had lost track of her own body's rhythms and had not prepared for this monthly ritual. She heaved an exasperated sigh, and as she began looking about for anything to stanch the flow, she realized that it was the glamour that had provoked this sudden release.

With both hands on her abdomen, she felt the soft slippery dark movement within and was tempted to use glamour to stop it. Immediately, she understood that such intervention would be unwise. It was one thing to eat of glamour so she could complete her quest and entirely another to use this power to withhold the offering of her sacred blood. That would only deepen her dependence on magic, and she had determined that her glamour would serve her son and their people, not herself.

Or was that simply a fanciful evasion, she wondered, rummaging through last season's mulchy leaves for a wad of moss. If she employed her glamour on this deepest most organic part of herself, it would be far more difficult later to relinquish her magic and live again as an ordinary woman. Bright Night believed she was promised to the dragonpit after the Graal was found, yet she cherished the prayerful hope that she might be spared, that when her mission was complete she would find herself back at Tintagel, once more a nun serving the sick, the dying, the impoverished of Dumnoni. She did not want to rely on glamour.

Fashioning a menstrual dressing was not easy in the drought-ridden land. Leaves crumpled to powder, and moss could not be found. Finally, she resorted to tearing the linen sleeves from her chemise and folding them to wads, one for now, the other a reserve.

By the time she finished, the rain had abated. The storm was just passing through. Fragmentary sunlight drifted across the gray fields, and Ygrane wished that the torrent had lasted longer. There had not been enough rain this season to nourish the summer flowers to come: The white shepherd's purse, the yellow snapdragons, the carpets of daisies would not arrive this year. An ill and ominous wind blew weather too quickly to sea. Perhaps when the Graal was found, its magic could be used to inspire sufficient rain to overwhelm this warscape of burned plains with dog roses, honeysuckle, and rambling bryony. For now, the land remained colorless, with its smoke-blackened trees and encrustations of dry ivy.

She stepped out from among the dolorous yews with their boughs of sere needles and looked about for her demon horse. It drifted out of the rock-strewn knoll where it had hidden during the downpour and came toward her with the cloud shadows, a deeper shadow itself, its ember eyes twin perforations into a sunset world.

Dewlights of rain sparkled in Ygrane's short hair and prismed the light on her lashes as the sun came out. Before mounting the black devil stallion, she watched the storm clouds hurrying away, and she used her glamour to lade her emotions upon those thunderheads. She needed to be calm though she bled and ached, and she could not carry fear and doubt as well as pain where she was going. Glamour lifted her uncertainties into the clouds. Then all the irresolute thoughts that had grievously troubled her about the loss of her gentle Savior and the necessity of this quest drifted away with those gray barges, those ghost ships whose cargo was her soul.

3

The Future Grows from Small Things

The Furor hung upside down from Raven's Branch, the topmost limit of Yggdrasil. He breathed in day and exhaled night. The powerful stratospheric winds buffeted him, twisting him on the axis of the leather thong binding him by his ankles to the silver bough that was also the uppermost limb of the planet's atmosphere. Gusts tossed him recklessly, and random blusters pummeled his bruised body, shaking him to the verge of unconsciousness.

He forced himself to stay alert. He had to stay awake or vision would not come. Destiny's strange and familiar where-abouts loomed just beyond the brink of utmost suffering. If he could hold on long enough, endure the random jets and blows of the thrashing wind . . . long enough . . .

At the limit of his anguish, music sifted into his brain from the far future: remote strains of Beethoven's *Eroica* entwined with the *lieder* of Schumann and Schubert and enclosing it all, at the audible frontier, Bach trembling with vital power, bringing him a pristine glimpse of what might be for his people if only he could embrace the agony a little longer . . .

The trammels of suffering peeled away day and night and grafted him onto emptiness. That blank space was the halcyon stillness of being, the ocean void of witness, the I Am afloat upon the nothing from which everything emerged. This was the nothing that made hands useful, the scintillant space around wings that opened into flight, the absence enclosing each question. It held him now in its augury, and the ripples of music from the future stilled to silence as the wind stopped and left him suspended unmoving above the huge, spinning world. Dark oceans and umber continents drifted below. They slid with planetary slowness from the azure daystruck crescent into blackness, the black orb of earth under the evaporations of stars.

Vision came as always with images of the iron cities. Factory towers spilled smoke into a hazy brown sky. Highways entangled the land in knots of concrete. Steel-and-glass buildings mazed every estuary and clotted the shores of every lake. Wherever he turned his one eye upon the future of the world, cities of towers loomed.

A white-hot glare silhouetted skylines to skeletal etchings. The cities scattered in carbon splinters before an erupting firestorm that billowed enormous clouds of flame and purple veils of lightning. Within this star-furnace radiance, the Fire Lords moved. The Furor saw them as motes of intense brilliance swirling through the columning clouds of fiery ash. They were dancing. They were dancing as the cities burned!

This was the apocalypse that the Furor had dedicated his life to avert. His whole purpose was to fend off this terrible destiny, and every sinew in his body strained to see past the fiery horror to a new beginning, a future hope. But all that his one eye perceived was a desert where the cities had been—ranges of lifeless talc.

"All-Father, why do you look so scared?" a small voice, a child's piping voice asked. "And why are you hanging upside down?"

The Furor twisted about and saw a smudge-cheeked girl with stringy blond hair and tattered smock standing barefoot on the frosty gravel under the Raven's Branch. She was Skuld, the youngest of the Norns, the Wyrd Sisters who possessed the power to witness all of time. "Do not tease me, little one. Away with you."

The Furor feared the Norns. They were not like the other gods. None knew their origin. They simply were. From before the time of the elder gods, they came and went as they pleased.

Skuld peered upward with ingenuous awe at the chieftain of the gods dangling by his ankles from the silver limb of heaven, his thick beard wind-twisted and fallen across his anguished face. "I would never tease you, All-Father. Verthandi says you want to speak with me. I have left my home on the Branch of Hours, and here I am. But why are you hanging upside down like a bat? Your hands are free. You are not in trouble, are you?"

The Furor peered at the child and saw that she was not laughing at him. She was sincere. As the Norn of the future, she had no immediate knowledge of his ritual hanging and how it drew the electrical might of the sun and the stars themselves through his legs and into his head to open a prophetic vista. But her Wyrd Sister, Verthandi, Norn of the present, had obviously beheld his distress and sent Skuld to counsel him. So distraught was he by what he had witnessed on the horizon of time that he defied his better judgment, and said to the Wyrd Sister, "I am in dire trouble, Skuld."

The child looked alarmed and reached her small hands up to grab his dangling arms. At her touch, the monstrous vision of the doomful future that had left him eaten half-away sank into him like an ice wind, deep as a memory, unavoidable as history. "Take my hand, All-Father. I will pull you down."

Alarmed, he pulled his hand away. "No, Skuld." He exhaled a trembling sigh and pulled himself up to his thong-tied ankles. With one deft tug, he released his legs and curled into his fall. He landed with bent knees and a forceful groan on the gravel beside the child. When she tried to steady him, he waved her off. "I'm fine, young one. Just tired. Just very tired." He staggered sideways and sat down, his legs in their wolfskin boots and leather-strapped trousers stretched out before him.

"You do not look well, All-Father."

"I am not well, Skuld." He wiped the sweat from his wrinkled brow and brushed his long and wild silver hair from his one eye. "I hung myself so that I might see what is to come."

"You hung yourself?" Skuld frowned, not comprehending, and sat beside the big-shouldered god. "Why? I can see what is to be. You've only to ask me."

"I wanted to see for myself. It was important that I saw for myself."

"And what did you see?"

"I saw the iron cities."

"And did you see the wagons without horses?" she inquired excitedly. "The metal wagons without horses? Did you see them?

And the metal ships that fly with wings that do not move? Did you see them flying faster than the wind?"

"Oh, yes. I saw them. All the wonders to come. The horrible wonders."

Skuld's excitement dimmed, and she nodded grimly and leaned against the Furor's bare, muscular arm. "It is horrible, All-Father. The forests are gone. And the sky has no birds."

"The fire—the storms of fire . . ."

"Plague first," Skuld whispered drowsily. "Plague makes the cities sick. Then comes the fire to cleanse them."

"You have seen this?"

"I see it."

"And after the fires?"

"No more iron cities."

The Furor regarded the child half-asleep at his side. She *was* a child, and that was partly why he had never pressed her to this revelation before. She saw with immature eyes. But now he had beheld this evil reality for himself, and he nodded with woeful agreement. "This world's age is over when the iron cities burn. But can we change what is to be?"

"You must ask Verthandi," Skuld mumbled, and nuzzled against the warm arm of the All-Father.

"No, Skuld." He nudged her awake. "I am asking you. Is there any other future for us?"

She blinked sleepily at him and shrugged. "Everything I see begins with Verthandi. Speak with her, All-Father."

The chieftain with the storm gray beard shook his head. "Listen to me, Skuld. I gave my right eye for the power to behold the future, and I learned from the dwarfs how to hang myself from this topmost branch of Yggdrasil that the strength of heaven would fill my head. I have seen what you have seen. But I do not accept it. I cannot accept it. For what purpose are we living if all is to be burned to ash? There must be a way to change our future. There must be a way!"

"Hush!" Skuld perked up, lifting her dirt-streaked face to listen to the wind moaning across the Raven's Branch. "Do you hear it?"

From afar came a song without music, a human voice soft and insistent with the cadence of a chant but without rhyme or meter:

Even our fear is not as old
though it will take our whole lives
to know for sure.

"Who is that?" the Furor asked, staring into the ice blue eyes of the child, suddenly afraid, remembering who he was with. "Who is singing to me?"

"Not to you, All-Father. To your wife, to Lady Unique." Skuld turned her bedraggled head to listen better. "It is the poet-king Wesc. He sings to your wife. He sings to the goddess of poetry, that she may favor him. Listen to his song."

The fatigue of smoke,
the torn mist rising from
the sea, the beard of the moon,
is the voice
that was trapped so long ago
in cages of light,
in mirrors
and dreams
trying to tell us
what will be left
after everything that might have been enough
is used up.

"Is that poetry?" The Furor's one eyelid lowered skeptic-ally. "I hear no rhyme or rhythm. It sounds like speaking, not poetry."

"It is speaking, All-Father. King Wesc writes for Lady Unique a poem that runs free from the heart. It is a love poem—so much in love it throws off rhyme like a lover undressing."

"Nonsense!" He gently pushed her away. "Why are you dis-tracting me with this, young one? I have come to Raven's Branch to confront evil and find a way free of it."

"But, All-Father, this poetry is free." Skuld knelt beside him and began to play with the leather laces of his boot. "Wesc loves Lady Unique—and she loves him. With her love, he rules the north tribes. And ruled by him, they will soon invade the West Isles."

"Child, you ramble." The Furor lifted his bearded chin to the indigo zenith and its crest of stars. "I have important work to do. Go now."

Skuld pouted. "Verthandi sent me to help you. And that's what I'm doing."

"By making me listen to poetry that doesn't even sound like poetry?"

"Wesc will kill Arthor with that poetry."

The Furor lowered his gaze and regarded more closely the young girl toying with his bootlaces. "Arthor? What do you know of the boy-king?"

She shrugged, distracted by the tasseled red leather of his bootlaces. And when he leaned forward and took her chin in his big hand, space wobbled, and he felt as though he were falling, toppling through the sky. He jolted, and a vision expanded through him.

Avalon, with rumpled green hills and valleys, sprawled on the horizon, an emerald gown discarded by the naked sea. The Furor's watchful mind moved closer, and the morning hills and dells became mountain cups of apple trees. On the high, verdant promontories, waterfalls fell in quicksilver threads that never reached the ground: These cascades blew away from the craggy cliffs in wild vapors and broken rainbows, disappearing in the air like a story that brims into nothingness on a book's last page.

The Furor yanked his mind away and found himself once more on the Raven's Branch, sitting in flinty gravel at the top of Yggdrasil. He felt drunk.

"What are you doing to me?" he moaned, both hands to his head. He reminded himself that Skuld only appeared to be a child. She was a Wyrd Sister, older, far older, than he. What manner of being was she? He could only guess. "Why did you show me Avalon?"

"Arthor's destiny is Avalon." Skuld untied his boot and intently strove to tie it again, speaking distractedly. "The Fire Lords have marked him. He will be a witness to the reign of chieftains. Ten thousand years of chiefs and kings and emperors are behind us. How many more years are ahead?"

The Furor began to comprehend. "When Arthor dies, he goes to Avalon . . ."

"To take the place of Rna. She is the oldest of the Nine Queens. Now that Arthor is born, she is free to leave Avalon." Skuld's fingers fumbled, and the bow she was tying fell apart. She frowned and began again. "Do you know how he was born?"

The chieftain of the north gods tugged his beard, wondering what Skuld was trying to tell him. Absently, he said, "Uther Pendragon sired him on the Celtic queen, Ygrane . . ."

"Skuld looked up at him abruptly. "See it!"

The Furor's mind slid backward through time eighteen summers and moved with the life mote inside the womb of Ygrane. He vaguely sensed the outer world around him—Ygrane and Uther asleep in each other's arms, a night camp of snuffling horses, distant owls sobbing, and the torn mist on the river adrift under a moon like a broken cup . . .

Closer, the entranced god sat with the tiny cellular life taking shape in the blood-dark. Already, the wee being only hours old glowed with bodylight, the radiance of creation held to the earth by the kitesilk of life's molecule—DNA. The molecule had a soul. The Furor recognized the ghost of a Celtic warrior who had lived centuries earlier: *Cuchulain!*

The cleavage of the ovum into morular cells followed the XY chromosome pattern of the male, shaping a sexual order out of helical waverings, carbon atoms, glucose molecules, precisely tangled bunches of proteins—a new life for an ancient soul.

Cuchulain glowed with the energy of chemical bonds. His DNA acted as antennae, resonating a waveform—frequencies of ultraweak photons in a pattern unique to him. The Furor watched with all that his astonishment could bear as the multiplying cells molded an individual identity, a human destiny reminiscent of a noble history that belonged now to the joys and sorrows of an undetermined fate.

With a strenuous effort, the Furor pulled himself back to the Raven's Branch, his one gray eye glaring in his amazed face. "Why?" he gasped. Like all the gods, he was a being of energy, and the organic powers that shaped planetary life were a mystery to him. "Why do you show me this?"

"All-Father, how can you destroy what you do not see?" Skuld finished tying a loose bow with the bootlaces and sat back satisfied. "There are many futures. Many. But only one comes to Verthandi."

"When Arthor dies, he goes to Avalon," the Furor repeated slowly, intently, fitting the pieces of understanding together as he spoke. "The Fire Lords will install him there to witness the consequences of one hundred centuries of rule by men, by chieftains and warlords. Apocalypse. Ragnarok. Death by plague and fire."

"The future grows from small things, All-Father." Skuld sat on his knee and gripped the leather braces of his leggings. "*When* Arthor dies determines what the future will be. There will be cities. The forests will fall. The rivers will stink with waste. Just as we see from here. But the weapons of plague and fire—they do not have to overwhelm the world."

"They do not?" The Furor took Skuld's narrow shoulders in his thick hands, then quickly withdrew his hands, afraid of falling into another trance. "If I cannot stop the iron cities, *how* will I stop the doom of plague and fire?"

Skuld's big pale eyes gazed openly at him. "Do you love your wife?"

"Lady Unique rules at my side," the Furor answered decisively. "The talismans she makes empowers the north tribes and holds them together under the sway of Wesc."

"But do you love her, All-Father?"

"She is my wife."

"Then why do I see you with Keeper of the Dusk Apples?"

The Furor stared into her candid eyes without speaking.

"She is your mistress," Skuld said with the frankness of a child. "And if Lady Unique were to learn this, she would be heartbroken—and the poetry, the free-running poetry of Wesc, would not sound so very good anymore to Lady Unique, would it, All-Father?"

> *How could we know*
> *though we listen*
> *and the black spot, the imperfection*
> *on the eye, goes on*
> *following*
> *full of love for us?*

The Furor put his hands over his ears. "Silence that damnable voice, Skuld . . ."

How could we know
when there is
nine
and the return to zero
in children's songs
and still
no way back?

"What are you doing to me?" The Furor pushed the child away and stood up. "My wife knows nothing of my affection for Keeper of the Dusk Apples. Are you going to tell her?"

How could we know
and not explain
if even to ourselves
the hazard, the
pieces of darkness
hardening
in our shadows?

"All-Father, listen to the poems." Skuld sat in the gravel where she had fallen, a shadow of sorrow between her eyes. "In these small words, the entire future opens."

"I hear nothing but gibberish." He gruffly turned away, angry that this—this entity had disclosed his secret love. "This is not poetry that Wesc writes. It is a premonition of the madness to come."

How could we know
the patient water was
speaking
our lives
through the salt
while we searched
the shores of the sleeping lake
for what we carried
in our mouths?

"If you won't listen to the poet-king," Skuld asked, "then will you heed the Dwellers from the House of Fog—will you heed the demons you have bound with your magic to topple Arthor?"

The Furor spun about to angrily confront the creature who taunted him—but Skuld was gone. The Raven's Branch had dissolved to mist, to the spiritous threshold before the House of Fog, the cold domain whence the demons came and went. Under the pressure of his stare, the haze parted to reveal a lightless abyss reeking with the tarry stench of hell.

Out of the blackness of the gorge, a giant rose. Onyx monster of leprous flesh, visage molting to a skull under blistered rags of skin, a demon glared with red eyes slant and malevolent. On rickets-sprung legs, the skeletal titan reared. "Who dares summon Lucifer?" A big voice shook cinders off the Raven's Branch so that they fell in shooting stars to the nightworld below. "Who binds my demons with magic?" Grave smoke drooled from a grin of black teeth.

The Furor stared speechless as the huge entity steadied itself in the void above the earth. Rotted cerements dangled from a brisket of chalk bones, its calcined hands bracing the cliff walls of the Raven's Branch to thrust its charnel body upright. Its tight stare found the startled god. "The Furor! Chieftain of the north gods!" Windy light stirred behind the decayed holes of Lucifer's skull, wormbores drilled into a brain of fire. "What is your purpose with my demons?"

The Furor motioned to speak, and all he had to say was said in a voiceless instant, snatched from him by the searing look of the demon lord.

"You lost my demon Lailoken!" Lucifer's wandlike arms swung with tantrum fury. "Your crude magic was supposed to bind him to your war against the Britons. He was supposed to rage with the other demons and destroy kingdoms! Instead, you lost him, and he fell into the hands of the angels! You dolt! Now he lives in a mortal body as Merlin, and his demon powers work against me, his master!"

Radium-fierce rays lanced from the skullholes of Lucifer's rotted head. "Now I must undo what you have done!" The giant's face ripped to smoke, ash dust subsumed in a widening radiance of thermonuclear glare. With star-fusion brilliance, Lucifer dissolved the darkness and laid naked the cankerous, pocked terraces of the pit that was the House of Fog. Souls in their tiny, swarming millions ignited like electric filaments, their cold suffering suddenly burning to hot pain.

The hot light dimmed—and Lucifer was gone. The Furor stood alone upon the Raven's Branch. Though it was a limb of the World Tree Yggdrasil, it also appeared as a landscape, a vast mosaic terrain of frost-splotched gravel and shattered plates of agate. A thousand hectares of rusty dunes rippled the horizon beneath an indigo sky with stars as big and evil as cactus flowers.

The Furor traversed this desolate ground stunned. The future of fire and plague, of the gods' own twilight, somehow depended upon his fidelity to his wife and also to the death of Britain's boy-king. But Skuld had been ambiguous. And Lucifer had been entirely terrifying.

At a cavern in a scarp of raw stone, he stopped. Inside were the entranced figures of his son, Thunder Red Hair, his daughter Beauty, and his staunchest allies among the Æsir gods. Their forms lay shrouded in white pumice, which had blown over them from the crests of scalloped eskers and dunes like sea swells. The lives of these gods were in suspension so that the Furor could harness their power and shape a magic strong enough to bind demons.

It had seemed like an able idea—using the combined strength of the gods to command demons in his war against the Fire Lords. But Lucifer, the fallen angel who was lord of the demons, was right to berate him for letting the demon Lailoken escape his magic. For all his magic, for all these brave gods who had sacrificed pieces of their lives, he had attained little. The trophy of Britain still eluded him—and the Fire Lords . . .

He shook his bearded head. He had not even managed to confront a single Fire Lord, let alone defeat them all. And now, they had Merlin, because he had been a dolt with the unwieldy magic of the sleeping gods and had inadvertently thrust Lailoken into their radiant hands.

Troubled, he sat on the sandy ledge before the cavern of sleeping gods and rested his hoary head in his hands. A voice whispered from afar. He pressed his palms tightly over his ears, not wanting to hear more rhymeless doggerel from his wife's worshiper. But the voice only sounded louder. And it was not the poet-king. It was a younger voice, speaking in Latin:

Mother Mary, Merlin says I must leave Camelot and tour my king-dom—but I am afraid. Magic frightens me. I want no part of it. I beg of you, Blessed Mother, pray to your Son and our Father that the curse that blights Britain be lifted.

The Furor removed his hands from his ears and lifted his head, astounded. He was hearing the intimate prayers of the boy-king Arthor. This was the work of Lucifer, he was certain. The magic that the Furor had culled from the sleeping gods and had used to bind demons to his will had also connected him to the demon lord. *Now I must undo what you have done!* Lucifer had groused—and this psychic peephole into his enemy's soul was surely the demon's work. He covered his ears again and listened:

Mother Mary, I have no fear of the sword. I know that your Son taught peace and warned that those of us who live by the sword would die by it. I am not afraid to die under the sword defending my kingdom and my people. But I am sore afraid of magic. I do not understand it.

When the Furor stood and walked just a few paces from the cave of the tranced gods, the prayerful voice of Arthor faded away. *It is indeed the magic of these Æsir faithful who give me the strength to hear my enemy's most private thoughts!*

He returned excitedly to the cave hole that looked in upon the sand-muted shapes of his children and allies and palmed his ears again:

By magic I have been duped into incest. Morgeu the Fey has doomed me. This I know. But I cannot accept it. Mother Mary, give me the strength to bear my sin, to rule though I am unworthy. And pray, dear Mother, pray for my forgiveness.

The Furor laughed with dark glee, and his shout of triumph echoed from horizon to horizon.

The dried scalps of slaughtered Britons and Celts strung on cords dangled from their hips. Wolfhide loinwraps and boots of human leather were their sole garments, and serpent-coil cicatrices and raven tattoos embossed their shoulders and backs. Each bore on their hairless chests the raised welts from wolf claws, received in initiation to their god the Furor, the one-eyed deity of the north tribes whom the Christians in their Latin tongue called Odin.

God of the Wild Hunt, god of the storm, the Furor was feared by ordinary tribal folk and worshiped only by sorcerers, poets, and berserkers, those warriors touched with his fury, his frenzied battle-fetter that bound them to killing trance. The

Wolf Warriors were his elite berserkers. All had served the Furor first as sorcerers, priests of prophecy, and then had run through the wilderness with the wolf packs until they had grown strong on pain and the voice of the wolf spoke in them.

The wolf and the raven were the Furor's familiars. The raven whispered to the sorcerers and told them of the terrible destiny that awaited the world. And the wolf's voice belonged to the berserkers. It sang to them of the Furor's passion to save the world from destruction. The wolf song lifted the berserkers above human conceptions of good and evil.

Determined to serve their god, Wolf Warriors sailed to Britain in the night. By day, they roamed the countryside in packs, hunting Britons and Celts, and stalking their own glorious deaths.

4

Dragon Psalm

All that remained of the mammoth trees that once flanked the old Roman highway north of Venonae were charred trunks, burned black and smooth as jet pylons of an ancient temple. The surrounding fields and hills had been scorched, and much of that land lay cindered and without definition. A few groves upon the ridges remained intact, but the dearth of spring rains had left them sere and winter-bare.

Clattering at a slow pace across the bare stone and gravel reefs of the remnant highway, five filthy, brutal horsemen rode. They wore dusty rawhide vests bleached and cracked like old ceramic, and their beards and scabrous hair hung in strings black and greasy as twists of singed candlewick. With an air of menacing vigilance, they surveyed the grim landscape and spotted through the ebony columns of incinerated trees a ramshackle roadhouse.

A broad cinder path led from the decrepit highway through a brambly garth of apple trees, past a run of chickens and a drowsy dog. The roadhouse had once been a Roman villa, and it retained a regal stature though its tile roof was largely missing, replaced by thatching, and its adobe walls had crumbled and relied on huge veils of browned bean vines to cover gaping holes. An old calf hide nailed to one wall had stenciled on it in rain-leached letters: THE BLANKET OF STARS.

Before dismounting, the feral horsemen rode to either side of the wide building, hands on their sword hilts, alert for Wolf

Warriors. They saw a burly young man in a crude hempen tunic grooming a gray palfrey, green flies spinning around him in a sunny haze of dust and horsehair. The clop of hooves, chink of metal, and creak of saddles elicited no attention from him, and the riders returned to the front courtyard and dismounted.

A scrawny, barefoot lad in gray breeches and chemise of knotted rags stood warily in the wide entryway. "Stable your mounts, sirs?" His voice quavered, and he kept his eyes averted from the dangerous men.

One of the riders grabbed the boy by the scruff of the neck and hurled him into the courtyard so forcefully the youth rolled into the dirt. "Unsaddle each in its turn only. We want them ready to ride quickly. Have you grain?"

"No cow parsley for these steeds, lad," another of the men demanded, "or we'll wring your neck."

The boy nodded and scrambled to his feet. "'Tis dear, m'lords. Three coins silver a bag."

The men laughed in unison. "Not for us, boy. We're king's men—with billeting privileges. A bag for each of our mounts. And look lively."

The five soldiers shambled like barbaric tribesmen into The Blanket of Stars, pausing briefly in the broad doorway. A graven and splintered gorgon gazed blindly above them. What once had been a greeting chamber and connecting servants' cells in a time long ago had coalesced to one large cantina with a floor of tamped earth. Holes in the thatched ceiling let down silver wands of sunlight among two long, ramshackle tables and warped benches. At the back, through knotholes and numerous cracks in a weathered partition of gray planks, stood visible the galley, with its lopsided stone oven and smoking charcoal grill. A young woman and an old man, both in rags and skins, warily stared at them through the steam like cavefolk.

The tables were not empty. A ragged monk and three road-dusted pilgrims with prayer beads at their wrists sat hunched over soapstone bowls eating cereal flummery and nettle soup. At the far end of the second table, a balding, one-armed man in a merchant's red leather jerkin did not raise his eyes from his bowl of salt fish boiled in milk.

Once assured there was no threat in this impoverished road-house, the soldiers went directly to the three wine casks stacked beside the galley partition, opened the bung, and, with much pushing and shoving, took turns filling their mouths with the brown wine.

From behind a moth-chewed curtain that draped the rickety stairway to the sleeping alcoves entered a barefoot woman in a matron's robe of blue velveteen so old it appeared crinkled as crepe. She possessed a rustic beauty, this big-shouldered woman with honey brown hair tied atop her head in a twist. Her eyes were small blue slits of sky yet proud under blond arches of brow, her cheeks ruddied by sun, and her long jaw and the lip under her pert nose dusted as with a haze of pollen. "I'm Julia," she announced in a voice of relaxed command. "Welcome, travelers, to The Blanket of Stars. Will you be having table fare with your wine then?"

"Not 'lest it's you on the table!" a soldier gibed, and the others guffawed.

Like fingers of a hand, the five men arrayed themselves in the middle of the cantina and leered at her as one. The short, stout one—the thumb—seemed their leader, and he spoke with a guttural authority: "Me and these men be king's soldiers. We're wanting bread and cheese and what fare we can take with us."

Julia shoved between the tallest—the stooped middle and ring fingers—and stopped the bung they had left splashing wine into the catch bucket. "Show me your silver, and I'll provision all your saddlebags."

"Best you let us talk direct with the innholder," said the greasy and scorched thumb.

"The innholder is my husband, Eril, a king's soldier, too, not yet returned from this battlefield wide as Britain. So, show me your silver, and I'll see to your provisions."

"We'll be taking what silver we find in this hovel," the thumb declared loudly, and nodded to the others. Immediately, pinky and forefinger went to the tables and stood threateningly over the diners. "We are here to collect what coin you have for our service in the war."

"The war is over," the one-armed merchant spoke up forcefully. "And I know for a fact that the king sanctions no quartering privileges among his soldiers."

"For a fact?" queried the forefinger, placing both hands on the table where the merchant sat and leaning forward with a malicious grin. "And how would you know that, monger?"

"I've just come from Camelot," the merchant replied coolly, "and I heard from the king himself that he will tolerate no looting. It is a hanging offense. If you are the king's men, you should know that."

The soldiers bellowed laughter at the merchant's refined tone and their own grim intent.

From the galley came the old man, a cleaver in hand. "Is there trouble here, daughter?"

"Nay, Father. These brutes were just leaving." Julia pulled from behind at ring and middle fingers' belts, tugging them with surprising strength toward the door. "Go steal from the Cantii Saxons, you louts—if you've courage enough. Now get out of here."

The soldiers' laughter frenzied to barks and howls. Thumb stepped before the old man and, in one motion, lifted the cleaver from his hand and smote him hard across the brow.

The aged cook collapsed with a moan, and Julia barged past the soldiers and rushed to him. "Father!"

"There'll be worse for you if you don't shut up and do as we say!" the thumb shouted. "Now everyone put your coin on the table. And you, woman, you'll show me the larder—you and me together."

The moth-chewed curtain jerked aside, revealing the beardless, brawny youth the soldiers had seen earlier in the back lot. He had a pale, rosy-cheeked face, his brown hair shorn to the temples like a farm boy's and bristly as badger fur, yet his yellow eyes held a baleful, intent look. He entered the cantina with a pronounced limp. "You dishonor your king," he said in a low and unhappy voice.

"Shut up, boy, or we'll pull out your tongue by its roots." The thumb waved the cleaver. "We've come for coin and provisions. But we'll take blood if we must."

"Only your blood will be spilled here if you don't leave this place at once," the boy said, a green vein suddenly ticking at his temple.

The thumb laughed darkly. "I told you to shut up! Now, gimp, I'm going to shave your head with this cleaver." The stout soldier advanced with a hostile grin and the cleaver held high to distract while his other hand swiftly drew a gutting knife from his belt.

"Stop!" Julia cried. "Leave him be! He's but a halt boy! You can have what you want!"

"We'll have it all anyway—and this gimp's scalp as well." The muscular thumb feinted with the cleaver and drove his knife upward, blade flat to slip between ribs. But the boy, calm as a dancer, had simply pivoted on his good leg so that the knife found only air.

In the moment that the thumb leaned forward off-balance, the boy's right hand swiftly slapped the assailant behind the head, throwing him forward, while his left hand twisted the cleaver from his grip. The lad waited a heartbeat for the thumb to scramble about and come at him again with the knife before he deftly flicked the cleaver, lodging the blade in the enraged man's skull.

Before forefinger could react, the merchant's one arm blurred, and a dagger pinned the soldier's right hand to the table-top where he had been leaning with vicious attention. Half a scream ripped from him, and the one arm grabbed him by the hair and pounded his head hard on the table, rendering him silent.

Outrage bawled from the three standing soldiers, and they drew their swords. As they came forward, the halt boy limped past Julia and her cowering father. He stepped with his bad leg on the end of an empty table bench, tilting it upright. With a mighty heave, he slammed the bench down on the upraised swords, catching two in the wood and yanking the weapons free. He caught the bench again as it fell and shoved it forward, throwing the front two soldiers off-balance.

The third soldier—pinky—dashed forward to skewer the adroit boy, but the staggering soldiers and the bench slowed his charge. The halt lad seized a sword from the bench, and with one swipe severed pinky's sword hand and stabbed the sword tip into the breastbone of the soldier pressing beside him. The stabbed soldier reeled backward with a grunt. Pinky collided into him squealing, arm stump jetting blood.

Thumb lurched upright, face slick with blood, and pulled the cleaver from his skull. The halt boy's yellow eyes fixed him with a cold look, and thumb dropped the cleaver and ran past, whimpering. Out the way they had come, the five soldiers fled. The one-armed merchant strode after them, dragging the unconscious soldier whose hand he had pierced. The monk and pilgrims followed timidly, anxious to see that the malefactors departed.

"Who are you?" Julia asked, as the lad bent over her father and examined the bump under his blood-matted hair.

"I am my master's servant." He helped the old man to his feet. "You should lie down. Your wound is not serious. A patch of willow's bark will speed the healing."

"You are a soldier," the old man muttered. "The way you move, lad—"

"I am just my master's servant."

"Your master is the one-armed merchant you came in with?" the old man inquired. "You both speak like lords."

"A Christian lord taught me well. And he is well traveled." He helped the hurt man to sit down on a table bench, and added comfortingly, "Those felons will be driven off without their horses. Those steeds belong to you now. Sell them if you wish and use the money to repair your inn."

"Who are you?" Julia asked again. "What are your names?"

The yellow eyes regarded her kindly. "I am . . . John Halt . . . and he is Elder John."

"Johns Halt and Elder." She smiled at him and kissed his cheek. "You shall have our finest vintage. Leoba! Open the Rhenish keg!"

A younger woman with strawberry hair came out of the galley with a wet rag for the old man's head. "The Rhenish keg?"

"Yes, you heard me aright, sister. Now, go and bring us two cups." She smiled again at John Halt, showing teeth clean and even as a Celt's. "We were saving that keg for my husband's return. But there'd be no home to receive my Eril if not for you and John Elder. You shall have our best vintage."

"Save your vintage for Eril." John Halt took both of Julia's hands and stared a long moment into her freckled and sunburnished face. "Your kind regard is reward enough for me."

"He speaks good as a lord," the old man said again. "Leoba— come meet good John Halt!"

The one-armed merchant returned with two sword belts in his hand. The monk and pilgrims followed, looking much relieved. "The malefasors are away and unarmed. They are now at the mercy of what brigands will receive them on the road."

"No doubt they will find comfort among the king's army of brigands," Julia griped, and finished securing the wet rag about her father's brow.

"You have no love for our king?" John Halt asked, and received with both hands the cup of well water Leoba brought to him.

Julia's upper lip curled. "We fared better when the warlords ruled Britain. My Eril was taken from me to secure King Arthor's throne."

"But now that the king has united the realm, surely there will be better times for all." John Halt looked to Julia's father for agreement, but the old man just shook his head.

"Arthor is a mere boy," the elder said glumly. "He made claim on the throne by right of birth, but the experience to rule all Britain, that he lacks sorely. Look at our fair land. He's made a botch of it already. That he might wear a crown and rule over us, he fought a war that laid waste the good earth. What kind of king is that?"

"A dangerous fool, I say," Julia answered irascibly.

"Yet, he united the warlords," John Halt pressed. "With our land one, we can better defend ourselves against pagan invaders."

"Aye, and will pagan invaders treat us less kindly than the five men of our own king's army you drove from our door?" the old man asked, and his daughters concurred with vigorous nods.

"I just want my Eril back," Julia added, "and each day pray he has not lost his life to put a crown on a boy's head."

"It's time we go," Elder John called from the doorway, where he had kicked out the soldier's severed hand. "We've a long way to travel this day."

"Go?" The old man stood up, then sat down again in a sway of dizziness. "You must stay, the two of you. You can sell your wares from here, merchant. Now that spring is come and the strife ended, there'll be travelers aplenty on the roads, and we'll be busy, you'll see. There's plenty work for your lad. Why wander in this dangerous world when Providence has led you to our haven?"

Elder John shook his balding head. "Thank you, good man, but I've business to attend elsewhere. Perhaps we will visit again before long. Get the horses, boy. Don't dawdle. We've far to go while it's yet light."

John Halt scowled, then shrugged and limped out the back way. After helping her father to his cot in a back room behind the galley, Julia stepped into the back lot, past the soldiers' five abandoned mounts, and found the big-shouldered youth saddling his gray palfrey. The stableboy, Julia's young brother, came forth from a rickety stable leading Elder John's stallion, a deep chestnut steed eighteen hands high and laded with the merchant's goods wrapped in burlap.

"I got a good eye for people," Julia said warmly. "An innkeeper's wife would, seeing all manner passing through. And my eye tells me, you're no common merchant's apprentice."

John Halt made no reply but kept his attention on securing his scuffed and worn saddle.

"Your halt leg—it's a wound, is it not?" Julia stepped closer, and continued in a conciliatory tone, "You don't fight like a brawler. You're proper trained in killing. What I just seen tells me you been soldiering for the king yourself. That's why you have good words for him." She put a hand on his shoulder. "I apologize for what ill we said of the crown. We all miss Eril. Sometimes I fear the worst—and I blame the king."

John Halt smiled, but before he could speak, Elder John called from the dusty lane with its trellis of dried bean cords and squash vines that patched the cracked plaster at the side of the inn, "Stop lingering, boy. We've far to go."

The youth swung himself into the saddle. "I'll pray for your Eril," he promised, pulling the palfrey around.

"And I'll pray for our king," she called after him, and waved.

"She said she would pray for me." Arthor grinned proudly at his one-armed companion as they rode away from The Blanket of Stars. "Do you think she is sincere?"

"What I think, my lord, is that you are taken with her."

"Taken, Bedevere?" The king cast a lingering look backward at the broken-down villa. "Is that why you insisted we depart? You were robust in your command of me back there."

"There was no point in remaining."

"What if those cutthroats return?"

"They will not, my lord." Bedevere lifted a pocket flap of his leather jerkin to reveal its mirror-polished brass underside and turned in his saddle until it caught the sun and winked three short flashes. A moment later, a star glinted from a distant cinder ridge. "They are still running north, toward Ratae. I signaled Bors to watch for them. If they turn back, they will be hanged."

"Hanged?" The youth let out a dry laugh. "Where will Bors find a tree in this devastation?" He gazed about with open despair at the scorched horizon: tree trunks angled like charcoal runes against a sky whose very blueness and toppling clouds seemed fugitive to the strange and barren world below. "This is so much worse than I had thought."

"Then the wizard was justified in sending us disguised into this wasteland, to witness this for ourselves." Bedevere rode his massive horse slowly among the broken cobbles. "Now you know what you could never have surmised within the walls of Camelot."

The king peered about for some living thing to stir among the black pastures and saw only cloud shadows running mutely across the ashen fields. "Where is Merlin?"

"Heaven knows—then again, my lord, perhaps not even heaven."

Merlin made his way along the ruins of an old wall and down a steep path to where silt from the river Nene had buried some ancient city. The donkey he had ridden from Venonae gazed about with its eyes of devilish merriment, as if amused that nowhere among the austere rocks sprouted any tuft upon which to graze. Except for a few scurrilous shrubs crowning the great masonry blocks atop the skewed wall, no flora had survived the purging fires. The landscape all about appeared primal and anonymous as the absolute shale delivered from earth's volcanic creation.

The wizard knew that this was unnatural. Something more terrible than the scorched-earth tactics of the king's enemies had charred the land. Dressed in sere and worn farmer's clothes, tattered as a scarecrow, he moved nimbly over silt-stained paving plates, seeking the deepest declivity among the rubble. He appeared an old scavenger, his bearded visage obscured by the black, floppy-brimmed hat he wore low and secured with twine. But when he leaped from the stone abutment of a collapsed bridge to a cistern filled with gravel, he lighted with feline grace and, fluid as a shadow, slid down among the old, tilted slabs of a littoral causeway.

In truth, he felt stronger than ever in this life, for he was growing younger each year. He was a demon in human guise. He was a demon who had once been a sexual fiend, an incubus whom the angels had lured into the womb of a saint, Optima, daughter of the King of Cos. And in that sacred darkness, he had lain with God Herself. For love of Her, he had been born into this brutal world a man growing younger.

He squeezed himself against the stone pylon of a sunken quay where ripples of the river tickled small, smooth stones, and he listened. His demon senses reached downward through the columnar rock into the alluvial soil that quaked with the singing burden of the river. Deeper, he listened, past the sonorous bed of the Nene, guiding his attention through strata of tile rock and tectonic densities into the magnetic flux of the planet's mantle.

There, he heard the Dragon's dreamsongs. The universe cried in those songs. The low, deep moan of the explosion that had flung all light into the void hummed through the Dragon's dreams with heat-noise—the vast thermal haze of a fire set by Whom. The flames had slaked long ago to starry embers, cold and drifting deeper into the cold.

Merlin shifted his attention. What he heard in the sibilant darkness around the Dragon jolted him. He recognized demon voices, incantatory singing—the mesmeric chants of his old cohorts. They were gathering the sleeping Dragon's energy, shaping its bright magnetic fire so like the Dragon itself—making evil miniatures within the Dragon's aura . . .

His listening was heard, and all at once, from out of the rock against which he pressed, a shadow shone. Through the stony granulations, the shadow thickened, bubbling to a tarry shape of ichorous outline. Too late, he pushed away. The living darkness stepped forth as a black reflection of himself and blocked his escape.

"Lailoken." The whisper of his name spurted like a flame and ignited the featureless thing of pitch and his own flesh as well. Together they burst into light and faced each other as they were in the beginning, white space, without intentions, pure energy of infinite frequencies, original light, without wanting, inside and out all at once, the plain truth before time, before fate.

This is an illusion! Merlin shouted in his mind. The light of heaven was long gone—except for the heat-noise in the Dragon's dreamsongs and what flames the Fire Lords themselves carried. *An illusion!*

"Lailoken, you cannot stop us," a voice deep as a drum spoke. "Britain will burn."

"The Dragon is asleep!" Merlin shouted, and his voice seemed to bound down an endless corridor. "How? How are you using it?"

"Britain burns, Lailoken," the drumbeat voice went on, "and your gutsack flesh will burn with her."

The wizard seized the dimensional shadow-thing, intent on pinning it to the rock and squeezing answers from it. But his hands closed on emptiness. As abruptly as it had appeared, the sticky blackness seeped away, draining backward through the rock crust. For one instant, a face with a smeared mouth and eyes hollow as bubbles hung like froth upon the stone. "You will die," it rasped, and vanished.

Merlin placed both hands upon the naked rock, feeling for the demonic presence and feeling only hard, insensate stone. Yet, he did not move. "I am as cruel as you are," he muttered to the rock. "I have not forgotten evil. Do you hear me? I will fight you!"

He waited for a reply. And though none came, he waited for long minutes in the mystery procession of time.

Morgeu the Fey, daughter of Ygrane and half sister to the king, breast-fed her infant Mordred on the piazza that her husband, the Celtic chieftain Lot, had built for her beside their black slate fastness on the northernmost isle of their realm. It was an arcade constructed in the Roman style with a colonnade of cedar pillars, white flag-stones, rose marble benches graven with caryatids, and—beyond a screen of gnarled apple trees—a commanding vista of the gray boreal sea. Vast mountains of cumulus drifted on the steely horizon. From embrasures in the wall of moss agate, scented wax purled a soothing scent of nepenthe that kept the usually colicky baby quiet.

Wrapped in a mantle of crimson silk and seated upon a cush-ioned divan, Morgeu regarded the group of islands that constituted her husband's realm. Water ouzels skimmed the bays, curlews rode rings of wind above the forested cliffs, and fishing vessels trawled the numerous firths and bays of the isles. She could have been happy here. The people loved her. Her enchantments diverted the big storms, encouraged the crops, and lured thick schools of fish. The North Isles had never flourished so well as since Lot brought her here as his wife.

Yet, she could never be truly happy, not so long as her half brother, Arthor, sat on the throne. His father, Uther Pendragon, had taken her mother, Ygrane, for his wife after the demon-wizard Merlin had arranged for Morgeu's father, Gorlois, duke of Dumnoni and *dux Britanniarum*, to die in battle. And with that death, happiness had become murder for Morgeu the Fey.

As a youth, distraught at the death of her father, Gorlois, Morgeu had retreated beyond the remnants of the Antonine Wall to the Roman ruins at Inchtuthil. In that windy hinterland, she had practiced demonolatry so intimately that she became the sum and meaning of those riotous ruins. The Picts, the ferocious tattooed warriors of Caledonia, feared her and called her the Fey—the Doomed.

With the infant Mordred in her arms, she felt the justice of that sobriquet. He was no ordinary child. She had conceived him by incest magic with her half brother, Arthor, deceiving him with a lustful illusion so that her womb would attract and hold the soul of her deceased father. But in death, Gorlois had been changed. The enemy of his former life, the Furor, had cut prophecy into her father's soul.

With the baby suckling at her breast, she could feel the strong eye that the Furor had carved within the reborn Gorlois. Vision expanded beyond the horizon of time. She glimpsed futures of unknown rank and order a dozen and more centuries ahead. Sitting on the piazza with the infant in her arms and her eyes closed, she saw what the Furor feared—and she indeed felt doomed: Monolithic cities of glass and steel glared to shadowy stencils in abrupt bursts of light, then dimmed to roiling fireclouds, giant trees of flame, each with its crown of ash. When they dimmed away, all that remained were horizons of imponderable ruin, burned-out lake beds of hell, and black ranges of barren cinderland.

In his oak chair set in the sun, Lot glowered at his dreamy wife from under a white bearskin cloak. He was old. His long gray hair and full beard enclosed a seamed and coriaceous face fixed to a permanent scowl. Since the birth of Mordred, he had begun to lose his mind. His two sons by Morgeu the Fey— Gawain and Gareth—pleaded with their mother to use her enchantments for his recovery. Morgeu claimed that the cure of his dementia was beyond her powers.

In truth, she was glad that Lot's age had stolen his mind. If he had possessed the clarity to suspect that Mordred was not his own child, the infant's life would be in jeopardy. As it was, he had sunk into himself, believing he had sired three sons by Morgeu.

His gray eyes gazed through an eagling frown at his wife nursing her baby, and he fixed first on her moon-round face and small jet eyes that gazed kindly at him. Sometimes he recalled that she was his wife. This afternoon, she was a stranger. He played his stare over her smiling but pugnacious features, her thick neck, and the gleam of her white shoulder between fallen tresses of crinkly, flame-colored hair.

He remembered his two earlier wives—long-limbed Elen, who had birthed him the warriors Delbaeth, Loinnbheimionach, and Cohar—and the lovely Pryderi of the Golden Hair, by whom he had sired the warrior twins Gwair and Galobrun. He nodded to himself with satisfaction and sifted back through those proud memories.

Morgeu watched him drift toward sleep, then rose from her cushioned divan and signaled with a nod for the nurse to emerge from the portico and take the sated infant from her. A young woman in saffron robes hurried to her side, and Mordred was bundled away.

Stepping lightly over the white flagstones to her husband's side, Morgeu bent to tuck the bearskin cloak more securely about his shoulders, and paused. A shadow of something invisible flitted across the limed wall beyond the stooped apple trees, and the air suddenly seemed to pulse louder with the sea's noise: The systole and diastole of the waves among the rocks roared with tempest fury though the bay was calm.

The smell of night surrounded her in the dazzling sun, and a chill frosted her bones. Magnificent and dreadful sorcery was moving toward her from many leagues away, a glamour so huge that it already cast its shadow upon her though her strong eye revealed no unusual presences to the very terminals of sea and land. Fear lit her up from within, a luminous terror that blanched all thoughts.

She sat down on one of the rose marble benches and waited for what was coming—something ancient, missing for centuries from daylight, already darkening the sun shafts in the tree vaults. Not since she first gave herself to demonolatry had she experienced such fear. But this was no demon coming for her. Demons were compact intelligences of destructive power. Each had a personality of evil love. What loomed toward her was something far more vast, full of blue rain and the sex of trees.

Faster than she had guessed, the presence was upon her. Candlelights burned in the wall of sunlight beyond the apple trees. *Faeries!* she realized in a frightful whirl of wonder. They came forward under the azure sky and towering clouds. *Faeries in daylight!*

Not since their exile from the Storm Tree five hundred years before had the pale people shown themselves by day. And not a mere handful but an entire nation of them came forward over the sea's curve and the low hills. Diamondglints burning among a mesh of sun rays, they came with the dense, overwhelming aroma of miles of grasses. A moneying gush of gold sparks, they poured over the motherless ocean and swirled toward her as wind-rushing atoms of noon.

Morgeu knew this was not possible. Without the sustaining energy of the Storm Tree, the Daoine Síd lacked the strength to withstand the heat of the sun and survived only because they took refuge by day underground, in the hollow hills. Yet, here they were, so brilliant that daylight bent around them in rainbow arcs.

They held no form but radiance. Solar particulates afloat in the air and in the choirs of sky beyond, they enclosed not only her but the arcade of cedar pillars and the entire black slate fortress. Like glyphs of a burning alphabet, they arrayed themselves in passages, shimmering yet still.

"Who are you?" she asked, feeling foolish and frightened, for she knew very well who they were. "What do you want of me?"

"A witness to truth," said a faint voice that she recognized immediately.

"Mother!"

Ygrane came striding forth from among the apple trees.

Morgeu knew that it was she, though she did not immediately recognize her with her hair shorn and the air around her viscous and dazzling.

Morgeu staggered upright, squinting to discern the familiar broad jaw, long, straight nose, and slant green eyes of her mother.

A softly hallucinated blur of light erased the space between them, and Ygrane stood immediately before her, within arm's reach. Morgeu sat back down on the rose marble bench, startled.

The *faëries* vanished. The gelid blue sky with its cottony clouds retained no remnant of their trespass into day. And the woman before her, in white kid riding boots with red laces, fawnskin trousers, and brown leather bodice, smiled kindly. "It is I, Morgeu."

"Mother—" She reached out and touched the woman's pale, naked arm, assuring herself of the solidity and actuality of this manifestation. With this one touch, she felt the same tranquil truth she had first experienced as a child and knew then that this was no illusion. "How?"

"The Daoine Síd have given me all the glamour I can carry—to find the Graal."

"The Síd? But you're a Christian—" Morgeu paused, and her mouth trembled for a moment before curling to a smile of comprehension. "You've forsaken the nailed god for power—the power of the Síd!"

Ygrane stared without flinching into her daughter's cold smile. "I must find the Graal, and you're going to help me, Morgeu."

Morgeu had been at Camelot, birthing Mordred, when the Graal had disappeared. She had believed it was the angels who had taken it back, and said, "The Fire Lords did not remove the Graal, or you would still be wearing your nun's habit, on your knees before god's tortured son. The angels can't help you—or won't. And so here you are, Mother, a witch-queen once more." Her small black eyes glinted with smug pride. "But look at you! You're more powerful than you ever were. Why is that? What did you promise Old Elk-Head in return for so much magic?"

"You saw the *faërie* hosts under the sun's blade." Ygrane bowed forward at the waist so that her face was on a level with her daughter's. "*I* am the power that anchors them in the day world. Do you understand, Morgeu?"

The smile slipped from Morgeu's lips. Though she hated her mother for abandoning her father and marrying Uther, she loved her for her strength and her glamour, and the enchantress's small black eyes glittered with pride and expectation. "Yes, Mother. You are the kingdom of yourself—the goddess in flesh rags—the one who makes shapes of pain—*Morrígan* herself."

"I am not *Morrígan*, but I have given myself to her."

"It is the same." Morgeu took her mother's arm and sat her down on the bench. Wonder pulsed in Morgeu, and fear. This was her flesh and blood, this creature of magic. She belonged to the pale people from childhood, and with that thought she grasped what was going to happen to her mother. "You are the sacrifice. When you find the Graal, you will be fed to the Dragon." She searched her mother's wide, sun-stained face for understanding. "But the Dragon is asleep. It was your unicorn that gave the Dragon sleep."

Ygrane said nothing, waiting for Morgeu to complete the pattern of her thought.

"And it will be your death that will rouse the Dragon again," Morgeu continued, "so that the Daoine Síd can carry their fight to the Storm Tree and the Æsir gods. That's it, is it not?"

"Yes."

"Mother!" The younger woman shook her head with disbelief. "You will never return to this world. Your soul will become one with the Dragon's dreamsongs, and you will never wear flesh in this world again. A wraith among the stars is what you will be. You know that."

"I know that."

"And you do this for Arthor?"

"He is my son."

Morgeu stood and stepped a pace aside. "I am your daughter and your firstborn. But that was not enough to keep you from giving yourself to Uther Pendragon."

"I loved Uther. I did not love your father."

"Gorlois was a good Roman." Morgeu's voice quavered, but the black bores of her eyes gazed steadily. Hurt twisted in her at the memory of her father dead in battle, killed defending this fickle woman, this faithless witch. "He was worthy of your love."

"Morgeu, I am not here to apologize for my past." Ygrane held her daughter's outraged stare—with difficulty. Queasiness blurred through her from her cramped uterus. Her menstrual flow was stronger than usual, provoked by the glamour coursing in her body, and she wanted to lie down. But she dared not show Morgeu her qualm, and she kept her voice strong. "I have made this sacrifice—and I have the power of Morrígan."

"The Síd will obey you, and you can lead them into the daylight. But what has that to do with me?"

Ygrane rose to her feet, ignoring the pulpy discomfort in her pelvis. "You are going to help me find the Graal."

"Have your faeries find it."

"They have searched all the Celtic lands and the hollow hills and found nothing. Now I must see if the north gods have seized it."

"And what has that to do with me?"

Ygrane stepped closer. "Mordred carries the soul of Gorlois—a soul that once dared ascend the Storm Tree. He was caught there by the Furor and cut into a shape that can see the timeshadows of the future."

"You will not touch my son, witch-queen." A frightened rage whirled up in the red-haired woman at the thought of losing her child to this sorceress.

"Ah, Morgeu." Sadness creased Ygrane's brow. "Why have you always been so difficult? Keep your silence, daughter. I know that the lack of love between your father and me hurt you. You would never accept that I was given to him against my will. I was just fourteen . . ."

"You will not touch my son."

"Yes, I will, Morgeu." Ygrane moved close enough for her daughter to see the stars of determination in her eyes. "And you will help me, because all that you cherish for your son is at hazard. If the north gods indeed possess the Graal, they are using it against Britain. And if they succeed in destroying your brother, Arthor, there will be no future at all for Mordred. You do not need the strong eye to see clearly this mortal truth." Pressing closer yet, she revealed that the stars in her eyes were really white birds, herons winging through darkness. "Take me to the child."

5

Weird Traveler

Mother Mary, my people suffer! Do you hear my prayers? Why do you send no relief? No rain. No aid from the Holy Father in Ravenna. Not even a cool breeze? Why? I tell you, Mother Mary, we are in despair. Merlin was just and sound in his demand that I tour my kingdom, for now I truly know the agony of Britain. War with the rebels has reduced the land to ash. Fishing villages have had all their boats burned. Farmers have lost their crops for the entire season. Drovers squat among the bones of their cattle.

Orchards and vineyards that had been cultivated over generations are gone! Even once-splendid inns and spas are destitute. Wherever I turn, there is mortal loss and suffering. What am I to do, Mother Mary? What am I to do? I am a wounded king. A sinful king.

Grief has me by the hair with both iron hands and pushes my face into the dirt, into the burned dirt of Britain, so that my cries and my prayers clog in the ash and dog shit and are not heard in heaven.

The Furor sat stitching outside the cave of the tranced gods among the whinstones and shale of the Raven's Branch. "Oh, heaven hears you, boy-king. The chieftain of heaven hears you, lad—and he is well pleased!"

The one-eyed god restrained a laugh, not wanting to disturb his stitching. These were rune sutures, binding the seam with spells to empower a pouch no bigger than his thumbnail. It was an earlobe, severed from an elf hunted down in the grasslands and divvied among the Rovers. He had taken the earlobe to fashion a listening amulet. Stuffed with sand from the cave of sleeping gods, it partook of his magic with the demon lord Lucifer. Now, wherever he traveled in the Storm Tree, this amulet would let him listen to the prayers of his enemy.

"Mother Mary!" He choked back his laughter at the anguish of Arthor's petitions. "Do you truly expect a desert tribeswoman dead over four hundred years to listen to your plaints, boy? You are so much the fool I cannot believe you have survived this long."

With a giddy heart, the Furor looked up from his stitching, into the cavern of the gods in their shrouds of sand. "Brave and trusting Æsir gods, I tell you now with certainty, your sacrifice is not in vain. I have heard the peevish obloquy of the West Isles' king for his nailed god—I have heard him weeping with frustration—and I tell you, when you wake, Britain will be ours."

Avalon was an island deep within its own dream. It could be reached only from the coast of the mind. And when one finally arrived there, one walked with the tread of the heart.

Each of us can listen to our heart inside our chest and hear the footfalls of selfhood. So also was it with the Nine Queens of Avalon.

Under immense clouds, luminously white and stacked miles high, the queens lived in immortal trance, because the magic of the Fire Lords enclosed them. Together, they experienced the invisible, disembodied ether that belongs to the long dream of life on this planet. Each of them could feel the enigmatic perfection of this ether that the moderns call mind. It enclosed the aching beauty of the dream in a secret purpose, which only now, fifteen centuries later, science has begun to disclose in its explorations of the cosmos and the atom.

None of the Nine Queens knew anything of the quantum mysteries that we wonder upon, yet they understood the true purpose of our faint, implausible dream within their own hearts. So also may it be with us.

Fra Athanasius rode a sumpter mule on the merchant road to Camelot. He kept as close to Chief Urien as he could among the pagan warlord's entourage of archers, lancers, and bare-chested Celtic cavalrymen. Urien had warned him that Saxon and Jutish raiders ranged freely through these badlands. With his weak eyes, the papal legate could see little of the surroundings, but what he did see disheartened him indeed.

The highway—what these primitive Britons called a highway—was an antiquated Roman road whose metal surfacing had eroded away and whose paving stones had buckled, revealing gravel beds worn to potholes. Every field they passed was burned, every hillside slashed with wrathful blackness.

Late in the afternoon of the second day, a weird traveler hailed them from the roadside. Urien called a full halt at the sight of him. He was of no remarkable stature and stood alone in the bleak terrain without so much as a walking staff or water flagon. Dressed entirely in black close-fitting garments, he seemed at first a shadow of a man. The company's sturdy dogs that ran ahead leaped about him with gleeful yips as if recognizing an old friend.

When the stranger removed his large, flat hat, he exposed a bald head and beardless visage tattooed blue and green with runes. Futhorc sigils in sinuous viper shapes framed a strikingly handsome face of merry, obsidian eyes, an exquisite nose, and strong chin, all stippled with tiny stylized symbols that together resembled the mottlings of snakeskin.

He smiled, and his teeth were perfect and white as a shaft of moonlight.

An infection of excitement spread through the war party at the sight of him, and he waved his big hat in greeting and advanced smiling—the dogs hopping joyfully around him.

Fra Athanasius, who could see none of this, asked worriedly, "Whatsoe'er do you see? Who stops our train?"

A Celtic lancer, who knew some Latin, whispered, "There is a supernatural being come to us. God or faerïe, I know not."

"God or faerïe!" Athanasius muttered to himself and clutched at the crude cross he had fashioned from whittled wood and twine. "What madness assails us in this broken land?"

The weird traveler in black held his floppy hat in both gloved hands and bowed his colorful and handsome head. When he looked up, he nodded at the gawking travelers and smiled again as if much pleased with the world. In flawless Brythonic, he said,

"I am come from the uttermost edge of the earth and am bound for Camelot to seek counsel with the king's wizard Merlin. May I ride with you?"

"What is your name?" Urien asked.

"Call me whatever you wish." The stranger's smile narrowed, and he cocked a delicate, stenciled eyebrow. "Men are not happy when they know my name."

"Stand aside," Urien commanded. "We will have no company with travelers we cannot name."

The bald head nodded sagely. "Then call me the Guide, for I am come to offer you guidance on these treacherous byways—in return for the favor of traveling in anonymity with your war party."

"Guidance?" Urien frowned. "We need no guidance in our own land. We know our way. Stand aside."

The stranger kicked at an ashen bank beside the road and out spilled an ossiferous cache of small bones and crepe skulls no bigger than fists. "Children in their place of murder." He shook his head sadly and gestured at the charred terrain. "You are among the dead. My presence in your company guarantees you safe passage. I am well-known to the murderers—and they will broker you no harm so long as I am with you."

Urien dismounted and took counsel with his warriors.

"What dost the chieftain say?" Athanasius queried the lancer who spoke Latin.

"The traveler before us has no dust upon his boots," the Celt replied in a hush. "Look for yourself. Not a flake of ash, not a mote of dirt upon his sable person. He is not a natural being, and our chieftain is loath to pass him by and offend such a divinity."

"Divinity?" Fra Athanasius hopped from his sumpter mule and strode to Urien's side. "My lord chieftain, this creature before us is unholy. Most obviously he displays every sign of a minion to Satan. I beseech you, set him behind us."

Urien regarded the lanky emissary thoughtfully. "I thank thee for thy counsel, No-Death. I was undecided, and thou hast made clear my mind."

Fra Athanasius returned to his mule relieved, grasping his cross, and mumbling a prayer of protection against the Devil.

"You wear the runes of our enemy, stranger," Urien declared from atop his powerful battlehorse. "What surety can you give us that you are not some scout of the raiders who savage our lands?"

"Indeed, I hail from the land of your foes, who know me well. My surety is my word. Your enemies have knowledge of me—and I of them." He fitted his large black hat upon his head, and his dark eyes glistened within its shadow. "Trust me once, and if I fail you, be done with me."

"You say you are the Guide," Urien challenged from his high mount. "Then tell us, what direction from here favors our journey?"

The stranger stuck an arm out and pointed across the cinderous waste. "Leave the road at once and make your way to the high ground west of here. You will recognize my purpose when we arrive."

Urien nodded once and waved the Guide into his company. The mysterious man bowed with exaggerated grace and strode through their midst.

The horses whinnied happily and bowed their heads to nuzzle him as he passed. He returned their salutes by cosseting several with his gloved hands. When he reached the sumpter mule that Fra Athanasius rode, he hopped on behind the rider. His arms tightened around the papal legate's soft midriff, and the wide brim of his hat folded against the back of the cassock's hood as he pressed his handsome face to the cowl, and whispered in fluent and contemporary Latin, "You think I'm the Devil, don't you?"

Fra Athanasius, shocked at his abrupt seizure by this stranger, made no reply. The Devil was a dissembler eager for discourse with his foul breath—but this devil smelled sweet as a meadow, and as they rode, the scent thickened pleasantly against the acrid stench of the slaglands.

Dusted with ash, Urien's war party moved through drifts of smoke and cinders and saw no other travelers in the barren land. They passed what had been a thorp, its wattle houses reduced to seared outlines in the chalken earth. At the central well, the travelers managed to draw water by lowering a boot strapped to a belt. Farther on, they found the skeletal remains of a shepherd, his herd reduced to clots of wool among bones smashed to the neuter simplicity of gravel.

The sunlight itself grew filthy with cinderous scurf as the day wore on. Shambling with exhaustion, the horses climbed a long slope where the war fires had staggered and left clumps of green shrubs. Ahead stood a massive forest that had been singed by the purging flames but largely spared. In the west, filaments of lightning stood like fiery witch scrawls over the woodlands.

From this high vantage, Urien and his warriors gazed through the blistered trees almost straight below upon a bend in the old Roman highway that, were it not for the eldritch stranger, they would be traversing now. There, they spied a band of Wolf Warriors waiting in ambush among the crisped hedges. At Urien's signal, the archers fired down at them and handily slew all of the Furor's fierce raiders.

Fra Athanasius averted his eyes from the slaughter and subsequent coup-taking and desecration of the enemy corpses. He dismounted and, coated in gypsum dust pale as a ghost, sidled away from the triumphant yells echoing off the highway. At a crooked and leafless tree, he knelt to pray.

"Pagans," a suave voice spoke from close behind. "That's what you're thinking, is it not? Were Urien and his men Christians, there would be no atrocity among the war dead."

Athanasius cast an unhappy look over his shoulder. The Guide knelt there, his black hat and tight ebony garments, gloves, and boots pristine, untainted by the ash and dust that coated the other travelers. "Keep away from me, devil."

The handsome man nodded politely. "Yes, to you I am a devil. But these others you call pagans—" His gloved hand motioned toward the jubilant cries of the Celts. "To these pagans, I am a holy one. And now that I have spared them the wrath of the Wolf Warriors, they are assured of my worthiness to be among them."

Athanasius clutched his wood cross and cast his gaze to the stony ground. "You are the Devil himself."

"Am I?" The Guide smiled gently, mysteriously patient. "You would be dead on that road below were it not for this devil."

The legate ignored him, concentrating on making his prayers

as focused and tight as his attention on the gravel he was study-ing.

"You live because of me and yet still you believe I am evil." His soft voice, for all its gentleness, was chilling. "And of a cer-tainty you must believe so, for you are a man of the cloth, Athanasius. In your heart, good wars with evil and what is at hazard is the soul. How strange that you put at venture what you so little understand." He laid a light hand upon the legate's shoulder, and the curly-haired man jolted at the touch. "What if I were to tell you that evil is itself a dispensation of good? And that good has no authority without evil?"

"Heresy!" Fra Athanasius hissed and began to pray more fer-vently under his breath, his brown, bovine eyes downcast.

"Oh, yes, heresy, from the Greek *hairesis*, the act of choosing. You choose to believe that evil is the privation of good. Any other understanding is heresy." The Guide removed his hand from the legate's shoulder and stood. "I will tell you a truth then, man of the cloth. Evil is *not* the loss of good." He walked away, paused, then over his shoulder added with a smile of conviction, "That is not lost which never knew a path."

Athanasius pushed to his feet and strode back to his mule. The war party were returning with blond scalps in their fists, and the legate mingled among them, preferring their blood-freckled faces and incomprehensible utterances to the tattooed counte-nance and taunting voice of the supernatural stranger.

Urien arrived burdened with several enemy swords and went to one knee before the Guide. The others of the company fol-lowed suit. Only Athanasius remained standing, and he turned his back and remounted the mule so that he would not have to see the gloating smile of the weird traveler.

The Celts offered the divine traveler their horses in gratitude for his protection, yet he chose to ride again behind the cower-ing legate. To the surprise and relief of Athanasius, the Guide kept his silence, and though his meadowland fragrance was obvi-ously another aspect of his demonic nature, the Christian was glad for it. The rancid stink of blood from the scalps curing in the windless heat mingled poorly with the acrid odors of the scorched land.

Later that day, they passed ruinous walls whose battlements

had fallen and lay strewn among bones and skulls like shattered earthenware, and Urien's riders, indigo with dust, their ash-powdered steeds festooned with scalps, seemed barbaric argonauts of a legendary world. What had been a city only a season past appeared to the dusty wanderers an ancient home for the wind. The day waned, yet none of the company would bivouac among those blackened stones.

They continued across the parched land through widening fans of crimson rays. To the Guide they looked for direction, and he sent them north into a chill blue evening among low, rolling hills of whitethorn and bramble trampled by the hosts of armies that had laid waste to the terrain two months earlier.

Twilight, blue and oily, found them approaching an ancient forest, where they could sleep through the night. The Celts dismounted and made camp in a cove that took shape from the light of their campfire breathing upon the arched boughs above. The warriors fawned on the Guide, offering him their best provisions and serenading him with harp music and song.

Fra Athanasius kept himself well apart from that happy band. Under a holm oak, he knelt in fervent prayer to the Almighty. "Holy of holies, protect me! This creature's unnaturalness is writ large, and I do fear him. Protect my soul if not my very life, oh Lord!"

"And who, may I ask, do you think hears your petition, man of the cloth?" The svelte voice of the Guide emerged from the darkness alongside the praying man.

Athanasius stared in fright at the sudden appearance of the tattooed man. He was leaning against the holm oak, his stenciled face afloat, framed by his jet hat and the blackness of night. The legate swung his wild stare toward the campfire and, with a myopic squint, discerned the bald, shining pate of the Guide sitting among the adoring pagans.

"My God—my God!"

"Your god is a silent one, Athanasius." The Guide spoke gently, as to a child. "If he hears you, how will you know?"

"What wickedness is this?" Athanasius staggered upright. "Is this a trickery of twins?"

"I am unique, I assure you." He smiled gleefully at the legate's wide-eyed distress. "It is no great difficulty for me to be in two places at once, for I am not corporeal in the manner of people."

"Not corporeal . . ."

"No, not corporeal. Not physical at all in any way familiar to you."

Athanasius pressed the crude cross to his chest as if to keep his slamming heart from bursting through its cage of ribs. "But I have touched you."

"And amused me as well, Athanasius." The entity proudly lifted the chin of his sternly handsome face. "I am quite alive. But I am not a material being. Oh, in the Great Tree I am solid enough. But here in Middle Earth I find it easy to work in multiples."

"Who are you?"

"I'll tell you if you promise on your god that you will not divulge my name to the others until we arrive in Camelot."

Athanasius winced at the thought of a secret covenant with the infernal creature and backed away. "Leave me be. In the name of God, leave me be."

"Come now, you are scribe and a man of five decades' experience. Surely, you understand that the world is ultimately not a knowable thing. It is a mystery that most deeply defeats us."

The legate's heels struck an upraised root as he retreated. He toppled backward and, with a yelp, sprawled into the leafy litter. Frightened cries squeaked from his constricted throat.

"They can't hear you. They are far too boisterous in my good company." The Guide stepped to where Athanasius lay and knelt over him. "Do you want to know who I am?"

Athanasius's stricken face shivered. "Do not impart such perilous knowledge."

"I am going to tell you anyway," the Guide said with an impish grin, and patted the frightened man's cheek. "But first you must promise. I have my enemies, and it is best my presence here not be bandied about."

In a crab-scuttle, Athanasius crawled away from the grinning apparition. "Why are you inflicting yourself on me?"

"Because you alone in our company do not adore me. You think I am your god's enemy. But I am not." The Guide's double sat cross-legged on the forest floor and removed his large hat.

In the darkness, the runes that stained his scalp seemed to squirm, and the round cope of his head shone as if greased. "Do you know who I am?"

Athanasius, propped on his elbows, peered over the quivering knees he had drawn up almost to his chest and shook his head.

"Promise you will keep my secret," the glowing head insisted.

Fearful of the consequences of refusing, the legate replied weakly, "I promise."

"Then I will tell you. I am not the Devil." His black eyes glinted like nails. "The Devil is older than the world itself, isn't he? I am not that old. No. I am a mortal being, such as you—only not of this dense realm. I was born higher in the World Tree, under the Rainbow Bridge and behind the great World-Mill that grinds the mold and fungus that makes earth. My mother was a white snake—a supernally beautiful being with eyes of gold flakes and milk that was blue as starlight. And my father—oh my father was a giant, a towering, muscular mute who turned the millstones of the World-Mill, grinding out boulders and rocks to build the mighty mountain ranges of this world. His sweat, his blood, his semen greased those millstones. And that was how I was born, when my mother came swimming under the Rainbow Bridge and received my father's seed in the foaming waters."

Athanasius's Latin face curdled with disgust. "You *are* a devil!"

"No." He scowled and smiled simultaneously, his jubilant face eloquently insane with anger and delight, and insisted, "I am the sworn blood brother of the Furor himself. In the Storm Tree I am called Loki, the Liar, because I am responsible for restraining my brother's wild enthusiasm for the truth. He's absolutely drunk with his need for it, you see—as if anything can be true in a universe whose most basic principle is uncertainty! Ah, but what would you know of that, you who have given yourself to dogma."

Athanasius blinked, hopelessly trying to bring his large eyes to focus. "You are a—god?"

"That is such a human word." Loki crawled forward on all

fours, reciting in a voice of pure joy, "'Is it not written in your law, I have said, You are gods?'"

"Those are words from the Gospel of John, chapter ten, verse thirty-four." Athanasius gusted with surprise. "You know the words of our Savior?"

Loki crawled over him. "Are you amazed to meet a pagan who is not ignorant of your faith?"

"I am bewildered," he said, averting his face. "You know of our Savior—you a . . . a pagan divinity. You know, but do you have faith in our Lord Jesus Christ?"

Loki rose and pulled Athanasius to his feet by the front of his cassock. "I have faith in everything, Brother! Everything! The bare stones themselves!"

"The bare stones?" The legate reeled, and Loki steadied him. "Stone is the coma of light."

"The deep sleep of light?" Athanasius blinked with confusion at the amused, sly face of scrawled runes. With the god's face pressed this close, the nearsighted man observed with fright that the futhorc markings were moving! Sinuously, they writhed, intercoiling to the proud shape of a crown—a crown of snakes. From far within, he heard himself plaintively whining, "I don't understand."

"Light, Brother, light!" Loki shook the scribe by his shoulders. "Everything is light, either asleep like the stones or awake like the cool fire shimmering off the living mud of your brain—the crackling brain-blaze you call mind."

Athanasius twisted free with a terrified cry and turned away. "You speak nonsense. Leave me be, Loki—*the Liar*. I am a Christian! I care not for your devilish talk. Leave me be. In the name of God!"

No reply came, and Athanasius was certain that the trickster was snickering at him. But when he glanced back, Loki was gone. At the campfire, the god inspired laughter among the Celts, and several of the warriors leaped up and began to dance for their divine guide.

The lanky, weak-eyed scribe shivered. Enclosed by a breezeless chill, he hugged himself. He was afraid to approach the campfire, where the evil god presided, and equally frightened to remain where he was, with the darkness breathing all around him and the leaves of the trees moving like tongues, murmuring in a language he could almost understand.

The infant that Ygrane held in her arms had been her husband Gorlois and the father of his own mother, Morgeu. He was a ghostly forefather to himself, because Morgeu's will to love him forever had lifted Gorlois's soul out of the astral realm of being and perishing before the spirit wind could shake the memories out of him and blow him into a different womb. His small skull fit perfectly in Ygrane's palm. She could feel the blood-pulse of his fontanel where his reborn soul throbbed at the top of his brain, not wholly fitting into his new body.

"He is beautiful, is he not?" Morgeu asked, her doting smile bright in the round, moon-pale face under her aura of ferocious hair, red and frizzy as a poppet's ridiculous mane.

The enchantress and Ygrane were alone in the nursery of Lot's stone fastness, where the gray slate walls had been covered with tapestries of battle scenes depicting the fall of Troy, the Greek victory against Xerxes at Salamis, and the sacking of Rome by Alaric eighty years before. Gorlois's armor, with its gorgon vizzard, embossed eagle cuirass, and ducal plumed helmet, hung opposite the tall windows so that sunshine drenched its polished brass. The short blade of his Roman sword pointed unsheathed down upon the cradle.

"He is a beautiful baby," Ygrane admitted, admiring the placid features of the child asleep in her embrace. The glistening fur of his head was black as Morgeu's small intent eyes, and he smelled of ferns. "But will he be a good man? Will you rear him to be righteous? Or is the vengeance that brought him back into this world the only destiny you cherish for him?"

"You should have stayed with Father," Morgeu replied, the hurt in her voice attesting to her irreversible sorrow. That pain was the core of her incest magic, the evil intelligence that plotted ways to use her own children as weapons.

"Your father was a cruel man." Ygrane met her daughter's pained look with the quiet suffering in her own green eyes. "I know you don't want to hear this truth, yet you must. You have returned Gorlois among us, and the Furor has marked him with a visionary power he never possessed before. As his mother, you must strive to redeem his failings."

Disgust twisted Morgeu's lips. "Gorlois's only failing was that he married a woman who did not love him."

"How could I love a man who brutalized me and my people?"

"Then you should have defied the druids and not married him at all. You should never have lain with him, never have brought me into this world." She placed her silver-ringed right hand upon the child's chest. "I live and Mordred lives and we defy your spawn Arthor, a spawn who exists only because of you and your faithlessness."

"I know that is what you believe, Morgeu. That is why I am here." Ygrane wanted to say more, but there was an air about Morgeu that defied reconciliation. She tolerated her mother only because of Ygrane's power. And now, despite her menstrual cramps and her heartache for her daughter and her fear of what the Síd's glamour was making of her, it was time to use that power. "We will find the Holy Graal, Morgeu, and I will leave you to rear this unnatural child as you see fit."

"So I shall," she said with vehement certainty. "And in good time, he will rule all Britain, and the child you conceived with the usurper Uther Pendragon will be toppled and forgotten."

"Enough prattle, child," Ygrane responded with force in her voice. She pointed to a nursemaid's stool. "Sit. And be silent."

Morgeu could not disobey. The nerves of her body had received the command before her brain could contravene it, and she plopped onto the nursemaid's stool. Her mouth jarred open as she forced herself to protest, then stopped. The air around her mother had jeweled. The nursery shimmered as with sunlight broken on water, and a slippery music began, a sighing rustle as of a willow breeze but coherent and subtle. The enchantress sat mesmerized by it, hearing single threads of voices, whispering cries, unweighted howls floating like wind-singing.

Faeries rode these unfolded wings of music through the open transoms, gliding on the sunslants and windowgleams into the nursery. They gathered over the infant, clustering like ball lightning.

Morgeu began to rise to go to her child, then paused. The

baby had become a cloud. The nimbus floated before Ygrane, lit from within and aswarm with hot points of fire. The very moment screamed—and the cloud became the phantom of Gorlois. He did not look like her father, for his face had been carved by the knife of the Furor so that he could see the timeshadows of what might be.

Gorlois gazed at her with surprise in the eyeball aslant upon his forehead and an unvoiced cry unlocked and skewed to one side of his lipless jaw like a laughing mule. A sudden inward-rushing wind sucked the smoke of him through a starhole into another world. The rawhide thongs dangling from Ygrane's vest lifted and waved like feelers in the draft, and the tapestries and cradle veils behind her billowed and snapped, eager to follow Gorlois's ectoplasm straight into the fiery perforation.

Morgeu clutched the stool under her, her crimson robes and frizzled red hair tugged fiercely by the abrupt undertow. In that violent moment, she was convinced her mother had deceived her and had used the faerie to snatch away her baby's soul. Rage flared in her. With all her might, she dug her crimson velvet slippers into the bunched carpet to keep her own lifeshine from whisking free of her body and following her father-child's soul into the netherworld.

Then, the wind stopped. Between herself and Ygrane hovered a chrome chalice laced in gold—the Holy Graal. Through its translucence she could see her mother's face, hollow-cheeked as a lynx and underlit by the ethereal glow of the beautiful cup. The baby was nowhere to be seen.

Morgeu lunged to her feet. "Mordred!"

For an instant, Ygrane saw a belled reflection in the Graal's chrome surface: A startling figure loomed there—squat, immense, and fierce. It was a dwarf dressed in studded leather straps that criss-crossed an iridescent tunic of firesnake skin.

The outrage in Morgeu's throat tightened to silence as she, too, glimpsed the creature half as high as a man but twice as wide, with huge, muscular limbs. He had a cubed head of tufty gold hair and red whiskers that swirled over pugnacious jowls. "The Furor's dwarf," she moaned. "Brokk!"

At the sound of her voice, the image wobbled and began to break up. Ygrane swiped at the vision, and it smeared to radiance, white and frosty.

"My baby!" Morgeu cried. She collided with her mother, and Ygrane pressed the infant into her arms. "Mordred!" She spun away with the child, and he began to wail. "Hush—hush!" Quickly, she examined the baby and saw that he was whole and unmarked. And when she turned again in the next moment to face Ygrane, no one was there. The nursery stood empty but for long rays of afternoon sunlight, their bright motes floating unperturbed in the stillness.

6

Beautiful Beyond Beauty

Marcus Dumnoni stood at the balustrade on the east terrace of Tintagel castle, peering into a golden broth of dawnlight pouring from the ladle of the hillocks across the wide swards and ponds. The long reach of his vision grabbed at the distant farmhouses on the moors and the streaks of woodsmoke from their chimneys. He was looking for some sign of the faeries he knew had to be there—for that land had been home for eighteen years to the witch-queen Ygrane.

Since seeing her ride past him on the black devil stallion, he believed that her life as a nun had been a lie. The Sisters of the Holy Graal continued to tend their trays of speedwell, yellow clover, skullcap, and bitterroot in the herb garden at the back of the castle, and each day they rode their dray carts to the hamlets of the countryside, delivering medicines to the ill and food for the indigent. Marcus had spoken to every one of the sisters, and none of them had a single recollection of their abbess practicing the old ways.

Before he was comfortable moving his entourage into Tintagel, he had carefully inspected each chamber, every alcove, searching for pagan symbols or implements. He had found none.

Yet, when he had seen Ygrane that day of his arrival, she was sovereign in her elfen power. She had barely looked human. Her face was dusted golden in faerïe powder, beautiful beyond the beauty of mortal women—but terrifying, with the faerïes themselves wafting about her like thistle tufts. He could still conjure the tang of autumn by remembering the rapt expression of her angular eyes, those eyes the color of trees.

He had feared then that Tintagel would prove a hauntful place, a portal to the netherworld, and a peril to himself and his household. And every day since arriving, he had been vigilant for eldritch signs. Nothing, however, had fulfilled his sumptuous fear. By night, he told himself he was relieved. But in truth, with the breaking of day, weary of having to face again the burden of administrative chores and the mundane terrors of Wolf Warriors and woodland gangs, he almost wished for a ghost to shuffle through the salt pines.

This morning, as sunbeams quivered in the clear deeps of the indigo sky, a shadow stirred upon the lawn. It was the gardeners with their reaping hooks and mulch pails, he was sure. He turned to change his nightdress of soft saffron silk for tunic and sandals, then paused. By the sharper sight of peripheral vision, he saw it distinctly—a black horse about a furlong from the castle.

The devil stallion!

No—not a stallion, not a horse at all. Standing perfectly still, he fixed his gaze and discerned a tusk upon the equine creature's brow. It was a unicorn, sable as the night.

Fetched up by the windless light of dawn, it pranced across the strath to the broken rocky ground where the heath began. There, it stepped into the sky, climbing among the gray cobs of clouds, a black hunter, a thimbleful of another world. Galloping among the orange peels of morning, it was exquisitely strange and robustly beautiful.

Without moving, Marcus watched it run, flying across the sky's kingdom until it disappeared in the ultraviolet remnants of night.

At noon, Bedevere leaned forward atop his massive horse and pointed down the hot and shimmering road to where a lone figure approached over the shattered stone plates and dislodged cobbles. The mounted rider trembled and bleared in the sun and finally coalesced into a farmer with a floppy-brimmed hat atop a donkey. "Merlin approaches, sire."

Arthor cantered Straif past several potholes to the wizard. "Where have you been, Merlin?"

The lanky traveler did not answer. He was looking at the leafless and jagged trees and the ocher fields cooking in the heat. Wobbly horizons augmented into gray hills under dusty haze.

Bedevere offered the old man a flagon of water.

Merlin waved it aside. "Have you seen aught of evil in the land, my lord?"

"Five brigands, my own soldiers, attempted to loot an inn, an impoverished inn at that." Arthor accepted Bedevere's flagon and drank. "And you? Aught of evil?"

"Yes, evil. But not brigands, my lord." He scanned the burned countryside with his strong eye, and green spectra flashed from where the roadway disappeared among the distant planes of heat. "Demons. My old cohorts are in the land, and thus we find this devastation."

"Demons?" Bedevere cast a skeptical glance to the king. "This land was burned by the rebel armies."

"Come." Merlin pulled his donkey around. "If the heat has not addled your bare heads, you will see more of true evil this day than the ravages of armies."

They rode on. Bedevere peered down uneasily at the wizard in his farmer's hat. "Why must we be here at all? Three days we have traveled in disguise among the devastations of war. What more is there for the king to see? Let us hie back to Camelot where we belong. There, we can coordinate the rebuilding of this savaged land."

Merlin regarded Bedevere balefully. "What I want the king to witness has eluded us these three days because we travel in disguise. Were the demons to know of our presence outside the protective bulwarks of Camelot, their monstrosities would have overwhelmed us."

Arthor shifted uncomfortably atop Straif. He did not want to hear about demons. He was happier thinking about anything else— about Julia, for instance, and her common woes. In his mind, wrenched about by the havoc of war and the cruel wiles of his enchantress sister Morgeu, the austere efficiency of Julia's inn seemed a paradise. He wished he could return there. He did not want to go where Merlin was leading. Yet, nothing could be changed. Even though he was king—*because* he was king—he could change nothing.

As they rode, the sky darkened. Sulfur smoke hung over the

land in a yellow shroud, and the king sat tall in his saddle, surveying the way ahead. "The balefires of war were damped weeks ago," he commented. "What is the origin of this evil pall?"

"Looters and brigands," Bedevere responded from atop his mighty warhorse. "Malefactors the likes of whom we routed at The Blanket of Stars abound in the wake of war, my lord. They set blazes to cover their wicked progress."

"Not brigands nor Foederatus raiders inspired these fumes," Merlin contradicted, and leaned forward across the neck of his mule to point with his whole body through the haze. "I warned you there was dire magic afoot in the land, sire. Now, behold— there, in the saddle of those hills ahead. What do you see?"

Arthor saw a scattering herd of sheep and several red cows galloping, and behind them a score of villagers in full flight. *Wolf Warriors!* he immediately thought, and hoped that the sulfur mist had not dimmed the sun beyond hope of sending a flash-signal to Bors Bona in the tableland to the north. Though Merlin had lured him beyond the walls of Camelot with news of a magical threat to his kingdom, Arthor had seen only the dreadful aftermath of war. He wished he had stayed at the drafting tables in the council rooms, supervising the rebuilding of this heartbreaking devastation. "A whole village is fleeing raiders."

"Not raiders," Merlin insisted. "Look again!"

"God in heaven!" Bedevere shouted, and his large horse reared and nearly threw him. "What in God's name . . ."

"'Praise the Lord from the earth, ye dragons!'" Merlin gusted Psalm 148 in giddy fright, and clutched excitedly at Arthor's arm. "Do you see how the earth is given to this dragon, my lord?"

Arthor made no reply. Through the brume, he spied what had stampeded an entire village, terrifying Bedevere and driving the wizard to a biblical outcry. A veritable behemoth walked the earth. It was a cancerous thing, spraddle-legged, imperfect, and malformed, its huge, tuberous shape hung with flesh like leper-rags: Swinging and slobbering its misshapen head on a delirious neck of parasitical lace, the lumbering thing emerged from behind the hills big and warty-shouldered as the hills themselves.

"What abomination is this?" Bedevere yelled, his big horse sidestepping and rolling his eyes like a parade dancer.

"It's a dragon!" Merlin called above the enormous roar of the beast. "It is a dream of the sleeping Dragon within the earth—a dreamdragon!"

"The ground itself shakes beneath the might of this dream!" Bedevere protested, struggling to control his sidling mount.

"It is a dream made of cold fire!" the wizard declared. "The demons themselves have provoked it!"

Arthor sat enthralled with fright. The dragon's breath wheezed smoke from a face like an earth-fetus, brow lobes cankerous, peeling away in fleshy tatters where the skin had split and pink bone shone among fungoid scabs and horned growths. Eyes colorless as phlegm glared from the torn and grotesquely swollen head in a rage of agony as the beast shambled moaning through the scalding sunlight.

"Daylight burns its hide!" Bedevere called out. "The dragon suffers under the sun!"

Merlin's teeth clacked on a startled oath when the mule under him bucked once. He lay forward again and placed a hand atop its head, gentling the frightened animal. "The demons who culled this dream from the Dragon's sleep have set sunfire upon the dragons to torment them into rageful acts."

"There are more?" Bedevere gawked in horror at the leviathan's warped stride, its bedrock claws plowing the ruined fields with each step. "Are they the blight upon the land?"

With a bone-jerking blast, the answer came: The dragon's gruesome face unflanged a jaw that opened deep as a cliff into a gorge of teeth, and blue-hot fire jetted from its maw. The blaze consumed half a dozen sheep and left oozing twists of black bone in a pool of melted earth that bubbled like tar.

"Stop this monster, Merlin!" Arthor commanded.

"I cannot, my lord. It is a demon's conjuration. If I break the Dragon's dream, the demons will rise out of the earth and swarm over us."

"You say this is an apparition of cold fire." Bedevere pulled his steed around with tight reins, thwarting his animal's urgency to flee. "Stir up a tempest and blow it away."

"No gale could stop this dragon," said Merlin with furious awe. "Cold fire it is but woven solid as rock. Behold its might!"

The dragon's hunched shoulders unfurled to spiked wings, and tattered membranes between pinions of varnished bone snapped like whips in the updraft of its broad span. The vortex it spun toppled the running villagers.

Arthor reached for a burlap sack upon Bedevere's jittery horse and unwrapped Excalibur. Its star blue blade mirrored the cindered world around them cold and clear as the cognizance of a vigilant mind.

"What are you doing?" Bedevere gnashed, pulling with his one arm to hold his massive horse steady.

"I have met gods before—in the hollow hills." Arthor brought his palfrey closer to Bedevere and yanked the burlap from the shield that rested atop the haunches of the warhorse. The image of the Blessed Virgin regarded him serenely. "The gods are beings of cold fire, and they fear Excalibur. Merlin drove off the Furor with this very sword."

"Metal will disrupt the Dragon's fiery dreambodies," Merlin admitted, glowering with consternation. "But the risk is too great. Sheathe your weapon. Let us flee from here."

"This is the evil that infests our kingdom," Arthor said, taking the shield in his left hand. "This is what you brought me here to confront, Merlin. Now I will fight it."

"Not now, Arthor!" The wizard flung a terrified look to where the colossus bellowed, peering through the steam of its own smoldering flesh for its prey. "You must gather your warriors."

Arthor swung his palfrey around and aimed her to charge. "That thing is going to destroy those people."

"They are but peasants, my lord." Bedevere's stallion blocked the palfrey. "I cannot permit you to throw your life away."

Arthor glared angrily at him and danced Straif around the frightened warhorse. "They are my *people*!" he shouted across his shoulder, and rode off.

"Stop him, Merlin!" Bedevere struggled to turn his big steed and charge, but the animal fought him. "By our Savior's wounds!" He leaped from the terrified stallion, drew his saber, and ran after Arthor, yelling at the wizard, "Merlin! Save the king!"

But Merlin shouted, "Halt!" and Bedevere's legs buckled under him.

Merlin walked his mule forward, leaned down from the animal, his floppy hat falling from his head, and caught the paralyzed man by the back of his jerkin. "The king has given himself to his fate." The wizard shook the limp man. "You cannot save him."

"*You* can," Bedevere moaned.

Merlin shook his wild head of hair. "If I stop him as I stopped you, he would not be king."

"Then stop that monstrous thing!" Bedevere struggled against the numbness saturating him, tried to run, and fell to his knees with a frustrated groan. "Surely, it will kill him!"

"Well it may!" Merlin raised both blue-knuckled fists in despair. "But if I use magic, the demons who shaped this dragon will know it is I. They will swarm us, and no one will survive."

The wizard nudged the mule out of the open into a field of gray winter grass and dragged Bedevere after him. From that partial cover, they stared transfixed at Arthor, who rode full tilt over the ashen terrain, kicking up clouds behind him. In his right hand, Excalibur spun, flashing stars of sunlight through the sulfur smoke.

Bedevere stabbed his saber into the ground and leaned on its hilt, heart thick in his throat, mouth agape. The dragon had spotted the charging horse and swung its obscene head toward the shouting rider and his bright sword.

Arthor pulled Straif up short and stood the palfrey on her hind legs, sword swinging over his head.

With a bellow, the dragon veered toward him, yellow steam wafting off its saurian hulk. The villagers fallen in its shadow scrambled to their feet and ran off wildly.

The gills of the dragon's rib cage pulsed in rhythm to its roaring stride as it descended on Arthor. The king lay flat over his steed, and Merlin, who had lifted himself to his knees atop his mule, stood straight up, and said in a voice barely audible in the shuddering air, "He's talking to her! What the devil is he saying to her?"

"What?" Bedevere croaked. "What is he doing?"

"He's talking to his horse!" Merlin wanted to turn away. The heart pumping in its darkness, drumming in his head, was his flesh and a stranger. The fright he felt was human and the despair as well. Watching the boy he had made a king, whose parents he had brought together by the use of magic, this boy he loved, in the very shadow of death broke all the hope in Merlin, hope that he had cherished since first becoming human. He would die if the boy died, he decided. He would be human no more. Let the demons take him back. Let him ride the darkness again as Lailoken if all he had struggled so hard to create was taken into the flames.

The jet of blue fire from the dragon's maw blasted the air like a stroke of lightning. Bedevere shouted with alarm. Merlin's unblinking stare winced, and in that blind moment, he lost sight of his humanity and became again a stranger to flesh and the dark beating of blood. Death was no revelation to him. He had ripped apart lives on worlds when earth was still just nuclear ash in the star furnaces. Life was never any part of what mattered. Only void was real to the demons. And the dancing atoms were but the motes that the angels used to create their illusions. Arthor had merely been the brevity of another dream . . .

"The king!" Bedevere cried when he saw Arthor atop Straif lunging through the dragonsmoke.

Merlin blinked. The palfrey had listened to the boy! She had not panicked under the blows of heat and bone-shaking thunder, nor under the stink, the lung-sore stink of the monster. With dazzling speed, Straif carried Arthor beneath the flame swath and between the dragon's massive claws. Excalibur winked like a star as the king swung it upward into the torn leather breast of the creature.

A scream ripped to the horizons, and the gigantic beast staggered upright, its cable-thick tendons stretched to their twisted limits. With one heaving throe, the dragon tore into gusty auroras and vanished.

To arrive in Avalon at the end of the fifth century was to find oneself immersed in a sourly sweet fragrance of sun-melted apples. Wild orchids flared colorfully among the gnarly apple trees, afoot in the syrupy brown mulch of their dropped fruit. On every knoll stood rough-hewn menhirs—single upright stones—that pierced the flowery ground in crude circles. Swift, soft clouds hurried from the south, swirling in sunny tatters as they flew through a blue sky darker than the enclosing sea with its tusks of foam. Emerald butterflies jostled among the season's leavings—ruffled cabbage flowers poking through the windfall apples with orange and violet intoxicants. White deer grazed upon the tall bracken between the bare frames of renegade elms. And beside a turquoise lake squatted a fat, lopsided mushroom dome, brown as ginger-bread.

Mossy rock shelves led to a crooked wooden door beside which glistened red shrubs—gooseberry, wild rose, and barberry. Within the odd round hut on the shore of the green lake was where we dwelled—the Nine Queens of Avalon. The hut's broad interior consisted of an earth-tamped floor and round walls decorated in spirals and wavy lines of warm yellow, blue, and red ocher.

Illuminated by slant rays of azure light from small, round windows high in the dome, we stately nine sat on bulky block-cut thrones all in a line. In our presence, the reek of the dying season lingered as though we lived in the brown hallways of the forest itself.

Who are we? And to whom are we speaking?

The eldest of us was Rna, queen of the Flint Knives. When she lifted her veil, she showed skin white as buffed bone, a crin-kled flesh that gleamed like minnow scales. Blue dusk had some-how been pressed into her temples, and though young of feature, with luxuriant hair the color of a thrush's breast, she appeared also very, very old.

She was, in truth, nearly a hundred thousand years old. She had come to Europe with the first people. No other people had ever camped or hunted among the fogpines of that land until Rna arrived with the Flint Knives. The angels with their faces of fire had kept watch. Through the blue doors of the glacier, they had watched, and one spring evening under the black pines they carried her off and brought her to this round hut.

And here she sat alone for ten thousand years. The angels gave her long life, and she remained beautiful in her exile. Long sight, too, the angels gave her, and she witnessed mammoth hunts, the taking of ivory for carving, and the leather chews of the women among the caves and along the streambeds, as the generations revolved. And after the last of the Flint Knives was dead, she observed the other tribes that followed. With the zenith sight that the angels had given her, she followed the flow-ing glaciers and then the ebbing ice sheets. And all the while, she sat invisibly beside the hunters reckoning with their stone knives and walked with the women listening for the bees' path to honey and hovered in the air around the lame ones and the blind ones coaxing music from the hollow bones . . .

One hundred centuries later, the angels brought a second queen from a nomad tribe to preside in mute witness with Rna. What does her name matter? Together they sat listening to the same birth screams and sun dances and mournful burial songs. They beheld the endless hunt. Fire was stolen from a lightning-struck tree and held ransom within the clans before it was lost and found again and lost again. The seasons delivered their idiot packages of snow and rain. Glaciers crawled forward . . .

Ten thousand years passed, and the angels brought a third queen from yet another tribe of wanderers.

Over and over, every hundred centuries the angels installed a new queen. In our attentive trance, we nine heeded all the particular instants of human life, tirelessly watching people thrive, struggle, and die. With our hearts as well as our strong eyes, we gave ourselves, mourning endless murders more plausible than love, lauding countless unsung heroes and their treason to evil. And slowly, as the stubborn ground of our own hard souls did relent and accept the nascent seeds of peace, charity, and mercy, a greening time began, falteringly, in the one joined soul of all women and men. The furrow of our chastened ways cradled new lives. Our remorse and praise and our prayers gave significance to a hundred, a thousand generations, and gradually a spirit of reconciliation and fellowship took root in the human heart. The plow of love dug deeper. Moral understanding—justice—common equality became important to the people.

And then—suddenly—the time of the queens ended . . .

Who are we—we nine?

The angels summoned no more queens to Avalon. Instead, a king would come as answer to the ten thousand years of kings before him. And Rna's soul would at last be free to return to the round of living souls that pass from form to breathing form. Soon, the angels would bring to this place the first male gage, the first pledge of man's rule, who would sit beside the last of the queens, Nynyve. And together with the eight queens, he would witness the indignities of man to his own kind and—worse—terrible crimes never committed during the long epoch of the queens—the indignities of man to the earth herself.

Indignities of a monstrous estrangement.

But who are we to say? And to whom are we speaking who will listen?

When the peasants who had fled the dragon returned triumphantly with Arthor to their hamlet, the boy-king was heartbroken by the devastation. Not one wattle house remained standing. The fields were scorched furrows, and byre and stable stood as blackened skeletons, the farm animals they had held reduced to stinking scrog. The king sent a sunflash signal that brought Bors Bona and his men down from the hills, and the remainder of the day was spent rebuilding the settlement.

At day's end, when amber sunlight fell the length of the world, Arthor lay numb with wretchedness atop Straif. The palfrey had carried him into a yard of crisped beanpoles, where the crusty ground hissed with each hoofstep. His thigh wound pulsed madly, enraged at the strenuous effort he had made baling thatch for the roofs with the other men, and the prayer in his mind was barely audible above the trumpeting din of pain: *Mother Mary, why do you not hear me?*

Bors Bona, stripped of the brass armor he usually wore, stood at the yard edge, stout and burly in a dirty tunic, his hands grimed from digging postholes, his gray brush-cut hair strewn with hay stems. He thought it a foolish use of his men to rebuild a peasants' hamlet, yet he had worked strenuously among them because their king had commanded them. Scores more villages, as savagely ravaged, lay between them and Camelot. Did the boy intend to bind wattle and weave thatch for all of them?

If it came to that, Bors knew that he would obey without complaint. This king had won more than his fealty. The fierce general who had torched pagan camps and had put to the sword the women and children of the invaders had given his heart to this boy. The lad was brave, his principles broad, and there was love in his soul for all his people. Bors had known no other warlord so selflessly devoted to the idea of a united Britain save Arthor's own father, Uther Pendragon.

Unwilling to approach his king unbidden, Bors Bona waited patiently beside a charred trellis of bean vines. Bedevere, watching discreetly from among fire-chewed hedges laced against the

sun's glare, advanced between the beanpoles so that Straif saw
him and turned in his direction, facing Arthor toward his general. Spotting his warrior, the king sat up on his barebacked palfrey and nudged her across the yard. "How fares the hamlet,
Bors?"

The general did not respond at once. The sight of the king
with his hair singed and his eyebrows erased by dragonfire startled him. Bors had not seen Arthor's marred countenance clearly
until now. Throughout the day, he had taken his orders from
Merlin while the king had labored at a distance, in the one
untrodden field, binding thatch. All the talk among the villagers
had been of Arthor's triumph against the dragon, but until this
moment Bors had not realized how close the boy had come to
losing his life. *For a hamlet!* he marveled, and felt his heart
swelling in his throat. He had observed dragons on his patrol
through the hills to the north and had been appalled at their
grotesque might. For a certainty, he knew he himself would not
have had the courage to charge such a beast.

He cleared his throat, and reported, "The grange hall is up
and roofed, and the peasants may sleep there this night. All our
provisions are at their disposal, as you have commanded, my
lord."

"Thank you." Arthor wiped the cold sweat of pain from his
smudged brow. "You are good to give your men to this humble
task."

"We are your men to command, sire."

"Yet, this is not a task worthy of warriors." He nodded
wearily. "I know. But I needed to know for myself that these
infernal monsters can be slain and their damage undone."

"You took a grave risk to destroy the dragon, my lord."

Arthor looked up in dismay at the high, flame-woven clouds
of dusk. "So I've heard all day from Merlin and Bedevere. Spare
me further opprobrium, Bors."

"I applaud what you did, sire." Bors nodded sincerely. "I
applaud it, though I would not have had the courage to do the
same."

"Were you king, you would."

"No, my lord." Bors waved flies from his beardless face. "I
am a warrior trained to fight men. I have no strength to confront
dragons."

"Aye. I understand. I feel much the same." Arthor bit his lip, distress in his yellow eyes. "Magic frightens me."

"Yet, you abide Merlin. He is an unnatural being, my lord." Bors read the immediate discomfort in his king's young face. "Forgive my outspokenness."

Arthor dismissed his general's concern with a curt shake of his head. "I want my warriors to speak openly with me. And I will be open with you. I fear Merlin. I fear magic. My own sister, Morgeu . . ." His voice faltered, and he covered his eyes with one hand, squeezing with thumb and middle finger the sudden hurt in his temples.

"Say no more, sire. We all know how Morgeu the Fey used her enchantments to beguile you into sin."

"I am so ashamed, Bors." Arthor lowered the hand shielding his eyes and spoke aloud his anguish. "I am unworthy to be king with this black sin upon my soul."

"Then send me to the North Isles," Bors insisted. "I will purge you of your wicked sister and her evil child."

"No!" Arthor sat up straighter, and the pain in his thigh flashed so hotly he gnashed his teeth. "That will only compound my sin. You must promise me, Bors, that neither you nor anyone by your charge will do harm to my sister or our child."

"But why, sire?" Bors glowered with bewilderment. "They are an abomination, the two of them. They should be purged at once!"

Arthor heaved a sigh, throwing off his physical pain. "We are Christian men, Bors. We are not murderers."

"This would not be murder. Morgeu has committed treason against the crown by lying with you deceptively and bringing an unholy child into the world. The law demands her execution and the destruction of her abominable offspring."

"She deceived me, yes. But I was not king when I lay with her. She committed no crime against the crown. And I will not have her murdered." The king leaned forward. "Is that understood, Bors?"

"Yes, my lord." Bors Bona faced away, squinting into the bright declivities of twilight, jaw pulsing.

"Speak your mind, man."

"You are too good to be king."

"Too good?" The boy scratched his itchy scalp. "What does that mean?"

"Only God is good, says the Bible." Bors faced Arthor with an earnest look in his bulldog visage. "You are king. You must do whatever is necessary to preserve your kingdom. Your aims and purposes are invested with an authority greater than all other men, and for the good of all sometimes you must extend your claims to what others consider fraughtful or even evil."

Arthor shook his head. "Bors, you sound like Merlin now."

"I am no wizard." The general advanced a pace, frowning. "I am a warrior. I know the darker nature of our enemy, and we will not stand unless we stand by the sword."

"Have you forgotten?" Arthor squeezed his thigh muscle above the wound, wanting to throttle the nagging hurt. "I was not born a king nor reared in noble luxury. I've lived most of my life as a thrall, and I know the darker nature of men and the brutal intent of our enemy." With steady, pain-bright eyes, he peered deep into Bors's gray stare. "That is why I insist that my rule be something greater—something that uplifts us beyond the reach of our darker nature—something truly noble that our people and those who follow us can emulate—a reign of mercy and Christian love whose radiance will shine forth no matter what darkness follows."

Bors Bona rolled his eyes to the darkening heavens. "That is a child's dream, unsuitable to this cruel world, my lord. You will not endure long embracing that simple and charitable vision, I assure you."

"That *is* my vision," Arthor insisted. "And I *am* king. And so long as I am king, I will abide by mercy and love. That is what our Savior preached even to his last breath upon the cross."

"And what of magic and Merlin?" Bors cocked his head. "Does your mercy extend to wizards and demons alike?"

"Merlin serves what is holy and good. And though I like not his reliance on magic, I trust in his goodness and his fair judgment." Arthor extended a hand and clasped his general's shoulder. "You have beheld dragons in the land. You know that we contend against unspeakable forces. We need Merlin."

"As you say, my lord." Bors felt a pang of sorrow for this idealistic youth. "I pray Merlin's magic is ample enough in the weeks to come. Clearly, his magic has done your leg wound no good. And if he cannot heal so small an insult, what hope against the invaders?"

"This is an unnatural wound." Arthor's hand rested heavily on Bors Bona's shoulder. "It pierces to my soul . . . and its pain pulses like a second heart, like the very heart of my shame."

"Morgeu—" The warrior's face tightened, indicating that something of the same had passed through his mind. "If you will not cast her into hell where she belongs, then what hope of breaking her curse upon you—and upon our land? What hope against King Wesc, who gathers a fearsome host in Jutland? His Foederatus legions will invade before the storm season is upon us. He will invade, my lord, and we have not the defenses to stop him on our shores. That battle will rage across Britain. And when it is done, our Saxon overlords will have little to say about mercy and Christian love."

Arthor made a fist of the hand that had clasped his general. "Then, when it is done, we must be the victors."

"I have small hope of that, my lord. We are too few, and they are so many."

"You have spoken openly with me, Bors. I thank you for that from my heart, troubled as it is." The king withdrew his hand and grasped again his throbbing leg. "Now, go and rest. Tomorrow, we will leave some men behind to finish the work here and we will return to Camelot—and slay dragons on our way." He pulled Straif around into the gloaming, horse and rider annealed to one shadow in the indigo darkness. Over his shoulder, he declared, "I have seen enough to know that Merlin was right. Much as I despise magic, we must find a way to use it against our enemies."

7

The Seven Eyes of God

Ygrane had the faeries lead her to Merlin and found the wizard at sunset on a hilltop of orange and brown weeds. He came alone as her faeries had instructed, his blue robes and conical hat gray with the powdery ash of the burned land.

When he saw her step forth from the scarlet glow of the low and watery sun, his silver eyes widened slightly. "It *is* you." With his common sight, he saw faeries crawling through her stubbly hair like flame moths—and the disembodied intelligences of the pale people moved through the twilit dust in ghost blurs only half-seen as though his brain had erred.

Within his demon vision, the lunatic shadows tightened outside human time to real forms with odors of the soul: In every brittle blade of weed, in all the tangled shadows, and in the very shine of the air itself, leafsmoke wore chameleon faces and red monkey grins. The sour incense of bog mud began moaning and gradually crescendoed in his head as the veils of dusk mist parted to reveal the Daoine Síd in their thousands and tens of thousands.

"By my holy mother!" Merlin gasped, and stepped a pace backward. Then he paused, realizing that he was surrounded by bodies thin as dreams yet stitched with flamethreads of desire so hot they could have burned him to the roots of his six senses. "What have you done, woman?"

"Steady yourself, Merlin." Ygrane came forward garbed in rawhide and a chemise of torn linen; she smelled of mountain mint and the deep quiet of the color blue. "I am queen of the Síd, daughter of Morrígan the Drinker of Lives. You are in my care, and no harm will come to you."

"Ygrane—Ygrane . . ." Merlin removed his hat and held it limply in one hand while grasping the astonishment upon his pale brow with the other. "You have forsaken your Christian soul!"

"That is no concern of yours." Her eyes in kohl shadows shone green as streaks of the sunset behind her. "I have summoned you here for the hope of Britain's soul."

Merlin shook his head in befuddlement, his sliding eyes staring uneasily at the many frosted eyes gazing back at him from faces slick as fruits—faces floating full before him, then slipping away behind other faces of seaweed hair, smoke hair, flametip teeth, starglint teeth, a pantheon of the angry red night. "You've given your soul to them—to the pale people. When Marcus sent word that he had seen you riding the night horse in broad daylight, I could not believe it. I looked for you in my crystals. I couldn't find you, not even in trance."

"I did not want you to see me." Feather-faces drifted between them and disappeared in the furnace air of the sunset. "I don't want Arthor to know."

"He knows. He saw the message from Marcus." Merlin pointed behind him to the lanternlights of the thorp in the dale below. "He is among his people, helping rethatch their roofs. This day he saved them from a dragon."

Ygrane's regal posture stammered. "You let him face the dragondream?"

"Then you know what the demons are doing in the earth to the sleeping Dragon?"

"Of course I know. The Síd have told me everything. The demons are bound by the Furor's magic and are ravaging Britain with nightmares culled from the dragondream." An ache of maternal fear for her son choked her silent for a moment, and she lifted her chin remonstratively. "You were foolish to let Arthor face such a terror. If he dies, everything we struggled and sacrificed for all these years will be lost. Britain will be shredded among the warlords again—and the Furor's tribes will sweep over us."

"You think I don't know this?" Merlin fitted his hat back on his long, bald skull. "Arthor is my king. I cannot command him."

"You are sworn to protect him."

"With my very life. I only brought him out here to show him the evil that assails us. Kyner reared him a good Christian, and he is averse to magic. I wanted to convince him that we must use magic as well as valor to protect Britain. I did not mean for him to attack the dragon himself. But once he did, I could not stop him."

Ygrane nodded with understanding, and the faeries blew around her like bright spores. "He is averse to magic because of his strong faith."

"And his sister's betrayal." Merlin did not hide the bitter unhappiness in his voice. "Her incest magic has damaged him to his very soul."

"Again, Merlin, you failed to protect the king. Why did you let Morgeu get so close to him?"

"My lady, you are mistaken if you believe I am infallible. I am as flawed as any mortal. My powers have their limits—human limits, I remind you."

The witch-queen sighed and turned so that the setting rays sliced across the notches of her profile. "Yes, you're right, Merlin. We are shaped by our flaws." The wizard could almost see her thoughts moving the way fire thinks, blazing with clarity and attached to forms yet reaching for the formless—knowing she was ultimately responsible for Arthor's life and with it all the attendant paradox of suffering. "Arthor is my son, and I fear for him in this contest of ruthless powers."

"That is why you have summoned me here—and why you have abandoned our faith in the love and salvation of our Savior."

She faced him full again, and her eyes were all pupil. "I am determined to recover the Holy Graal for my son."

"You know where it is?"

"I will find it. It was given to me by the Sisters of Arimathea—who are the Nine Queens of Avalon. And it was lost, because I brought it too soon to Camelot."

Merlin stepped closer, his stare avid. "Where is it?"

"I don't know," she lied. She dared not tell him what she knew, for Merlin was only his human name. He would always be

Lailoken, a transfigured incubus, and his demon cohorts might easily hear his thoughts and warn the dwarf Brokk and his master the Furor that she was coming. "But it is important that I find the Holy Graal and return it to Camelot."

"If you can, you must." Merlin wanted to reach into her mind, to discover more about what she knew. But her power was strongest at the day's apocalypse, a power of soul-snatching madness, a power good to dread. Staring hard into her face, her lynx cheeks, her wide brow, and long nose all gleamed, shiny as the first plastic centuries away. "The Graal is an antenna, an implement for receiving and focusing cosmic energies . . ."

"I did not call you here to tell me what I already know." Her hand took his arm and gently, as if drawing the lonely near, pulled him close. "I am again queen of the Síd, and I am privvy to knowledge that can protect my son and all Britain for his lifetime. Know this, Merlin: High upon a remote branch of the World Tree, there grows a singular blossom cultivated by the old gods in the age before the Fauni or even the Síd dwelled in Yggdrasil. It is known among the pale people as the Vanir Lotus."

"I never heard of it."

Ygrane's slim smile floated palely in the darkening air. "Nor has the Furor or any of the Æsir gods. The Síd stumbled upon it only after having dwelled in the Storm Tree for many years. And it meant nothing to them then. But now that they have endured life in the hollow hills all these centuries and have become intimate servants of the Dragon, they have realized the magical purport of the Vanir Lotus." Her lips approached his ear, and a dense smell of summer rusting to autumn dizzied him. "If a single teardrop from the Dragon is immixed with the nectar of the Vanir Lotus, the elixir that results is a fusion of the most high and the most low of this planet. Whosoever partakes of it will be endowed with the strength of Yggdrasil's root and branch. No one—not even the Furor and all his Rovers of the Wild Hunt—can do him harm. And if the one who collects the Dragon's teardrop and blends it with the nectar of the Vanir Lotus is king, then by the magic of emblem and correspondence, his entire kingdom receives infallible protection for the life span of that king after he drinks of the elixir."

"Can this be?" Merlin surged with hope. But no reply came. Only a dark wind pressed against him where Ygrane had been.

The sun was gone, and she had vanished with the last light into the night's immense quiet.

Gawain of fourteen years and Gareth of thirteen climbed through the branches of the apple trees at the edge of the piazza to better view their father, Lot, wrapped in his white bearskin cloak asleep in his large oak chair. "Did Mother put a spell upon him?" the youngest asked.

"Yes, she has blessed him with sleep." Gawain propped himself against a knobby trunk. He was a large lad, muscular and long of shoulder. "He's earned his rest."

"No, Gawain." Gareth, more slight yet as freckled and russet blond as Gawain, perched on a smaller bough above his brother. "Did Mother put a spell upon him to forget us?"

Gawain shook his head, though he was not sure himself. "Mother would not do that. Our father is old, Gareth. Nigh on fourscore years."

"But he remembered us before the snows melted. How could he forget us so quickly?"

"The war. He fought hard for Uncle Arthor. It wasted what was left of him." Gawain saw his mother Morgeu emerge from the doorway to the nursery, holding their baby brother Mordred to her breast, and he stiffened. She stared directly at them. Though their covert of apple bramble would have rendered them invisible from her vantage, they both knew she saw them, and they *felt* her watching them. "Come on, Gareth. She knows we're here. We'd best return to our studies. No dinner if we can't complete our ciphers and write our verses."

Morgeu met her sons as they climbed down from the apple trees, and both boys were startled that she had crossed the piazza that quickly with the babe in her arms. Before either of them could say a word, she waved one hand before their faces and passed them into a waking dream.

For a moment, she hesitated to fulfill her intent. She was not happy about beguiling her boys. They were her dream of strong sons become a reality. Looking at Gawain's freckled youth already relenting to the ferocious hawk's face of his adulthood filled her simply and naturally with pride. Gareth—still more boy than adolescent, his features clear and light as the weight of a flame—appealed strongly to her maternal urge to protect him from the inevitability of adult power that soon enough would burden him.

Nevertheless, she had to act. She had to use both Gawain and Gareth and use them at once. The reality of Mordred was already well beyond her and her two older sons. The incest magic she had provoked two springs past had its own horrific energy that would not be denied now that she had seen the powerful Graal vessel in the crafty hands of Brokk the Æsir smith.

The incest magic wanted it for its own, for Mordred, for madness itself, and it would try to take it from Brokk. It would risk her life and Mordred's for this unspeakable need, and she could do nothing about it. She had become the victim of her own magic, and the evil she had wrought against her brother now bound her as well. She would find a way to steal the Fire Lords' chalice from the dwarf. The Graal would serve Mordred if it served anyone. Of that, she was determined.

To fulfill her ambition, she had to distract Arthor and his warriors from the true Graal. She would use her own children to do this, for they were her own flesh, and so easiest to manipulate thoroughly. They would carry to Camelot the illusion that God had hidden the true Holy Grail and only the most noble of men could reclaim it. The quest would scatter Arthor's warriors across Britain and offer opportunities for her to destroy them while she sought the actual Graal that Brokk held. With his best generals driven to distraction by this deceitful quest and perhaps even killed, Arthor would be weakened and the opportunities for Mordred's eventual ascension to the throne enhanced. Morgeu could not ignore this chance to do her brother crucial harm.

And so, even though it hurt her heart, she pushed Gawain and Gareth deeper into her enchantment. With obedient eyes, they regarded her.

"Boys, you have seen the true Grail, the Holy Grail," she told them in a voice with a texture of moonlight. "Not the Graal that you saw in Camelot. That Graal, with its chrome jacket and gold filigree, is the false Graal. The genuine Grail is made of wood. It is the true cup from which Jesus drank wine at his last meal with his disciples before the Romans crucified him."

Gawain and Gareth stared at her softly in the cloudshift of

late afternoon. They loved her with a grief hard as gravel, and her voice was the streamflow smoothing all their sharp hurts.

"Behind the apple garth, you saw the true Grail floating above the six-foot grass, floating in a sunflash as off a lake. But there was no lake. Only the sunflash and the floating cup of wood and a voice of blue hugeness, the voice of the sky, that spoke, 'Behold the sacred vessel of our Lord and Savior Jesus Christ. This is the true Grail, sequestered in Britain, where only the pure of heart and most sincere of faith may find it. Return the Holy Grail to Camelot and the blight of the land will be healed.'"

"But we are Celts!" young Gareth declared proudly.

Morgeu smiled with shameless guile, and no tenderness broke in her heart when she said, "The sky has said to you, 'The true Grail is revealed to you both for you are pagans. How else are the other Warriors of the Round Table to know this vision is authentic except by the messengers who are pagan and do not need to believe what they see and whose seeing, therefore, is all the more valid? Go now and inform Arthor and his warriors of all you have beheld.'"

Gawain and Gareth swallowed hard, accepting this tranced moment with dread, grimacing as if drinking dark medicine.

Merlin said nothing of his meeting with Ygrane to Arthor. He wanted the king safely returned to Camelot before discussing the dangerous hope that the witch-queen had revealed. But Arthor wanted instead to rally his warriors and track down the other fire-breathing dragons devastating his kingdom.

"Swordplay is not sufficient to end this plague of dragons," Merlin argued hotly to the king in the hamlet they had helped rebuild. They stood beside a well where Bors Bona's men had created a makeshift derrick to dredge the ash-clogged water table. "For every dragon you slay, the demons within the earth will cull two more from the sleeping Dragon's dreams."

"I refuse to believe that magic is the only way to break this evil assault on our land," Arthor insisted stubbornly. His previous day's attack against the dragon had singed his hair to a brush of dense hedgehog bristles, and he looked more like one of the hamlet's farmers than the high king of Britain. "Exorcism and the ministrations of the Church will not avail against these demons?"

"Easier to pray the sun backward on its heavenly course, my lord," said the wizard. "These demons are not theological creatures subject to priestly command. They are older than time and subject to cosmic laws so wide of our faith we must needs call them magic. Camelot itself is designed on those cosmic principles, as a magical instrument to strike at the demons and to protect Britain from them. Our purpose in the outlands is accomplished now if only you can be convinced of the need to use magic against our enemies. Mount up, sire, and we will be in Camelot this time tomorrow, and there I will show you how we can use your fortress city to thwart these demons and restore Britain."

Arthor, though still sorely troubled, resigned himself to Merlin's argument and did not hesitate any longer. The morning was bright and songless, the sky blue as a lake and rippled with clouds. During the day's ride, thoughts kept returning to him about the dragonfight, about the sulfur stink and the beast's radiant flesh, iridescent behind the scabrous peelings. It must have been a beautiful creature before the sun's blast drove it mad.

At night, asleep in the watchful forest at the foothills of Cymru, the air around him throbbing with owl calls, the king dreamed that Straif had not listened to his assurances. In his dream, the palfrey believed the sulfur stink, the scorching heat, and the vehement roaring were far more than the usual troubles of battle. So, Straif hesitated. The dragonfire struck them and cast them into hellfire, a river of blue flames dragging them downstream through searing pain. Blistered, boiling, dripping flesh, and exploding bones, the glowing embers of their souls were swept into hell . . .

Arthor woke in a sweat, and the hauntful feeling of the nightmare polluted him with his fear of magic. What if Straif had not heeded him? What if the magic of the dragon had been more persuasive to the animal than his soothing words? They would be dead now. And next time? Would his training, his palfrey, his shield, and his sword be sufficient to overcome magic next time?

The low, throbbing pain of his wounded leg, the vacuity of his prayers, and this fear of magic, of Morgeu and Merlin, too, and his own mother Ygrane—all this troubled him until Camelot finally hove into view.

The strange beauty of the fortress revealed something new to him each time he let the parabolic walls and twelve-sided spires fill his mind, and his pain dimmed. He wanted Merlin to reveal more of the citadel's secrets. But there was no time for digressions. Valets waited with bath sponges, a fresh poultice and dressing for his wound, and a change of garments—a blue velour tunic with a crimson sash and a regal chaplet of gold laurel leaves.

When the two travelers reached the narrow, ouroboros-graven portal to the wizard's grotto behind the throne in the central hall, Merlin quietly took his leave. The wizard had magic to forge against the dragons. A herald, meanwhile, informed the king that a distinguished emissary from the Continent awaited him in the main council chamber.

The spacious elliptical room gushed with sunshine. Seven shafts of prismed light, seven colored beams of radiance arched across the room in a perpetual rainbow that Merlin had dubbed the Seven Eyes of God. Honeycomb baffles in the geodesic ceiling doubled as mullions for the crystal windows and focused sunlight to individual pools of illumination throughout the barrel-vaulted hall. The daylong rays, directed by swivel mirrors atop the citadel, fell upon tapestries and bas-relief depictions of ancient and exotic courts: Curly-bearded Menelaus and his lovely queen Helen greeting the beardless emissary Paris from Troy; Imhotep, the Son of Ptah, surrounded by dung beetles and mooncalves; Gautama Siddhartha in the floriate Deer Park at the very moment he became the Buddha; and from Cathay, the Goddess of Mercy, burning joss sticks at her beautiful ivory feet, instructing King Monkey how to defeat the yellow prince of hell.

One of the sun shafts fell upon a potted dwarf pine, and beside it stood a stately woman who looked as though she had stepped out of the surrounding artworks. Her skin glowed with cinnamon heat, her sable curls shone slickly as night itself, and her large Persian eyes glistened with darkness like a song before the sun is up.

"Selwa—" the king identified her at once. Months ago, she had helped him to flee Londinium when her uncle, the *magister militum* Severus Syrax, had imprisoned and threatened to murder him.

The lissome woman, swathed in long, white Ægyptian robes and a belt of amber beads to ward off the evil eye, lowered a tinsel-trimmed green veil and let out a soft, spicy laugh. "The king without a beard—you remember me."

Bedevere stepped ahead of Arthor and, on pretext of greeting the emissary, took both her hands in his one and inspected them for poison rings.

Selwa ignored him, and spoke directly to Arthor. "I am not here to assassinate you, young king."

"You saved my life once," Arthor acknowledged. "I am indebted to you for that. But my debt to Bedevere is even deeper, and so I beg your forgiveness for my suspicions. I have many enemies."

"I am not one of them." She lifted her arms to her sides so that Bedevere could see she bore no weapons. "But search me if you must."

"My lady." Bedevere scrutinized her loose hair, then swiftly passed his hands over her body as he knelt before her. Satisfied, he rose and stepped aside.

Selwa motioned for Arthor to come to her, yet he stood unmoving in the tall entryway. "Do not fear me, boy-lord. Remember that I am a woman of culture and finesse. My merchant family is so venerable that, seven centuries ago, it sent trade factors with Alexander the Great to establish posts in the Kush and in India—posts that remain important mercantile offices for us to this day. We have exporting agencies in all the Mediterranean countries and estates across North Africa, in the Levant, in Iberia, and in Gaul. So, why am I here in this chilly and insignificant island of the remote north?" Her indigo lips smiled as she lowered her chin mischievously. "Because you defeated and hanged my dear uncle, Severus Syrax, *magister militum* of this desolate land's oldest city. And my family, the estimable Syrax family, hold me personally responsible for his death—because I took pity on you in Londinium. As punishment, I have been given the unsavory assignment of residing in Londinium and representing the Syrax trade interests among the Foederatus—a rather uncouth and rancid crowd of tribesfolk."

Arthor swallowed pain to cross the room without limping,

anxious to hide his wound from this woman who bore his enemy's name. He took Selwa's arm and guided her to a mahogany settle whose sides were carved to flying eagles and a backboard cushioned with purple squabs. "My lady, I apologize " he said, sitting down heavily beside her.

"Your apology does me no good, Arthor." She pouted at him mockingly. "Is that the best you can do for the beautiful woman who saved your life at the most crucial time in your royal career?"

The king grasped her topaz-ringed hand. "What can I possibly do for you?"

Selwa cast a brief, surly look to where Bedevere stood off to one side with the sunlight dazzling on his balding head. Then she faced Arthor with a small, demure smile and a hopeful glimmer in her fawn-dark eyes. "Marry me. Make me your queen." Her hand tightened on his. "Don't look so startled. You insult me. Does not my physical beauty match your manly virtues?"

Arthor's grip on her hand went limp. "You are indeed beautiful . . ."

"Her blue-powdered eyelids narrowed. "But?"

"My kingdom is in jeopardy." He removed his hand from hers. "I am not prepared for marriage—to anyone."

"The threat to your kingdom comes from King Wesc and his filthy hordes of savage warriors." She leaned closer and enclosed him in the sapphire aura of her perfume. "Marry me, and we will buy them off. The Syrax family will hire the whole brutal lot as escorts for our caravans and protectors of our trade routes. They'll be scattered from here to Cathay. And you and I together will make of Britain a paradise of profits and peace. We will usher in an age of abundance the likes of which not even Rome enjoyed."

"Your offer is magnanimous, my lady."

She tilted her head forward so that she stared at him through her jet curls. "But?"

"I am a Christian—"

"Then, I will become a Christian, as well. The pope himself will wed us."

Arthor sighed, and his burned eyebrows shrugged haplessly. "I am a Christian intent on marrying for love."

"For love?" Selwa sat back with a jolt, as if slapped. "What mad notion is that? Kings marry for the good of their kingdoms. No king has ever married for love."

"You spoke of Alexander," said Arthor, crossing his arms. "After he defeated Oxyartes upon the Sogdian Rock, did he not marry that chieftain's daughter Roxana for love? His troops were amazed."

"And you compare yourself to Alexander?" she asked with a supercilious chuckle.

"I compare myself to no one, my lady." He strove to keep his tone free of umbrage, yet pride whetted his words keenly. "I am simply Arthor, high king of Britain. Battle blood sanctioned my title against those your uncle raised to challenge me, including the Foederatus that the Syrax family now offers to buy into passivity. Though I am flattered, at seventeen years of age, I am not prepared to marry anyone—even a woman as beautiful and influential as you, Selwa."

"Do not spurn me so quickly." From under her robes, she unfolded a parchment. "My offer may seem more palatable once you read this missive from your worthy enemy King Wesc, chieftain of the Foederatus."

"It's a poem," the young king noted with surprise. "And he misspells my name."

"It is not a misspelling. The king of the Foederatus believes that your name mocks his god Thor, Thunder Red Hair, the son of his war god Odin. He simply respells your name Arthur, a form more pleasing to his pagan sensibility. Read the poem."

A few quick passes of his yellow eyes took in the poetry and immediately moved on to the terms of peace attached to two extra leaves. "The poem is formless yet elegant," he declared as he finished taking in the concluding passages of the diplomatic attachment. "He sues for peace. But these terms require British fealty to *earls*—pagan lords who will oversee our dominions. I cannot accept that."

"I knew you would not accept," Selwa responded triumphantly, "which is why I offered you my hand. If you refuse King Wesc his portion of your kingdom, you know he will swarm over your little island and take it all. At this moment, he assembles a massive invasion force upon the shores of Jutland. With a moment's notice, he can descend upon you like a hawk stooping to a fat pigeon."

Arthor spoke through a tight jaw. "This pigeon is the white dove of the Holy Spirit—and I am His claws."

"Brave words, Arthor." She smiled coolly, amused at his ire. "But by summer's end—mark my words—before you see your nineteenth autumn, King Wesc will drink a salute to his warlords from your skull." She stood up. "Think about my offer. If you think hard enough on it, I believe you will see that you can learn to love me."

"Wait, Selwa," he called as she turned to depart. "Return a message to the poet-king. I will consider his terms. But I must counsel with all my warlords—Christian and Celt alike. This will take time."

Selwa frowned with disapproval. "He will know you are stalling."

"If he truly wants peace, he will not deny me the chance to champion his terms among my people." Arthor rose and, mindful not to limp, walked over to a long conference table of ebony, where parchments, inkstones, and quills were arrayed upon its polished surface. "I will meet with him—on my birthday, this Mabon, the twentieth day of September—in your city, Londinium. And there, he will have my answer."

"If it is the same answer you gave me, there will be war." She shook her head ruefully, rocking her thick, black curls. "And it will be a quick war, for his forces are formidable."

Arthor bent over the ebony table, writing deftly, heedless of the emissary's warning. "Give him this," he said, blotting the ink carefully before passing the parchment to the lean and dusky woman. "It will make it easier for him to understand me—and to hold off his invasion for now."

Selwa read aloud, astonishing Arthor with her fluent command of Saxon, for he had written his lines in the latinized rendering of his foe's language:

> *Let us not waste our breath*
> *on threats of war.*
> *For what is breath, after all?*
> *Spirit of the wheel, apparition*
> *of beginnings, it is breath*
> *that shapes the words as if*
> *to meet us*

halfway
with its own meaning,
the anguish of its source,
the caged wings.
Your brother of the pen,
high king of Britain—Arthur.

Selwa allowed a cunning smile to touch her empurpled lips. "Very clever—Arthur with a u. You flatter your enemy well through his weakness for the rhymeless, broken-line berserker poetry he loves. I learned their guttural language for trade—but how do you know not just their tongue but also this strange and pagan form they call poetry?"

"Not so long ago, I believed I was sired of a Saxon plunderer," Arthur answered quietly. "I took their language and songs for my own, the better to mock them in battle. But I no longer seek to taunt them. I am king now. I am strong enough to respect my enemies. And as of this day I will spell my name in a manner less offensive to them. King Arthur seeks not to enrage but to win peace and security for his people."

"Well then, dear Arthur with a u, if you are truly as clever as you seem to be, you will marry into the Syrax family and accept our protection." She tucked his poem under her Ægyptian robe. "Otherwise, I assure you, the berserkers you have mocked will rip your lungs from your rib cage and those wings will carry you out of this world forever."

8

A World of Dreams

Ygrane rode the devil horse with her naked arms tight about its neck. The loss of menstrual blood had left her tired and achy, and she was strongly tempted to pack her womb with glamour and staunch the troublesome blood flow. But she did not. Cramps, the itchiness where the linen pad chafed her thighs, and fatigue were ties to her humanity. So long as she felt this discomfort, she knew that the glamour she possessed still belonged to the Daoine Síd and had not yet transformed her entirely into a spirit being. She remained a woman, though she outpaced the wind on the devil horse and rode it straight through the stone face of a mountain, disappearing among cliff rocks like a ghost-bride.

The devil horse carried her into the hollow hills. It was like riding into a sunset that never ended. Baggy shadows fell to either side, and ahead shone the gaseous red sun.

But it was not the celestial sun. It was the magma heart of the planet. It was a ball of red light, spinning inside the earth, weaving the magnetic threads and cords that were the roots of the Storm Tree—Yggdrasil.

In that tangle of magnetic brilliance and suffocating heat, the Dragon slumbered. And around the Dragon, the demons hovered, stealing dream energy—wisps of dreamsong—to shape the monsters they loosed upon Britain.

The demons were cold drafts in the pouring blaze. They had no shape. They loathed shape and all forms. When they took shapes, they wore the most hideous, most disgusting guises they could devise. In their nascent state, they were formless, as close to the nothing they worshiped as they could get.

Ygrane felt her heart hide from these cold drafts of demon intelligence. If she had been simply a woman, they would have effortlessly ripped her to atoms and scattered her into the nothing that they loved. But she was the witch-queen of the Daoine Síd. And when she pulled her heart out from its hiding, it came forth shining.

A vast magnetic ocean of wind flowed through her. This was the power of the Síd, who had lived centuries in the hollow hills and had made the root-tangles of planetary flux lines their own. The whiplash force of the spinning core, big as the whole inner horizon of the world, spun the demons out and away.

The cold drafts of rageful sentience shot beyond the rocky skin of the earth and streaked upward through the atmosphere like green meteors. Somewhere beyond the moon, they slowed down and flapped into the void like the blackest of ravens, wondering what had struck them.

They would be back. The Furor's magic bound them to the earth and to the will of the storm god himself. They would return to the dazzling core of the earth and to the sleeping Dragon there—and they would butcher its dreams again.

But for now, the way into the hollow hills was clear for Ygrane's son, King Arthur . . .

The Furor felt discomfort as the demons he had bound were flung into space. At first, he was not sure what troubled him. He lay with his mistress, Keeper of the Dusk Apples, in a dell of dense grasses and trees like wands seventy leagues above the earth. The spongy ground of red moss seemed to quake. But it had not moved. The Furor's soul had shifted as his bond to the demons swerved inside him.

"What is wrong, my beloved?" Keeper asked, as her lover disengaged from their embrace and propped himself against a large tooth of rock inlaid with gold lichen. "Have I displeased you?"

The Furor swept back his mane of silver hair with both hands and shook his head. "No." His one gray eye had glazed over as he peered inward. "Someone works magic against me."

"Lady Unique!" Keeper of the Dusk Apples spoke her immediate fear and pulled about her the golden tiffanies and yellow taffetas that the Furor had peeled away during their dalliance. "Your wife has found us out!"

"She suspects nothing."

The Furor's mistress heard no great certitude in his voice, and unhappiness swirled up in her at the thought of the Furor's infidelity coming to light. She had no thought for herself. She was but a hunter's daughter who had surrendered to her chieftain with no expectations. By his favor, she had been appointed to forage the forests of Yggdrasil for the rare dusk apples that the Brewer pressed to the golden wine favored by the Æsir. Her work carried her far and wide, to remote branches of the World Tree—wild places where often the Furor would seek comfort with her unseen by the other Rovers of the Wild Hunt.

"The Lady's magic is great," Keeper of the Dusk Apples expressed her trepidation. "Her talismanic power—"

"She would never use it against me." The Furor reached for his wolfskin boots and tipped them to be certain no asps had curled within. "I have not always told my wife the truth, yet she knows I have always loved the truth, and that has been sufficient to put off her suspicions. No. Some mortal dares thwart my demons."

"The sleepers!" Keeper fretted, thinking of the Furor's children and allies entranced on the Raven's Branch who had given their life strength to empower his magic. "Are they in danger? Lady Unique would never forgive you—or me—if anything were to happen to her children."

"They are in no danger." The chieftain sat still, contemplating what he had felt, and Keeper of the Dusk Apples looked with undisguised admiration upon his nakedness: his mighty limbs, broad chest, and carved torso so faceted with strength that his pale flesh seemed cast of white iron. "My power is not challenged, merely—diverted. And only briefly. I must go and see who dares."

"Seek out first the Liar," Keeper advised, and lifted the gray cord trousers that the god had tossed carelessly among the asphodels and ferns. "Your blood brother has no love for you."

The Furor considered her words with a distracted expression.

"Loki is gone from the Tree or hiding. Perhaps this is his mischief." The clarity in his one eye sharpened. "I must go."

"At once?" She held his trousers against her chest. "Can we not sport just a little longer, my love? Who knows when next I will see you."

He smiled, his teeth in the shadow of his beard like a white mist of stars. "You are my passion and my counsel, Keeper. You alone of all the Æsir know my heart and love me with the simple caring that I need to be whole."

"Lady Unique loves you." Keeper lowered her head demurely so that her long, silver-gold hair covered her face.

"As a wife," the Furor replied. "For her, all is poetry. We, she and I, are a good rhyme: the daughter of the old gods' gate-keeper and the hunter's son who broke down those gates and overthrew the old order. We are the mother and father of the Æsir kingdom, a good rhyme to start a long epic. But her status as queen is more vital to her than her concern for the terrible visions that swarm in me." He shook the boots of silver fur he held in his hands. "She was appalled that I would entrance our children—appalled that I would use their power for the binding of demons so I might take the West Isles and make a stand against the Fire Lords. The only reason she helps me now with her talismans is for our children. Not for me." His angry stare unclenched. "Ah, but you've heard all this before, my love. I trouble you."

"I want you to trouble me." She lifted her face, a visage of solar beauty, peach-fuzz cheeks burnished ruddy by her long wanderings under the forest sun. "I want to shoulder your cares."

That evoked a broader smile from the Furor. Here was a woman not dismayed by the eye socket he had emptied to win prophetic sight—unlike Lady Unique, who thought him addled to mar himself that he might see events flare uncertainly in a dark future. "Then, you do not think I demean myself by enlisting demons to break my enemies?"

"Your wife so thinks?"

"The Dwellers of the House of Fog disgust her. Yet, they are entities as old as time itself. To move them is to turn the very axle of the universe."

She stepped closer, watching him brightly, a sigh in her eyes. "You have accomplished what not even the Old Ones dreamed."

"The magic I needed to bind those demons was so much more than any talisman could harness. But did she care?" He dropped his boots and meshed his thick knuckles like gears. "My ingenuity was to unite the strengths of many gods and meld a power that not even the demons could defy. Did she praise me for my daring? No. She berated me for endangering Thunder Red Hair and Beauty. But I am trying to save our world!"

"Trouble your mind no more of this." Keeper of the Dusk Apples sat beside him on the large rock among the pale trees like wands. She rested her head on his shoulder, and her gold-streaked hair smelled sweet as a lawn. "Take a moment's refuge in my arms. You will be stronger for it. Come." She drew him down to the red moss floor of the forest in a dell of dense grasses seventy leagues above the turning world.

Mother Mary, I fear for my soul. Grasshoppers crackle in the weeds. It's nigh on autumn and no rains. I have prayed to you time and again to protect the few grain boats we bought so dearly in Gaul. And each time, the Saxons have caught them at sea as if the devil were receiving my prayers instead of your grace. Forgive me. I am cantankerous these days. My leg blazes like a Yule log.

Mother, help me.

"Democritus was right, you know," Loki whispered from behind Fra Athanasius on the sumpter mule. "Atoms and the void—that's all there is. The precious light itself is made of little bits, restless little bits that never stop moving. And even space, so-called empty space, is composed of tiny parts, threads and knots so minuscule that familiar space around us appears smooth and featureless. Space and time are one thing, you must understand, and it is not continuous, I assure you. It is a foam, a froth of unbelievably small geometries."

Fra Athanasius shrunk inside his cassock, hood drawn up over his curly head, trying to ignore the devilish god at his back. Under his breath, he recited prayers and Bible passages and paid no heed to what the demonic voice said.

When Urien announced the appearance of Camelot through the trees, the legate gave thanks to the Almighty that his mind had not been seduced to confusion by the pagan dissembler. He squinted to see their destination, and his weak eyes offered him a blurry image of a large, bright stone edifice among the blunt mountains of Cymru.

Once through the massive pylons, Loki leaped from the mule and was gone. Fra Athanasius felt his lungs expand with relief. And then a tantara of horns announced his arrival in the outer bailey, where a small crowd had gathered to greet the papal legate. Urien and his warriors dispersed among the market stalls while grooms led the weary, dusty mounts to the stables.

The scribe was greeted by a deep, resonant voice that he heard as much with his chest as his ears, "Emissary of our Holy Father, welcome to Camelot. I am Merlin, the king's counselor, and this is our bishop Riochatus, who will assist you in your ecclesiastical offices while you are among us."

Athanasius peered blearily at the indistinct figures and knelt before the crozier-shape. "Bishop Riochatus—that such a one as you comes forth to greet me applies far more honor than I deserve! The vagaries of fortune—or more truly misfortune for my own beloved bishop—has untimely bestowed this charge upon me. But you—blessed Riochatus—you retain steadfast renown and dearest respect from Arles to Ravenna for your efforts both staunch and tireless to carry the good news of our Lord and Savior among the pagans of Britain. My lord Victricius, whose soul now resides with God in heaven, oft spoke of you as an equal to Patrick of the Gaels and Non of Cymru—a saint of the Church."

Riochatus, stooped and doddering under his mitre and leaning heavily on his crozier, dismissed this flattery with a sputter and bid the priests on either side of him lift the legate to his feet. When the papal emissary stood erect, the bishop spoke in an enfeebled tone so small and bodiless that Athanasius almost toppled forward bending closer to hear. "Blessed Victricius remains a true prince of our Church in his heavenly station," he wheezed. "We are deeply saddened that the Lord God has called him from us so soon. But we are heartened at your arrival in his stead, dear Athanasius. Please, do not kneel or bow to me. Lift your head. I am your servant, for you carry the mandate of the Holy Father himself, and by your good judgment our island kingdom will be found either worthy or wanting of the Church's favor."

The deep voice of the counselor resounded again, this time from behind him, startling the legate and jolting him upright. "In anticipation of your arrival, I have prepared for you a small gift. If you would humor me for a moment, please—" Merlin placed a wafer of glass to Athanasius's left eye, and inquired, "Can you see better through this lens?"

The legate's mouth gaped at the sudden clarity that revealed before him the haggard, grizzle-bearded Riochatus in his gold-and-ecru ecclesiastic robes and mitre, his aged hand firmly gripping the shepherd's crook. Around him, seven priests stood in the gray, brown, and black cassocks of their individual orders.

"Urien's messages mentioned your weak eyes," Merlin continued, removing the glass disk. "I took a reasonable guess about the curvature of the lens necessary to correct for your blurred vision. We can make minor adjustments later, but for now I believe these will serve you well."

Reaching around from Athanasius's back, Merlin fitted two lenses framed in gold wire over the legate's eyes and hooked the armatures behind the emissary's ears. Vision sharpened with miraculous immediacy and force, and Athanasius gasped aloud. Before him, in crisp and colorful detail, stood the crowd that had gathered to greet him: Riochatus with every gray whisker aglint in the bright sun's rays; the seven priests revealing their yellow, snaggled teeth with their broad smiles at his astonishment; and four lancers in the king's black leather cuirasses embossed with wide-winged eagles, sunshine glazing their bronze helmets. He could have stared a long time into each of their exquisite faces and gazed into the very mirrors of their souls so clear in their watchful eyes, but his newly sharpened vision pulled his attention beyond them to the citadel that loomed above.

Initially, he was not sure what he was seeing. The geometries baffled him. The ramparts were not vertical as in every other fortress he had visited but curved and smooth, devoid of masonry seams. Atop them, stone shells—chevron parapets—each twice as tall as a man, fretted the battlements, and trying to discern their function filled his head with a meaty ache. The spires that lofted into the blue afternoon carried pieces of sun among their many facets as though angels stood in the turret windows.

Then he turned to the counselor Merlin. Instantly, all thoughts fled, his heart a frantic movement, for this personage had the face of Death with diamond eyes.

One finger raised, the wizard stopped Athanasius's scream in his throat before it reached his mouth. The scribe did not see the glorious light of that finger but felt its warmth just behind his face, a warmth in his brain that was a mixture of comfort and splendor. On the walk across the bailey to the king's court, the wizard put his arm across the legate's shoulders and told the astonishing and improbable story of his origins as the demon Lailoken and his birth as a human in the womb of Saint Optima.

Athanasius listened attentively, his soul smoothed like a linen sheet by the wizard's strong voice. At the central ward, before a tall fountain of carnelian and green tourmaline, where waterspouts emptied onto interlayered basins all carven with images of dolphins, salmon, squid, conger eels, and mermaids, Merlin took his leave with a fateful smile in his grisly countenance, "Anon we shall speak further on matters of spirit and soul and their opposites whirling to one center."

Before Athanasius could reply, Merlin hurried away, and Riochatus and his entourage approached, ushering the emissary into the main hall.

The king received the legate in a large room vaulted by a dome that was more glass than stone and ablaze with solar fire. Between high-manteled open hearths, tall windows exposed the fortress city's luxurious and enigmatic architecture: Buttress terraces of Irish yews banked an inner ward of roof ridges, cottage gables, turrets, and airy spires, bastion upon wider bastion joined by arched footways between which fell artful and artificial waterfalls that fed the tiered households with running water and powered fountains in diverse yards and gardens. And indeed, the sun had already passed below the colossal battlements, yet sunshine dazzled the windows and the skydome.

The Round Table—ashen silver as a storm cloud backlit by sunlight—occupied the center of the hall. Its high-backed ebony chairs, carved with dragons and unicorns, sat empty. Aromatic sandalwood pillars inlaid with gold encircled the great studio, separating the perimeter into individual alcoves decorated with statuary and hangings of figured silk. Spectators filled these enclaves—churchmen, merchants and their families, warriors and their attendants—all gathered to witness the arrival of the pope's legate. A sennet of brass horns from the musicians announced his entry.

With his restored vision, Athanasius skittered his attention among the alcoves, wanting to focus on everything at once. Never had he beheld such sumptuous appointments: settles upholstered in leather of peacock blue, silver lanterns of topaz lights with chains twined in a verdure of creeping plants, red-lacquered doorways jambed by jasper columns—and the people attired in a magnificence of divers-colored textiles cut to Roman and Celtic fashions.

The music ceased, and the emissary's bespectacled eyes alighted upon a throne of dark wood cut with the image of a dragon and a unicorn fused to one fabulous creature. The king who sat on that strange seat was, as foretold, a boy. He wore the gold chaplet of monarchy and regal garb of deep indigo blue with figurings of crimson. But his hackled hair, his rosy cheeks, and his sharp quadrangular jaw devoid of beard could more readily have belonged to a yeoman.

Still, Athanasius went down on one knee. The king admonished him to rise, and as he stood, his sharpened eyes fell upon the one-armed warrior standing behind the dais vigilantly watching the assemblage in the alcoves. Blood shrank from the legate's face, then rushed back in a flush of shame. At once, he dropped to his knee again, hiding his consternation.

"Legate, rise," the king repeated, and leaned forward, almost standing to help the stricken emissary to his feet. "What troubles you in my presence."

"Sire—the soldier attendant upon you at your dais is Bedevere of the Odovacar," Athanasius said in a voice thick with disgust, squinting his gaze to be certain that the wizard's lenses did not deceive him.

Hearing his name, Bedevere stepped forward. "I am Bedevere of the fallen kingdom of the Odovacar, former servant of our Holy Father, Pope Gelasius and also of his servants Theodoric, king of the Ostrogoths, and his brother-in-law, Clovis, the Merovingian king."

"You recognize me not, Bedevere?" Athanasius's upper lip curled with revulsion. "A score and ten years ago, I served as *notarius*—civil notary—for the emperor Julius Nepos in Dalmatia when the holy bishop and now blessed saint Severinus excommunicated you. I am the very scribe who recorded the minutes of your hearing before the ecclesiastic judges."

Bedevere shrank where he stood, his face suddenly pasty as hot murmurs ran through the assembly.

"Excommunicated?" Arthur gave a bewildered look to his personal guard. "What was the offense?"

Bedevere remained silent, his head hung low.

"Sire, his offense is unspeakable." Athanasius leveled an expression of horror upon the king. "I am shocked to find him in your presence—for you are at an age still prime to be corrupted by his evil."

"Never!" Bedevere shouted. "My offense was thirty years ago! I have redeemed myself since in numerous righteous battles for our Savior. Gelasius himself accepted my sword in his defense full aware of the ban upon me."

"And yet it is obvious you have told nothing of your heinous offense to the Christian monarch you now serve." Athanasius shook his head grimly and faced the perplexed king. "My lord, my first responsibility as the legate of our Holy Father is to warn you that this—this swordsman who serves at your right hand is a convicted sodomite."

Merlin descended slick and uneven stalagmite steps into his grotto beneath Camelot. The cavern was illuminated by an array of small glass spheres that burned butyl blue. Hung from among the stone teeth of the high ceiling, the multiple spheres focused white light to a dozen rays that crisscrossed the haze. Their spotlights revealed stone niches where tar-oil burners blazed under galley pots and alembics. Large jointed pipes and coiling copper tubes connected hissing brass kettles to numerous carboys and stained-glass jars that percolated with incandescent distillates.

"I know you're in here!" the wizard shouted, and his angry voice echoed across the uvular dome and along the ribbed walls of the cavern. "I smelled your electric stink leagues distant. Come forth, trickster!"

From inside a tall, primeval stone carving of the Original Mother, Her features rubbed smooth an epoch ago on the glacial moraines, Loki emerged. He removed his floppy black hat from his bald, rune-marked head and gestured at a mural of archaic starcharts hung between gleaming stalactites. "Ah, Lailoken, the maps of mortal destiny writ large upon the sky—do these celestial signatures apply to demons and angels, as well?"

The wizard strode angrily up to the god, seized him by his shoulders, and shook him to a blur of voltage. Swiping an amber wand from a table-rock cluttered with pliers and tongs, he pierced the fox fire and quickly carried it to a maroon stump with a lode of hematite iron. Then, robes flapping and hat flying from his head, he rushed to a stone shelf, grabbed a bell jar, and hurriedly placed it over the pulsing flame.

"Done!" Merlin huffed, and stepped back with a proud laugh. "It will be a small aeon before you slip these shackles, Æsir god."

Loki's face formed within the bell jar, fetal and bloated. "Lailoken, I have not come to you in strife."

"So you say now, Liar."

"If I had meant you harm, demon, would I have presented myself to you so directly?" He opened his tiny arms guilelessly. "Do you not think I knew you would smell my body of lightning from leagues distant? I relied upon it. That is why I sought refuge with Urien and his war party. I have come not in secrecy from *you*, remarkable Lailoken, but from the other Æsir gods." His bulbous head rolled forward and pressed his scrawled scalp against the glass jar. "Read the futhorc upon my pate. Read it. These are inscriptions to ward off detection by my brother and all the Rovers of the Wild Hunt. I am here with you unbeknownst to them."

Merlin glanced at the runes and saw that they were shapeshifter incantations meant to hide Loki from the earthward gaze of anyone in the Storm Tree. "Why? Why have you put yourself so easily in my hands, Loki? You are brother to the Furor, the sworn enemy of my king."

"That is precisely why I am here with you. For years I have disagreed with my blood brother's arrogant nostalgia for the past. And now I require your help, Lailoken."

"You will not call me by that name." The lanky old man

picked up his hat and dusted it off. "I am Merlin, the king's counselor."

"But it is Lailoken who can help me, for I am come to ally myself with the Fire Lords—the angels of your king's lore."

"The Fire Lords are not mine to command."

"Surely not." Loki's disembodied head stared passionately from under a halo of silver electricity. "But you are a demon they have favored. Was it not the Fire Lords who lured you into the womb of Saint Optima and wove you a human body? With your help, I would ally myself with them."

Merlin donned his hat and sat on a stob green with malachite. "Why would an Æsir god want anything at all to do with the Fire Lords, whom they despise?"

"*I* do not despise them, because I know they will have ultimate victory in this world." Loki's dark eyes expanded plaintively. "The Fire Lords are the future. The Furor's ambition to hold them at bay is futile. The knowledge of numbers and alphabets that they have brought to our world has forever changed us—gods and mortals alike. The primeval age that the Furor loves is long gone, never to return."

"To what end would you betray the Æsir, your own clan?" Merlin crossed one leg atop the other and curiously tilted his head. "To what end, Loki?"

"Not all the Æsir share my brother's fanaticism for the days of yore. Many of us know that change is inevitable. The Christian faith will soon enough supplant us. Science—that is the knowing that the Fire Lords gave to the Babylonians, the Chaldeans, and the Ægyptians. Each of these peoples used it to know greatness for their moment of history. Science is what made the Fauni of the Greeks and the Romans strong enough to conquer the world for their moment. Now the Angles and Saxons want that power. We want the future and our moment of glory."

"You will serve the Fire Lords?" Merlin threw up both hands. "Say no more. Whatever you say, I will not believe you."

"I do not ask you to believe. I have come for your help, not your faith."

"What help do you want from me?"

Loki lifted his rune-marked face and closed his marked eyelids. "I want the sword that Brokk forged when the Furor was exiled to walk the earth. I want the sword Lightning that the

Fire Lords stole from Brokk for your king. I want the sword that you call Excalibur."

Merlin uncrossed his legs and stiffened. "That is the king's sword."

"It is the Furor's weapon stolen to serve your king." Loki's eyes flashed open and held the wizard's adamant stare with determination. "I want it back. With the sword Lightning in my hand, I will lead a revolt against the Furor and take Yggdrasil for those who serve the future instead of the past."

"Excalibur is not mine to give you. And even if I could, why would I?"

"To save your king from the wrath of the Furor." Loki's visage expanded to one dark staring eye. "The sword Lightning is the first weapon that Brokk fashioned for my blood brother in his war against the Old Ones. The dwarf proportioned it for a human hand, because in those early fugitive days our chieftain could safely assume no greater stature. But now he is a giant among gods—and the sword still fits a human hand, this dangerous sword forged of diamond-edged steel, this lethal sword Lightning designed to rip the waveform flesh of gods as savagely as it tears human bodies. Put that sword in my hand, and Yggdrasil becomes a home to gods friendly to your king and to Britain."

Merlin's mind reeled at the possibility that this god fabled for his deceits and betrayals was speaking sincerely. "How can I trust you, Loki, whose name means Liar?"

"Trust begins here—with me putting myself in your hands." The god's face shrank to dewdrop size. "That is why I came to Camelot with the king's warlord Urien, to place myself in your hands and trust that we can make an alliance."

Merlin stood up from the brassy green rock and stroked his forked beard. Loki had arrived at a destinal moment for the kingdom. His help could be crucial in reaching the Vanir Lotus—or his offer could very well be a deception that planted a vicious Æsir god in their midst. For a long while, he gazed languidly into the calm light of the nearest oil lamp, one of a dozen glass orbs dangling by fine chains from the carinated ceiling, its fuel clear as water and a flame afloat upon it like a leaf.

No hope in fear, he heard his mother, Saint Optima, advise from far back in his soul, and he stepped to the trapped god and removed the bell jar. When he took away the amber wand, a thousand fiery snowflakes swirled up from the hematite stump and solidified to Loki in his black garb sitting cross-legged on the maroon rock.

His handsome, stenciled face smiled without rancor. "I knew I could trust you, Merlin. You were a demon once. You know the uses of fear. But trust, that's something new for you, isn't it? And we all want what's new."

"I can't give you Excalibur," Merlin said flatly, and sat down again on the malachite stump. "Not unless the king gives it to me first. And he won't. Unless I trick him. And I won't trick him. Unless you help him to take from the World Tree something more valuable than the sword."

Loki's scrawled eyebrows lifted inquisitively. "Are you going to scare me?"

Merlin told the god about his encounter with the witch-queen and what she had revealed to him of the Vanir Lotus.

"Are you mad?" Loki's bald head rocked back with disbelief. "You'll never get your boy into Yggdrasil without the Æsir knowing, let alone climb with him to some distant bough. The Æsir are *hunters*. They will track you down like animals. And when they catch you, they'll nail you to the Tree and feed you alive to the ravens."

"You will distract them."

Loki hid his face in his hands. "Just put the bell jar over me again and forget I'm here."

"The sword Lightning is not easily won, Loki." The wizard stood. "If you want the king's sword, you will have ample share of his risk."

Loki peeked through his gloved fingers. "When do we leave?"

For ninety thousand years and more, people wandered the earth and their dreams fitted the contours of the earth perfectly. Whirlwinds of light, the people moved upon the open hand of the earth. When they died, they disappeared completely, vanishing like dreams into the very depths of emptiness.

Then the Fire Lords taught the people numbers and alphabets. The people learned spelling—and with these spells, the world changed forever. Dreams became bigger than the contours of the earth. People still died, but they did not disappear completely anymore. Their dreams remained behind.

We Nine Queens were placed here on Avalon by the Fire Lords to witness this change that came upon the earth with the first kings. History is their enduring spell, etched in fired clay, chiseled in basalt, inked onto parchment, printed across bond paper. We have seen these spells change the earth we once knew into a world of dreams we do not recognize.

Why are we here?

Why else but to be with you? We are in your spell, this most intimate spell of reading the written line that carries us deeper into your light . . .

9

Love Like Wrath

"Are you a sodomite, Bedevere?" King Arthur asked awkwardly in a narrow studio behind the central hall. He had dismissed the valets and now stood alone with his bodyguard in the blue tiled room.

Bedevere faced the king with his back to the spired windows. Along the armless side of his body, rose trellises framed the bishop Riochatus and his clerics, marching with Fra Athanasius to chapel.

"My lord, you were perhaps too hasty in your dismissal of the papal emissary." Bedevere cast an apprehensive look out the windows at the colorfully attired crowd filing through the garden maze. "Without the approval of Athanasius, our requests for grain and livestock will be denied. Famine will devastate hundreds of communities across Britain."

"Bedevere!" The husky boy stepped forward angrily, winced, and leaned against an oaken chair. His right leg ached into the bone. "Are you a sodomite or are you not?"

Bedevere straightened. "I am."

The king sagged into the chair, his pallid face expressionless. When he spoke, his voice was anguished. "For over a year—you lied . . ."

"I never lied to you, my lord."

"By omission—you lied!" The hurt in his stare twisted to anger. "We are humiliated—shamed before the entire court—learning this intimate truth in a public denouncement!"

Bedevere dropped his chin to his chest.

"You hid your passion well, and well you should have," Arthur said grimly. "I am a Christian king."

"You are my king, and I revere that truth with my very life." He addressed Arthur's boots with a stricken look. "No hint of my feelings would ever have been known to you had not the legate made the issue public."

"By God's wounds, man, how can you speak so to me?" The king pounded both fists on the arms of the chair. "What of shame? Have you not given yourself to Christ?"

Bedevere's throat tightened. "You cannot imagine the intensity of my love for our Savior. I love him with a fiery ardor that wracks my bones."

Arthur sat back in his chair as if shoved. "You *are* shameless."

"No, sire." Bedevere looked up sharply, his gaze firm. "I know shame. But not for what God made of me."

"God?" The king's mouth hung open, voiceless, as he measured the man before him, astonished at his apparent sincerity. "It is Satan who has corrupted your soul, Bedevere."

Bedevere lifted his eyebrows sadly. "When I was your age, I so believed. I tormented myself with fasts and endless prayer vigils, striving with all my might to drive the evil one from my soul. It took years for me to realize—there is no more evil in my soul than in any of us created of mortal clay. I am simply a man who loves men."

Arthur could not believe his ears. "That is abhorrent."

"Is it, my lord? Our Savior never spoke against it. He taught us to love one another."

"Not in the way you love. In the eyes of God, that is a love like wrath."

"I love with my heart, as did our Savior—as do you. Never have I inflicted my desire on anyone, neither by force of will nor cunning."

"I cannot believe that God has put such desire in your soul, Bedevere." The king sagged in his chair, shaking his head. "It is unnatural."

Bedevere nodded softly at this brutal censure and its inevitable consequence. "I will leave Britain at once."

Arthur gnashed his teeth. "No."

"The other warlords—the people of the land—now everyone knows my heart." The warrior shielded his eyes with his one hand, twisting inside to see ire and disappointment immixed in the young king's face. "I must leave your kingdom."

"Exile?" Hues of blood patched the king's cheeks, yet his brow gleamed white as stone. "After you've slandered my reign and implicated me in your sin, do you think I will release you?"

"My lord—" Bedevere looked up, baffled. "Of course, you must release me. Never have you executed or imprisoned a subject. You *are* the true Christian king that the Holy Father seeks. To win his blessing—and his grain—you must denounce and banish me."

Arthur sank deeper in the chair, pulled by the weight of a decision.

Bedevere unclasped his sword belt and offered the weapon. But the boy-king stared past this gesture with a peculiar sad outrage. The sword belt slipped through Bedevere's fingers. "Do I detect behind your hot dismay, cool pity?" His bewildered look pressed to a frown. "You think—you think I am humid in my heart? You think to redeem me through charity and mortification. Sire!" His mouth worked soundlessly a moment, then said, "I will not be changed. I am *not* infirm of soul."

"Be silent." The king curtly waved him aside. "I can't think on this now. Pick up your weapon and get out."

Kneeling on one knee, his hand atop his sword belt, Bedevere did not move or speak for a tense moment. Finally, he dared announce, "Perhaps you should execute me, my lord. Athanasius will surely deny you the pope's grain—thousands of families will suffer in the months ahead. Many will die. I am to blame."

"Your sins have caught up with you at a critical time for Britain," Arthur said quietly, and pressed a knuckle into the ache at the center of his brow. "I know about sin. Fair breeds foul. Morgeu—Mordred—and now you, Bedevere? I can't think on all this at once." He brusquely pointed to the door. "Leave me alone. Stand watch outside. I don't want my prayers disturbed."

Head bowed, lashed by the king's silence, Bedevere exited.

Mother Mary! Arthur cried out from his soul. *Carnal sins pollute my life and my kingdom! Evil propels us on an infinite course. You must pray for us, Mother—or we are damned.*

The Furor heard Arthur's cry. The dim, mortal voice echoed like a prophetic haunting, a summons from his blind side, tattered with echoes.

. . . pray for us . . .

The chief of the Wild Rovers was surprised to hear this voice from the earlobe amulet he had stitched to his vest. He had climbed to Fallen Wing, the highest twig on Raven's Branch, the tallest bough of Yggdrasil. Amulets rarely held their power so close to the abyss. For as far as he could see around him, silver sands rippled under the stellar winds and nothing living stirred. Overhead, constellations hung their lamps in the void.

. . . we are damned.

Was that truly King Arthur's voice—or was it Lucifer's?

The Furor had felt a jolt in his soul while lying with his mistress, an abrupt torque of mood that could only have come from disturbing the power he had borrowed from the sleeping gods. He had climbed to Fallen Wing alone to find out if his demons were still bound to his magic. He expected treachery from demons; nonetheless, he had not asked for help from the Rovers of the Wild Hunt. This was a chieftain's risk, and belonged to him alone.

Crags of black clouds towered against the star mist. Their thunderhead darkness stretched for distances so unreckonable that light itself took centuries to cross them. Infinitesimal, an atom smaller than sight, the Furor stood before the House of Fog.

He called for the demons he had bound, and cold rushed out of that vast pit of smoldering darkness, brushing back his beard and flipping the brim of his wide leather hat. The black wind poured into his head with knowledge from the demons, who had been driven out of the hollow hills by the Daoine Síd.

"With the Dragon asleep, the Síd are feeble ghosts," the Furor said to the pit. "They could not have driven you out. There must have been a Fire Lord among them."

The one-eyed god did not wait for a reply from the gulf but turned and hurried away across the whispering sands. He leaped from Fallen Wing like a rainbow. If there was a Fire Lord below, he would find that radiant being, and the angel would tell him why they had come with their spells of numbers and alphabets. For the sake of all time to come, the angel would tell him.

• • •

Under a cloven moon with the northern sun smoldering like an ember in the cauldron of night, Morgeu the Fey wandered through a desolate field. The torchlights of the black slate fastness that she shared with her husband Lot glinted on the ruddy horizon. When she felt that she had hiked into the remote interior far enough from the watchful eyes of Lot's warriors and the ever-curious witnesses of the fishing hamlets, she called for the Furor: "All-Father, Great Father, One-Eye-All-Seeing, Furor and Rune-Master, Frenzied God of the Wild Hunt, Sacrifice of the Storm Tree, come to me! I who birthed her father call to you. Come, First of All Magicians. Come to me that I may offer you alliance!"

Morgeu felt forced to this desperate summons by news from her spies in Camelot that her brother had received Selwa of the wealthy house of Syrax, a seductress who had proposed marriage to the king. That news inflamed Morgeu, and her breath jetted forcefully in the cold. An agony of frustration cramped her so that it was difficult to stand straight. Everything she had done to destroy Uther's son had come to nothing. All the good in her life that she had sacrificed to defeat Arthur had been twisted and damaged by her incest magic: her husband, her children . . .

A visceral shriek flung spittle against the stars. She had given away too much of her life to let Arthur live, let alone flourish. The king's alliance with the aggressive Syrax family would deny Mordred his claim to the throne. She had to act at once. She had to trump Arthur by giving herself in bond to an even greater power. "Chieftain of Yggdrasil, hear my cry!" she called into the night with all the strength she had won from her demonolatry.

A star moved free of its tethers of darkness to the north and tracked across the black horizon. In moments, it expanded to a radiance sleek as a comet and swift as a meteor. Among the enormous mansions of night in the northern constellations, it swerved, journeying brightly toward her.

"Skidblade!" she cried in awe. The self-propelled launch designed and built by Brokk, the master smithy for the Furor, approached. A ship without sails, without oars, floated in the sky upon the shadow of the earth, its seamless hull shining softly, fashioned from chrome of moonlight. When it settled down through the glycerin layers of the atmosphere like a silver pearl, she noticed that it did indeed possess sails—tenuous and ruffling scarves of auroral iridescence that whispered around it with the transparency of star fumes.

The luminous vessel hovered soundlessly an inch above the rocky ground, rotating slowly, displaying the smooth contours of a porpoise as it rocked gently to a complete stop. An oval doorway irised open to a glittering interior, and Morgeu lifted her scarlet robes so that her sandals could carry her in a full run to the ship the god had sent for her.

Cold, gelid air poured from inside with the purple smell of a squall, but she did not hesitate to enter. Immediately, the door winced shut behind her, and she gawked about at the blue-yellow centers of flames all around her and then, abruptly, clouds of steam drifting through each other with a hum that widened gradually to a whistling wind as over fifty-foot crests on the arctic sea.

Skidblade was flying, she realized in the swathing steam that embraced her with a touch like the sun. Skidblade was flying, and she felt no motion, only the kiss of the dry steam. And then, the calm flamecores flared around her again, the door gaped, and an icy breeze hurried her out.

She stepped onto a moraine of flaking shale before an ice-sludged sea; on the horizon a small, frosty sun was lodged in a nest of green clouds. She flung a look backward, and Skidblade was gone.

"You would speak with me, woman?" the voice of a hammer spoke.

Morgeu whirled about and faced a one-eyed man with the visage of a storm cloud: his beard gray as the North Sea, wild as a war song of kettledrums and trumpets. *No—not a man,* she realized instantly. Though he stood upon the gravel banks in big wolfskin boots and bear-hide vest, his turbulent mane was an aura of blizzard force, his empty socket a skullhole into night, his one boreal gray eye a crystal of the future. One glance into it and her life was a shadow as time roared down inside her.

She fell to her knees and gazed hard at the frost-veined stones. "All-Father, you see into my heart. You know why I have called to you."

"Ygrane knows that I have the Fire Lords' Graal," the voice

of thunder said. "And you are here to help me—and to help your son Mordred, who is your father Gorlois."

"My brother Arthur cannot stop you from taking Britain for yourself," Morgeu said to the ground. "I know this, and so I give myself to you that you will have mercy upon my son who is my father. Use me—and find a worthy place for Mordred when our islands fall into your hands."

"Such a vengeful heart beats in your breast, Morgeu." The Furor's shadow fell upon her deep as a night without stars. "You rage at the demon Lailoken for your father's death, though death is certain for all. And you rage at your mother Ygrane for marrying Uther Pendragon and birthing Arthur, though birth is what love sows in answer to death. Is it not existence itself that you spite?"

Morgeu's mind reeled among bitter memories and fierce thoughts of smashing those who had stolen her father from her, stolen his life at its prime and mocked his death by filling his absence so quickly with another.

"Look deeper," the voice of avalanche said from above, reading her thoughts. "Look for the crow in your heart. Look."

It was there. The Furor's voice of command brought it out to where she could see it: the living shadow of hot anger—the rageful darkness that had always dwelled within her. That black intelligence was never a child. Always it had taught her another way to think: *Life is useless. It begins in spasm. It ends in spasm. A brief fever in a cold world.*

"Yes—that is your truth, Morgeu the Fey." The voice of the tempest covered her. "You have always disdained life. The death of your father is only an excuse for your hatred of your brief dream, your brief brightness."

Morgeu lifted her face angrily. Above her, the one eye stared coldly like light held in wet ice and beside it the empty socket with darkness pouring out, the aftermath of all light. Her face tightened to a fist. "Why must any of us live at all?"

The Furor nodded, satisfied. "I will tell you. But you are a Roman woman, and you will not understand me. Yet, I will tell you anyway. We live so the stars can caress us. We live so that when we do perish the earth can receive us into her sweet home. Yes, the earth that you call dirt is holy, and she is sweet. Certainly, the world is cold, but we are its warmth. Who kindled this fire in us? Know that and you will understand why the animals share their wisdom with us: They curry our spirits during the hunt so that we may wear their skins proudly and eat their flesh with joy. Joy! Do you hear me, Morgeu? Joy. That is the location of life. Whatever happens, the one, simple truth of life remains always unchanged. All our troubles and all our pain are merely pathways back to joy."

Morgeu turned her face spitefully to one side and peered at the blue mountains of icebergs on the dark sea. Despite her fear of the Furor's wrath, she heard the crow in her heart squawking: *Clown—clown—clown!*

"I *am* a clown to the Roman mind—the modern mind," said the Furor like a grinding of glaciers. "Only a clown can find joy in a world of suffering. Yes? That is why the Fire Lords have taught you numbers and alphabets to make science, to protect yourself from suffering. And now, the modern people kennel whole tribes in walled cities, cage people in boxes with numbers, imprison entire races in grids of roads, while slicing the open country with fences. Keep out the suffering. Protect yourself with boundaries from all that is other. But all you do is isolate yourself, for joy cannot be contained."

Morgeu stood up and cocked her head defiantly. "Strike me dead if you will, god of the one-eye—for I have two eyes, and I see clearly that there is no joy that does not rot to pain sooner or later. Strike me dead, just stop dunning me with your righteous noise about the glories of nature. Nature eats babies. So, strike me dead, All-Father. I find no joy in this miserable world."

The Furor sighed, a pine breeze full of creaking sorrow. "I will not strike you dead, Morgeu, because I need you. You are a powerful enchantress, trained by the demons themselves. You will use your craft for me."

"Will you provide a worthy place for my son Mordred when you take Britain?"

"First you must do a difficult thing for me." The Furor's storm silver eyebrows tightened to a frown. "When the Fire Lords wanted to steal my sword Lightning to arm your brother, they sent Rna, the eldest of the Nine Queens of Avalon. She came here and strode past Garm, my wolf-ogre, entered my dwarf Brokk's underground workshop unfazed by the smelting pots of boiling metal he poured upon her, and took my sword. I fear that the Fire Lords will send her or her ilk again, this time to retrieve the Graal—a device of their own fashioning. I want you to stop them."

Morgeu scowled with disbelief. "How? I don't even know where Avalon is."

"Skidblade will take you to Avalon." The god spoke with his eye raised to the slow revelation of clouds in the twilit sky as if reading there the future. "You will hex-dance around their abode and weave an enchantment that will contain them. In that way, the Graal will remain here, where Brokk can continue studying it and interpreting its secrets."

"What if the Fire Lords themselves come for their Graal?"

A smile opened in his beard as he scrutinized the first stammering stars. "I am hoping that is exactly what will happen. I have longed for such a confrontation since I first heard gossip of them. They are older than the gods, you know. And unlike the demons, who are as old as they but so much more cowardly, they still carry the light of creation, though it burns them with an indescribable suffering. Think on the revelations my prophetic eye will discern in that glorious fire!"

"And if I fail?" Morgeu continued to stare contemptuously at the god, who shone with a rainbow aura in the gathering darkness. "If my enchantments will not contain the Nine Queens within their abode?"

"You will not fail, Morgeu." The Furor held her with a baleful expression. "You who mock the joy of life will be hurt by what you mock." His naked, muscular arm pointed to where long rays of scarlet from day's end illuminated a startling figure half as high as a man but twice as wide, with huge limbs and a cubed head of tufty gold hair and red whiskers that swirled over pugnacious jowls. It was the dwarf Brokk, and in his arms he held an infant.

"Mordred!" Morgeu's cry elicited a frightened wail from the baby, and she moved to rush to him—but the ferocious strength of the Furor's stare held her in place.

"Nature eats babies." The Furor's face was a cliff in the red darkness. "My wolf-ogre Garm will devour your beloved Mordred in one bite if you fail me, Morgeu."

• • •

Merlin found the king in the rose maze on his way to the chapel. The choir's threnodies unraveled among the trellises like invisible veils, and the hardy spiciness from censers and thuribles overlay the summer scent of the dusky roses. The wizard removed his hat and glanced around while the wounded king painfully lowered himself onto a stone bench. No others were visible among the rose arbors—save Bedevere, several paces back on the grass walk.

"I heard the valets chattering about the uproar that the pope's ninny, Athanasius, inspired during his audience with you." The wizard turned his hoary head and nodded to the one-armed guard. "I am sorry, Bedevere, that you were made the foil of such a fool." Then he lifted his robes and sat on the bench beside the king. "Sire, how have you decided to resolve this controversy?"

Arthur cast a weary, troubled glance at his bodyguard. "I am too angry to resolve anything. I don't want to talk about it."

Merlin clucked and pulled on the tines of his forked beard. "You are king. You make a decision even when you don't decide."

"Look at this leg." His limb was swollen and green as a toad's. "This is going to kill me."

"Nonsense." Merlin touched the glossed flesh and felt no pestiferous forces. "There is no poison here, my lord. Only a septic soul. You suffer a malady of the mind." He hung his long face close to the boy's ear. "Conscience."

Arthur nodded and moaned, "Morgeu."

"Deeper."

The king squinted as he tried to understand.

"You do not trust God's election. You crave the freedom of failure, because your hour is upon you and you must prove that you are not the slave Kyner reared. But your conscience questions you: Are you yet a slave? To magic? Or Morgeu? Or to me?"

The king hung his head and confessed, "My prayers turn against me, Merlin. Mother Mary spurns me. I am an abomination in God's eyes."

The old wizard clapped his hands loudly. "And what then am I, an incubus squeezed into the skullcase of a man? We are all abominations, Arthur. Now stop sulking and make a decision about your personal guard."

"What do you recommend, wizard?"

"I recommend you make a decision immediately." Merlin stood up. "Accept God's election. You *are* king, no matter how you feel. Decide."

"As you say." Arthur beckoned Bedevere and, when the guard knelt before him, stated resolutely, "I have decided not to decide. You will continue for now as my guard. We will ignore whatever calumny that inspires. And when I am less pressed, I will deliberate on your fate." He motioned Bedevere aside, then turned to his aged counselor. "Satisfied?"

"Superlative decision, my lord." Merlin wrung his bony hands together. "Men are to be judged by their deeds, never their desires." He bent closer to the king. "Now then, we have a far more ticklish situation to settle. I have just come from a meeting with Loki."

"The Æsir god?" Arthur stiffened with incredulity. "Here in Camelot?"

"In the grotto," the wizard replied. "He seeks an alliance with us, my lord."

The king looked into his counselor's silver eyes and saw he did not jest. "Merlin, he is *the Liar*."

"True." The old man nodded, and his hair looked like a moult of feathers in the warm breeze. "Yet, his rivalry with his blood brother the Furor is famous. He believes that the Fire Lords will ultimately dominate our world, and he wants to be included among the victors."

"Dare we believe him? He's a trickster—and a god."

"Ah, but I possess a demon's soul." His face, resembling nothing more than cold gray wax, smiled both grave and complaisant. "I gazed into the flamecore of this god's mind, and I believe him to be sincere. As much as one such as he can be. Should our defeat ever present greater dividends than what injury he can inflict on his brother, I don't doubt that he will turn on us, of course. But for now, he means to serve our cause."

"How?"

"Sire, you are convinced that only magic can now save our kingdom?"

Arthur removed the chaplet of gold laurel leaves and rubbed his burned hair. He felt immersed in a nightmare. Could it be that God and the Holy Mother had given him over to magic and pagan gods? It could not be. And yet it was, and that left him feeling scared and adrift in a reality as absurdly wild as battle itself. He gritted his teeth before the inevitable, determined to save his kingdom. "My encounter with the dragon has overridden all my previous reservations. If magic is what we need to save Britain, then I will certainly use magic—however reluctantly—even if we must go to the Devil for it."

Merlin winked with satisfaction at the king's hard-won mettle. "Loki may well be that devil. His magic is strong. And we will need that magic and his knowledge of Yggdrasil to defeat our enemies." He again sat beside the king and there, with his mummied hand upon Arthur's arm, informed him of his encounter with Ygrane and her hope of winning protection for him and Britain with a Dragon's teardrop and nectar from the Vanir Lotus.

Worry stamped the king's brow—worry that Ygrane had voluntarily damned herself for him—and he took a deep sighing breath. "This is knowledge my mother won with her soul, Merlin. I must speak with her."

The wizard turned his hands palm up. "Even I cannot find her, my lord. She has given herself again to the Daoine Síd, the pale people who have been her companions since childhood. Be assured, Ygrane and the Síd strive for Britain as valiantly as we. As soon as she can, I know she will find you."

Arthur shook his head and cocked a cynical eyebrow. "Can we ever succeed at this improbable quest, Merlin?"

"No venture is certain, my lord—least of all one as dangerous as this. But victory means the salvation of Britain for your lifetime and a golden moment for your people." The wizard suppressed a hideous chill at forethought of the dark age to come, and added quickly, "With Ygrane preparing the way, and with Loki to guide us and distract our enemies, victory is foreseeably within our grasp. Now we must take the risk."

"There is little time." Arthur straightened his right leg painfully and shifted his weight. "I have met with Selwa of the Family Syrax. She has arranged an audience for me with King Wesc. I have won us an uneasy respite, at least for these next few weeks. However, if by Mabon we have neither a magical victory nor a willingness to capitulate to the Foederatus, the pagan hordes will sweep over Britain."

"And what of the papal interlocutor Athanasius?" Bedevere

spoke up, tentatively. When he saw that the king regarded him, he continued more strongly, "Once you deliver the Dragon's teardrop to the Vanir Lotus and drink of the protective elixir, there is still the famine of Britain to defeat. My lord, without aid from the pope, you will reign over a nation that will endure suffering for generations to come."

"That will not be," Arthur replied softly but with determination. "Athanasius must be won to our love of Britain. He must no longer regard us as a nation of lost souls cursed by God."

"Athanasius is a simple matter, sire." Merlin stood and fitted his tall hat upon his head. "I will entrance him."

"No. You will not." Arthur spoke brusquely, holding the wizard's silver stare with unblinking resolve. "Magic shall not be the solution to all our problems, Merlin. Athanasius is not a simple matter. He is the emissary of the pope, and so he is the very emissary of my Christian soul. He will *not* be entranced. He will be convinced that we are faithful to the teachings of our Savior and that our purpose is just and good in the eyes of God."

Merlin lifted his owlish eyebrows and tugged at his wispy beard. "That may be more difficult than bringing the Dragon's teardrop to the Vanir Lotus."

"Then we will take the legate with us on our quest," the king decided, and shoved himself to his feet. "We will show that sanctimonious Athanasius that we are not devils but God's own champions."

"Hu Gadarn Hyscion—Hu the Mighty, who led the Celtic people to Britain—Mighty Hu was a descendant of Abraham the father of the Semites," Gawain declared in his clear, vibrant voice. He had arrived at the court of King Arthur, his brother Gareth at his side, and now both stood before the Round Table, their russet hair mashed with sweat. They had marched directly into the central hall in their riding leathers and interrupted a security conference, where all the warlords were present save Lot. The boys had ridden well ahead of their father, arriving in time to occupy his position at the Table and speak in his place. Eyes shiny with zeal, they shared their vision of the Holy Grail. Only Urien, affronted that senile Lot was losing his two boys to the nailed god, demanded to know why Celts should have anything at all to do with the drinking cup of a Hebrew prophet.

"The Celts are a tribe of the Hebrews," young Gareth explained with conviction, and all laughed but the king.

"Our altars remember," Gawain pressed when he saw that his uncle Arthur listened intently. "The dolmen shrines. The menhir boundaries. The great slabstone circles. We Celts build altars from unhewn stone, and that has been recorded in the Hebrew Book of Exodus. Uncle, look at chapter twenty, verse twenty-five: 'And if you make Me an altar of stone, you shall not build it of hewn stone; for if you use your tool on it, you have profaned it.'"

"Our vision is important," Gareth insisted. "We must find the Holy Grail to heal Britain."

"Who will search with us?" Gawain looked directly at the king. "Who will fulfill the angel's command?"

Arthur smiled warmly. "All in time, boys. For now it is enough that we prepare to stand against the Foederatus."

"And what does your father say to all this passion for the nailed god?" Urien demanded of the youths, and stood up angrily. "Does he mandate you to speak of Celts as lost Hebrews?"

The king motioned him to sit. "I've heard all that before, Urien. And it may well be true. The desert prophets Isaiah, Jeremiah, and Zechariah all named their coming messiah 'the Branch.' The druids, too, taught that the Celtic deliverer was the Branch—the All Heal symbolized by the mistletoe."

"And on the rare oak where the mistletoe grows, do not our people mark a cross?" Gareth challenged Urien. "And do we not name that branch All Heal, in our oldest dialect *Yesu*?"

"Yes, yes, all that is true," the king acknowledged, and directed a mollifying look at Urien. "I've spoken to druids, rabbis, Persian magi, and yogis. The ancient history of the Celts is wide and touches much of the world. Even so, boys, Urien is right to return us to this Table. The fate of Britain holds us all to the tasks at hand. I've no time just now—even for the Holy Grail."

"No time for God?" Gareth asked in shrill disbelief.

Arthur laughed at the dismayed expression on the thirteen-year-old's face. "I've used up what time God has given me," the king confided, and motioned for the boys to sit. "But of course He's always making more, isn't he, lads? And if He gives some to me after we drive the Wolf Warriors from our shores, we will quest together for the Holy Grail. I promise it."

Ygrane determined to visit her dead husband, Uther Pendragon. The way through the hollow hills to the sleeping Dragon had been cleared of demons for her son, Arthur, and there was nothing more she could do for him in these scarlet-shadowed depths of the planet. So, she turned her devil steed about and galloped through the featureless terrain following the red and green threads of eternal twilight.

Eventually, the shadow plains brightened under a sky like an ocean of blood. Out of the abstract shadows emerged the skeletal shafts of fire-ravaged trees—echoes of scorched Britain. Ygrane rode faster, and soon bluesmoke forests appeared in the crepuscular dark, followed by sprawling meadowlands that were at once curiously cultivated and wild.

She slowed down and walked the devil horse into the netherworld forest so that the pines' tufted boughs floated above her like islands in the sky. The lurid light had paled to opal hues streaked with raspberry smudges and lemon rinds of clouds.

She drew her steed to a full stop and listened to the faint piping of the oldest music, the rhythms of wind and water. Dismounting, she felt soggy and heavy. She leaned against a pine and took the time to change the pad she had fashioned from the torn linen sleeve of her chemise. Thoughts of Homer's and Virgil's heroes presenting blood offerings in the underworld crossed her mind as she buried the soaked cloth in the soft mulch of the hollow hills. This was the presentation of her lifeblood to the dead, and when she stood she whispered the name of her dead husband, "Uther Pendragon."

A foam of laughter and song sifted through the slanted apertures of the woods, and she discerned human shapes of luminous mist frolicking and cavorting in the distance like an assemblage of fauns.

"Uther," she called quietly. "Come forth."

The misty figures in the bosky woods continued their roisterous dancing like passing smoke on a wintry river.

Ygrane called again, this time summoning her husband by his original name, "Theodosius Aurelianus—come to your wife.

Come to Ygrane of the Celts. Come forth, Theo."

A spry figure separated from the troupe and stepped closer through the forest's purple shadows—a man of floss and cobwebs, chimerically lovely in his tatterdemalion silks.

"Theo!"

Her beloved came full into view, his raven hair darkly shining as it was in life and his yellow eyes bright with surprise and ardor. "Ygrane! It is you!" His stare winced. "Are you dead?"

"No—not yet, my love."

He shifted his gaze to the devil horse with its glossy black sinews and slant red eyes. "What is this beast? It smells of magic—you smell of magic." His Roman face showed concern, but his voice betrayed his disappointment. "Why, Ygrane?"

"Only magic could bring me here to see you."

He stepped back from her. "You must go—and quickly. There is no magic here. The Lady of the Wild Things dwells in these woods, and her glory is eternal spring." The mists subsumed him, yet his words continued, frantic and crazed with echoes, "Can't you smell it? The flares of pollen? The rain mists? Ygrane—this is a place of life! You can't stay here. You belong in the world of the dying."

10

The Valor of the Worm

In the main council chamber, Merlin paced before the long conference table under the Seven Eyes of God, where the king sat staring at his reflection in the highly polished ebony. On a faldstool
to his right, Fra Athanasius slumped, avoiding looking across the
table at the god Loki, who leaned forward on his elbows, black-
gloved hands clasped before his tattooed face. Nearby, Bedevere
stood in a pool of sunlight let down from the crystal skydome.

"Fra Athanasius, you have seen the devastation of our island
kingdom during your journey here," spoke the wizard. "Will
you help us? Will you inform Pope Gelasius that we are worthy
of his Christian charity?"

The legate cleared his throat, thumbed his spectacles higher
on the bridge of his long nose, and passed a dark look from the
boy-king to the wizard. "Sir, I have but one mind and heart
here, to make firm the will of our Holy Father. The mandate
given me remains the same as was laid upon my beloved master,
Victricius, the original papal legate, a saint more than a church-
man, who paid with his very life that I should come before you
as emissary of the papal see. I durst not betray my love of him or
his lifelong love of the Church by assessing your kingdom by
any less brave measure than the truth."

"And your assessment, Fra Athanasius?" Merlin pressed. "Let
us hear it."

Athanasius's jaw throbbed beneath his peppery beard, and the wings of his nostrils whitened before he spoke in an angry but frightened voice: "By my faith, you are all devils, every jack of you! The king's warlord Urien and his men who escorted me to Camelot are pagans all. The king himself is but a boy, a child who abides sodomites and wizards. And opposite me sits the very Devil himself, a supernatural creature in mortal disguise." His large eyes blazed behind his lenses at Loki's smiling face of tattoos. The legate turned to the king and did not flinch before Arthur's outraged scowl. "You dare ask the Holy Father for charity? You dare? The fire of God's wrath hath blown upon the land of the Britons to make it desolate, a grim and terrible testament to the wickedness of your unholy ways."

"Shall we take that as a no?" Loki asked through a snide grin.

"Be silent, Loki," the wizard snapped. "Not one more word from you."

Loki bowed his scribbled head in mock submission.

"And you as well, Merlin—be silent," Arthur said in a tight voice. "The king will speak for himself."

Merlin clasped his hands behind his back and directed his irate stare to the sunny skydome and the rainbow cope.

"Athanasius, I am but a boy." Arthur's rose cheeks glowed with anger, yet his voice was mild. "And you, you must acknowledge, you are but a scribe."

"Be not deceived, young king, I am full warranted by the Holy Father himself."

"I do not question that. Yet, I say again—you are but a scribe. Do you dispute this?"

"Take not too great scorn at my humble station. Yes, I am a scribe, a former *notarius*. But I serve the most high offices of the Church and am fully sanctioned to act in full capacity as legate of Pope Gelasius."

Arthur accepted this with a gracious nod, though he made no effort to disguise his indignation. "I am a boy who is a king, and my station is as properly sanctioned as yours and more so, for I was born to noble parents. Accident alone made you an emissary, whereas God Himself warrants my status by birthright. Nonetheless, I am but a boy—as you are but a scribe. Both of us must strive against our limits to fulfill—properly and rightly—the tasks that God has put before us."

"Your boyhood is not constraint upon my judgment, sire.

But a sodomite at your right hand and a wizard at your left—that is the vile part of you I dare not condone for love of my own soul."

"The man you brand a sodomite came into my service by recommendation of the very same Holy Father whom you now serve. Pope Gelasius was master to my Bedevere with full knowledge of his—his . . . predilections, and yet he relied on his skill for protection against assassins." From the sheaf of parchments before him, the king removed a vellum trimmed in papal cochineal. "Here is the document of recommendation bearing our Holy Father's signature and seal. As a scribe you are qualified to affirm the authenticity of what I am showing you."

Athanasius accepted the document with both hands and recognized it at once as an official papal commendation. "Verily, it is genuine."

"Pope Gelasius is not a sodomite." The king's voice fell into silence like a stone down a well. After a significant moment, he went on, "Nor am I, Athanasius. I am a devout Christian and accept Bedevere as my personal guard for his abilities as a warrior. Surely, you will not hold that against me any more than you would question the judgment of our Holy Father—will you?"

The legate blinked and wiped sweat drops from his high brow, visibly flustered. "No, my lord." He noticed Merlin peering intently at him from under his bent hat with its esoteric stitchings, and he stabbed an accusatory finger at him. "But that wizard with the direful countenance, that creature who speaks freely of his former existence as a demon—an incubus! Carnal Merlin! Surely, he is not right flesh nor blood."

Arthur laughed good-naturedly, and his golden eyes glittered merrily in his boyish face. "Merlin is a marvel of God's love, Athanasius! That God could transform a hateful demon into a benign mortal devoted to the furtherance of all that is holy and good is a genuine marvel. A miracle! His mother was Saint Optima, daughter of the King of Cos. From her, he learned compassion, and now all his demon powers are directed by a will of love and truth. There is no deception in him. And there is no wickedness. Do not judge him by his face, man. Look to his soul—and you will find his soul in his deeds. What evil has he done? This was an island of strife and warfare until God sent him to help us unite our land against the pagan invaders. Look no farther than your own nose if you would measure this wizard by his works. Did he not restore your sight?"

"I am well pleased to see most clearly again," the scribe admitted, then confided in an anxious tone, "but I fear magic, my lord. It is unchristian. It draws a veil of illusion athwart our eyes."

"I tell you this, Athanasius, I *am* a true Christian, and there is nothing unholy in my court. What we call magic here in Camelot is not supernatural at all. It is nature itself. And I will prove that to you—if you are sincere and will fulfill properly and rightly your role as legate."

The emissary placed both palms flat on the table, and averred, "You will indeed resolve all my doubts if you can show me that what appears magic to my restored vision is not supernatural."

"What is supernatural is beyond the knowing of this world." Arthur looked to the legate for acknowledgment. "Of that you will agree?"

"Of a certainty." Athanasius bobbed his curly head briskly. "The supernatural is *gnosis*—understanding that descends to us from the ultramundane. The Church forbids such apprehensions, for they originate with Satan and come forth to take us unawares and confound us."

"But the natural world," Arthur continued, "the world of God's creation—that is within our knowing, within our capacity as mortal beings to grasp and understand with our minds."

"Indeed." The legate regarded the boy-king curiously, wondering where his argument was leading. "Such is *scientia*, and all the Church fathers concur that this knowledge is given us by God that our minds may better encompass His creation and we may know Him more truly."

"Then, I tell you Athanasius, all the magic here in Camelot and all the magic practiced by my wizard Merlin is *scientia* and can be explained in a way that anyone of common intelligence will understand."

The scribe thrust out his lower lip and nodded contemplatively. "You have spoken well, sire, and I am moved now to recant my uproar of words and my dark condemnation of you and your court. But I shall not depart one tittle from the article of my faith before the inexplicable. Thus said—" He slid his gaze toward Loki, who was watching him with a bemused smile. "How do you adjudge by *scientia* this adversary of reason?"

"Merlin, show Fra Athanasius the truth of our guest, the god Loki."

The wizard nodded to Bedevere, who with a swift, lunging step came up behind Loki. As the Liar gripped the table edge to push away, the blur that was Bedevere's saber thwacked through his neck and sent his bald, tattooed head rolling across the table.

The legate shrieked when the head tumbled into his lap, black eyes agape, mouth still moving and speaking. "You've gotten a head of me, Athanasius . . ."

Merlin plucked up the severed head by its ear, and it winced, and cried, "Ouch!" He exposed the tulip-bright underside to the scribe. "Behold—no blood. Just this longing to appear mortal." He reached his hand into the red frills and pulled the head inside out. Like a hand puppet, the fuchsia crisscrossing of muscles, the tangle of blood tubes, the hard-boiled eyes, and the complete absence of brain bobbed before Athanasius's horrified face. "You see, it's fake. An illusion." He slapped the flesh rag against the tabletop, and it splattered into green sparks and crawling blue volts. "It's a kind of ectoplasm—like Saint Elmo's fire, the colorful flames one sees on the masts of ships in a storm. Like will-o'-the-wisps. Or ball lightning."

"My God—my God!" Athanasius blubbered.

Out of Loki's severed neck, a sparkling blood mist rose and crystallized into a precise replica of the head that had vanished. "Would you like to see that again?"

King Arthur doffed his gold chaplet and regal attire and rode out from Camelot dressed in the hempen tunic and frayed sandals of John Halt. Merlin made no attempt to stop him, for he understood how thoroughly the boy had taken upon himself the distress of Britain. Only outside of Camelot would he find the resolve necessary to overcome his bewilderment at his mother's desertion of their faith and his own anguish at the powerlessness of his prayers to overcome without magic the dangers that threatened his kingdom. Merlin only prayed that the boy would avoid dragons and encounters with wildwood gangs and roving Wolf Warriors and return safely to Camelot.

Meanwhile, Merlin occupied himself by taking Fra Athanasius into Camelot's grotto so that he might be educated in the *scientia* of magic. The legate gawked in dismay at the wizard's underworld basilica. Mineral steps curved downward into a cavern of amorphous coral shapes and shadowy alveolar depths lit by phosphorescent orbs. On rock shelves and ledges, bubbling glassware and steaming kettle pots filled with cuprous green fluids crowded against distilling coils and stacks of scrolls and moldy tomes. Among the measureless rock ducts, drains, and gullets, echoes of dripping liquids clocked their dull chimes.

Apprehensively, the legate stepped past chalk pillars and under wet stone fangs, frowning with obvious disfavor at the gravid icon of the Original Mother that seemed to preside solemnly over the entire infernal panoply.

"Ah, this is the oldest God, Athanasius, the true Creator," Loki said, striding past the scribe and slapping the pregnant belly of the statue. "Her dugs have squirted the Milky Way, and from between Her legs came skidding forth the whole of earth among the placental stars."

Merlin lifted an amber wand from a stob of rock cluttered with knobs of resin, opals, and drilling tools. He held up the wand for the emissary to behold, then rubbed it vigorously between the folds of his robe.

"What are you up to, Merlin?" Loki backed up against the crude and featureless statue as the wizard approached.

With a swipe of the wand, Merlin cut Loki in half. "You see, Athanasius, what the pagans call gods are in fact entities of astral fire, a cool, protoplasmic form of lightning."

"Stop that, Merlin!" Loki shouted with annoyance as the wizard slashed the amber wand through the god's body, breaking him into hovering, disjointed pieces. "I'll not be your toy!"

"On the contrary." Merlin whirled the wand vigorously, and Loki dissolved into a luminous frosty green haze. "You will prove a most entertaining subject for my first lesson in the *scientia* of cold fire." He gathered the radiant cloud above a ferrous rock stump of rusty hue, where it pooled to a vaporous swirl of spectral refulgence from which Loki's cries of protest squeaked like the rage of bats. The wizard smiled at the openmouthed legate. "We will begin with a demonstration of attraction and repulsion in the realm of atoms . . ."

• • •

Bedevere groaned when he realized that Arthur was returning to The Blanket of Stars. "Our kingdom is plagued by dragons, King Wesc gathers a massive invasion force in Jutland to swarm upon our shores, the papal legate who decides whether we are to eat or starve is in the care of your *wizard* while the Æsir god Loki wanders freely about Camelot, and you visit again with an innkeeper's widow?" He drew his horse alongside the king. "Are you mad, sire? You realize, we are without protection. Bors Bona has withdrawn his forces to his fastness in Parisi to prepare for the coming assault. You and I alone are out here among wayfaring brigands and pagan raiders."

"Look at the land, Bedevere." Arthur motioned to the broken road before them and the leafless trees. In the brittle fields beyond, a neatherd marched his spindle-shanked cows along the broad stony bed of an exhausted river. "The Furor has already defeated us with his magic. If we are to reclaim Britain, we must use magic ourselves." He turned a narrow look on his guard. "That makes me feel—unclean."

"Surely, your faith is unbesmirched by these forces that are dark only because the light of reason has yet to illuminate them." The swordsman tugged uncomfortably at the sheepskin collar of his threadbare mantle. "You yourself convinced Athanasius that magic is but *scientia*."

The king nodded gravely. "I should be as attentive a student as our Latin brother and sit at Merlin's knee. But, in truth Bedevere, I fear for my soul."

"And the innkeeper's widow offers salvation, my lord?"

"Perhaps you are right to chide me." Perspiration mottled his hempen tunic and had wrung his hair to spikes, and he appeared every inch a farmer's husky son. He spoke hesitantly, unable to look Bedevere in the eyes and pretending to adjust the linen bands that dressed his swollen leg. "I am the king and should have loftier affections, I know. And yet, somehow I sense that Julia, this common woman, can be my anchor in this world. She is a good British woman, a caring daughter, a hard and proud worker, who has paid in blood with her husband's life to put me on the throne. I would—" He paused awkwardly. "I would see her face again before I give myself to the netherworld and Merlin's magic." His yellow eyes glittered. "She has a face I find agreeable, that is all. And if I hold close the memory of her, it is only to guide me back to this world."

Skidblade swept Morgeu the Fey across the face of the earth toward Avalon. In its billows of dry steam that smelled purple as a storm, she felt no motion, though she knew she was flying because the Furor himself had so commanded the clever vehicle. To the nacreous interior she spoke: "Set me down in Britain, in the forests of Crowland."

She did not know if Skidblade would obey her, so when the calm flamecored lights dazzled around her and the door widened, she peered out anxiously. The black night baffled her, and she had to exit before she recognized the tattered pines of Crowland. Skidblade had alighted upon a bluff overlooking the willow spills of a lone island in a turgid stream where starlight reflected like broken lightning. The moon, a bird of wish, a wing of bright stone, stood high above the ragged treetops.

Skidblade waited while Morgeu made her way down the rocky slope, over fallen trees and desiccated bales of weeds. She lifted her crimson robes to her thighs and waded through the muddy shallows and razory grasses to the slender island. There, with nothing more than moonlight and marsh vapors, she wove a chapel.

Of moonfire and stardust, Morgeu raised a small, holy house on the willow isle. Its blackstone lintel bore the cross in the circle of the Celts, and under the sonorous trees the little building appeared entirely real, dark as the peacefulness of death, its spired doorway ringing with deeper darkness. Inside, in a silence serene and overwhelming, she raised a bituminous altar, black as oblivion. Upon it, she set the Grail.

It was just a wood cup. It was not a real wood cup, any more than the feldspar blocks of the walls were real or the jet tiles of the roof, or the votive flames flickering upon the tall, pale candles in the windy chancel. All were insubstantial as tomorrow yet borrowed solidity from the ache for mystery in the human breast.

Satisfied with her illusion, Morgeu walked three times around the dark chapel, singing to the demons who served the Furor. Her voice floated unearthly over the treetops. The demons heard her, and their hardy musk thickened in the willow air.

"Send a dragon," she instructed. "Send a dragon to lie in the swale. Soon, my brother's warriors will come . . ."

Smiles of raw meat widened under the willow manes.

Morgeu splashed across the shallows laughing bleakly. Ahead, shining atop the pine crest in emerald hues of the night's breath, Skidblade waited to carry her to Avalon.

Fra Athanasius sat alone in a shadowed alcove of the main hall. Out of the vestry, he had selected a white alb and a blue dalmatic to replace the cassock that had become tainted with the fumes of Merlin's grotto. The hellish stink had troubled him. It had smelled like a medicinal church, full of the unholy incense of distillates and mentholated vapors. He could not think with that dire stench in his nostrils, and he had doffed the offensive cassock and rummaged through the liturgical wardrobe for something appropriate to wear. In his current station as a papal legate, he felt entitled to don ecclesiastic garments, though as a scribe and *notarius* he had only been allowed to put on a simple smock and, for formal occasions, a tabard embroidered with clerical emblems.

The priestly garb, for all its starched crispness and fresh scent, did not assuage the uneasiness that accompanied all he had learned from the wizard. A whole other order of beings existed, he discovered—entities who dwelled far up in the sky and deep within the earth, creatures fashioned by God out of electricity. *Electricity.* The word troubled his tongue. He, of course, recognized the cognates as *electrum*, the Latin term for amber, which itself came from the Greek name for the same substance, *elektron*.

Then, with his amber wand, Merlin had disassembled Loki, demonstrating the general properties of electricity and its relationship to the mysterious lodestone. The scribe was familiar with lodestone, having taken transcriptions for the emperor Zeno from Moorish navigators out of Gujurat who had employed what they called a *bait al-ibrah*, a "house of the needle" to identify north: The device was an iron splinter that had been in lengthy contact with a lodestone before being affixed to a cork afloat in water; no matter how it was spun, the splinter always aligned to point north.

Using spools of silver thread and spinning a lodestone in their midst, Merlin had made the ends of the silver filaments spark and had even woven cold fire inside a glass sphere. He had told the scribe that a vast lodestone spun below the earth, generating huge currents of energy invisible to the human eye. The Dragon was a God-created creature made of this energy, who dwelled in this underground ocean of invisible currents and tides. Likewise, the wizard explained, an enormous sea of similar energy floated at the top of the sky, where the sun's wind generated charged particles. But to understand that celestial sea, one would have to know more about the structure of atoms—and there the scribe had raised both hands in dismay and stopped Merlin. He needed to absorb what he had already been told, and he had come to this alcove to sort through the demonstrations he had witnessed in Merlin's infernal grotto.

Athanasius's head swam with the many notions of *scientia* that the wizard had introduced, and he sat on the stone bench that jutted from the alcove wall, head cradled in both hands, muttering to himself. "Electricity. God's natural power in the world, so the wizard says. Indeed, what he showed me was as visible as bolts of lightning, fox fire, and no doubt the tongues *as of* flame that touched the apostles on the Day of Pentacost. Not fire, but *like* fire. It must have been electricity. And perhaps, too, the burning bush that spoke to Moses and was not consumed . . ."

A gruff voice intruded on his ruminations: "Fra Athanasius—may we have a word?"

The legate looked up startled and adjusted his spectacles. Before him stood two tall, burly men with ruffian faces, pugilist eyes narrow and shielded by thick cheekbones and heavy browridges. One had a ponderous red mustache that covered his mouth entirely, and the other was clean-shaven, a younger twin of the first, with a merciless mouth. Both wore their red hair long and tied to topknots in the fashion of the pagan Celts. But these two brutes displayed Christian emblems: the eldest with a scarlet cross emblazoned on his overblouse, and the other, a golden cross of Celtic design on a thong that dangled before his black leather cuirass.

"I am Kyner, chief of Cymru," the eldest introduced himself in a voice rough as gravel. "And this is my son, Cei, the king's seneschal."

Athanasius stood, jittery as a deer in the sudden presence of these imposing warriors. His first thought was that they had come to admonish him for speaking to their boy-king with such bold ire, and he nervously observed that both carried swords—the younger a giant weapon that could cleave armor, and the elder a thick saber with an ivory handle yellowed from use and with two intaglio Latin words written upon it: "Vita Brevis."

"Sir, do not stand for us." Kyner motioned for the legate to seat himself. "We are humble servants of our Lord and Savior Jesus the Christ, and we are come to you in his name—for your blessing."

Athanasius sat and demurred with a hand splayed upon his chest. "Sirs, you hazard mistakenly to seek blessing from my hand. The Church abides me for my services as a scribe and has conferred upon me no power of benediction."

"Nay, you are too humble, sir." Kyner bowed slightly in deference. "You are the Holy Father's emissary and even now wear the attire of God's servant, which rightly displays your sacred purpose to any who set eyes on you. Your blessing would be significant to us as any from the pope's hand itself."

"Verily," Cei added in a more confidential tone, edging a half pace closer, "the king has all my love. We were reared together by my father as brothers, and I know his heart as well as my own. Yet, I tell you, sir, I was gladdened to hear you reproach his tolerance of Merlin, a wizard too like a demon for my good faith. And Bedevere—on my word, we had no knowledge of his sin—his alleged lust for catamites. Is this truly so, good sir?"

"Of a certainty, Cei." Kyner glowered at his son. "Don't ask doltish questions. The legate speaks with the voice of the Holy Father. Bedevere, for all his bravery in battle, is a miscreant and a felonious debaucher. We will have none of him."

"As you say, Father." Cei inclined his broad face toward the emissary. "Even so, several ambassadors from the Continent have confirmed that Bedevere fought barbarians on the Italic peninsula for Pope Gelasius. The king believes that the Holy Father himself is full cognizant of Bedevere the sodomite and has forgiven him. Do you know this to be true?"

Kyner struck his son's shoulder with such force he turned the younger man half about. "How dare you pose such a flagrant question to the legate?"

Cei muttered an apology and returned his strenuous stare to the cringing legate.

"Hold your disapprobation, Chief Kyner." Athanasius rose and raised a restraining hand between the two Celts. "I am not offended by your son's question, for it accords with my own understanding of our most Holy Father, whom I served for several years in Ravenna myself. Gelasius *has* forgiven Bedevere the bane that the Enemy of Christ placed upon him. My sole objection remains that what the pope in his infallible wisdom can suffer to forgive, a boy-king—a *boy*—is by deficit of years too callow to comprehend fully this wicked offense's properties for ill and so stands in jeopardy of evil suasion."

A laugh like a shout escaped Cei. "Arthur's no sodomite. If he were, we'd have seen that by now, eh, Father? All those years in the servants' hovels and soldiers' barracks when we thought he was just a rape-child! He was subject aplenty to evil suasion then, let me assure you. Miscreants abounding in those quarters. And I can attest from our travels through Gaul with Father, the lad has no *suasion* for men but a vigorous liking for the ladies. Well, not ladies so much as servant girls, which is all would notice him before we knew him to be royal."

"Enough, Cei." Kyner urged the legate to sit again. "Please, sir, we have not intruded on your meditations to pelt you with questions but to receive your blessing—the blessing of our mother the Church, which the Holy Father has granted you to bestow on all worthy Christians."

"How would I know you to be worthy Christians?" Athanasius asked, then shifted his weight uncomfortably under the worried stares of the two warriors. "Have you been baptized?"

"By the missionaries, who delivered the good news to the hills of Cymru with Saint Non when I was a lad," Kyner acknowledged proudly. "Bishop Riochatus baptized both Cei and Arthur in their seventh and fifth years respectively, at the first five-year festival during the construction of Camelot."

Athanasius nodded with satisfaction. "And do you renounce the heresy of Pelagius?"

Cei turned a perplexed expression to his father, and Kyner rubbed his thick jaw. "We are not versed in theology, sir. We are simple Christians who have utmost faith in the salvation offered by our Lord and Savior."

"Stout of heart and faith, you are," the emissary declared. "Of this, I can see for myself. But I must try you against the most common heresy of this remote island, and so I ask you, is Christ a man, a child of Eve as are you and I, or divine, an emanation of God Himself, Who existed before his physical appearance as a man?"

"'Before Abraham was, I am.'" Cei quoted from the gospel. "Christ is divine." He shrugged as if this was obvious and looked to his father for approval.

Kyner nodded. "To believe that Jesus was a man is the heresy of Arius. We in Britain have no faith in Arian blasphemy, for to believe that Jesus was a man is to say that he is separate from God—and that denies the one God and throws us back into the pagan chaos of polytheism. Jesus *is* God the Son, not *like* God but God Himself, for only He Who is truly God can reconcile us to the Godhead and win our salvation."

"Well-spoken, Chief Kyner—for a man unversed in theology. Now answer me this—" Athanasius thumbed his spectacles higher on his nose and paused to carefully phrase his next question. "Do you believe that our salvation comes to us by God's grace or through our own will?"

"Our will, of a certainty," Cei answered forthrightly. "Unless we *want* to do good, we're victims of Satan."

The legate arched a critical eyebrow. "Do you concur, Chief Kyner?"

"I stand by my son in this assertion, sir." Kyner squared his shoulders. "Our fate before God is in our hands. He has given us free will to choose between good and evil, and it remains entirely up to each of us to determine by our powers of volition how we will live our lives when confronted by temptation in all its guises."

"Such as I had suspected." The legate shook his head grimly. "Such as I had suspected, for Pelagius was also a Briton. The errors he found in this land he carried to Rome, Africa, even Canaan. Yet, for all his far-flung travels and hot debates with Augustine and the bishops of many nations, his falsehoods gained not one whit of veracity. Accursed wretch that troubled our minds with such skillful blunders, he has put your souls in jeopardy! Sirs Kyner and Cei, you are both heretics."

"By our faith in Christ, we are not!" Kyner glared at the

bespectacled man. "We are true Christians. In what way is our thinking false?"

"You believe that your will can save you." Athanasius shook his curly head ruefully. "Fie! You are the thrall of your own instruments, the victims of your misplaced faith in human strength. You benighted souls! The human will is flawed. Abased by the original sin of Adam, the sin that has condemned us to the riot of this fallen creation, the will is weak. It succumbs. And so our Savior preached forgiveness and charity. Only God's grace can save us. Else we stake the eternal hope of the soul upon mortal foibles."

"That's the faith of weaklings, cowards, and poltroons." Kyner jabbed a stout finger at the scribe. "You are obviously a man who has thought more than he has done. For a man of deeds, will is everything. Do you think it's God's grace holds us fast in the heat of battle?" He turned to his son with a mocking grin under his big mustache. "What do you think, Cei? How much good is God's grace against a berserker swinging a battle-ax?"

"How much good?" Cei pondered this with a tug at his ear. "God's grace in that situation is all one needs, Father—to get into heaven."

"In truth, for God 'makes His sun rise on the evil and the good.'" Kyner fixed the legate with a harsh stare. "There are Christians here in Britain today because we've a will to fight. Without our will, *sir*, God's grace would have to content itself with naked worshipers in blue mud and tattoos leaping about a bonfire singing praise to the Furor."

Athanasius cringed behind his raised hands. "For all your fierce and disdainful lip, in the eyes of the Church you remain heretics nonetheless."

"*Heretics?*" Cei's square face darkened, and he would have lunged forward to grab the scribe had not his father restrained him with both hands. "We have defended our faith with our lives, you glassy-eyed . . ."

"Enough, Cei!" Kyner pulled his son back and stood between him and the legate. "Our love of our Savior is beyond reproach, and we do not require insults to defend what we love. We are men of deeds, not scribes who build their reputations on words. We will show you and the Holy Father that we are beloved of God."

"Show me?" Athanasius's big eyes widened behind his lenses. He feared that these two huge men intended to pit their faith against his in some trial of endurance or suffering, and he tried to dissuade them with an apologetic smile. "We have sore mistook one another, brothers. I am no priest. I opine merely as a scribe. Please, go hence and put out of mind my unruly commentary."

Kyner and Cei shared a look of bafflement. "We will go forth," Kyner asserted, pounding a fist against his heart. "And you will regret calling us heretics."

"I am the king's seneschal." Cei glared in disbelief. "I cannot abide such slander of my faith. I will prove my sincerity to you, *sir.*"

Athanasius bowed his head, mumbling, "It were wrong of me to say aught of heresy or faith. My post as legate has raised me above my harvest. I am simply a scribe, a man of books. All I truly know is that the sparrows have their heights, the wolf its horizon, the lowliest worms their kingdoms. I know naught of the soul's stature."

"Every worm has its valor," Cei admonished the scribe. "We are all God's creatures and are to be judged by Him alone. Even a humble *notarius* should know this."

Kyner bent forward and spoke strongly to the skullcap atop the legate's fleecy head, "We will bring you and all Camelot proof of the purity of our hearts and the strength of our faith. This day, two young Celts, Gawain and Gareth, have revealed a blessed vision, an encounter with an angel. This messenger of God has told them that the Holy Grail is to be found in Britain by true Christians alone and no others." He poked his thumb into the center of the scarlet cross on his overblouse. "I tell you now, my son and I are those true Christians. By God's grace *and* our undaunting wills, we will find the Grail and return it to Camelot."

"With such high hearts and strong faith, I am certain you will succeed," Athanasius readily agreed, relieved they did not intend to challenge him. "I have intelligence of the Grail from your bishop Riochatus. It would be a sweet sight to behold and a wondrous achievement to report to Ravenna. Go forth, great chief and scion of the Celts, and bring honor to Camelot and our Savior by retrieving this sacred vessel."

As the two hulking warriors departed, Athanasius removed his spectacles and wiped the perspiration that had beaded above his dark eyebrows. "Oh, Lord Almighty, when you had able Victricius, a learned and experienced bishop, in your service, why did you cut short his life and deliver me, an insignificant scribbler, to this distant land of manifold strangeness?"

Even as he spoke his complaint, the unhappy thought occurred to him that Victricius had not been snatched away untimely but in truth saved, whisked off by angels and spared the maddening experience of Britain, this bizarre threshold to hell whereupon had been cast in the bishop's stead the lesser soul of Athanasius.

PART TWO

BOOK OF THE GRAIL

Lord, how long will the wicked,
how long will the wicked triumph?

—Psalm 94:3

1

Crown of Fire

A construction gang worked on the highway that fronted The Blanket of Stars. Men tamped gravel into potholes and chipped cobbles to fit precisely. "It appears better times have visited the road to Ratae since last we were here," Elder John said, turning his horse onto a cinder path where workers knelt to lay flagstones. "And the humble inn itself seems to be under repair."

John Halt regarded with satisfaction a crew of roofers atop the inn unloading blue tiles from a pulley cart and hammering new rafters into place. "Perhaps the king has bestowed a widow's gift upon the kindly woman who dwells here with her young brother, unmarried sister, and elderly father."

"What a fortunate woman," Elder John noted drily, observing the pruned apple trees and the lime-washed wickets of a large and boisterous chicken coop. "An especially fortunate woman considering how many other widows throughout the land have received nothing from the king."

"I suppose the king cannot help everyone in these difficult times." John Halt shrugged good-naturedly. "With the stucco repairs and fresh paint, this sad inn is beginning to look like the villa it once was."

"Indeed," the one-armed merchant replied, and dismounted before a scaffold of laborers toiling to repair the building's two-story facade. At a trestle table, a craftsman bent over a star-shaped sign, meticulously chiseling smaller-faceted stars, framing the inn's name with the constellations of Orion's Belt and the

Great Bear. "Blanket is now too humble a name. This hospice should be called The Palace of Stars, don't you think, John?"

John Halt did not answer. One of the two main doors—big mahogany portals with panels carved in astral motifs—opened, and a handsome woman stood at the threshold, her honey blond hair flowing over broad shoulders and a bodice embroidered with hyacinths and braided vines of stephanotis. "John Halt and his master! It's me, Julia! Methought I saw you through our *windows*." With a strong smile, she motioned at the glaziers fitting hinged lattice panes into casements that the week before had simply been holes in the wall obscured by bean vines. "Isn't it a wonder? The king's fund has bestowed a lordly endowment on us. For my poor Eril's life." She came forward and took the reins of the palfrey. "Would he ever have thought to be worth so much more away from us than here toiling at our side?" she asked with a sigh.

Her young brother, no longer barefoot or in rags and hardly recognizable in his leather groom's apron and ankle boots, approached the master's giant horse and set about busily removing its burden of canvas-covered goods. "We've hearty feed now for your mount, sir. Not just hay but good oats. And new brushes. Your horses are sure to be happier than last they were here."

Elder John smiled and dismounted. He passed the reins to the boy and offered his one hand to his apprentice.

"That wound is livid yet, John?" At the sight of the puncture with its blackened lips, Julia's thin eyes widened, showing their pale blue irises. "I'll want to send Georgie to Venonae to fetch a leech for that, I think. We'll get this gouge cleaned out and dressed by evening."

John Halt eased himself off the palfrey onto his good leg. "Don't bother. My master had the finest surgeons look at it, and there's nothing can be done."

"It looks no worse than last you were here," she admitted, taking his arm to walk him inside, "but no better. There's a wicca-woman lives at a stream nearby, a crone who does magic with herbs . . .

John Halt interrupted her. "Please, no magic." His ruddy, boyish cheeks paled, and she was not sure if fear or anger tightened through him until he added, "I'm a Christian—and magic offends me."

"Oh, but we're all Christians here." She squeezed his arm reassuringly. "Let's find comfort for you in prayer, then, if the surgeons and the crones can't help."

Cheerful golden rays slanted into the villa through the restored windows and illuminated cedar rafters hung with dark red roses. The thick vines climbed the walls out of great clay vases painted with images of Persephone in spring. Julia explained how these urns had arrived among wagonloads of stores that included amphorae of Spanish claret, casks of Rhenish brandy, white wine in barrels from the Gironde, and tubs of British beer.

"The king has truly been most generous," Elder John noted coolly, nodding to the tables carved round and flat in the likeness of tortoises, their stubby legs supported by carved dragons standing on their hind feet. Puce-colored goatskin covered the benches, and upon the window ledges stood onyx pots planted with yellow roses. "Are you now more inclined to find favor with our majesty than you were when last we visited?"

Julia's golden eyebrows bent woefully. "All this I accept for my family. But in truth, I'd as soon have sent every stick and nail back to Camelot. I'm yet sore at heart with the king. Wasn't it he who took my Eril away? None of this bounty is worth even one hour in his arms."

John Halt met the older man's cool, reproving stare with a frown. "I know my master would be pleased if your young sister—Leoba is her name, yes? Might Leoba show my master to a chamber where he could bathe and remove the dust of the road?"

"I myself would happily oblige. But all our rooms are filled." Julia led them through the empty dining hall to a staircase with a yet-unvarnished newel post and raw wood steps. Laughter and overlapping voices floated from above. "A caravan from Uxacona is carrying wares to Londinium. Tin goods, bolts of cloth, and such. They're the only ones in the land with coin. A week ago, they'd have passed us by, and now they've filled the inn and we're all busy as starlings. But our family's suite is yours during your stay. We'd not even be alive but for you. Come along. Father and Leoba are in the galley. We'll get you some victuals and then a bath."

"Well! I am glad that fortune's wheel has turned for you." Elder

John pushed open a swinging door whose panels displayed a cornucopia spilling fruits and sheaves of grain. Oven fumes laved them with redolences of braised meats and boiling broths. "But since we *are* imposing on you, Julia, I'd like for us to be of some real use to your household. With his bad leg, my apprentice will be no good with the guests. But I have some experience working with people. If it pleases you, I'll take over some of your responsibilities with the guests. And perhaps young John can help with your sit-down chores. He's a good conversationalist—and a marvel with a scrub brush."

With excessive brightness, we see you. From inside our round hut on the solemn island of Avalon, we see the wonder and pain and beauty of who you are.

You are this: the serpent and the grail—blue bunched bowels coiled hungrily in an upright pelvis, the overflowing cup of the sacrum, sacred vessel of bone that is our humanity.

Together with you, we wander the wooded slopes of destiny, losing our way as in a forest. Your thoughts are sunbeams gleaming in the somber darkness of the forest that is your body, that is the bodies of all the physical things about you. Your thoughts are sunbeams, and by their light we find our way through the physical world in which we are lost. Your thoughts are sunbeams, bright pillars of nothingness in a universe of atoms and void.

Life-enchanted animal, who are you?

The stars sing in their fiery kingdoms. Cosmic rays. Gamma rays. X rays. Ultraviolet rays. Rays, like burning angels with blazing wings lifting over us forever, stand fiercely atop the sky. One angel falls to earth, the angel of visible light falls into our world under the clouds: The rainbow is our own rapturous angel. The spectrum of visible light walks ahead of us upon the gathered roads, and this angel with seven faces is our own guardian fallen to earth. His blue face fills the sky.

The shells of darkness beyond resound with the singing stars and the fierce songs of the invisible and dark angels—but down here, beneath the uncaring heavens, there shall be light, and within it we shall dwell in wonder among these spelled words, these thoughts we share, these bright pillars of nothingness.

• • •

The shade of Uther Pendragon vanished in the mists of the netherworld, and Ygrane stood alone where ocher light sifted through crazed pine boughs. The ground quaked underfoot like a bog. She looked for her demon stallion, and it was gone.

Starwebs dazzled in the gloaming, and the shadows around her looked darker and butchered. She thought the sparkling air was her faerie escort, but as the energy began to take form, she knew it was not the magical power of the pale people but of their antler-crowned god, Someone Knows the Truth.

"Why do you torment Uther?" a rumbling voice asked out of an elk head perched atop a shaggy human form twice as large as a man. "His soul belongs to me."

Ygrane dropped to one knee before the primeval deity. "Lord of the Wild, forgive me. I trespass in the Happy Woods to see again my husband."

"Uther Pendragon is no one's husband." The black lips of the animal head did not move; the god's voice poured itself directly into her brain. "You took from me Cuchulain's soul and fleshed a body for him in your womb. Uther was given in exchange. He is no one's husband."

"Yes, lord. Forgive me." The elk-god's shadow stretched over her, and cold shook her bones. "I acted foolishly."

"Most foolishly, Ygrane. For you have come into my suzerainty—and so, you are mine."

"No." She dared raise her face and saw flakes of light drizzling through a human shape crowned with antlers. "Lord of the Wild, I am not dead. I came to drive off the Furor's demons from the Dragon who sleeps deep below the hollow hills. I have done that, and now I must depart."

"How will you depart, Ygrane?" The sparkling form scattered to emptiness, and only the giant antlers hovered before her, their points merging with the pine boughs like a tangled misperception, an error of her brain. "No mortal walks free of the hollow hills."

She lifted her arms toward the invisible voice. "I have an agreement with the Daoine Síd . . ."

"I am god of the Síd." The voice throbbed angrily. "I know all about your agreement. Bright Night will throw you into the dragonpit to wake the planetary beast and ride it into the World Tree. Ha! He is an arrogant minstrel of madness. Does my name mean nothing to you? Someone Knows the Truth—a name I have carried for longer than you can know. I have seen the ice sheets come and go. Of all the elder gods, I have survived, because I do not wage wars I cannot win. I will not sacrifice my subjects to the wrath of the Furor."

"Prince Bright Night has given his word," Ygrane pleaded. "I have spilled my blood in pact."

"So long as you are here, mortal flesh, there is no pact. And here you will stay, for I will not release you."

The pines stood empty, and the wind stirred among them a babble of shadows. "Wait! Don't leave me here! The Síd have given their word!"

Someone Knows the Truth was gone. She was alone among the pinefog. The black iron woods imprisoned her, and the Daoine Síd could not rescue her. They would not defy their god, not within the hollow hills.

Ygrane approached a tree and pressed her forehead to its black, twisted middle. She knew better than to wander. In the netherworld, all directions were the same and led deeper into dusk, into the resinous light that was the primordial fire that had forged the earth. Not long ago, when the Dragon was awake, the pale people led the living there and fed them to the beast. Now the planet was a vast stone room. In the hearth at its center burned the dreams of the Dragon.

She listened for those dreams in the pine that was not a pine but an illusion of the underworld. It was an illusion full of voices in the uptwisting branches, and she used all her training from the druids, all her experience among the pale people to listen past the fury of noise. She heard the yammering of souls in rapture and terror. The elk-god's gristled power sizzled like lightning, and behind that was the scraping, grinding thunder of the planet's smoldering interior. Deeper yet, she found the silence in which floated the dreamsongs of the Dragon.

If she had not heard it before as a younger woman, she would not have recognized its waft of repose. It was the soft phosphorescence of the one cosmic Dragon communicating with its many parts scattered among the floating worlds of the stellar islands, the galaxies adrift in the void. Touching its serene power with her mind, she reached beyond the netherworld, higher than the sky. And there, she found the wild creature that could save her.

Even before she had called for it, it had known she would call, because it was an entity that dwelled at the perimeter of time, where the future echoed back into the present. It was a black unicorn, a shadow-creature projected into darkness by the sun stallions that ran in herds upon the solar wind. She would have preferred to summon a white unicorn, for her magic had bonded her with one of those bright animals in years past, and she knew their ways. But they would not come for her in the hollow hills. They were creatures of radiance.

The silk of its nearness touched the back of her neck, and she pushed away from the tree. The black unicorn swayed before her, a wild bulk of darkness, rearing and wheeling away, then sliding close, bending low, its tusk an inch from her amazed face, its eyes slants of animal clarity, opal blue. In their mirroring near-ness, she saw the emerald light of her own eyes, twin sparks of a hollow-cheeked mask covering the astonishment within her.

She had not expected it to come so swiftly. Nor had she anticipated the psychic exposure she felt before its sentient gaze. The beat of her heart deepened. She could hear the unicorn as she had heard the elk-god, only softer and more intimately. *Hold on to me,* it breathed within her. *He is coming. And he is angry.*

The ocher light between the black trees jellied to an antlered shape. "What is this?" a big voice rumbled. "What witchery have you brought into my domain?"

Swiftly, Ygrane flung herself onto the black unicorn. As soon as she touched it, a vibration of bliss coursed through her. She experienced the masterful elation of escape even before the uni-corn took a step. She felt the certainty of it echoing across the gusty distance of the future.

In an instant, the black animal under her would charge directly at the shaggy giant, exploding him to fiery shards. And his roar of pain would rush into the wing-space above the trees and stretch to helpless silence behind them.

Merlin took Fra Athanasius and Loki through the upland fields to the high woods behind Camelot. "To win your confidence in what lies ahead for us, it is important that I show you how I designed this fortress," he told them proudly.

On one side of them, the land plummeted to a gorge of

immense boulders and clinging trees where a cataract poured its blur of mist and rainbows into the River Amnis. On the other, scorched terrain mottled the meadows and forests marking the sites of battling armies from earlier in the season. Between the verdant river canyon and the seared countryside, Camelot appeared like a flight of thought captured in pure geometry.

From this vantage, the luminous fortress city looked almost pyramidal, with terraced edifices and ziggurat-style stepbacks. Morning light reflected brightly from its various skydomes and curving windows. Sculpted friezes and projecting entablatures adorned the facades, familiar contours that offered refuge to the eye in the midst of strange polyhedral turrets and paraboloid jacket walls shining brightly in the sun.

"The stone is dressed with crushed coral and powdered seashells immixed with alabaster concrete," Merlin proudly explained. "That is why the towers and walls shine like poured light. It is a technique I first observed in Ægypt thirty-five centuries ago."

Athanasius hugged his dalmatic tighter about himself. He nervously edged away from the wizard, in the process tripping over an upraised root. Loki grabbed the legate's arm and kept him from falling. "Steady, man. You represent the Rock of Christ. Stand fast."

"Mock not my faith, unnatural creature!" The scribe tugged his arm free and glared at the stenciled god who was smirking at him from the shadow of his large black hat. "I say unto you, if you had tasted the truth of our Savior, you would not address me so insolently nor regard me with looks that smack of ridicule."

Loki stepped back, smirking. "Next time, then, holy man, I'll leave you to fall on your rump."

"Will you two pay attention?" Merlin scowled at them. He pointed a gnarled hand at the bright towers of Camelot. "See here now. That citadel is no mere edifice. It is a portal into the very Storm Tree itself. So, Loki, if you are sincere about taking that Tree from the Furor, you'd do well to heed what I have to say about how we will get there."

Loki stiffened, then nodded once, curtly.

"As for you, Athanasius—" Merlin leveled a stern look at the legate yet spoke in a softer, more conciliatory tone. "How can you judge my king fairly if all you see is magic where, in fact, there is science? Loki is no unnatural creature. I thought I had explained that to you in the grotto?"

The scribe stood silent for a moment, feeling the uncomfortable weight of his responsibility—as had been charged to him by his holy office. With his forefinger, he pushed his spectacles higher on his nose, then sifted a sigh between his clenched teeth and turned to the god. "I apologize, Loki. You, too, are a creature of God by Whose omniscience you have been shaped of stuff different of substance yet not of kind. I was wrong to declare you unnatural."

Loki accepted the apology with a lopsided grin. "It must be difficult for you, a man of the Church, to stand here with a demon and an Æsir god. So what say you? Do you believe Jesus loves us as he loves you?"

"Enough!" From under his midnight blue robes, Merlin extracted an amber rod coiled with silver wire. "Your insolence is a dangerous distraction."

"What did I say?" Loki opened his small eyes wide with mock innocence and placed both black-gloved hands upon his chest to stay a startled breath. "I have asked the man a simple question. I would but know if Jesus is our Savior, too. Is that insolence?"

The wizard rolled his wrist and twirled the amber baton around his hand so fast it blurred. "Enough of you, I say! We will talk later." With one pass of the wand, the god spun on his heels, a black vortex with a pale smear of startled eyes and woeful mouth. "Go to the grotto and wait for me there. And don't make any mischief, or I'll expel you from Camelot altogether!" With a mighty twist of his body that sent his robes and conical hat flying, Merlin whipped full around and pointed the rod toward the radiant battlements of the fortress.

A wild moan trailed behind as the man-sized whirlwind that was Loki rushed off, tilting down the slopes through the sizzling grass.

"Upon my soul!" Athanasius blinked into the gust of chill magnetic wind that smelled of thunder and straightened the curly hairs of his head. "I took in earnest his question, Merlin, and would have offered him tender bond of our Savior's love."

"It was a mistake to bring him along." With his nimbus of white hair fluffed about his ferocious countenance, the wizard resembled a wrathful prophet of the Bible. "You must understand, I thought to take advantage of Loki's restrained situation. He is here secretly among us. Those runes he wears upon his flesh are designed to keep him invisible to the other Æsir gods, in particular his irascible brother the Furor. He dare not use his powers too overtly, or he will expose himself and face the dire consequences of his brother's fury. Believe me, Athanasius, gods oft use their strength cruelly upon people. If Loki were not restricted by his need to remain discreet, he would be too dangerous to tolerate anywhere near us."

"Might and a high heart are Loki's divine philosophy, it seems." The scribe picked up the wizard's fallen hat and handed it to him. "How would you reply to the god's question? Does our Savior love the gods as he loves humankind, or is Loki's hope for salvation a vain purpose?"

Merlin cocked a pointy eyebrow. "Is this another theological test from the legate?"

Athanasius looked askance at the path of parted grass that Loki's vortex had left behind. "On my word, Merlin, the need to know this kingdom's Christian merit is all that keeps me here."

"And your judgment thus far, legate?"

"My judgment remains in suspension." The scribe nervously twisted the whiskers on his small chin. "Yet, I would know your understanding concerning pagan gods and the salvation proffered by our Lord Jesus."

"'No understanding avails against the Lord.'" Merlin wiped broken leaves from the brim of his hat and fitted it upon his hoary head. "So we are told in Proverbs twenty-one. Hence, my thoughts on this issue matter not at all. It is by our deeds that we shall be judged, Athanasius. By our deeds. And that is why I have brought you here, that you may comprehend the scientific means by which the deeds before us shall be accomplished and not mistake them for magic. We are a Christian kingdom, and all that we achieve here is done by the grace of God and the natural powers He puts at our disposal."

Athanasius removed his spectacles, filled his head with blurry light, then fitted the lenses back upon his face. It gave him unspeakable satisfaction to see again with such sharp acuity the tiny grassheads swaying in the morning breeze and pollen motes afloat in their millions. "Throughout my tenure here, you have answered me with reasons supported by logic," he began slowly, weighing his thoughts carefully. "The unpeace that first assailed me is for the most part at rest. Despite the strangeness of much before us on this remote island, you have freed me from the thralldom of fear. No longer do I believe that the mysteries I have witnessed will necessarily lead your kingdom to bane. But I reserve my judgment until I more fully comprehend this alleged science." Arms akimbo, he turned decisively to regard the chevron-hooded battlements of Camelot. "Reveal to me what you will of this—this teeming edifice."

Merlin smiled approvingly. "What you see before you is an electrical resonator. Surely, you are familiar with harmonics—the simultaneous combination of musical tones that are pleasing to the ear? Such harmony is possible also among the electrical properties I revealed to you earlier."

"The cold and quenchless fire of flowing electrons may be harmonized to other such currents?" the scribe asked through a frown. "Harmonized as singing voices do harmonize in lofty relationships of chord and pitch in a choir?"

"Precisely. Our bodies are electrical. The earth itself is electrical. And the air and the oceans and the moon and the sun themselves. All atoms in the world about us relate by electrostatic force."

"'Atoms and the void'—from the mouth of Democritus, as you have fully expounded to me." Athanasius leaned back against an elm's stolid trunk, eyes glazed, searching inward for comprehension. "The physical world all about us, as well as our own corporeal forms, are, of a great majority, void. Atoms, tiny beyond sensate perception, float in soft effulgence upon the void, most tenuous."

"Most tenuous, indeed, Athanasius. We are almost entirely void and would easily pass through the ground and each other like clouds if not for the electrostatic force in the enormous spaces between the atoms. It is that force that Camelot is designed to work upon." Merlin gestured proudly at the bartizans and spires of the citadel. "The architecture resonates specifically with the electromagnetic field of the planet—the field that the gods regard as the World Tree, Yggdrasil. The dodecahedral towers have chambers designed to harmonize with the highest branches of the Tree, far above the earth, while the grotto is a

resonance cell for the roots of the Tree. The courtyards, the terraced levels of the ramparts, and the battlements correspond with
the intermediate strata of Yggdrasil."

"Like unto a portal to Yggdrasil is Camelot." Athanasius
pinched his lower lip while he mulled this over. "Science ordains
that the very atoms of our bodies lie suspended upon the void by
the contrary powers of electricity whereupon like charges repel
and opposites attract. How then does Camelot serve as a portal? I
am vexed to understand."

"There are secret passages in the fortress that only I know of,
for I designed them." The wizard watched the scribe rocking his
jaw, trying to digest what he heard. "These passages open to
Yggdrasil at precise times, when the electrical field of the earth is
appropriately amplified or diminished by the energies of the sun
and the moon and their alignment with the planets."

The legate shook his head. "This smacks too much of astrol-
ogy's heresy with its beneficent and malignant stars."

"Harmonics, Athanasius. Above our heads is an immense sea
of electrical energy created by the solar wind that strips electrons
from the atoms of the atmosphere and generates a powerful
charge. The alignment of sun and moon have much to do with
the disposition of this charge, and I have shaped Camelot to take
full advantage of the potential difference between the earth and
this electrical sea in the atmospheric heights." He knelt on the
ground and swept dead leaves from the loamy earth. In the soil,
he began to sketch schematics for oscillating circuits and a wave
guide. "Here, let me show you how an electrical charge can be
shaped by the geometry of space . . ."

Merlin found Loki at the top of the castle, in a bartizan, a small
chamber of an overhanging turret attached to Camelot's highest
tower. The god was regarding a wall hanging of knotted sable
cordwork tinseled with gold and platinum threads. Embroidered
in the tapestry were winged men in battle gear, numerous as a
whirlwind of hail flying above a plunging darkness wherein
uncoiled a seemingly endless red-gold serpent. The serpent was
flanked by bat-winged warriors of brawny sinews with fanged
faces upon their abdomens and malevolent eyes staring from
their buttocks. Woven around the perimeter of the hanging were

silver purl words from Revelation 12:7—AND THERE WAS WAR IN HEAVEN . . .

"Tell me of your time as a demon, Merlin." Loki stood at the window and gazed down upon the scorched parkland and singed tree-roughs that fronted the River Amnis. Silhouetted in radiance and dressed in black sarcenet, the bald god seemed an anonymous shadow graced by the crown of fire that was the sun. "Tell me what it was like to destroy worlds."

"It was hateful, Loki." Merlin removed his hat in the sun-warmed room and sat on a sandalwood bench fashioned to the lithe shape of an antelope. "Demons hate. They hate losing heaven. They hate living in the cold and the dark, which is all that creation really is. A huge void of unbelievable cold and darkness sprinkled with dust and a smoldering of wan stars. They hate it. They want to rip it all to nothing—to void. And when there is nothing left, nothing left to hate, nothing left to remind them of the heaven they lost, they will sleep, formless in the void."

"How did you lose heaven?" Loki asked in a whisper, still gazing upon the campestral and the mountains floating like blue pyramids upon the horizon. "Why did you fall into such darkness?"

"Love." Merlin's wiry eyebrows lifted ruefully. "We loved Her. We loved Her more than anything. More than our lives. We would have followed Her anywhere. To hell itself." He snorted. "And we did."

"Who?" Loki turned about and sat on the sill, gloved hands bracing himself against the casement. "Who are you talking about? Who is She?"

Merlin smiled. "How can I possibly explain? There were no names in heaven. We simply existed, whole, integral, one with Her. And She was one. We were all one." He saw Loki's perplexed expression and sighed. "Look—heaven is not what you think or can hope to imagine. It's outside time. Time and space itself did not exist until we followed Her out here."

"Whom did you follow? Who is this beloved woman you left heaven to follow?"

"God." Merlin scratched his bearded cheek and shook his head. "That's the only human name for Her. But it's misapplied and misunderstood. When She departed heaven, She arrived here, in the vacuum, the emptiness, the void. And She filled it with Herself. And for a moment, for one beautiful instant, we thought it was going to be just fine. She was so glorious. So radiant. Until then, we had simply been one with Her. There was no sense of anything else. But out here, we *saw* Her. We weren't with Her anymore. She had stepped back, away, and we *saw* Her. And we *saw* each other for the first time. Before that, we believed, each of us actually believed, he was the only one with Her. But in truth there were many of us, so many of us. And only one of Her." The soft light in the wizard's silver eyes hardened. "Then it began to get cold. And She was gone. She was just—just not there anymore. And we were alone, all of us alone in the cold. We panicked. We flew every which way looking for Her. But She was truly gone." He rubbed his jaw, still astonished at this fact. "We were alone."

"Where did She go?"

The look of sad remembrance on Merlin's face fell away, and he straightened and nodded knowingly. "It took me a very long time to figure that out. I was one of those who believed She had abandoned us, tricked us into falling out of heaven. I was furious. It was cold and dark, and the light of heaven that remained burned our bodies so fiercely I couldn't think. I couldn't figure what had happened to us. So, I threw off that light, and the burning stopped. But then the cold ate into me instead. I raged. I tell you, I raged for a long, long time."

"So where did She go?" Loki rocked forward from the window ledge. "Did you find Her?"

"Oh, yes." Merlin smiled expansively and showed his snaggled teeth. "I found Her. Or, I suppose, She found me." The wizard abruptly stopped smiling. "But I've already answered your initial question, Loki. I didn't come here to reminisce. We need your help. Stop harassing the pope's legate."

Loki hissed derisively. "He's a dogmatic fool. He hasn't an original thought in his brain, and he's insulted your king and your own person. Why do you tolerate him?"

"His approval will assure that Britain is fed this winter."

"So, put that conviction in his curly head with magic and send him back to Ravenna, where he belongs."

"Yes, that would be simpler." Merlin pursed his lips, thinking just how very simple that would be, then shrugged. "Ah, but the king forbids it."

"And you always obey the king?" Loki asked with a skeptical twitch of an eyebrow.

"He is my king."

"But you are older than time!" Loki cocked his bald head, mystified. "Why do you serve this—this boy? *You* should be king."

"Bah! I don't want to be king." Merlin edged his voice with scorn and in the next breath spoke rapturously. "I serve God. I serve love."

"So, you think God is love?" Loki smiled grimly. "How quaint. But, of course, you were a demon until recently. And love is something new for you, isn't it? We all want what's new."

Merlin scowled. "Love is not new for me. It's older than my hateful life as a demon, for I remember heaven." He pointed a warped finger at the god. "Your obsession with what is new is a weakness, Loki. You think you can usurp the Furor because he is old in his ways. You seek alliance with the Fire Lords because they herald a bold, untried future. But the new is always an ordeal. Are you strong enough for what is new?"

"I am here," he replied with a glint of humor in his dark eyes. "I am here in the newest capital on earth."

"But we cannot stay here." Merlin gestured to the velvet carpet. "Soon we will descend into the hollow hills, where the king will collect a teardrop from the eye of the Dragon. I want you to come with us."

"Not me." Loki leaned back into the casement, hands raised before him. "No chance of that, Merlin."

The wizard stiffened and stood up. "You have sought sanctuary among us, Loki. You say that you want to overthrow your benighted brother. And we have an agreement. The sword Lightning for your full cooperation with my king in his venture to win protection from the Furor."

"Yes, yes, I know." Loki turned his back on Merlin and peered down at the sunny sward. "But I'm not going down there. Not ever. For the last five hundred years, the Daoine Síd have been feeding to the Dragon anyone they catch down there."

"The Dragon sleeps."

Loki looked over his shoulder with a frown on his scribbled face. "I'm not going to be the one to wake it."

"Then what good are you to me?" Merlin snatched his hat

from the antelope bench and brusquely placed it on his head. "Unless you help my king, we have no agreement."

"I will not go into that dreadful underworld." Loki hunched his shoulders and watched clouds crumble in the blue void. "But I will serve you in Yggdrasil—if you survive your visit to the hollow hills."

2

Road of Solitudes

From atop a pine bluff, Kyner and Cei peered down upon a wide and shallow stream freckled with sunlight. They believed faith had led them there after two days of hard riding across plains of shifting ash and through forests burned to fields of black axletrees. But the enchantment that Morgeu the Fey had stamped into the air was what had actually summoned them to this precise overlook.

They surveyed a vista where light struck gold among reflections of copper beeches and shimmering birch banks. On a willow island enclosed by the stream's slow dismantlings, Morgeu's spell opened just wide enough to fit into their brains, and they glimpsed a chapel behind the swaying withes. A deep serenity touched them.

Kyner should have known better. He had accomplished grisly deeds for the bishop, tracking down the abominations that the Phoenicians and Romans had brought to Britain over the centuries—shapeshifting African weredevils, oriental lamia with their viperous poisons, and the too-human vampyres. He was an intimate of evil and had the experience to be more cautious. But the dream-strong allure inspired by Morgeu's enchantment combined with his eagerness to prove himself a worthy Christian to Fra Athanasius and defeated his usual wariness.

Cei's shouted greetings went unanswered, and the riders dismounted and led their horses down the tussocky embankment. Kyner took the lead, intending that the scarlet cross upon his tunic should allay the fears of any Christian souls watching from within the blackstone chapel. Cei kept his hand on the hilt of his sword, alert for berserkers and wildwood gangs. The chuckling stream and sighing birch breezes offered no cause for alarm.

They tethered their horses to a stooped tree ledged with fungus and slogged out of the stream, through the willow veils, and onto the isle's spongy turf. The chapel's stone blocks were too heavy for the soft ground, and the small building had sunk into the sedge grass so that the seekers would have to stoop and step down when they entered. Sullen red candleflames hovered upon tall tallow sticks, and the interior darkness was flavored with twilight.

Cei knelt before the square-cut doorway and gasped. "Father—behold! The Holy Grail! The vessel is just as Gawain and Gareth have described!"

Kyner did not respond. His heart was chiming against his ribs, and his battle-wise hands suddenly felt thoughtless as they reached for the hilt of Short Life but could not find the strength to draw the saber. Behind the chapel arose a vast face, luminous and maimed as the moon—a dragonskull hung with torn flesh. Eyes of blue diamond gazed malevolently from sockets like jagged craters.

"Cei—" The name fell like a stone.

The dragon's deformed mouth leered open upon ranks of blood-gummed teeth, and an oily black tongue slithered forth with a stink of rancid offal.

"Da, the Grail!" Cei called again, then cocked his head as the stench burned his nostrils. "Something big and dead rots nearby."

"Cei, come away quickly!" Kyner drew his saber, and it felt heavy as sorrow in his hand. "Quickly!"

The fright in his father's voice drew Cei's hand immediately to his sword, and he stepped back from the chapel. A groan like an airy sigh escaped him at the sight of the dragon looming above them, its waxy brown wings unfurling, the hungry stare in the shadowed dark under its horned brow like starlight squeezed through coal.

"Run!" Kyner commanded, ponderously backing away on legs like marsh stumps. "To the horses!"

Cei could not move. He stood entranced by the bewildering madness of pinworm parasites aswirl upon the black tongue's rainbows—and purple silks of tattered flesh hanging from the warped jaw like throat-frills—and the mineral beauty of this colossal skull shining like moonlight through its ripped and moldered face.

With a shout unraveling to a howl, Kyner dashed to his son and grabbed him by the back of his leather cuirass. They ran bent over, and blue flames slashed above them through the air, igniting the thickets ahead. Ashes whirled with the crazed bellow of the beast. Seething with fright, the two Celts plunged backward through draperies of willow.

The horses tugged at their tethers in a panic to flee. Kyner untied them, and Cei flung himself atop his steed in one leap. They splashed into the shallows with savage cries, Kyner riding hard, hugging the neck of his horse. But Cei, gripped by some lunatic fascination, swung about to catch another glimpse of the enormous monstrosity.

With a squeal, he realized his stolen look would cost him his life. The dragon had trampled the willows and stood in sunlight steaming, bellowing with huge power and torment directly behind him. If he had not turned, he might have outpaced its burning hulk. But under its heavy shadow, he felt the heat of its putrid breath and could not elude the reach of its flames.

He swung his round shield from the horse's flank to his back and hunched over. Fire lashed over him, and burning pain unpinned all his joints, flinging him like a blazing rag doll into the shallows. He rolled about in agonized terror and saw that his steed, in wild fright, had reared over him, unintentionally protecting him from the brunt of the fiery assault. It blazed with skeletal radiance, a fire-blown silhouette of a horse.

Hooves splashed beside his head, and a gruff hand reached down and lifted him out of the water. He clung to the strong arm of his father, his body incandescent with suffering.

Kyner yanked his son onto the back of his own horse and bolted away as cobalt flames descended upon the smoldering carcass of Cei's steed. The dragon staggered backward, hurt by the sun, seeking sanctuary again under rafters of brambles and nettle to await the next intruder upon the dark chapel.

John Halt sat on the edge of a trestle table before an outdoor hearth stirring a steaming cauldron of soiled bed linens. A drying rack to one side held the napery he had already soaked and rinsed in the washbasin beside him on the table. His face was flushed from the steam and his hands were chafed red, but he did not mind. Julia had kept him company during these chores, and they had chatted amicably about themselves while he stirred the cauldron and scrubbed the linens on the washboard.

He learned that she had grown up on a farm outside Venonae. It was an ordinary story. That was what pleased and comforted John Halt, for it assured him that there were lives that belonged to the seasons, to the daily round of toils and simple pleasures, to the connectedness of things.

Violence and magic had shaped his whole life, but he told her nothing of that. He pretended for her that he was no different from any other common man and continued to turn her questions back on herself. She spoke of her seven brothers and sisters, all gone from the homestead except for the two youngest, Leoba and Georgie. Julia had stayed with the inn, because it was shelter for these young siblings and her aged father—and it was all that remained of Eril.

"An orphan he was," she reminisced while she folded the dried table linens. "He worked as a common laborer in Londinium, saved every copper, and bought this place when it was the ruin you first visited. He had big plans for it, but the king had bigger plans yet, and Eril went off to war." She smiled, thinly, briefly. "Won't he be surprised now when he sees what's become of it?"

"You still hold faith he's alive?"

"Ah, with all my heart." She paused in her folding to brush back a strand of golden hair from her proud face. "But I've sense enough to know he must be gone to heaven, for the king does not award every widow so handsomely for a lost foot soldier. He must have distinguished himself for the crown, he did. And now we've got ourselves more than a hovel by which to earn our way. But where is my poor Eril's body? By my faith, he's alive—until I dig his grave in my breast."

"John—we're away!" John Elder called from alongside the sawyer's wagon under the scaffolds at the north side of the villa. "Be quick about it. Our horses are already saddled."

"So soon?" John Halt called, but his master had turned away and the query was lost among the loud hammering of the carpenters. He shrugged to Julia and gingerly slid from the table onto his good leg. "I must go. I hope your faith is fulfilled and your Eril returns. Short of that—" He dared a gentle smile. "I hope you learn to love again."

She took his ruddied hand and squeezed it affectionately. She felt ashamed for the feelings of desire he stirred in her. He was a boy—and yet not. Unlike her Eril, swarthy and rugged to look upon but gentle within, John Halt's rosy cheeks and gentle features belied the fury she had seen in him when first they met. He was not a common man as was her beloved. By his own admission, he had lived in a chieftain's fastness, even if as a thrall. Hearing the strength in his voice and the caring, she could give herself to him—if she were not yet in love with Eril, and she told him as much, "Were I to find a man as kind and able as you, perhaps I would learn to love again."

Arthur limped away light-footed under the scaffolds and the fresh-painted trellis of a future vineyard to the apple garth, where Bedevere already sat upon his big chestnut stallion. Though the older man said not a word, his urgency was obvious in the way he tossed the reins of the palfrey to the youth. "Don't dawdle, boy. We've a long ride ahead of us. Put some life into that gimpy leg or find yourself another master."

Once their horses had clopped over the new-laid flagstones and gained the highway, the king said, "You'd best have good cause to remove me, Bedevere. Julia is like family to me."

"You've another family, sire, who needs you now." Bedevere hurried his horse to a canter. "The sun signals I've received tell me that your brother Cci is burned—scorched by a dragon. He lingers at death's threshold."

Arthur spurred Straif to a gallop and rode her until she was spent. By then, Bedevere's signals had brought fresh steeds from the garrison at Venonae, and the king and his personal guard continued without stopping. Under the breathing stars of the Milky Way, they charged along the Roman Midlands highway, taking new mounts at Letocetum, Pennocrucium, and Uxacona. By dawn, they swept into Cymru and ascended the steep trails at a full run, their swift shapes reflected in the mirror world of the high lakes. They passed Cold Kitchen before midday and arrived at Camelot with their coursers half-dead under them.

On an airy terrace enclosed by potted mint ferns, Cei lay

abed, mummied with wet windings soaked in cooling unguents. His swollen face looked unfamiliar and tinted green, and through the thin slits of his eyes stared a blackness in which starlight whispered.

"The Holy Grail," Kyner said, rising from a folding chair beside the bed and bowing to the king. "Cei saw the Holy Grail in the Chapel Perilous and would have restored it to you, my lord, but for the dragon."

Arthur embraced his stepfather, then bent close over Cei, and whispered, "I am here for you, brother."

"Save the king," Cei's blistered lips mumbled from deep in his suffering, from far away on pain's road of solitudes. "Save the king from fire—fire of the last day. Apocalypse . . ."

Merlin gently led Arthur aside. "He raves, my lord, about the Christ's return and stern judgment. He sees hellfire."

"Restore him, Merlin," Arthur beseeched.

"You know I would if that were in my power, sire." The wizard placed both big-knuckled hands on the king's shoulders. "Cei suffers from flames of the Dragon's dream. If he is to live, you must drink the very elixir your mother has foretold. Only by imbibing a teardrop of the Dragon combined with nectar of the Vanir Lotus will you heal these wounds—Cei's, yours, and Britain's."

Arthur's jaw seized up tightly as he absorbed this fact, but his golden stare did not flinch. "Lead the way, wizard. Lead the way into the underworld."

Skidblade crossed time as well as distance. That was Morgeu the Fey's conclusion when she commanded the wondrous flying ship to deliver her to Londinium: The ark of moonfire landed upon the roof of the governor's palace, and when Morgeu stepped through the dilated portal into the black twilight, she noticed that the disposition of the wandering stars had shifted. Jupiter and Mars had transited slightly among the constellations, signifying the passage of days, though she felt as though she had stood before the Furor in the arctic twilight of Brokk's island only hours ago.

Fear widened in her like the frayed end of a rope. With the lapsing of so much time, surely the Furor would know that she had not gone directly to Avalon as he had commanded. A groan twisted in her with the voice of stones in an ice-locked stream as she thought of Mordred. *What will they do with my baby in their wrath?* When next she entered Skidblade, she might well be returned to the Furor's presence to find her baby maimed or dead, sacrificed to the righteous fury of the Æsir gods.

I must be swift, she realized, and marched across the rooftop past ornamental cornice urns to the bronze utility door under its wooden canopy. It was locked, and she knelt before it and urgently whispered a summoning chant. Moments later, the latch clacked open, lamplight sliced the darkness, and a matronly servant woman peered out.

Morgeu spoke sleep to the servant and took the tin lamp from her as she slid unconscious onto the steps. Her crimson robes jumping, she pranced quickly down the stairs and through an open door of sturdy oak strapped with iron into a narrow and dark corridor of the upper floor. She spoke to the yellow tooth of flame at the mouth of the handlamp: "Take me to the mistress of the palace."

Following the directional sway of the flame, Morgeu strode swiftly among hallways lit with ceiling lanterns and scented with braziers of fragrant wood. She intended to finish her business there as expeditiously as possible, as she did not want to leave Skidblade unattended too long. When she encountered servants or guards, she curtly informed them, "You do not see me." And they did not.

The lampflame led her to an opulent chamber of potted palms, pink marble pillars, and an enormous round bed under a canopy of saffron veils and blue taffeta drapes. A dark-skinned sylph of a woman sat perched upon a teak chair; before her was a mahogany table laden with silver platters of figs, dates, blood oranges, nut pastries, and honey confections. Her glossy black hair fell in tight ringlets to small shoulders covered by translucent pastel fabrics trimmed with gold tinsel. The dark, heavy-lidded beauty of her Persian face betrayed no fear or even surprise at the arrival of the large moonfaced woman with bright frizzy red hair.

"Good evening, Selwa from the house of Syrax." The enchantress placed the tin lamp on an ivory stand. "Am I disturbing you?"

"Not at all. Come in and sit with me." Selwa motioned to a sofa of silk cushions embroidered with trumpeting elephants. "You must be the king's sister, Morgeu the Doomed. You are famous even in lands as distant as Araby and the Levant."

Morgeu stepped past copper kettles overflowing with ferns and helped herself to a glazed date. "I have heard from Camelot that you have visited my brother—with an offer of matrimony."

"A prudent offer, which he foolishly declined." Her suspiring eyes did not flinch before the cold stare of her guest. No look could intimidate her. She had peered too often into the dark bores of men's widening pupils as they had died, poisoned as much by her beauty as by the toxins she had slipped into their drinks. Inured to death and thus immune to life's threats and blandishments, she herself viewed all the world's ugliness and beauty through a viper's eye. "The king would do well with me at his side. An alliance with the Syrax family assures prosperity to Britain."

"It is not Britain's prosperity that interests you." Morgeu nibbled at the date with her small white teeth. "You would control the king with your wiles. You are a seductress. And you are out of your depth."

"Am I?" From around her long neck, she lifted an onyx amulet whose crystal planes radiated a demonic visage—a pike's thrust jaw and a grin of fangs that reached to its shelved brow and malevolent eyes: a Chaldean devil. "My efreet is older than the pyramids!"

The devil-face lifted out of its onyx matrix slow as a cobra's sway, then rushed forward in an ectoplasmic blur of needle teeth.

Morgeu continued nibbling the glazed date in her right hand while her left twirled and wrapped the green smoke of the efreet about her wrist. "Your magic is old, my dear, and tired. In the eight thousand years since this devil was trapped in its crystal cage, the planetary powers have moved north. The south now belongs to the Fire Lords and their world-conquering science. You would do better if you allied yourself with them instead of these worn-out relics from the Euphrates."

Selwa pushed to her feet, astonished.

"Sit down," Morgeu commanded, and the small woman's legs gave out and plopped her inelegantly into her seat. "I want to talk with you."

"I will not see your brother again," Selwa insisted with a lilt of fright in her voice. "I will never return to Camelot."

"Of course you won't exert your wiles upon my brother again." Morgeu snapped her wrist, and the efreet's eelish body thwacked against the table edge and blurred to an effluvial vapor that seeped back with a squeak into the onyx amulet. "But you will return to Camelot. And you will use that seductive body of yours to entice the man closest to the king."

Selwa closed her open mouth and winced. "Bedevere is a sodomite. He'll have none of me."

"Not Bedevere, you foolish girl." Morgeu put her hands upon the ebony table and leaned toward the frightened woman. "Merlin."

"The wizard?" Selwa scowled with disgust. "He's old."

"You speak more truth than you know." The enchantress took a honey confection from a silver dish and admired its amber inclusions of almonds and yellow raisins. "Merlin is very old. Yet, his flesh is growing younger. And with flesh comes desire. You will give yourself to him and baffle and distract him with desire. But—" She popped the confection into her mouth and turned to depart. Without looking back, she said, "You will not conceive a child by him." The potted palms clacked as she swept through the doorway, and only the musical enchantment of her voice remained behind. "If you do, I will have to kill you."

Birth. Love. Death. Those are the icons we worship, the oldest devotion. What was true for the great earth mother and the most ancient female spirit—what was true for Rna when she danced as a priestess, primitive and wild upon the open hand of the earth—what was true a thousand centuries ago remains true today, for you. Though you live in the labyrinth of steel, though the invisible angels have fallen from atop the sky to dwell among you as your servants—X rays for your teeth and bones, radio waves for your entertainment, microwaves for your food—you still obey the oldest devotion, you still worship the icons we worship. Birth. Love. Death.

And so?

The heart's secret self makes a covenant with the darkness from which we are born and with the darkness into which we die. Ardent and voluptuous, passionate and tender, that covenant is our common bond. The whole population of humanity from time immemorial to your time in the steel labyrinth wonders what it is for, this covenant of love that stands between birth and death and that holds them apart with such ardent and passionate tenderness.

We are the Nine Queens who have watched the lonely and enchanted children of the forest become the proud warlords of the planet—and yet we ourselves do not know what love is for. Though we sit upon the highest mountain of time, we ourselves do not know.

The portal to Merlin's grotto appeared as crude as a cave hole. An ouroboric carving of a snake swallowing its tail encircled the entryway, and mephitic odors sifted from within.

The wizard, the king, and the papal legate stood on the threshold garbed like desert nomads, black sendal head scarves drawn across their faces to protect themselves from the Dragon's breath. Bedevere, bareheaded yet dressed for combat in his leather cuirass and sword belt, protested, "You must reconsider, my lord, and keep me at your side."

"No, Bedevere," the king replied, leaning heavily on his cypress-wood crutch. "It is Merlin who commands us in the underworld, and he says the fewer the travelers the better our chances of returning."

"You cannot protect the king where we are going," Merlin confirmed. "I would have to watch after you in the netherworld and thus diminish my capacity to guide the king. Loki, himself a god, refuses to accompany us. Without his help, I will not have the wherewithal to assure your safety."

"My lord, it will not gall my heart to stay behind," Athanasius spoke, the jittery eyes behind his spectacles looking first to the king and then the wizard for reprieve. "This demonstration of telluric science that you offer me, Merlin, I say to you it is an addition I desire not."

Merlin's chrome eyes narrowed above his mask of black silk. "Then, on your word as legate, as the pope's own emissary, you will commend our king a true Christian and immediately request provisions be shipped to Britain from the Continent?"

"On my word?" Athanasius lowered his eyelids resignedly. "I have tasted the truth of what you claim is science but not yet digested it. In good faith, I cannot swear that this kingdom is other than a false jewel of righteousness in a rich casing of deviltry justified by sophistry and specious reasoning."

"There you have it." Merlin put his arm about the legate's shoulders and led him down the grotto's steps. "Your papal commission requires you to accompany us and ascertain that it is not magic and supernatural powers with which our king cavorts but the natural forces of God's creation. Come along, Athanasius."

The king met the concern in Bedevere's gray eyes. "I need you here in Camelot. Attend to all matters of state while I am away."

And with that, the king departed, leaning upon his crutch. Bedevere returned to the court with a heavy heart, because he knew he could not fulfill the king's charge. Since Athanasius had exposed him to all Britain for a sodomite, none in Camelot would have anything to do with him. He was a sinner useful only to the king. Kyner and the other warriors acted as though he did not exist and responded to him only when in the presence of Arthur. Worst of all, Bishop Riochatus insisted on preaching to him at every encounter and sprinkling him with holy water, striving to drive away the carnal devils that possessed him.

Bedevere determined to prove himself as righteous as any man, and on that day, as the king entered the hollow hills to claim a teardrop from the eye of the Dragon, he himself left on his own quest for the Holy Grail. When he returned with that sacred vessel, he knew that no one would ever again question his faith or his worthiness to serve the king.

Following Kyner's directions to the Chapel Perilous, Bedevere soon arrived in Crowland, on the pine bluff that overpeered the willow isle in its shallow stream. Egrets waded through their silver reflections in midstream, and the dragon that had mortally wounded Cei was nowhere to be seen.

Bedevere loosened the girth straps of his horse, fitted his plumed bronze helmet upon his head, and led his steed down the slope of reed brakes. With the day scattered like crushed topaz in the water, he mounted and drew his sword loudly from its sheath so that its echoes rang across the glade. A deep growl replied from behind the willow isle, leaving a trail of darker echoes.

Fear boiled up in Bedevere, and he had to use all his strength to hold the reins and the hilt of his sword firmly in his one hand as his mount danced beneath him, eager to turn and run. But there was no place to run to. In Camelot and across all Britain, he was an abomination. His salvation awaited him in the Chapel Perilous, and the sole obstacle was the dragon. In that moment, the dragon became the hatred of the people who had forced him to this cruel contest. All the prejudice that had tramped upon his honor, all the fear of others at his own hopeless love, all the murdered joy of his life had taken form in this vile and vehement creature.

His fright hardened to an ivory anger at this realization, and he shouted, "Come out, you filthy beast! Come out and end my suffering once and for all! Make me a man among men—or kill me!"

From behind the vale of willows, the dragon rose. Its tonnage of torn flesh and encrusted bone reared against the sky on ruined wings, and it lunged over the isle with one stride. Fumes poured from its skull-grin like the smoke of a squall, darkening the day, and the flags of its ripped tissue flapped with the force of its bounding charge.

Bedevere's horse would not be restrained. It twisted about and bolted away hopelessly under the steaming shadow of the monster. A roar pounded the air to deafness, and Bedevere took that as a signal to jolt his loosened saddle rightward, toward his armless side. He slid under the galloping steed as blue fire blasted over him and the world blurred and disappeared in a blind glare. Heat scorched him, and the stink of roasted flesh filled his lungs.

The burned horse crumpled, sliding into the water and collapsing into mud and gravel. Bedevere rolled, with his sword pressed flat against his chest, his cuirass and helmet taking blows from the river rocks. Fast as he could, he shoved to his feet and ran for the shrieking behemoth, remembering how Arthur had slain his dragon.

The hissing bellows of the beast deepened, and he knew another blast of burning death was coming. Screaming inaudibly against the oceanic roar of the dragon, Bedevere swung his sword hard over his head. Above him towered legs big as pylons, the iridescent hide ripped raw to shining, pink-fleshed wounds. And above the mighty legs, a torso of tattered crimson banners. And above all that, the gaping maw with its slithering tongue of black oils and the smoking red teeth. Eyes like yolk jellies in horned sockets fixed him where he stood, and the jetting blue flames exploded with lightning force as he threw his sword.

"Earth is a globe in the void," Merlin explained to Fra Athanasius, as they entered the hollow hills. Layers of ether light glowed in the long sky beyond a horizon of narrow trees. Moments earlier, the wizard had led him and the king down natural steps of flowstone to the grotto where the scribe had first learned of electricity. Vapors continued to leak phosphorescently from the distilling vats, galley pots, and carboys that cluttered the limestone crannies.

In passing, Athanasius had glanced into lamplit side chambers of vermiculate rock formations crowded with drafting tables, brass instruments, and more glassware. He had been nervously looking for Loki but had found only a few bats flurrying around the hanging spires of the cave vaults. And then the wizard had taken a sharp turn, past stobs of green rock mired where the ceiling dripped puddles of mineral liquor, and suddenly they were in a sparse woods lit with minty colors of twilight.

"The flat earth is an illusion," Merlin went on, striving to calm himself as well as his companions. Well he knew the risks of wandering in the hollow hills. On prior visits, the wrath of the elk-headed god had nearly killed him, and once had even made him a spirit fugitive to his own body. "What the eye perceives is only apparent. In truth, the earth . . ."

"Has a spherical shape," Athanasius concluded the wizard's thought. "For centuries reason has been in mutiny to perception. Aristotle observed the curved shadow that earth casts upon the moon in eclipse. Oh yes, Merlin, I am a scribe, and I have read scrolls in the libraries of Rome and Alexandria full of wonders past expectation. Such as Aristarchus of Samos, whose mind was bent to high enterprises and noble attempts three centuries before our Savior's birth. Aristarchus proposed that the ponderous notion of celestial spheres upon which are fixed the stars and planets is a luxuriant illusion. He claimed that earth is simply one of the wandering planets, all revolving about the sun. The nocturnal parade of stars across the heavens appears thus because earth rotates on an axis."

"Your erudition is a happy surprise," Arthur said, braced by his cypress crutch and gawking about uneasily at the crepuscular forest. He, too, had known horror in the hollow hills and fervently regretted that this magic required him personally to collect the Dragon's teardrop. "Can you perhaps arrange for those scrolls to be copied for our library in Camelot?"

"I will see to it upon my return to Ravenna, my lord," the legate replied, avidly praying in silence that God would allow him to fulfill his promise and deliver him whole and sound from this unsavory venture. Apprehensively, he looked about and saw the sky like watery blood and the trees thin and knobbed as charred spines. He shuddered and strode closer to the wizard. "How then, Merlin, if we journey subterranean, do our senses perceive ourselves at cockshut time in a wood of eerie quiet where one might well expect to behold steaming out of the loam the departed dead rebated from hell?"

"The earth is electrical as is the brain," Merlin answered. "What we see in the hollow hills are the thoughts of the earth, or I should say the thoughts of those beings who live in the earth, the Daoine Síd. They have imagined the world above. For them, twilight is perpetual, for in their exile from the World Tree, they are the light fallen into the earth. We wander in their dream, in our minds, while our bodies stand entranced in a cavern beneath Camelot."

The wizard stopped abruptly. From among the red shadows of impending night came a rider. Dead leaves swirled under hoof, and the air shimmered about the steed.

Athanasius tilted his lenses, and breathed in awe, "A unicorn!"

"Fear not," Merlin said, and grasped Arthur's forearm. "It is the king's mother, Ygrane."

Lit by a faint pale aura, the witch-queen came to a stop upon her black unicorn a few paces away. "Do not approach," she warned. The space around her appeared fragmented or feathered, brushed with streaks of northern lights. "I have broken free from the god of the hollow hills. His glamour is upon me, and if we touch, you will be enthralled."

"Mother!" Arthur limped forward and pulled the mask of black sendal from his face. He had never before seen her without her habit. Bareheaded, her pale hair cropped close to the facets of her skull, her eyes a green rhyme to the sunset, combustive stars in the dark hollows under her high forehead, she seemed malfeasant, an apostate to all that was holy. "It is true then? You have forsaken your immortal soul and given yourself to the pagan gods?"

Ygrane made no reply. Aqueous reflections wobbled around her and smeared her countenance with a radiance propagated out of emptiness. Upon the brow-tusk of the black unicorn palest fire spiraled, and within the bestial curves of its opal blue eyes Ygrane sat again upon the black unicorn, both drenched in sunlight, already arrived in the dayheld world beyond the hollow hills.

"Mother—why?" Tears tracked Arthur's cheeks. "You were a holy woman, and now—you are a witch!"

"Do not tarry," she counseled him, unfazed by sorrow or a mother's sentiment. Contact with the unicorn flared a serene and voiceless joy through her, a prophetic joy that washed over her and passed on through the beast's horn to the three before her. Arthur would endure. He would endure beyond his flesh. The slippery body that had somersaulted in her womb and that had squeezed forth from her would find a way back to daylight and the deeds that would defy silence and death and give themselves in a fusion of memory and dream to become legend. "Do not tarry," she said again, and smiled, her heart broken and its pain arrogated by the might of a greater love.

3

Lo! The Dragon!

Inside the nacreous foglight of Skidblade, Morgeu the Fey writhed with remorse. She had endangered her baby Mordred to use the Æsir god's magic ship for her purposes. No matter that those purposes ultimately served the child if by her delay in going to Avalon she had enraged the Furor. He would flay the infant for a skin-patch on his breeches.

When Skidblade's hull circled open and revealed a sun-basked vista of knolls and dells crowded with apple trees and the standing stones called menhirs, Morgeu leaped out and skidded on a slick mound of rotted fruit. She fell to her haunches and sat there in the apple muck, staring at high thin serifs of cloud printed against the blue like some undeciphered legend. On the verdant promontory below the cloud runes, a cascade fell in a single silver thread into a gorge of lichen-covered rocks splotched yellow, red, brown, and green as tapestries or carpets flung into the chasm.

She laughed, realizing she had arrived in Avalon and had, for now, eluded the Furor's ire. Muttering Mordred's name fervently as a prayer, she scrambled to her feet. With her crimson robes lifted almost to her knees, she ran nimbly, a happy servant of the Æsir chieftain. From among the gnarled apple trees, she glanced back and saw Skidblade floating blue and white as a cloud in a glade of clover.

The death of her baby would extinguish all her foolish pride, she realized, acknowledging to herself that her pride in the child born of her incest magic *was* foolish. She and her baby Mordred were but a momentary dream. The warmth of the sun stretching itself on the meadows of Avalon and the perfume of those meadows, enigmatic and pianissimo, assured her of that. And she slowed her run.

We could have stopped her then. We Nine Queens were not without magic of our own, and this was our island. But millennia of watching and not interfering, of witnessing birth, love, and death with divine patience had left us empty beyond illusion. *Let the enchantress work her spell,* we thought to ourselves. Eight thousand five hundred years of spelling had not unraveled the knot of the human heart and its tangled bloodways of mammalian hungers. Ninety thousand years of our attentiveness and attunement had only just begun to loosen that knot. Compassion, mercy, and love still could not match strength with the heart's avarice and vengefulness. Murder, rape, and the venom of lust that molested children and made of them monsters filled our unblinking sight day after day across horizons of time. Only the rare soul knows what love is for.

So—*Let the enchantress work her spell,* we thought. None had dared before, but we were unobstructed by expectations, fearful or otherwise. Morgeu came slowly through the trees, already sensing the pointlessness of her rage and the truth of what the Furor himself had told her: *You have always disdained life and hated our brief dream, our brief brightness.*

We cooled the heat of her disdain by our mere presence, but that only slowed her. She came on through the apple trees and down the slope of cloud shadows and swaying grass like a sleepwalker. The chanting had already begun inside her in the woods, before she saw the large round hut of packed earth, with its circular windows and small red door. When our hovel finally came into view she gave loud voice to her spell, her gaze illumined with purpose.

Barbarous words they were—full of harsh sounds and discordant rhythms—abrasive cries that weakened the strength of our watchful trance. Dancing her circles lighter than leaves about our hut, her crimson robe aflutter, her arms jangling over her luminous head of frizzy red hair, she stalled our soulful visions. We slumped in our block-cut thrones, and our pulses clicked like ice in our wrists.

For that moment, we were just women again. The magic had stopped, and we were simply nine women lowering our gauzy veils, blinking away sleep, and staring at one another anxiously. Were we wrong to let the enchantress dance her spell? What would we do now? Would we live or die?

The youngest of us, Nynyve, who had been out in the world recently to help the high king of Britain whom the Fire Lords had marked to take Rna's place, said, "Wait. The Fire Lords who chose each of us for this beautiful work want us to finish. They will not let Morgeu or the Furor stop us. But the radiant ones are few and scattered widely across the cosmos. Wait, and one of them will come."

We agreed to keep to our places, and so we sat and chatted about how eerie and lovely the world was, and ruminated why each of us had been selected for this task. "We are victims," one of us said, recalling the Germanic kin word *wih* from the Sanskrit *vinakti*—"he sets apart." "We have been set apart to carry the dream of the universal family," chimed another. And a third added, "Because that dream is a dream, no one believes it, and so we must bear its weight across the generations until love becomes more plausible than hate." And a fourth suggested, "We are lucky the universal family *is* a dream, for dreams are light and our road is long."

Before anyone else could speak, the spacious chamber with its tamped-earth floor flooded with dazzling light. A Fire Lord arrived, as Nynyve had known he would. We drew our veils once more across our faces, and the magic of the radiant ones lifted us taller in our seats. The trance seeing began again, every unique human life in Europe floating before us like foliage upon the branches of a sturdy bough.

Outside, Morgeu the Fey stopped her frenzied dance, and the barbarous spell went silent in her throat. The Fire Lord stood before her so bright that even the vivid red of her hair and the crimson of her robes drained to white outlines of themselves. In the sugared radiance, the enchantress stared silently, aghast that her blasphemy had summoned a fiery angel out of heaven's closed eternity.

Loki sat upon red jasper flagstones in a narrow and remote terrace under Camelot's north wall. He plucked sulkily at the livid toadstools growing through the joints and pondered summoning the Fire Lords directly. Why did he have to wait on Merlin? Why truckle to a demon who had lost the stature of a demon and become a man? For the promise of a sword? His blood brother the Furor had employed high magic to draw demons from the House of Fog for his conquest of Britain. Why not summon the Fire Lords themselves and conquer Yggdrasil?

"But would they come?" he wondered aloud. Looking about him at the evergreen arbors and the flight of black marble stairs that descended to a water garden in the inner ward, lifting his tattooed face to the ranks of beech trees against the espaliered bulwark, he felt a moment of pride. Of all the Æsir gods, he alone had dared to enter the citadel of the Furor's enemies. Merlin could have trapped him in a jug and thrown him into the sea to languish for aeons. His courage and his wits had prevailed.

Bolstered by this evidence, he decided to call out to the Fire Lords and appeal for their direct support in overthrowing the Furor, who despised them. Merlin had claimed that this citadel was designed to resonate with the Storm Tree and thus presumably with the universe beyond; if the angels could be reached at all, they would surely sense him from here.

He stood up and sent forth a single shout, not daring more for fear of alerting the Æsir to his presence in Camelot. "Fire Lords!" he called. "Come forth!"

No radiant beings appeared. Instead, the air darkened, though the sun remained unobscured by clouds, and a frigid wind broomed dead leaves across the terrace, gathering them into a scuttling whirlwind. Out of the tossing wind emerged a naked man big as two men, a giant with pomegranate skin, and where his face should have been, rusted twists of jagged wire stitched every orifice—eye sockets, nostrils, mouth, and ears. A living face thrived on his belly with goat eyes of clouded quartz for nipples, a hog's nose at his sternum, and an impossibly wide grin of fangs like a serpent's jaw dislocated to devour prey.

This was Succoth, one of the demons driven off the Dragon by the witch-queen, Ygrane. The Furor's magic bound him to the will of the Æsir, and an immediate telepathic understanding passed between him and Loki: The demon would devour the god, would rip him to plasmic shreds and scatter the ions of his dead flesh into the solar wind, where they would be blown into the void and drift forever through profound and absolute darkness.

Terror sliced through Loki, and he anchored his wits on the espaliered bulwark beyond the beech trees. When Succoth came for him, scythe claws slashing, the god sprinted across the terrace, through the trees, and up the curving bulwark with monkey agility. Succoth followed, his abdominal jaws rending wet and grinding cries.

True to his word, Merlin had designed Camelot for connection with the Storm Tree, and when Loki reached the parapet above the inner ward, he slapped the tattoos from his scalp and face and ascended toward Yggdrasil in a geyser of auroral fire.

Succoth's claws swiped the empty space where the god had stood, and the demon soared after him. His sticky red flames yawed to a shark's mouth, and he shot with a flowing voracity through the tangled layers of the Tree.

Loki intended to lose the demon in the dense forests of Yggdrasil. He ducked under hanging moss and air plants and entered a riotous world of ghostly tree boles, strangler vines, and thick walls of blossoms. A crested eagle, surprised by the fleeing god, screamed, "Lokee! Kee! Kee!" And its laughter at the Liar's plight directed Succoth faster along the ivy lanes and the high galleries.

When Loki realized he could not hide in the forests of Yggdrasil, he fled to the marshes. There, mist strayed in whorls among cypress stumps and skeletons of fallen trees. He banged on the lichenous doors of trolls, hoping they would hide him. But the wet, gnashing cries of the demon frightened them. They heard the toads of the mere responding to the dark angel by shouting at the sight of Loki, "Suk—ut! Suk! Suk! Suk—ut!"

In despair, Loki ran full out across the open fields of the upper world, bounding away uphill with furious vigor. The other gods, alerted by Loki's loud shrieks, watched in astonishment from their bowers and the forest trails of the endless Wild Hunt. None stirred to help him, because all immediately sensed the Furor's magic upon Succoth. Like a howling wind, the demon passed among them, intent only on Loki.

The sky's broad blue glare darkened toward indigo and wisps of eternal night as the terrified god climbed higher in the Storm Tree. Stars tight as silver seeds glinted where the cold hardened and the silence roared. If Loki ran any higher, he would plunge into space itself and be swept away in the solar wind. Desperately, he searched about for his blood brother, and called to him by his childhood name: "Wo-tan! Wo!"

The cry flapped across gypsum dunes to the Raven's Branch, where the sleeping gods lay, the gods who had loved the Furor so dearly that they had given to him their wakefulness to strengthen his magic and his tether upon the demons from the House of Fog. Loki's bitter cry fell into their dreamless ears, and they heard him not. Sister Mint, whose husband, the Brewer, had concocted the sleeping potion; Blue, sea-dweller and oldest friend of the Furor; Ravager, storm-rider and sorceress; Silver Heart, huntress; and the two children the Furor begot on his wife Lady Unique—Beauty and Thunder Red Hair—stirred not at all. The Liar's screams reached them, but they heard him not.

Elsewhere in the World Tree, in the oak-wood palace called Home, Lady Unique did hear the despairing cries of the Liar, and she smiled, for she detested his deceits and trickery. Yet, she knew her husband would not tolerate his blood brother's death by a rabid Dark Dweller from the House of Fog. That was too humiliating a death for any Æsir god, and the Furor was proud as he was bold. That he had not quickly responded gave her pause for thought.

Lady Unique, robust and big-boned, her white-blond hair strained back from a serene brow and gathered in deep folds at the back of her head by bands of moonstone, wore only the simplest gowns of brown hunter's cloth embroidered by her own hand with ferns and wood pigeons. She did not value opulence, nor did she favor weakness of any kind. For many years, she had believed her husband admired these sturdy qualities in her.

But of late, since he had convinced their children, Beauty and Thunder Red Hair, to give him their life strength for his magic, he had seemed more remote, and she sometimes wondered if perhaps he savored her less than before. Such thoughts were themselves a betrayal of weakness, and she always drove them quickly from mind. She was the queen of the Æsir gods. Upon the blond rafters of their Home gleamed the shields of battles won against Fauni and Síd. The skulls and bones of enemy champions had been crafted into flambeaux to light the tall windows of Home, and they reminded her of her pride and her purpose as the Furor's wife.

While the Furor gave all his strength to his magic, binding demons to serve him and conniving against the invading Fire Lords, she worked daily to gather the mortal troops necessary for the conquest of the West Isles. Their king, Wesc, was devoted to her, and his poetry pleased her with its profundity and its beauty. She had embroidered lines of his verse in gold thread upon black baize, framed it in gazelle horn, and placed it among the skull trophies, battle flutes, and skin drums of the hearth den to inspire humility in her husband:

What has not become of you
continues.
How it has helped you you
will never know.

Daily she inspired King Wesc's Wolf Warriors and his snake priests. Daily the invasion force grew, pulsing with the energy that she gathered for them through her talismans: She wove them from bryony twine and set them with polished beryls so that they focused the magical power of the upper world and directed it to her chieftains and wizards as battle luck, courage, and orphic visions. This work lately occupied most of her time, and she had no strength left for suspicions and the weakness of jealousy.

And yet, with the Furor's blood brother shrieking for his life and making a spectacle of himself before all the Æsir, she could not help but wonder why her husband was so slow to reply. She resolved to question him about this the next time he came Home to inquire about his mortal troops. She would ask him where he was, though already her pride insisted that he was in trance, using their children's strength and the strength of the other gods who loved him to protect Yggdrasil from the Fire Lords.

In truth, the Furor lay in tall ambrosial grass beside his mistress, Keeper of the Dusk Apples. Tall and slender, Keeper dressed in laces, tiffanies, and veils set with gems like dewdrops and scented with angelica. Her love for the Furor was fiercely passionate, and there was little talk of invasions, talismans, demons, or Fire Lords when they were together. Staring into her adoring eyes, he heard the Liar's screams as in a dream.

Loki dared not wait another instant for his brother's aid. The demon Succoth came flying across the gypsum dunes like a red razor. The god leaped from the Raven's Branch and fell through the World Tree, through the azure sky and clouds like white hills. He landed upon the Branch of Hours—the bough of the Storm Tree that belonged to the Norns.

This bough was a mere of ice and mists, where dim forms of snow ranged mutely across a vast boreal tract to a cold jade sky. Noon stood like a golden column, warming a small girl with strawberry hair and a tattered frock, the Wyrd sister Skuld. Her face smudged, her thin limbs gray with grime, she played with bright pebbles, blue diamonds marked by runes, a gift from the Furor.

When Loki fell into a nearby drift, splashing snowdust, Skuld did not look up from her game. "The red blade is coming for you, Liar." She tossed her pebbles onto the slate ground with one dirty hand and gathered them with the other. "You cannot live here. Not now."

"Where can I live, Skuld?" Loki asked, tumbling out of the drift and skidding and slipping toward her. "Be quick, girl! Where is the way out of here?"

"Under the lamp of the moon," she answered simply, the tossed pebbles clacking. "But you have to run, Liar. The red blade is coming."

Loki spun about and found the moon under the scales of night in the far distance. He ran, veering and sliding on the ice, forcibly quieting his breath to listen for the wet, grinding chops of the red demon. He heard a glittering growl and then Succoth's claws clattering onto the ice panes, and he did not look back.

The sky grew darker as Loki fled across the winter bough into the future. Night reared before him, a black flame of star vapors. Half a millennium later, he slowed his mad dash across the glacier of time and threw a fearful look over his shoulder. No one was there. Far back from where he had come, he saw the claw of the sun and winter light, pale, silent, diaphanous as smoke—the smoke of the past, like fumes rising from a grave.

• • •

The Dragon slept. In its sleep, it dreamed. And in its dream, the universe was an enormous instant. The beginning burst like a star upon the silence, throwing its spears of light into darkness. From a point smaller than an atom, smaller than an electron, tinier yet than a quark, the explosion threw out prophecies. Time began.

Stars emerged out of densities of hydrogen gas. Out of gravity and stars came beryllium-8, carbon-12, and oxygen-16. And out of the fusion of these nuclei in other generations of stars came calcium, magnesium, and iron. Out of—out of—out of the zero of void, the light. Wombs inside wombs: the womb of light delivering matter into the envenomed cold, into the bitter darkness of space-time.

The enormous instant plunged outward into itself. Billions of years, tens of billions, and the swarming galaxies flying apart thinned away like so much smoke. Outward, faster and faster— forever.

In the Dragon's dream, the enormous instant of the universe expanded to absolute darkness. The dreaming Dragon of earth saw back to itself across that precipice of nothing, back through vacuous aeons to the fiery delirium of spinning galaxies, then down to one yellow star and earth falling through its orbital years, down to earth spinning its wobbly circle of days, down to the Dragon's own slumbering self coiled deep in the cooling core of the planet.

Three diminutive creatures approached—animalcules made of stardust—tiny entities of calcium and carbon and effervescing water, mere fantasies, fleeting blurs so close to nothingness that the Dragon in its sleep almost did not see them there at the tiniest boundaries of time.

"Where are we?" Athanasius shouted into the roaring air. His spectacles glared red against his black mask, and he raised his hand to shield his eyes from the blinding refulgence of the sun. *No, not the sun!* He had to remind himself that the king, the wizard, and he were miles below the earth. The illusion of trees had vanished long ago, and they had been scrabbling through rocky terrain for hours, relentlessly pursuing the flaring sunset. The stench of sulfur and the heat disoriented him. "I weary myself with probabilities, Merlin! I crave certainties! For what, in this world, has God wrought this chthonic luminosity?"

"The fire of Vesuvius!" Merlin yelled above the din. He waved the legate closer, to the jagged brink of a titanic ravine where he and the king stood. "Lo! The Dragon!"

Across an abyss of fiery cliffs and gulfs, magma flowed in arteries of incandescent blood and cataracts of dazzling white-hot radiance. Waves of lava splashed against black rock islands and columnar walls of carbon and corundum, while overhead the shadowy glare reflected off crystal vaults frosted with diamonds. By the prismatic light that breathed in those gems, the vascular arches and cupolas appeared organic, like effloresced tissue and mottled skin.

"Who would have dreamed?" Athanasius bellowed in awe. "A great life inhabits the interior! Self-effulgent and fiery!"

"Relax your gaze!" Merlin passed a hand before Athanasius's face. "See deeper!"

As the wizard's hand fell away, the legate saw the desolate patterns of bare rock as camouflage. Suddenly the colossal gorge became the skin folds and wrinkles under an eye gigantic as a mountain. The glowing currents of lava were but capillaries branching among the scleral vastness of the eye. Its crystalline cell structure pulsed with radiant life-force on an orb so immense that even craning his head all the way back, he could not see beyond the lower curve of the diamond eye white to where the dragon's iris began. He staggered backward and sat down on the warm stone floor, stunned.

King Arthur, too, limped back a pace when he recognized the stupendous eye. By swinging his head side to side, he saw that the pupil had rolled up into the socket. The Dragon was asleep.

"Use Excalibur to retrieve a teardrop!" Merlin instructed the king, and pointed to the rock face that was the lower eyelid of the dragon. Mineral outgrowths knobbed its surface and gleamed with a chimeric light.

Arthur did not immediately hear the wizard. Nor did he feel the throbbing pain in his leg that had escorted him from Camelot. He stood entranced by the behemoth. Before him slumbered the worship of gods and ancestors. *There is that Leviathan which You have made . . .* Psalm 104 rang from his stammering heart and in its echo the portentous words of Job 40:19—*He is the first of the ways of God.*

Within its heat, he felt all the veins of his body shooting

blood, hammering his arterial walls and his brain with awe. An ecstasy of wonder transfixed him. He did not feel his wound or hear the jarring cacophony.

Merlin grasped his shoulder, pointed at the wall, and shouted, "Use Excalibur!"

The king drew his sword, and it shone slick as blood in the fiery air.

Merlin walked alongside, fearful for the king. Arthur alone had to retrieve the teardrop to assure that the magical operation was fulfilled. The wizard was not certain that this was necessary, yet he thought it wise to take no chances, even though this required the king to climb with his wounded leg above the pit of flames.

Magic was helpless to heal the puncture or stop its pain. Arthur set aside his crutch and favored his good leg as he pulled himself onto the ponderous shelf of rock at the fluorescent brink of the gorge. Merlin placed himself at the edge of the plummet to catch the king if he fell.

Fortunately, no demons were anywhere near. The wizard searched for them and felt only the Dragon's sense of being, a repose at the point of transparency, opening upon star depths and a vertigo of galactic distances. Ygrane had kept her word and had cleared the dragonpit for her son.

To steady himself, Merlin focused upon the king's precarious ascent. By the ultraviolet glow of the superheated rock in the chasm, lachrymal drippings shone above Arthur as purple stalac-tites, nacreous oozings from the cliff. The boy perched on an overhang above seething magma and balanced himself on the toes of his good leg to reach a bubbled spill of crystals.

Wedging the blade of his sword beneath a globular excres-cence and using his strong leg for purchase, he twisted from the waist and pried loose a pearl big as a skull. It fell into his arms. With a whooping shout silent under the roar of the heat, he jumped down.

"My lord!" Merlin shouted triumphantly, and ran a knobby hand over the iridescent sphere. "We must hurry from here! Already the sleeper senses our presence! Should the Dragon dream of us, we will never find our way out!"

· · ·

"Falon!" Ygrane called, and the black unicorn carried her north over Britain toward the Celtic warrior who had protected her since her days as a child-queen chosen by the druids. The scorched land flew below like black-and-brown mottlings of a serpent's skin. Then the lake country reflected the sun in wild flashes, and clouds fell to mists among the highlands and dark ravines of Caledonia—

And they arrived.

A canopy of chestnut trees framed a mound of mossy rocks—a gravesite. Rhododendron and barberry flourished around the cairn, and a path of pebbles and rivershells led from the burial tumulus into a pine forest so that the warrior's soul could walk away from the fallen animal in the grave and return to the spirit world.

Atop the unicorn, Ygrane saw through time and a corpuscular haze of matter so that the grave became a window into the magnificent disorder of the corpse. Millipedes, beetles, ants, and a ferment of minuscules thrived in the loam that had been her guardian. Naked bones moldered with a brown decay of new life. New desires flourished inside the amber cage where his heart had been parsed out to countless tiny creatures. And in the domed cave, in the sludge that had been his brain, worms writhed, singing about paradise.

She dismounted and slumped when separation from the unicorn drained her of prescience. She stood dull with grief before the burial site. The disposition of the stones, well joined along the sides and aligned awkwardly at the crest, told her that Falon had prepared his own cairn and had lain down in it and covered himself with prepared stones when he was ready to die. She found braids of ivy net and twined creepers that he had used to lower the last cache of rocks upon himself from where he had hoisted them in the bough of the overhanging chestnut, and she wept.

That he had died alone did not grieve her. He was fiana, one of the fabled horsemen of no home who had served the Celtic queen by defending her highways and countryside from marauders. No fiana were lonely, because they were married to the wind. When she had put on the habit of a nun and married herself to the Cross, he, who had no love for any outlander religion, had left her and had wandered with the wind to this wild place.

She wept for the grace lost between them, seventeen years of absence.

Presently, she stopped crying and sat down on the mossy rock mound, troubled that Falon would not accompany her into the Storm Tree. She needed a companion she could trust on her dangerous mission, and some of her tears carried her loneliness. After Uther's death, her devotion to his faith had led her to Miriam, the Savior's mother. Miriam had been sweet company throughout those years of service among the sick and impoverished. But who would help Ygrane now that she was queen again with the last of her fiana dead?

She pressed her hands against her abdomen, massaging her cramped insides. Menstrual pain and grief mixed poorly, and she felt battered in body and soul.

"Creature!" A muffled shout echoed from under the needle floor of the forest. A moment later, sunthreads let down by the forest canopy parted like draperies, and Prince Bright Night of the Daoine Síd emerged, red hair in radiant disarray, tapered green eyes wrathful—"You faithless creature! You pierced our god! Someone Knows the Truth lies on the floor of the hollow hills bewildered with pain."

Ygrane glared with outrage. "You abandoned me in the hollow hills!"

"Our god commanded us."

"Your god!" The witch-queen stood up, surprised. "What about our blood pact?"

Bright Night nodded impatiently. "Yes, you spilled blood for our pact, Ygrane, and I am bound by our agreement—to retrieve the Graal." He wagged a finger slowly before his angular face. "But I am not bound to defy Someone Knows the Truth. He is my god. You were a foolish woman to seek out your dead husband in the first place. What did you expect? That you would take him back with you, out of the hollow hills?"

"Of course not." She picked up a spiky chestnut and held its urchin pins against her palm, feeling the glint of pain as a temporal reminder of what she had sacrificed to see her Theo again and to help their son hold his kingdom. "I am a mortal woman, prince. If I am to be cast into the dragonpit, never again to be reborn upon this world but to journey in the great beast's dream-song as exiled as starlight, then I am entitled to see my husband a last time."

"Entitled?" Incredulity stiffened his stare. "You risked the entire enterprise for your *dead* husband. You're a living woman, Ygrane. You have no entitlement to see Uther at all." He kicked the chestnut tree as if it were a door he could force open. "Don't you realize what we've mobilized here?"

She nodded angrily. "All the Daoine Síd are at my command."

"Faerïes. Sylphs. Hobs. Elves. We are your servants—after our devotion to Old Elk-Head."

"Was that part of our blood vow?" Ygrane stepped slowly toward him. "You said that the Síd will make certain I have the power to terrify the Furor. You said you would empower me with a magic that would shake the Storm Tree. You promised with blood that I would have at *my* disposal *all* the magic of the Daoine Síd—not what magic remains after your devotion to this Old One."

"This *Old One*, as you slanderously tar him, is the last in Europe." Bright Night stood touching boot tips with the witch-queen and did not turn away though her face looked slant as night. In the green-rimmed dark of her eyes, his shining form was an ashen smudge, and he knew that with a shout she could dissolve him to rainsmoke and send him spinning through clouds for the next hundred years. Yet, even so, he bitterly spoke the outrage of all the Síd: "Wotan—Zeus—Vishnu murdered all the Old Ones, to take power for themselves. And look at what those vehement gods have done to our Mother: the land torn into empires, ripped by war, and scarred by the avarice of human ambition. You of all mortals must feel the numbness, the dead-ness the Romans have made of her body with their cities and roads. The ancient lines of power in the terrain are broken. Our rivers are filthy with city waste. The forests shrink. All this in a mere thirty centuries. For three *hundred* centuries, the Old Ones have led us through the tides of ice, and we have moved like waterbirds in and out of the valleys since long before there were mortals in the north forests and on the snow plains. We were lords among the beasts. Where did you come from?"

"We have a blood pact, Prince Bright Night." She pressed

closer, of a height with him, her vexed expression tight as a stone. "For the price of my *soul*—a soul in love with Jesus—you said I would command *all* the might of the hollow hills."

"It was understood, the Daoine Síd obey Someone Knows the Truth above all others." He did not budge before her ire. "It is ancient knowledge. You cannot plead ignorance of it."

"Then you are mistaken." Her voice gleamed cool as ivory. "I took you on your word—and you broke your word."

"What are you saying?" The elf prince raised his beardless chin proudly. "We agreed to return the Holy Graal to your son, not overthrow our eternal devotion to . . ."

"Don't dun me with your eternal devotion!" Ygrane gnashed her teeth so tightly her jaw locked, and for a moment she glared speechless. When her words came, they were viscous with wrath. "I lost my eternal *salvation* in those three drops of blood. I want *all* the magic of the Síd. *All* of it. You won't abandon me in the hollow hills again. Look what I had to do to get out!" She gestured to the celestial beast that was silently watching them.

The black unicorn floated in the tremolo shadows of the forest, its eyes hot slashes of sunlight, its tusk the sharpest needle of night. The floor of dead leaves did not rustle under its weight.

"They are not uncommon." The prince lidded his eyes indifferently and did not waver before the witch-queen's close, irate stance. "They come down from the void and wander the wild spaces—what wildness is left after empire."

"But when they come," Ygrane said, and tilted her shorn head impatiently, "the branches of the World Tree reach through time and blossom into the future."

"It is no concern to us." The elf touched noses with the witch and winced playfully. "No invaders have yet swarmed us from times yet to come. And who can help those few of us who wander through the Tree? They return more rarely than the unicorns themselves."

"That is my fear, Bright Night." Her callused hands seized him by his blue tunic, and a crow cried in his heart. When she laid hands on him, she took him into her brightness. Her light stripped him naked of form, reduced him to moon mist trembling in the breeze. "To get Arthur to the Vanir Lotus, he will have to cross among the branches—and risk losing himself across time."

"Have no concern for that, my lady." Bright Night's smoke seethed through Ygrane's fingers and re-formed to his human shape a pace away. "The Síd will not permit your son to wander aimlessly the ranges of time like some homeless wayfarer. He *will* return, he *will* win the Lotus and the Graal—and you *will* be ours. That is our pact."

The witch edged closer. "What will you do when Someone Knows the Truth summons you from my side again?"

Bright Night crossed his arms. "We cannot defy our god."

"Why not defy him?" Ygrane put her hands on his arms and made him feel her interior space and the tragic dimension of her sacrifice. She had given herself to a decision that made time and the emptiness of the world shimmer. She wanted him to feel the same power. "Why not boldly overthrow him? You are the more able leader, Bright Night. You have vision and daring. With you as god, the Síd can return to the World Tree."

The prince laughed and pushed away from the witch. "I am not a *god*! I am but a prince of elves who can win this great victory for my god. I will return Someone Knows the Truth to heaven."

"Unless we fail." Her voice deepened somberly. "And if we fail, if you let the Old One thwart me again, you will not have my soul to waken the Dragon and win your fight. Yggdrasil will never again be home to you or your god. To win my soul, the Síd must devote themselves to me above Someone Knows the Truth. *You* must cut through him if he blocks my way again. Let the pain bewilder him. He will restore himself. But what you take from me, I lose forever."

Bright Night mulled this over, his shining eyes lidded—and an acid tang of hate poisoned his thinking. He did not want to balance odds against stakes to decide faithlessness to his god. That assailed his integrity . . .

With a jolt, he understood that this was also what enraged the witch-queen—the resented blood pact that had turned her from her nameless god. He unlocked his arms and straightened with surprise. "We are thrown together as one!"

"As one," she confirmed with a grim nod. "I'm glad you finally understand."

"It is a dark pact we have forged between us, my lady." Bright Night pulled his fleecy hair back with both hands. "We are a pair of infidelities."

"To one purpose." Her eyes were pits above the hollows of

her cheeks, a shadow of the Crone. "My leadership. My sacrifice. Simple and certain."

Bright Night nodded once, committed to the ruthless symmetry of their pact. "Our god will not block your way again. Until your soul is in our hands, we set him aside." He looked at the slinky darkness of the unicorn. "And you will control your beast. It is not the same creature as the white unicorn you rode when you were a young queen. This breed is treacherous."

"I am not afraid." She smiled at him, bright-eyed with unconcern for the future. "After all, you are guarding me."

4

Unwrinkle the Stars

Why have the masters written nothing? Jesus was a rabbi, Siddhartha a prince. Both literate and famously well-spoken teachers wrote nothing.

Why?

Because they were spell-breakers, not spellbinders.

Morgeu the Fey cringed before the Fire Lord, hands upheld to shield her squinting eyes from the heatless brilliance of the angel. In his glare, shadows appeared more darkly real than physical objects, and colors detached and floated away. The round abode of the Nine Queens, the apple groves, and the languid hills of Avalon shone white and featureless.

Darkness intervened. A human figure massive as three men eclipsed the Fire Lord, and in the giant's shadow Morgeu sat down, stunned colors and vaporous hues rippling across her brain. The dark soul in her dark blood crawled away somewhere, and for a long moment, she remained just a shape of herself, like the chalk patterns of the trees and hills she had glimpsed in the angel's radiance.

Voices locked in ice hissed and cracked. The sense of the words was unreachably distant, yet Morgeu the Fey knew that the giant and the angel were conversing in great seriousness. When her senses thickened enough for her to open her hands in the brown sunlight and touch the grass stalks she had trampled with her barbarous dance, she remembered herself.

The giant who stood in flame-edged silhouette was the Furor. She recognized his wolfskin boots and his wild hair shining like tangled lightning. Startled, she scuttled backward. His heavy shadow crawled with ribbonworms of light. The rays of the Fire Lord moved inside the god, burrowing through his astral form.

Morgeu rolled to her feet and dashed away. The god did not see her. He was in the angel's grip. That was what he had wanted all along—for her to evoke the Fire Lord with her noisy, delirious enchantment of the Nine Queens so that he could confront the fiery being, his fateful enemy.

She ran from the Furor and did not glance back. Every shadow pointed the way, stretching from the white dazzle of the angel into the honeycomb dark of the forest. She did not care what transpired between the two titans. Her promise was fulfilled, and now all she wanted was to get back to Skidblade and use the shining ship to find Mordred.

The Furor paid her no heed. All his attention was upon the luminous entity, because he stood before this adversary without a weapon. He cherished no hope of winning a fight with such a formidable and otherworldly being and determined instead to confront the invader with himself, leader, and—if need be—sacrificial offering of the Æsir. "Who are you?" asked the chieftain.

No reply came. The being's light fitted his thoughts as water in a skull cup. Wherever the prophetic power of his one eye searched, he saw only himself in the diamond rays, in the blinding white, in the endless vacuum white of the Fire Lord.

"Why do you come to my world with your magic?" The Furor still smelled the crushed-grass musk from Keeper of the Dusk Apples. He had rushed to Avalon as soon as he had heard Morgeu's raving chant, and the mint scent of his mistress breathed from his furs. Along its perfume trails, deep into the Furor's psyche, the Fire Lord shone his radiation from the first pulsebeat of time.

The Furor fluoresced. The atomic haze of his ionic plasma resonated with the energy of the Fire Lord. The angel expanded to fill the full mosaic of the Furor's physical body. Shining with the refulgence of the Fire Lord, the Æsir god saw his thoughts and feelings as cut crystal, inexorable, definitive projections of his corporeal form.

"You say there is no choice! Is that what you are telling me, Fire Lord?" He realized that to this entity he was merely a form, a shape, barely sensate. The Fire Lord illuminated one facet of the Furor's crystal soul, and the angelica perfume of his lover brightened in his nostrils. The Furor listened to the silence, not a bird or a leaf rustling. The white intensity of the angel had blinded him, and the passionate smell of his lover returned him to the ambrosial grass in the dell where he lay with Keeper of the Dusk Apples.

"Why did you rush away?" she asked him, her hazel eyes surprised, caught picking feathers of grass from her gauzy veils. "What is going on?"

"I am with a Fire Lord . . ." he began to say, and the dream scrap of his mistress slipped away. He squinted into the fathomless glow of the Fire Lord until his one eye hurt, then he turned his lost eye to the light—and he saw with it once more!

He saw his wife Lady Unique at Home, in their palace of blond wood. She sat under a quince tree beside the lily pool braiding more of her beryl-and-bryony talismans for King Wesc. Her faithfulness to their cause stung his empty eye with a teardrop of lye.

The Fire Lord touched again the first facet of the god's soul, and the rhapsody of longings the Furor felt for Keeper of the Dusk Apples swelled once more with voluptuous insistence. His whole body reeled like a cliff, rigid yet threatening to topple at any moment into the depths of his passion.

"Stop!—touching me!" The Furor bowed his head and squeezed his eye shut. Golden light hazed to the silver shadows of her hair and that fragrance again, fathoms of desire full of unremembered dreams. "Yes. She is my lover. The great secret of my life. Should my proud wife ever discover us, I will lose my strongest ally. Is that what you want me to admit? That I have put my whole noble purpose at risk for faithless lust?"

The Furor sank to his knees, hands over his face, his voice a sob of muffled thunder in his big beard. "I admit it then! I am flawed! Thick desire stands in me! And you are perfection come to earth? Then why do you break the land with roads and walls and fences? Why do you kennel people in cities? And why, tell me why, why do I see you always in our future?" He uncovered his face, and the Fire Lord was gone.

"Come back!" the Furor bellowed, lurching half-blind to his feet. Colors burned to their opposites and staggered back into place—red hills, green apples . . .

"Come back and answer my questions!" He stamped his feet angrily and shook his fists at the black clouds. "Why do the cities burn in winds of fire? I have seen it. The cities of glass and metal burn! Why? And why do you dance in their flames?"

Bedevere's flung sword exploded the dragon, and the blast ripped through him like a bolt from the blue void. All the tips of his body burst into silver flames. Shrieking, he threw off his sparking helmet and collapsed into the water. The shallows crawled momentarily with green firesnakes.

When he stood up, his blackened nose and the charred tips of his ears wisped fumes, and ashen hair drizzled from his bald head. A red star etched in soot upon his pate marked where the helmet had arced to his scalp. With the tattered fingers of his one hand, he reached for the willow isle and its veiled chapel. He shambled through the canes and willow withes, moaning through his roasted lips. His swollen eyes rolled with each tortured step, as if inspired by the tragedy put upon him, as if pain also had a muse.

He entered the blackstone chapel on his knees. The serene flames on the tall candles cast a uterine glow in the dark interior and seemed to pulse with his own heart as he reached for the basalt altar and the holy chalice. The wood cup did not diminish his agony, but it filled his hand with wood that had filled the hand of the Savior and it gave him a focus: He fixed his mind upon the terrible beauty of the Lord's suffering, and his mind, already tried beyond endurance, found strength.

With the Holy Grail grasped in his black, frayed fingers, he shoved himself out of the chapel, lumbered through the willows, and slogged downstream. He would carry this glory to Camelot, never suspecting its unreality and Morgeu's trickery. The glory was all that the burning pain would allow him to hold in his mind. He would carry to Camelot this holy emblem of his Christian fidelity. The warlords would kneel in awe before him . . .

Kneel in awe . . .

He marched through the night, the stars burning coldly in

their deep cavities. By dawn, he shuffled across sand on a windy gray beach. Dunes scalloped the coast as far as he could see. A fisherman's shed occupied a cove of black boulders—driftwood thatching and walls of wind-slotted planks. Pale seaweed draped its doorway and parted before a lank man with a salt-stained beard, fish-skin raiment, hollow eyes, and a crown of starfish. A wide, vermilion scar glossed his brow.

"Hail from the Fisher King!" The shaggy man strode through the gloaming toward the one-armed wanderer and presented himself. "Let your journey's ache end here, stranger. You are come upon the Kingdom of the Sea, and without a boat it is shut to your coming as rock. Stop and climb prayers with me, prayers for the quick and the dead, and I will share the high room of the soul with you where we are all kings above our made graves. Stop and give prayers to these answering skies and praise with me the love who dies for our grave truth."

Bedevere stalled before the seeming madman. He wanted to shove past him, to keep walking, on to Camelot and his redemption at the Round Table. But the jabbering hermit blocked his way.

"Speak, man!" the Fisher King commanded, and lifted both fists in the gray, predawn air. "Have you knelt at the empty grave? Do you know who rolled aside the stone? Speak, man!"

"The Holy Grail!" Bedevere shouted, and held forth the chalice, but only a moan emerged from his crisped lungs.

The Fisher King recognized the embossed eagle upon the wayfarer's leather cuirass. "Even a king's officer must reply to the whirlwind silence! To God! Know you His son? Are you deathless? Is the Word in you? Or are you yet trapped in the mire of love, in the guilty flesh appointed to dust, caught at the endless beginning of suffering? Speak, I say!"

Bedevere grunted once more, "The Holy Grail!"

The Fisher King seized Bedevere's scorched face in his greasy hands and pried open his jaws to see what wound impaired his speech. "Heaven's host confound evil!" he shouted, and danced away with fright. From the wanderer's mouth stuck a black tongue split at the tip into a pink five-pointed star. "Are you the Devil that will unwrinkle the stars? Are you come to set aboil the waters of my heart and plunge me into darkness like some pitch moon? Begone! I do have the Word in me. And winds of light surround me. And I am protected by the original love."

Bedevere sagged to his knees. He reverently stood the sacred chalice upon the wet sand and wrote in Latin under it, *This is the Holy Grail, taken from the Chapel Perilous by Bedevere—Protector . . .* He had not the strength to scrawl *of the king* and instead simply sagged over, unconscious.

The Fisher King read the dark words in the silver sand over and over—until the sea turned the page with a white wave. He flung himself into the churning sand and grabbed the wood cup as it rolled away. Cæsar's man had found the Holy Grail and delivered it to him. Surely, this was the purpose of his birth—and this officer's as well. He could almost see the burning ciphers aflame in the round of space above him, the spirit fire that once touched the crosstree, the tomb, and the apostles' heads.

The Fisher King took the Holy Grail to his crude shrine at the back of the stony cove. He stood the chalice beside a crucifix of splinters, a savage outline in slivers of a man nailed to the boards. Then he fell to the sand and writhed with sobs. "Praise to the conjured spirit on my shrine of spindrift! Praise to you, Cup of our Savior—you who knew him before the prodigies of his suffering won us from Adam's sin! Praise!"

While Bedevere's body rocked back and forth in the lapping waves, the hermit wept and prayed. Inspiration followed, and he cobbled together a raft from the wood of his shed and vines of sea grape. He sang the Lord's Prayer as he pushed the makeshift raft down the beach, into the sliding water. Out on the seabound current he sent the gray boat with the devil-marked body of the Cæsar's man lashed to the thwarts. It rode the outbound surge of the tide and soon dwindled under a horizon that shone like dirty milk.

Three nomads masked in black head scarves hobbled across a night landscape toward a deep twilight flat as a blade. The infernal glow of the hollow hills dwindled behind them. Ahead a sky of laminar opal marked a new day under the sun. On all sides, swales of grass breathed with silver shadows, and the air smelled cool and algal. The path underfoot was a ridge of packed turf, one of many that crisscrossed above the marsh, trails of ancient drovers.

King Arthur, Merlin, and Fra Athanasius stopped their laborious hike, momentarily bewildered by chattering birds and warbling frogs. They tugged the black scarves from their faces and drank sweet air.

"We are in the Fenlands, sire." Merlin smelled the ocean's spices in the dawn wind. He reached with the brails of his heart into the twilight and summoned a raven. "The Wash of Metaris is a few leagues ahead. Banovallum, then, cannot be far north." The black bird lit on his shoulder and waited under spread wings as he withdrew a strip of parchment from his pocket, stretched it across his palm, and began writing on it with a stub of lampblack. "The garrison will get this message before the sun rises, and horses and provisions shall arrive soon thereafter."

The king lowered himself to the turf and sat hugging his cypress crutch, searching the star pastures in the western darkness for any sign of the netherworld. He saw only familiar constellations and curlews flapping through the gray air above the marsh grass. With a whispered prayer, he pressed his chin to his chest, grateful to be returned to Britain.

Behind him, Fra Athanasius sat cross-legged on the path, holding the Dragon's teardrop in his lap. They each had taken turns hauling the ponderous orb of smooth stone and had each experienced the clarity of its boundless nature. In the pearl glow of first light, the mineral mass gleamed, aswirl with oily rainbows. Timelessness suffused from it, and Athanasius felt erased. He was no longer a special point in the universe, a soul. Consciousness extended beyond his solitude into the whole of God's creation. And he sat amazed under the skywide realization that his immortal soul was not inside him: *He* was inside the cosmic immensity of his soul.

Wingbeats thrashed, and the raven Merlin had conscripted as messenger flew north, tossing irate cries behind. The wizard took the teardrop from Athanasius's lap, and the legate continued to peer beatifically through spectacles powdered with rock dust of purest mauve.

"I don't believe our blessed emissary will have aught to say till past noon." Merlin showed his snaggled teeth in a hideous grin and held the nacreous sphere before the king. "My lord, your trophy. Let the lachrymose strength in the Dragon's tear ease your burden of time. Soon enough, we will be in Camelot."

Arthur waved the geode aside. "I'm not returning to Camelot. There is naught I can do for Cei anyway, not until we reach the Vanir Lotus in the Storm Tree. I must prepare myself for that."

Merlin made no reply. In his spidery hand, the glass stone dripped reflections of greasy light from the lowering dawn, and fear for the king expanded in him. After a moment of clamorous thinking, he bowed and backed away. He had no faith that this boy could act wisely on his own behalf. Arthur lacked sufficient self-love and cared only for the tribal imperative, the greater good of those Providence had placed in his care. For that selflessness, Merlin felt respect. But for the personal disregard that enabled such nobility, he feared for the king.

Before the brightening coals in the east and the charcoal expanse of the nightbound marsh, the demon Lailoken hefted the Dragon's tear in one hand and then in the other, balancing his decision to say nothing against everything he could say about the unforeseen consequence and the inscrutable heart, everything he had learned over millennia as a destroyer of souls.

Silence felt preferable in the mind of this counselor old as time. Let the king have his dalliance again with the common lot of men. That was how he had been reared by Kyner, as a thrall, and that was where the comfort of his identity remained. The elections of fate that made kings were no less than the hates and wants in the dismal ambitions of men.

Let him take rest among his people, the wizard intoned to himself, using magic to assuage the disquiet in his heart, the foreknowledge of evil festering in the king's petite incautions. *We have survived the Dragon. We have yet to face the Storm Tree. And before that, in the days ahead, there is the encounter with King Wesc in Londinium—the suit for peace without concession.*

Merlin mouthed a silent unhappy laugh, knowing the brutal devastation that the Furor would visit upon Britain for defying him. War was inevitable—and the outcome a terrible thing to dwell upon. All they could hope from their king was that he could buy them time, a respite from chaos.

How will our lad handle himself before a king twice his age and tenfold stronger in military might? Merlin tilted the globular rock so that it reflected the red fetal eye of dawn. *Wesc is no fool to magic. He will be prepared to annul all my cunning efforts. Arthur must face this king on his own.*

The wizard placed the teardrop before the secret center of

himself, that unique space in front of him where the right went invisible and the left took hold. Holding it in that way, he felt inside the relic to the whirlwind of stars, the collision of suns that was the metabolism of the Dragon.

Time is deep—and lives are glittersparks . . .

At that moment, Merlin silenced himself, because he sensed us, the nine watchers installed in Europe by the Fire Lords. He regarded us quietly, the way a demon would, rubbing our softness, our watchfulness against his face of emptiness.

An irreparable shiver chilled us. We were wont to see into human hearts. Our sudden glimpse into the abyss of Lailoken curled three of us in our chairs and threw the other six to the dirt floor. It was a vision with no boundaries, and it damaged us.

We had never contemplated such unreckonable emptiness, and we were unprepared to save ourselves. We fell through absolute darkness into the sleep that stone dreams upon.

Formless void—beyond witness . . .

Arthur handed his chaplet of gold laurel leaves to Merlin in the presence of the camp commander from Banovallum and instructed him to convene the Round Table in his absence, make ready for the Londinium meeting. He would join his entourage on the Tamesis, at Corinium after a fortnight. His sword Excalibur he entrusted to the papal legate, saying, "For our Savior came to bring a sword into this world. This is the sword of the Christ in my kingdom. Guard it with your soul."

He doffed his leather armor and his silk tunic for a hempen robe and a boot dagger. Even his cypress stave he relinquished. The camp commander gave him a sorrel stallion, for Straif was stabled in Camelot, and he rode that horse swiftly out of the Fens. Divested of all power save himself, free of the wizard and the watchful grooms, the vigilant warriors, the attentive women and curious children, he charged over the peat trails.

Farther west, among bare rounded crests of scorched knolls, he wished he had brought Excalibur. But no dragons stalked him across the wide vales, and he rode unmolested into the cedar fastness of Causennae.

Arthur recalled a market plaza crowded with pens of live game, vegetable bins, fish tubs, and meat stalls. Shops lifted upon wooden pillars above the boggy ground had offered cooking pots, farm equipment, and cosmetics from perfumes to eyebrow-black and false hair. Now, those shops stood empty. Two fruit barrels and a run of chickens occupied the plaza sward.

He spent the night outside the city in a rowan stand above a creek and dreamed of a church bell tolling over the shimmering grasslands—but no tower or edifice stood upon the bleak swales—only the sun in the quivering sky echoing like a well.

The next morning he galloped for a while with a flurry of birds skirling behind. Towers of white cloud rose with their implausible dreams above ink-and-pearl hills. Like an emerald blazon upon gray heraldic fields, the irrigated orchards, vegetable plots, lawns, and spinneys surrounding The Blanket of Stars could be seen from the highway for many leagues.

The king's engineers had learned their science serving the wizard Merlin during the long construction of Camelot, and restoring the ruined Roman villa had served as a model for the renovation of Britain. Rills and creeks had been diverted, wells unclogged and pumped by small windmills so that water flowed in clay pipes across the estate. From grassy slopes so green they were jewels, shepherds stood among their flocks. They watched the beautiful sorrel move like visual music through chords of sunlight and shadow cast by the highway's colonnade of trees.

A score of local people displaced by the war had come to the villa to work on the grounds. Their thatched cottages covered the sunken floor in the gutted ruins of a Roman granary, and their children gamboled with a white dog under walnut trees. A young woman watching over the smaller children pointed to the beautiful horse and waved.

This pastoral community that weeks before had been cinder-land cheered the king with hope for his realm, and he rode on jauntily. Ahead on the road, a caravan waited to be stabled. The wagon tents glared with swastikas painted in bold black lines—crossed hammer and tongs, emblem of the ironworkers' guild.

The wood shingles nailed to the side planks identified the caravan's sponsors from the Orders of Iron: swords, arrowheads, lances, helmets, shields.

Armorers and weapons masters all, Arthur groaned to himself. They were on their way to Londinium for the Meeting of Arthur and Wesc and for the commerce of kings—war.

5

Powers of Angels

Blue heather and amber gorse clad a hill craggy with black rocks.
Into a cleft of this mossbound scree, Ygrane rode her black unicorn, and the Daoine Síd followed. They glittered around the
witch-queen as bright shadows of their eternal kind, lit with
inner light. Halo moths cut fiery signs in the air above her. And
smiles like thin scarlet threads streaked the darkness in her wake.

She rode across indigo sands with her bare head uplifted, surveying the nocturnal terrain. Imponderable horizons of darkness
pulsed with mystic blood, the red auras of volcanic cones pouring
lava streams. Their throbbing glare matched the pain of her menstrual cramps. Grimly, she held herself upright with the thought
that this anguish was just the mask of herself. Behind the incandescent pain was the bloodtide of the moon. That was the knife
turning inside her, peeling away another slice of her life for its cal-
endar cult. It was a divine torture by whose spilled blood the irre-
vocable promise of endless life was assured. So, she spoke to hold
herself above her pain and nausea.

"Why have we returned to the hollow hills?" Prince Bright
Night called through waves of heat. "My lady, where are you
taking us?"

Ygrane rode silently, her attention focused on a plutonic eye
of flames that had opened in the planetary depths. It watched
her wrothful and unblinking, and she pointed at it with her
right thumb as though she held a scepter. "I want to talk with
you, elk-god."

"What are you doing?" Bright Night whispered hotly from the swarm of chambered lights tumbling in the darkness behind her. "We don't need to involve Someone Knows the Truth."

"Be silent until I command you to speak." Ygrane lifted herself high upon the unicorn's velvet back and raised her voice. "You call yourself Someone Knows the Truth. Come out before me that we may speak. I command you by the might of the Daoine Síd, by all the faerïes, elves, hobs, and sylphs without whose power you could not survive at all."

The glowering eye expanded, and the black range under them dwindled away as the staring flames billowed larger, a huge, silent explosion of burning gas. It filled the darkness with ramparts, spires, and domes of dazzling energy—a palace made of fire.

Bright Night said nothing, but Ygrane could sense him tighten with anxiety. She walked the black unicorn beneath a portcullis of lacy flames. They entered a radiant court, where tiered galleries glowed red as cauldrons of magma and pillars woven of fire throbbed. Yet, no heat assailed them nor din of combusting rock. The magic of the Daoine Síd protected Ygrane—from all but her feverish cramps.

The witch-queen rode directly toward a luminous throne of burning topaz, where a naked giant of a man sat, bearing the head of an elk.

"I am queen of the Daoine Síd," Ygrane announced dourly. "And you are one of my subjects."

The centroids of darkness that were the eyes of the elk-god visibly brightened. "I am no one's subject."

Ygrane's jaw tensed, all her patience eroded by her lavish menstrual pain. She lifted both arms above her head, made fists of her hands, and pulled them quickly to her sides. "Bring down the palace!" she ordered the Síd—and in that instant, the fiery walls, resplendent balustrades, bright columns, and archways collapsed to darkness. Dimly, a rimland of mesas and anvil shapes appeared, backlit by a scarlet glow.

Someone Knows the Truth fell from his vanished throne and landed on his haunches with a mighty groan. "Children of the hollow hills!" he shouted—then moaned when no reply came. "Why do you betray me?"

"You are not betrayed, Old One." Ygrane leaned forward upon the withers of her horned beast, teeth gnashed against the hurt cradled by her pelvis. "The Síd are as loyal to you as ever. But they are obedient first to their queen—and I am not happy with you."

"You are not happy?" Someone Knows the Truth bellowed and pushed to his feet, arms fisted at his sides. "Who are you to stand against me? You are a mortal woman, and I am god of the Wild Things, god since the time of ice!"

"The time of ice is long past." Ygrane spoke from her ulcerous pain. "And I am no common woman." Words came angrily, and she voiced them without thinking, believing that what she said did not matter so long as she expressed what was ripped, what was torn. "Through lifetimes far older than the ice, I have bled. What do you know of time? I have paid in blood since time stood on two legs." She straightened upon her beast and pulled achingly against the twisted knots in her belly. "You are as a child to me, elk-god. And I am not happy with you."

The furry chest of the god swelled, drawing breath to speak strongly to the Daoine Síd, but he stopped when he saw the witch-queen shake her pale head and gesture to the watchful dark. The pale people materialized in a spectral host, ranks and tiers of them in the darkness, a broken motley of shapes and echoes of shapes—leaf people, winged gazelles, human skulls with scaly flesh and eyes like spinning water, fleeting faces of the wind with brush sparks of lashing hair, and those thin, unraveled smiles.

The more that the god looked, the deeper he felt himself intertwining with the misty throng of the Síd. His own bestial humanity began to dissolve, drawn away from him into the squalid haze of phantasmal shapes. Dizziness seized him, and the astral crowd began screaming and jabbering excitedly to feel his glittering strength joining theirs. Their noise was a welter of monkey howls and chittering trills, and above it all, a sustained and eerie lilt of human singing.

Someone Knows the Truth covered his hairy ears and sagged to his knees.

"You *are* queen of the Daoine Síd," he acknowledged, antlers almost touching the ground. "Do not be angry with me, my lady. Spare my life, and I will serve you."

She fisted her hands over her sore womb. "You have held your form longer than most, Old One. But true power resides not in form. We are as shadows, all of us. The source of our being is the greater light that casts us into these lives, a light in whose radiance the sun is itself but a shadow."

"I will not forget, my lady." With the legions of luminous creatures crowding around him like seething fog, he pleaded, "How may I serve you?"

Ygrane wanted to ask that her husband be brought to her so that she might speak again with him and assure him that their son had become monarch of all Britain, that his sacrifice had been fulfilled. But the vibrant power of the unicorn dulled in her at the thought, and she knew that the echoes from the future did not rebound from that hope. She would never see Theo again.

"You serve me by serving the Daoine Síd," she informed the elk-god, then turned the black unicorn and rode away with her cramps through the shining mists of the animal powers.

Merlin placed the chaplet of gold laurel leaves at the center of the Round Table. In chairs engraved with dragons and unicorns sat the warriors Bors Bona, Urien, Kyner, Lot and his two sons, Gawain and Gareth. All apprehensively watched the bareheaded wizard pace before them, hands clasped at his back. None was at ease in the presence of this demonic being, and they listened unhappily to his account of the journey to the dragonpit.

Bors Bona, a small but powerfully built man with a face as stout and small-eyed as a boar's, lowered his gaze. He stared at his square hands pressed palm down upon the Table, so that only the flat top of his gray, brush-cut hair faced the wizard, and hid his dismay. "We are men, Merlin. We have gathered around our king to defend our island from invaders—Jutes, Picts, Angles, Scoti, and Saxons—men all. We are not sorcerers and necromancers suited to do battle with dragons." He lifted his pugnacious face and looked to Kyner. "Cei is a great warrior, yet he fell before a dragon. Is that to be the fate of us all?"

"We must slay the monsters!" Kyner shouted, and practically stood up. "We must answer Cei's suffering with death for all dragons!"

Bors conceded this with a reluctant nod and rubbed his square, beardless chin. "Can we not slay these creatures with our arrows? Must we hazard their breaths of flame?"

"Arrows have not sufficient concentration of metal to kill a dragon." Merlin placed his hands upon the back of an empty chair and slowly swung his craggy visage around the Table. "We leave soon for Londinium and the crucial conference of our king and the Foederatus. We have the word of King Wesc that no raiders will be set upon our shores during this meeting or immediately thereafter. But those are assurances given for Foederatus raiders. The dragons will swarm."

"We will be ready!" Kyner thumped the Table with his fist.

Lot parted the long white locks that had fallen over his face as he had dozed and blinked at the jowly, red-faced man pounding the Table beside him. "Who are you?" He glared at the stranger in the white tunic crossed in scarlet. The man appeared like a Celt, with his long mustaches and all else shaven from above the ears, his gray-streaked hair pulled to a horsetail topknot. But he wore the blood cross of the nailed god.

"Da!" Gawain leaned close to his father's ear. "This is Chief Kyner!"

"Kyner?" Lot's drooping white mustache puffed outward with a gust of surprise as he suddenly recognized the arctic-wolf eyes in the ruddy, sun-scarred face of the burly man beside him. "Nay, nay. You are too old. You are Kyner's father, Owain. You and I hunted the white bear in Cimmeria."

"Aye, you and Owain hunted the white bear in Cimmeria." The wolfish eyes in Kyner's russet face crinkled kindly. "He wore that giant snow fur the day he died in his lodge, three days after he was wounded defending Cymru against Scoti raiders. That was my nineteenth summer, and Owain was my father."

"Forty years ago," Gawain whispered in Lot's ear.

Lot nodded somberly, absorbing this.

Merlin came around behind the senile Celt and laid a long-fingered hand upon his shoulder. The wizard felt the vacuoles of forgetfulness in him, clustered chambers of a darker heart pumping emptiness through all the interstices, from the immense gaps between atoms to the spongiform darkness of intergalactic space. He was beyond the wizard's help.

Gawain and Gareth regarded Merlin hopefully until he shook his head and strolled away, hands clasped once again behind his back. The boys shared a knowing look. They had discussed this eventuality earlier. Merlin could not heal their ailing father, because his magic was demonic. They would have to find the

Holy Grail themselves and use it to serve Lot holy water and thus clear his mind.

Dressed in tunics that displayed a gold-wire circle enclosing a silver-studded cross, the brothers revealed their conversion to Christianity without alerting and offending their father. To him the Celtic cross was a primeval emblem of sun and earth, and its significance to his sons would only be disclosed to him, they decided, after the Grail had healed his mind. Until then, the boys made no public announcement of their new faith, though they wore tunics of soft lambskin, Gawain's stained maroon for the blood of the Christ and Gareth's pure white as the Savior's soul. God and His servants knew they were sincere: The day that they had arrived in Camelot with the news of their Grail vision, they had been baptized at midnight by Kyner and Bishop Riochatus while Lot snored in his suite.

"Where is No-Death?" Urien inquired, breaking the awkward silence. Naked above his braided belt and buckskin trousers, save for a shouldercloth of plaid, the chieftain of the Durotriges appeared restless in the high-backed chair. "Why is the legate not among us to hear of our plight?"

"The king has entrusted Excalibur to the legate," said Merlin as he paced slowly about the Round Table. "The holy emissary is presently in the chapel praying for our deliverance from the Beast he viewed in the hollow hills. He knows not whether it was Satan Himself or the most rare of God's creatures seen by mortal eyes."

Urien's white-blond hair fell across his face when he pressed forward upon the dark, lacquered Table. "Are you saying, wizard, that this minion of the nailed god yet refuses to request aid for us from his masters?" He stood up, ready to stride out of the council room. "I will go speak with No-Death, and we will have the Church's tribute."

"No, Urien." Kyner rose, jowls dark. "I am a Christian, and I will speak with the legate. My son put his life in the dragon's fire for love of our faith. He can deny us no longer!"

"Sit—" Merlin hissed the word softly, and the two Celts sat. "Grain and livestock are little good to our people if the meeting with Wesc turns against us. Until that is decided, we must defend our land from dragons. Marcus Dumnoni guards the south. Lot will remain here with Kyner to oversee the west. Bors, you shall hunt in the north. And Urien, you will escort the king to Londinium." The wizard stopped behind Gawain and Gareth. "As for the two of you, who have seen the Holy Grail, I have an important task for you to fulfill."

"We shall hunt dragons with the chieftains!" Gareth declared boldly, and Lot rapped his knuckles proudly and gave a hoarse laugh.

"Let us come with you that we may speak again to our uncle and discuss our vision with him once more," Gawain entreated Merlin, not flinching before the wizard's unearthly stare. "We have petitioned him since we arrived, and he has made no reply. We are his own kindred, nephews by his sole sister. Take us to see him, that he may understand that our lives are changed utterly by an angel of God."

Merlin nodded sagely. "Lads, the angel came to you, not to your uncle, by design. *You* are messengers. Arthur is your shield. Leave him to protect us so that you may reveal all of what God has disclosed to you."

"We have revealed all." Gawain's young, kestrel face darkened. At fourteen, he was as big as a man, and he wore his strawberry hair shaved to well above his ears and pleated across his crown in mystic knots like a warrior. "We would speak to the king about what must come of our vision. All the warriors of the Round Table should give themselves to the quest for the Savior's chalice. For Christian and Celt alike, this relic must be found."

"Yes!" Merlin clapped his hand upon the boy's thick shoulder and touched his soul, feeling how crushed it was under Morgeu's spell. Like white ivy, like almost-death, the young soul's true brightness was obscured, veiled by enchantment. "Your vision is valid and must be revealed not only to our king but to the pope himself." The wizard's head, bald, long, and speckled like an egg, intruded between the two boys, and his silver eyes slid side to side. The moment that he felt Morgeu's shadow in them, they had become prisoners of Camelot. "There are two drafting tables in the library behind the central hall. Go there and each of you write about your vision. Illustrate profusely. I will ask Fra Athanasius to assist you. Pay him heed. He is not only the papal legate, he is an experienced court scribe. With his help, you will create illuminated accounts that will convince our Holy Father that Britain is a true Christian isle. And when he sends the grain that saves us from famine, I will be there to see that the king and all the warlords praise you for saving Britain."

We are in a place between dreaming and wakefulness, between absence and presence, that is violated by travel. When the Furor kicked down the red door to our hut and stamped in, six of us lay on the dirt floor and three sat twisted in our block-cut chairs. Contact with the demon soul of Lailoken had nearly cast us out of our own bodies. We peered unhappily at the fierce chieftain with the storm gray beard.

The Furor advanced into our clay dome and saw the round windows like wells where he could drink deeply of sunlight. He saw the nine block-cut thrones of rowan wood arranged in an outward-facing circle. But he did not see us.

He strode mightily around the hut. On the earthen floor and curved wall of pastel spirals and flowing lines, shadows whispered yes and no as clouds sped across the sun. The one-eyed god stepped backward out the door, muttering oaths at the empty chamber.

We are in a place between dreaming and wakefulness, between absence and presence, that is violated by travel. Until you are here, there is no way to get here. Once you are here, there is no way out.

"I want to learn all your secrets," Selwa told Merlin in the western gallery where he received her. A ribbon window curved the length and breadth of the slate wall, facing the west quarter of the outer ward with its winding cobbled streets and rooftops of green and purple tiles. The wizard stood with his back to the afternoon, an angular silhouette among the potted mimosa trees. "For so long as you will teach me, Merlin, I will stay at your side and please you, attentively please you, in the manner for which I was trained in the seraglio of a Persian prince. He owed the house of Syrax a small fortune and repaid it by giving me a most excellent education."

The wizard regarded the petite and lithesome woman silently

for a moment. No guile showed in her large, obsidian eyes. Those windows opened on elemental feelings he recognized as sincere—avarice, yearning for mastery, hunger for power—and he inspected again her outer form. She wore a long silk robe of green moons and nightingales. She parted that raiment and revealed, behind a sheer gown of creamy white gauze, the cinnamon shadows of her breasts, the antelope curve of her belly, and the dark tuft below.

"You are beautiful," he said, removing his peaked hat. He stepped to the side so that the window light fell full upon his strange countenance: metallic eyes in skullpits, a swerved blade of a nose, and a forked beard drooping like catfish whiskers. "And I am grotesque."

"Who you are is beautiful to me." Her fingers languorously touched the bone dents of his temple and the long ridge of his maxilla. "You are the greatest wizard who has ever lived."

"I am a demon locked by angels in this lurid body." He ran his knobby hand over his long, sallow pate, his scalp blotched brown and ocher, a map of mysterious countries. "I am growing younger each year—as a man. And as a man, I suffer the physical cravings of any man. But for now I am not young enough in the flesh to win affection by my appearance. And I am sworn on my good mother's soul never to use my demon powers for ill—and surely it would be grievous ill to persuade any woman to embrace me."

Selwa stepped close enough for him to smell the sumptuous fragrance of her glistening curls and the minty spice of her breath. "Embrace me then, Merlin. The angels meant for you to be a man. And to live fully as a man, you must know a woman."

Merlin reached into her mind once more with penetrating clarity and confirmed her greedy urgency for magic. No demons lurked within, and no enchantments lay upon her. She was simply a mortal woman with the audacious notion of giving herself to him for his capitulated knowledge. "You are not appalled by my hideous form?"

"Hideous?" She stroked the long white hair above his gristly ears. "You who have lived since creation first forged stars and firmament—you are not hideous in my eyes. You are unsurpassable! The angels themselves have shaped you, and you are a virile form, most august and terrible as the knowledge you bear. Share that knowledge with me, Merlin, and I am yours, in body and deed."

Athanasius knelt in an alcove of the chapel lit by red glass oil lamps. Excalibur stood unsheathed in his hand, rays in every hue of fire fanning from its naked blade. Since the king had entrusted him with the royal sword, the legate had kept the sheathed weapon under his clerical robes. The journey into the under-world had left him shaken and determined to flee Britain and its demon-wizard, gods, and dragons. He would have departed from Banovallum on the Fenlands in a bull-hide boat with one oar and no provisions, risking Belgic pirates and Saxon raiders to get back to any Christian realm—war-torn Trier, remote Bordeaux, or even the slums of Rome. But the king stopped him by giving him his sword. That was a trust he dared not betray before God, even on the frontiers of hell.

Huddled in the holy darkness, he gazed with endless aston-ishment into the blade's flawless mirror. He turned the airy sword in his hand, and reflections spun around him bright and quick as birdsongs. He observed a light within the light, where the reflected world of lampflames, statuary, window lights, his whiskery face, and star-thistle eyes hung like tattered muslin.

Beyond this shaggy scrim, light drenched itself. A voluptuous ocean of light, where all his thoughts drowned in transparencies of brightness and his whole life floated before him like a great lesson.

Not until later did his thoughts return, in the indigo darkness of his canopy bed with Excalibur sheathed and lying lengthwise atop him, his hands crossed over it in funereal composure. Then he remembered who he was and who the Church had made him, and he told himself that his vision of drowning in light was a spirit visitation. His master, the drowned bishop Victricius, was praying for him in heaven, and his prayers had inundated him in grace. He was sure of it.

I am not to flee, he believed, and reflected on the smallness of his soul adrift in God's light, his whole life a great lesson, an illumi-nating experience for his immortal self. *This vision fixedly confirms me. I am to stay here 'mongst what I fear and do not understand—and I am to learn.*

Athanasius convinced himself that his mission, his suffering, and perhaps even his death in this hinterland, were sponsored from heaven. And Victricius continued as his teacher, even before the face of God. To fulfill that good bishop's work in this world, he determined to remain in Britain and to use all his faculties to answer the problem originally posed to Victricius by the Holy Father: *Is Britain blessed—or damned?*

The draperies of the canopy ripped away, torn off as by a gale wind, and Loki jumped onto the bed. Screaming with garish pain, he reared over the legate. His wild face was stenciled once more with futhorc sigils in a vain attempt to drive away the demon pursuing him. The bedchamber had filled instantly with the demon's ichorous heat and the cries of a razorous wind, and above these shrieks, Loki bawled, "Give me the sword!"

Athanasius squealed and rolled over the scabbard, cringing with fright.

Loki seized the back of the legate's sleeping gown and lifted him off the bed. "Give me the cursed sword!"

"Merlin!" the scribe yelled.

The chamber doors burst open with a radiant gush, and the wizard, bareheaded and draped in a leather chemist's apron, stalked in, waving a torch. The flames flared larger in the fetid atmosphere and blazed green, as Merlin shouted, "Loki, release him!"

Loki dropped Athanasius onto the bed and, with his gloved hands clutching his bald head, threw himself at the wizard's sandals. "Help me, Merlin! Get the demon off me!"

Merlin swung the torch over his head, his wispy beard and tangled white hair brushed back by the vortex force he released from the gates of his body. Using the brails of his heart, he snatched the demon out of the thick heat and with one blow from the torch dressed him in fire.

"Succoth!" He recognized the warped limbs and chewed visage of his former accomplice from the void. "I break the Furor's hold on you! Go back to the abyss! Now!"

A frigid pallor descended from the groined ceiling, and the cutting wind ceased abruptly. In the ensuing icy stillness, the flame-woven demon crackled, "Lailoken—traitor—we will chew your bones . . ."

With a backhanded swipe of the torch, Merlin smashed the

fiery shape to dazzling dust. The sparkles billowed to emptiness, and the frigid pall dispersed.

"Sweet blessed Jesus, pray for us in this furious moment of trial!" Athanasius prayed ardently, clutching the sheathed sword to his chest with both hands.

"I will take Excalibur now," the wizard declared, and removed the sword from the legate's grasp. "I leave soon for Londinium, where the king will require his sword. I am sorry that this responsibility has cost you such a fright."

"I am not stony-livered enough for life in Camelot," the legate admitted, glad to see Excalibur taken from him. "For my happy deliverance from the spoiler of souls, I will spend the night in prayer to our Savior."

"Pray to Merlin." Loki spoke with awe, peering up from where he lay on the carpet and seeing no demonic sparks other than the silver pins in the skull sockets of the wizard. "It is Merlin who saved us." He pushed to his knees. "Succoth *is* gone?"

"I snapped the Furor's bond with him." The fluttering torchlight rippled over the pits and rills of Merlin's long face. "Succoth will fall for a while through the blind depths. But soon enough he will come to his senses and report to the others—and to the Furor. Loki, your presence in Camelot will not long be secret. Why did you draw Succoth here?"

Loki looked hurt as he pushed to his feet. "I grew impatient waiting for you, Merlin. You abandoned me." He glanced into the shadowy corners of the chamber and shivered, still hearing the demon's echoing cries in his bones. "I called for the Fire Lords—and Succoth came instead."

Merlin scowled irately and grabbed Loki's ear. "Come with me. You have jeopardized us all. Now I must find a place to keep you until we are ready to climb the Storm Tree."

"Ouch!" Loki grabbed the wizard's wrist but did not dare pull the hand away or shapeshift, fearing he might be cast out among the demons. "Let me go. I will come with you freely. I have much to tell you of my flight through Yggdrasil—onto the Branch of Hours and into times yet to be. I thought to lose the demon, but he followed and chased me back here. Ouch! Release me, Merlin. I must tell you of the Tree . . . the Branch of Hours . . . and the phantom worlds. Ouch!"

The wizard led the tattooed god out the door by his ear, and

Athanasius sat in bed watching, appalled. Torchlight faded down the corridor, and darkness closed over the disheveled chamber.

Cei lay in silk windings on a pallet under the ivy spills of a terrace wall at the north side of Camelot. There the sun did not touch his blistered face nor the moon glare across his swollen eyes. By day, mountain breezes bodied forth clouds above the gorges and laved him with conifer fragrances. At nightfall, veils were drawn about the pallet and braziers of scented woods sifted through the starlight.

A surgeon, a priest, and a harp player attended Cei at all times, yet he remained unresponsive. Three times a day, the surgeon inserted a tube down the seneschal's throat and fed him broth and herbal infusions. The bedding was changed regularly, and the scorched body anointed with plasters Merlin had devised of willow seepings, spongy blue moss, and duckweed. But this had no more obvious effect than the prayers or music that graced the terrace.

Cei hovered free of his burned body. He rose past slick cascades of ivy and looked back at green flagstones grouted with yellow moss—and a pallet with bed linens folded like white petals around a bandaged figure with his face.

The more he looked at himself, the more he felt the gummy pain, viscously stretched over the length of his body. Every movement was dragonfire. He threw his attention outward, away from the terrace and his suffering, and he soared across the sky's blue gulf.

A gilded barge with crimson gunwales and an ivory hull floated placidly in its moorings at a river wharf crowded with pavilion tents and awnings. Cei recognized the royal barge and the pebble shoals and silver birch groves at the headlands of the Tamesis River, the waterway that flowed to Londinium. *Arthur's meeting with Wesc!*

With that loud thought, Cei found himself wandering in the memory forest under a bewitching moon of dreams. The shadowy runes on the face of the moon spelled *raidho—mannaz*, journey—step back. All around him, shades of his past closed in: Wolf Warriors in scalp cloaks, his mother at White Thorn, only much younger with her wheat gold hair twisted over one naked shoulder as she breast-fed him, and there was Arthor the boy, six summers old, cheeks smudged, huffing to keep up with the dogs as he lugged quivers, bows, and water flagons, a good servant on a quail hunt . . .

Cei began to pray, and despair came on like a star when he could not remember the words to any of his prayers. The phantoms circled closer. Berserkers hoisting battle-axes, Bishop Riochatus swinging the chain of a fuming censer, bent crones lopping grassheads with their short scythes, and the rasping coils of a dragon slid in and out of sight among the memory trees.

Each tree was an interval of forgetfulness in his exiled mind. When he threw himself at one and pressed his face against its trunk to avoid looking at the wraiths lifting around him like sea mist, he entered not-knowing, the darkness of dreamless sleep. For a while he rested. Upon awaking, he floated out of his body again and slipped up the ivy wall onto a blue causeway cobbled with clouds.

Descending over the pebble shoals of the Tamesis, he watched the royal barge sliding downriver. The gilt naiads at the prow with their unbound hair painted in gold flake gleamed in the sunlight above the frothy wake. He wove among the red-and-white pennants streaming from the rail spars and glided above the blue caps of the bearded bargemen.

Under a tasseled canopy emblazoned with the royal eagle, Merlin and Selwa sat together on a divan of dove gray velvet secured to the observation platform. She lay curled against the wizard, her glossy black tresses spilling over his shoulder. Pastels of diaphanous veils and the silk netting of a bathing thong hid little of her dusky beauty.

Simultaneously inflamed with sudden desire and cold with astonishment to see horrid Merlin so embraced, Cei looked away. His attention shot beyond the billowy coppices at the riverside to fields and hedgerows where hearthsmoke wreathed farmsteads. The bosky obscurities calmed him, and he drifted high over the river through clouds like hanging gardens, like powers of angels.

6

Beauty Shines Invisible

Bedevere woke on a terrace, ocean mist and valerian scenting the air. A cloud of pain filled him. Rolling his head to one side, he faced a prospect of seacliffs clothed with pine forests and primrose glades. "Tintagel," he mumbled, recognizing the majestic headlands.

"He awakes," a woman's voice called forth softly. Distantly, chimes glittered and dogs barked. A nun in a white habit bent over him with a moist cloth fragrant with myrrh, and she smiled and daubed at his crusty eyes.

The barking dogs grew louder. The nun whispered a blessing and stepped aside. Chalk pillars coiled with vines framed the maritime view. There stood the silhouette of a man with shaven cheeks and a stout chest cased in a jerkin of silver studs. A large dalmatian sat to either side of him, and when he stepped closer he revealed a square-jawed face and ruffled hair blond as a hay nest.

"Duke Marcus . . ."

"Be still, Bedevere." The warlord showed no dismay as he regarded the burned man, though his stomach winced at the sight of the blisters that nubbled the blackened face, blisters like seed pearls. "The nuns found you on the strand, washed ashore during the night. We've sent news of your arrival to Camelot."

Bedevere sat up, and pieces of light swarmed across his vision until he lay back down again. "The Grail," he husked, relieved that his tongue was less swollen. "I found the Holy Grail!"

"I doubt you not." Marcus spoke soothingly and adjusted upon the scorched man's head the wreath of blue spikenard that the nuns had woven to help him sleep. "But tell me first of the king. Where is Arthur?"

"With Merlin." His eyes gleamed from under their eaves of charred darkness. "In the hollow hills."

"Why are you not at his side?"

Bedevere grimaced, remembering. "Merlin forbade me to go with the king. I left Camelot . . . expelled by shame." He raised a glossy hand to his trembling lips and confessed in a tremulous whisper, "Lord Marcus, I . . . my past is revealed to all by Athanasius . . ."

"Say no more of that, Bedevere." Marcus laid a comforting hand upon the shoulder of the swordsman's missing arm. "I ask not of your past, and you need not tell. I've heard enough of that from the minstrels and gleemen who delight in parading sordid news from Camelot."

"You are not offended at my presence?"

"We fought together on fields of battle with the king, and I know you for a brave warrior. All else is between you and God." Marcus bent closer. "Now, tell me—who burned you? Brigands? Wolf Warriors?"

"A dragon."

Marcus cocked an eyebrow and retracted his chin.

"It guarded the Chapel Perilous," Bedevere insisted, straining to lift his head and deliver his conviction directly into the duke's skeptical eyes. "I slew it and took the Grail."

"A dragon?" A crease of sadness deepened across Marcus's brow. "Bedevere, there are no dragons."

"The king slew a dragon outside Ratae. I killed one in Crowland, and it burned me."

Marcus fixed him with a stern look and spoke harshly, hoping to jolt him free of his delusion. "You are distraught. The anguish that drove you from Camelot has distorted your memory. Raiders or a woodland gang torched you. Remember."

"I found the Holy Grail, I tell you." The one-armed man sagged back onto the couch, defeated by his pain and exhaustion. His voice dimmed. "A dragon guarded it, and I slew the beast."

"Rest now, Bedevere." Marcus straightened and motioned

for the attending nun to approach and continue her healing ministrations. "Rest, and we will talk more later."

"No." Bedevere's hand clasped the duke's wrist. "You must believe me. There are dragons in the land. Many have seen them. Surely, you have heard reports."

"These are dire times." Marcus pried away Bedevere's hand. "The gleemen sing of dragons. Traveling tinkers whisper of them. But neither I nor anyone here at Tintagel has seen such a beast."

Bedevere fell as abruptly into sleep as a body into the dark earth. The airy part of him rose like a gravepit vapor, and he floated outside of his flesh. He looked down at his blisters, bright as gems against his seared skin. Buoyant as a fragrance, he drifted away. The nun beside his couch, white as a moth wing against the black bough of his body, dwindled as he slipped through the rafters of purpling valerian and hovered on the seawind.

Hours poured from the cup of the day moon before he understood that he was not dreaming. Time had become something new. The sea washing its laundry among the black rocks under the cliffs had enthralled him until he realized he was not inside a dream. Time was a kingdom of light, its riches hammered to gold upon the ocean and spun to opulent threads in the loom of the forest. Under the tall columns of white clouds, he could be anywhere at all. He flew with feathers of sea mist over the limestone turrets of Tintagel, eager to find his way back to his physical form.

But the pain of his blistered flesh drove him away from his comatose body, while the fear of the sky's undertow pulling him into nonexistence lured him down into the great yew avenues and oak-houses of the forests north of Tintagel. He was attracted to his clothing that Duke Marcus had taken with him into the woods as a scent marker for his dogs.

The duke knew that Bedevere was no fool. If the one-armed master swordsman claimed he had been burned by a dragon, then Marcus determined to see what manner of beast roamed the land. With Bedevere's charred clothing to inspire his dogs, the duke and three lancers followed the dalmatians north. By day's end, they arrived at a grove of evergreen magnolias. Bright citrus rays shone through the trees while the hunters searched about for a glade in which to bivouac for the night.

Bedevere's shade bobbed past them, following the excited dogs under the twilight jellies toward a knoll of black hemlock. He knew what lurked there. A dragon lay curled among the pines, waiting for the hateful sun to set. Bedevere tried to stop the dogs. He waved his arms and shouted. But he was a ghost, and the animals did not sense him as they bounded over the knoll.

With their broken yelps and shrill cries behind him, Bedevere flew back toward the duke and his men. The tide of night flowed with him. Moonlight like glue pasted the black cutouts of trees to the silver darkness as he swept toward the horsemen, who were shouting and whistling for the dogs. He danced and pranced and tumbled before them, but they did not see him.

And then the dragon came. The ground quaked, and pine needles sizzled from the drought trees. Two of the lancers were thrown from their mounts, and the duke fought with both arms to steady his steed. A sump stench thickened in the darkness, and then an evil shape reared against the white fires of Spica and Arcturus in the western sky, an eclipsing behemoth among the steadfast stars.

"Jesus, Lord and Savior!" Marcus cried out.

A blue flame blazed above the treetops, illuminating a gaping maw wide as a sunset. Clusters of fangs flashed, razorpoints of stars in an ulcerous visage of lizard jaws hung with wattles of torn flesh. Under a barbed brow, eyes of smoky blood glared, and the roar that followed sent clods of torn tree bark flying like startled birds.

The first stroke of dragonfire smote the treetops in a lightning blast that ignited the stand of dry evergreens. Through the wall of flame, the dragon crashed, and its second gust of blue fire combusted a thousand autumns of fallen leaves.

The thrown lancers abandoned their weapons and leaped upon their horses. Marcus drove them ahead and charged after, bawling for them to, "Run! Run to the sea!"

In tatters of inky blackness, the dragon spread its wings, blotting whole constellations. It swooped overhead, whipping flames, sparks, and dead leaves into vortices that ran alongside the galloping horses and their terrified riders. Bellowing another cry, the dragon's talons seized the lead runner, plucking the lancer in one claw and the horse in the other, and hoisted them into the night's crystal darkness. Their screams were lost in the concussion of the roar, but moments later gobbets of flesh, lopped limbs, and slashed viscera rained down upon the duke and his men.

"Into the trees!" Marcus shouted, and the riders plunged off the forest trail into the woods' dark alcoves.

Wings whistling like a stormwind, the dragon dived. Blue flames sheeted the trees, and the crisp forest exploded. Tree trunks burst, scattering hot fléchettes of burning wood in fiery arcs. With a horrified scream, one of the lancers' horses tripped and fell, and before it could rise, the blazing canopy collapsed over it, immolating steed and rider.

Marcus and the remaining lancer shot out of the woods onto the highway two lengths ahead of a surging firecloud. They rode full out, hugging their horses necks, not daring to twist a look toward the deadly sky. Moonsmoke flowed upon the sea as they came across the moors.

Overhead, the dragon circled. Occasionally, its roars swelled out of the night, and the riders cringed. But the demon beast did not stoop to kill. It glided on the high wind mesmerized by a sensation akin to the power that had created it. Bedevere's ghost lay upon its horned head, singing to the rageful creature. While neither dogs nor men could hear him, the dragon did. It heard him singing "Grandma and the Widower" and "I Have No Money for My Ale to Pay" and other ditties, and it was soothed.

Bedevere wished he had known sooner the power that his phantom songs exerted upon the dragon, so he could have saved the two lancers. At least, the duke and the third lancer were spared certain death. The disembodied man kept his focus upon his singing until the horsemen reached the citadel of Tintagel. Then he dared quiet himself and listen.

The dragon's congealed face of scabs and leprous sores appeared like a battle mask battered by a hundred years of enmity, and it moved Bedevere to pity. He heard a drowsy music within the beast, a melodious form of divination that carried this dragon's hideous will within a larger will—the dreamsong of the Dragon at the center of the planet. Hearing a dim echo of that energy, the ghost experienced an implacable clarity expanding within him, widening him toward a unity of existence. If he went with it, he knew he would enlarge beyond himself. And he broke away.

Night rushed across the enormous edge of time.

Bedevere jolted awake. He was inside his body again, inside his pain. Nearby, nuns were chanting vespers. And in the distance, from somewhere in the fastness, Duke Marcus shouted with distress.

Flesh and shadow—for thousands of years, we were both. Then, we peered into Merlin's demon depths, and our trance was broken. We Nine Queens fell back into our lives on the edge of time. For an interval we became again as you are, mortal, ephemeral, each of us a consciousness exiled in pain and unknowing.

How do you go on?

Knowing what we know, having witnessed for thousands of years the same pains, hungers, and ignorances of people, we gaped at each other and wanted to die. We did not want to live as human animals ever again. We wanted to die into emptiness, into absolute forgetfulness.

But then, you go on, because you have not seen all that we have seen, over and over and over again—the same cruelties of murder, rape, and despair—over and over and over again. None of the living has witnessed these eternal hostilities with our clarity, and so you go on, perpetrators of evil and victims of ignorance, believing your crimes and your sufferings are unique to you.

That is why love fails.

And that is why, deprived of the Fire Lords' power, we felt ruined. We knew everything. And so little of it was good.

The sun blazed in the doorway to our round and earthen hut. Not the sun. A Fire Lord. His radiance penetrated our stunned bodies and burned away our despair. Once again, we were lifted above the mystic biology of pain to our vantage outside time. And from there, we saw the living souls of Europe like grains of sand before us, each grain a tiny, magnifying lens revealing to our unblinking minds the redundant malice, suffering, and loss—Yet, we also saw what could comfort us: the dreams from where your strength comes—the compelling reason you go on—

the dreams, the hopes, the ambitions of the pitiless love that is life.

"John Halt is the king, I tell you," Leoba said to her sister as they drew water at the tile-canopied well in the kitchen yard outside The Blanket of Stars. The drum-windlass that had been installed by the king's workers made easy work of lifting the heavy bucket that before had caused the simple pulley to whine and groan; even the small, strawberry-haired girl had no difficulty raising the three-gallon container. She rested it on the stone lip of the well, opened its spigot, and began filling terra-cotta carafes for the guest rooms. "Think on it, Julia. He's of an age to the king and shows a leg wound."

"A thousand boys in the land are of an age to the king and a hundred of them got leg wounds," Julia countered, fitting the filled carafes into a push wagon festively painted with starlings and garlands. "And if he were king, where are his soldiers? The king goes nowhere without his men. Not with gangs on the highways and raiders in the woods."

"Ask him then, why don't you?" Leoba challenged. She topped off the last of the carafes, placed a wood lid atop the bucket, and left it on the well ledge for guests to help themselves. "He talks right proper, and Georgie says his horse got noble lines, a sorrel courser fit for the upper cut, not a merchant's boy."

Julia laughed and pushed the cart to the kitchen. There was much to laugh about: Every room of the inn was filled and paid for in advance by ironwork guildsmen on their way to Londinium for the grand conference of King Arthur and the pagan lord, Wesc. These guests would carry glad reports of the handsomely renovated buildings and grounds at The Blanket of Stars, and there would be no lack of business ever again. Only the absence of her beloved Eril left a stain upon her heart. He had paid in blood for the king's craftsmen and their materials.

"Leoba thinks you're King Arthur," Julia informed John Halt when she came through the hanging leather strips that guarded the kitchen door from flies. "What say you to that charge, John?"

John Halt did not look up from the chopping block where

he minced chives with a cleaver. "Leoba is right, of course. I was unhappy in Camelot and thought to ease my soul by chopping vegetables and washing dirty linens at your fine inn. She's an observant lass."

Julia laughed again and ladled dishwater into the window boxes of cooking herbs flourishing on the sunny sills of the long casements. "Why are you here with us, John?"

"I'm the king, even as Leoba says, and I'm hiding from my woes." He smiled at her, happy to tell her the truth. The upcoming confrontation with King Wesc and the ascent into the Storm Tree to end Cei's suffering were burdens that felt lighter in her easy company, accomplishing small tasks, living much in the same manner he had known when he was Kyner's thrall in White Thorn, before magic had made him a king—and an incestuous sinner. "I'm also here to court you, Julia. I want you to be my wife and to live with me in Camelot."

More laughter poured from her, and she set about stirring the stewpots and sauce pans simmering on the gridiron charcoal stove. "As if God and the king have not already got everything for me I want—short of my Eril back in my arms." The laughter drained from her, and sadness imposed an inner watchfulness over her strong and freckled face. "But heaven has received my Eril. A hero for the king, he is. And I'm right proud of him. So, if he is in heaven, and you are the king, how will you woo me?"

"With the best oysters from Rameslie," he answered at once. "And a dozen robust sunsets at Land's End. And our own houseboat on the Nith River."

"No gold?" Julia feigned surprise. "No fine perfumes from Persia? And a palace in the Eildon Hills with valets and footmen?"

John Halt laid down the cleaver, and answered earnestly, "When you are queen, you will see that those things are far less enjoyable than the simple pleasures. That's why I'm here."

"Ah, then you *must* be king to appreciate a simple woman like me." She gave a self-mocking laugh and tossed a pinch of salt into the soup. "If you add to the bargain the sharpest cheese from Droitwich, I will be your queen."

Julia's father entered the kitchen with a peck of elecampane roots to be pared and diced for the stew. He made no secret of his ambition that John Halt would take fifteen-year-old Leoba for his wife. The older man admired the youth for his courage, his eloquence, and his industry despite his war injury, and wanted him for his son-in-law.

At every opportunity, he paired them, but with the inn full, there was so much work to do that tasks quickly separated them. By night, after the galley was cleaned, the dining hall cleared, and all the guests had drunk their fill and sung themselves hoarse under the stars in the atrium and gone to bed, John Halt and the innkeeper's family were too exhausted to mingle.

Dreamless sleep soothed Arthur. He was happy at The Blanket of Stars and hopeful that, if he could convince Wesc to forestall the pagan invasion and if he succeeded in working the magic that his mother, the witch-queen, had devised to protect Britain, he would be free to make Julia his wife. Then there would be no more of magic in his life, he swore to himself. He would rule by charity and love with a woman at his side who knew from hard experience, as did he, the everyday needs of the people.

In the dark before dawn, John Halt rose from his straw pallet in the granary and, with the scythe pole he used as a crutch, limped to the woodshed to gather birch bark and straw. The earth oven outside the kitchen had to be fired early to bake the day's bread, and during his stay he had taken this task upon himself.

Leoba, roused earlier by her father and sent to intercept John Halt, awaited him by the domed oven, arranging hazelwood tinder in the fire hole. "You are the king, ain't you?" She squinted at him in the gray light from where she squatted, her loose hair straying across her face in the dawn breeze. "You're King Arthur."

John Halt threw the bark and straw into the fire hole and leaned full upon the scythe pole. "I don't think you much like me, Leoba."

"I liked Eril," she said almost without moving her lips. "He was a kindly man. He took us in. That he did. He gave us this home. And the king killed him."

"He died in war, Leoba." Among the jointed shadows of the vineyard, morning mist drifted like wraiths. "A lot of people died in that war."

"So that you might be king." She withdrew a tinder pouch from the ample pocket of her frock. "You should be in Camelot. Why do you want to live with us common folks?"

"I'm happy here, Leoba." He gestured to his common tunic and rope sandals. "I grew up a thrall in Chief Kyner's clan, and I'm more at ease in a stable than a stateroom."

"There are lots of stables in Britain. Why are you here with us then?" she asked, striking a spark with flint and firesteel.

"I love your sister."

"I know that." Red light jerked in her eyes from the combusting torchwood. "I seen you looking at her, smiling at her, touching her. I told Da that. He says you ain't old enough to know what you want. He wants you for me."

"I'll wager you already have someone you love."

"And he loves me, too, Tom does." She stoked the kindling until the hazelwood took the flames. "Not that we see each other much since you fixed this place up and brought in the caravans."

"I didn't fix it up, Leoba." Standing crooked, spiked hair awry against the right and God-made stars, he looked every inch the peasant he claimed to be. "The king's men did this work. And there's so much more work to do for this inn to be successful. Why don't you ask your Tom to serve here at The Blanket of Stars? You could use the help."

"He works here already." Leoba pointed to a hillside beyond the orchards where a herd floated like fog. "They're his. Them sheep. Well, his da watches them for my da. But Tom tends them, he does."

John Halt shifted his weight on the scythe pole and turned about in the plum light. "I'm leaving soon. Perhaps your father will ask Tom to work in the inn with you."

"Them sheep were bought for my da with the king's coin." She stood, hands on her hips, her jaw irately thrust to one side. "Now Da thinks Tom ain't good enough for me no more. Da wants the likes of you."

Julia called from the kitchen for Leoba to bring charcoal, and the young woman shoved past John Halt to reach the coal bin.

The busy day left no time for further talk about personal ambitions for any of the workers. The caravan of guildsman packed to leave early that morning, and by midafternoon another caravan had arrived, textile merchants from the north cities on their way to the port city of Noviomagus to ship their wares during the lull of hostilities from the coming negotiations. The day's work was not done until near midnight.

John Halt lay weary on his pallet when the granary door opened narrowly and admitted a shadow figure against the flare of stars.

"Leoba says you leave us soon." Julia spoke in the round darkness. "Is that so?"

"Aye." John Halt sat up in the dark and felt Julia settle beside him on the pallet. "I must finish the work my master has given me to do. I stopped here first to be with you, Julia—to see if you would have me for your husband."

She pressed her face close to his, and he smelled the kitchen smoke in her hair as she whispered tenderly, "You're yet a beardless boy, John."

"I'm eighteen years old this month." He dared put his arm around her waist, and she did not object. "You're but two years older."

"I'm a married woman," she said, and covered his hand on her hip with hers. "I gave myself to another man."

"Your vows are not wider than death."

"But is my Eril dead?" She turned in his embrace and put both hands on his shoulders. "I've seen not body or grave."

"I'm not asking you to marry me at once." Noses almost touching, they gazed at each other, eyes glimmering like vague stars subjugate to the dark. "If you will have me, we will wed in the spring. It will be a full year since the war. If Eril is not returned to you by then, he would not want you to wait."

Her nose did touch his, playfully. "How do you know that?"

"I love you, and if I were gone a year from your side, I would not want you to wait for me." His voice carried sad certitude. "From all you've said of him, I know he loved you as much and would feel the same."

"How can you say you love me, John?" She sighed and gently pushed him away. "You hardly know me."

He would not let her go and urged her closer. "That's why I stayed here, to know you better. And now I know for sure."

"And now you know for sure, my beardless boy?" Her laugh shimmered, then fell suddenly quiet. Her breathing sounded close to panting. "You know you want this woman who has given her heart to another man?"

"You're a woman who can give her heart, and that's what I love about you, Julia." He drew her close to him, his strong arms tight about her. "I want you to give your heart to me. I want that, and I will do whatever I have to do to win your heart."

"And Leoba?" she asked when he released her. "Da wants you for her, you know."

"Leoba wants nothing to do with me. She's for Tom."

"And what a happy family we'll be then—you and me, Tom and Leoba, and father and Georgie." She laughed again, and his heart swelled in his chest with the joy he heard in her voice. "We'll make The Blanket of Stars the best inn in Britain, won't we?" She gently brushed his hair back and kissed his forehead, slowly and with passion. Then she stood up to leave. "Let me think on your love, my beardless boy. Let me think on all this, and we'll talk again, won't we? When will you be back?"

"When I can." He rose, put his hands to the sides of her face, and spoke to the stars that were her eyes. "And if I'm gone more than a year—don't wait for me."

Morgeu the Fey squatted in the dry, fragrant mists of Skidblade, the flying machine's control lights clicking their bright colors in her wide stare. An ocean divided her life. On one shore, her baby Mordred cried for her from Brokk's island guarded by the wolf-ogre Garm. On the other, she trembled, a speck of dust, a shivering mote in the radiance of the Fire Lord who had crossed the universe to confront the Furor. The backs of her eyes still ached from her glimpse of that fiery angel.

Morgeu commanded Skidblade to take her to her mother. As if the world were a thought, the portal sighed open on a drowsy dazzle of daylight in an ivy grove enclosed by mossy trunks of rowans. A black unicorn lay in the bracken under a broken rain-bow, its tusked head turned toward her, its opal blue eyes watching, dream-free and attentive.

Ygrane sat on the cracked clay floor among drifts of leaves, white butterflies opening and closing themselves in her cupped hands. She smelled of the hollow hills, a pungency of cauterized stone. Her mind had been deep in contemplation, pondering the best way for her to climb into the Storm Tree unseen, when Skidblade stole the birdsongs from the forest and flashed between the trees like raucous sunshine. No joy lit her long eyes at the sight of her daughter.

"Mother, I need your help." Morgeu threw herself onto the glade's hard floor, arms outstretched before her. "The Furor has taken my baby and holds him captive on Brokk's island."

"Who is to blame for that, Morgeu?" The butterflies scattered from Ygrane, world wanderers once again. "You saw with me that the Holy Graal has been stolen away to that island—and you went there yourself, did you not?"

"Mother, I only thought to broker a bargain for the chalice," the enchantress whined. "That evil dwarf Brokk is using it to direct the Furor's demons and create dragons from the dreams of the one Dragon. Why should Britain suffer? Let us come to an agreement with the Furor, I thought . . ."

"You thought to usurp Arthur." Ygrane spoke dryly. "But the Furor is not to be bargained with, is he?"

"Mother, don't do this to me." Morgeu beat her fists against the clay, her face pressed to the ground. "If you will help me in this, I will never again oppose you—or Arthur. Help me get my baby back, and Mordred and I will swear fealty to the king."

And Ygrane thought: *She deceives herself. But—how could she not? Her mind is twisted around her grief for her father, the very soul she has captured again in Mordred with her incest magic. She will say anything to get him back.*

"Speak to me, Mother!" Morgeu lifted a smudged face tracked with tears. "Don't stare at me so coldly. Mordred is your grandson. And he is held on the same island as the chalice. Come with me now in Skidblade. With your authority over the Síd, we can free my baby and take the Graal from Brokk. That is what you want, isn't it?"

"Yes," spoke a darkly gleaming voice. "That is what our queen wants. And this is our opportunity to fulfill our blood pact with her." From the shadow depths between the rowans stepped a tall man with florid red hair and green eyes. His torso and legs appeared transparent, weirdly empty and blue as the deep sky, and like the air's endless nowhere, a luminous being who, for all his light, was as much nothing as darkness.

This startling apparition rolled Morgeu onto her haunches. She had never seen him before, yet she knew who he was from legend. "You are the elf prince—" She studied him as his empty body, his slender figure with its suggestions of effeminacy, took on the figurations of a blue tunic, red leggings, and yellow boots.

"I am Prince Bright Night." Behind him, in the forest's dark alcoves, glinted lizard eyes, candled skulls, and wide scarlet animal grins. "I speak for the host of the Daoine Síd."

The resonant voice touched Morgeu's spine with a torpor that almost rolled her onto her back. Only her training as an enchantress kept her from slipping instantly into trance. "Mother—"

"Leave her be, Bright Night." Ygrane tossed a twig at the elf prince, and it passed cleanly through him. "She distracts us from our purpose."

"Distracts us?" Bright Night glared with incomprehension and gestured to the cold disc of palpitant light shining between the trees, like fire fallen from the planet heavens. "There is our passage to the sacred cup we seek. Let us seize this opportunity at once and complete our quest."

"If we enter Skidblade," Ygrane warned, "we will become as imprisoned to the Furor's will as she is."

Bright Night's shoulders sagged, and he cast an unhappy look at Morgeu. "Is this true? Are you bound to the Furor?"

"Don't play the fool, Bright Night." Ygrane nodded to Morgeu. "Tell him from where you have come."

"Avalon," she answered before she could help herself. Her mother's power was too strong to resist. It reached into her like a cold wind and gripped her viscera. "The Furor made me chant a binding spell upon the Nine Queens. And a Fire Lord came—"

Bright Night stepped back into the rowan depths of the ivy glade, afraid of the Fire Lords, those luminous entities alive beyond beginning.

Ygrane placed her focus upon her uterine cramps, anchoring herself with her pain so that her excitement did not betray her intent to Morgeu. *The Furor is hunting the Fire Lords!* she grasped, excitedly. *Now is the time to climb into Yggdrasil. Now is the time to find for Arthur the way to the Vanir Lotus.*

"Mother, please—my baby Mordred . . ." Morgeu entreated.

But Ygrane was already on her feet. The frightful carnival of faerïes, hobs, sprites, and elves in the woods began rushing through the forkings of the trees like windblown mist, like a storm front rising into the sky. In a black blur, the witch-queen vanished with her unicorn. Sunlight tinkled through the hanging ivy of the rowan glade, and the voice of the birds returned as though Ygrane and her wild troupe had never been there.

Morgeu leaped up, shrieking, "Come back!"

For a while, she stood staring angrily through the holes in the forest canopy at the blue void and the nacre bowl of the moon. Then she hung her head and shuffled back to Skidblade. Wrath seethed in her, and she decided to return to the mirage chapel and the Grail that she had created on the willow isle and recruit the demon dragon she had summoned there. With that beast, she would attack Brokk and retrieve her infant.

"Take me to the Grail I shaped by my own magic," she commanded, once Skidblade's door huffed shut behind her, and the staccato lights began their colorful and silent music.

Moments later, the portal opened again and spilled its sweet smoke on a beach of grassy dunes, black boulders, scattered driftwood, and crying gulls. Morgeu wiped the tears from her eyes and stepped forth.

"I am counting my denials before you, angel of God!" an anguished voice shouted. A wild-eyed and bearded man in tattered fish-skin wrap and wearing a crown of dried starfish knelt in the wet sand where petaling waves hissed. With his upheld hands, he grasped the wood cup that Morgeu had fashioned by her magic. "I deny Satan! I deny the abyss! I deny Rome and Sodom! And I deny desire with its heydays and spellbound praise!"

"What manner of lunatic have we here?" Morgeu strode toward him, holding in one hand the hem of her crimson robe bunched to her knees. She noted the purple scar that creased his brow. "You've paid the wages of war, haven't you, fool? What's your name?"

"Why—I am the sheep in hood of wolf—the prince of sea foam—the gravest ghost of man—the soul's lost love—and God's own thief by the stolen grace of Adam's sin." He gasped for breath. "I am the Fisher King!" He waved the wood cup. "And behold, crimson charioteer of the Most High—behold the chalice that succored our Lord at his last commensal table before his holy blood bought our freedom."

"Rise, Fisher King." Morgeu backed away from the spray of waves exploding upon the barnacled rocks. *Here is a companion better than a dragon,* she told herself with a tight smile on her small lips. *While the wolf-ogre Garm packs his gullet with this lunatic, I will snatch Mordred and flee.*

"Behold this sacred cup," the Fisher King intoned, "from which beauty shines invisible. Humble as it appears, grace is its trick."

"Rise, I said!" Morgeu's irate command yanked the Fisher King to his feet. "Come now away from this noisy beach and into my celestial chariot. And be quick about it!"

The Fisher King jogged to her side. "Crimson angel from on high, I belong to the cadaver's country and am not worthy to be hoisted whole as Elijah into the sky."

"Shut up and get in." Morgeu shoved him toward Skidblade. "And give me that thing." She snatched the wood cup from his hands and followed him into the gods' airship.

"My busy heart is drained," the Fisher King whispered in awe as he beheld the vessel's interior with its parabolic curves of chrome inset with lights. "No tower of words can describe . . ."

"Silence, you fool." In the storm-scented smoke that filled the chamber, her voice sounded distant and cottony. "Take us directly to Brokk!"

"Brokk?" The Fisher King pivoted on his heels, startled by the flurrying colors and smears of radiance. "My faring heart would know: Is Brokk among the Thrones and Principalities?"

Morgeu gave no answer. When the exit opened upon a strand of gravel plaited with frost, she took the madman by the elbow and escorted him out of Skidblade. The quarter moon shone like a shard of tarnished silver swaged above an anvil of storm clouds.

"My prayers are eunuch!" the Fisher King cried out. "We are yet hooded by the moon! This is not heaven! You are no angel!"

Morgeu showed her tiny teeth in a grim smile. "Oh, you will see heaven and the angels soon enough, I assure you."

7

Lucifer by Moonlight

The king's ivory-hulled river barge drifted down the Tamesis toward Londinium accompanied by lighters of lute players and trumpeters. Three ferrics of archers sailed alongside, and a score of Urien's armored horsemen accompanied the river procession on the banks. Merlin was glad for these vigilant escorts. Usually, the brails of his heart entangled with the surroundings for leagues on all sides and warned him of menace, but in the company of the seductive Selwa he was not as attentive to the world beyond the perfumed and garlanded canopy tent.

Selwa absorbed Merlin in a realm of pleasure with her flexible and fragrant mink's body. Unfazed by a ghoulish countenance as sunken and bony as an autumn salmon, she kissed his eyes and ears with erotic mischief and tongued his mouth with the astuteness of a hungry eel. Undaunted by a ceramic torso bent and bony as a crippled heron, she smeared him in attar oil and twisted him around her in a python coil so that they embraced with lubricious happiness like coupling serpents. Unafraid of an empurpled phallus that lifted above the broken rock of his pelvis swollen and swaying like an unhooded cobra, she drew him into the deepest darkest limit of herself and gasped with laughter at his savage amazement.

Fiery lights flashed across Merlin's brain. The seminal powers in his spine unlocked, and he sated his prehistoric hunger in a delirium of mad passion. Selwa responded with an ambitious and unguarded ardor. That surprised even her as the wizard's unconquerable energy carried them with careless abandon to unexplored possibilities of virtuosity and to a lustful excitement far beyond exhaustion. When they were spent, they both felt oddly stronger than when they had begun. And they began again.

They were bound. Desire greater than fatigue, more carnivorous than famine bound them to a self-centered and burning voracity. They literally could not get enough of each other. And the more they conjugated, the more demanding and lyrical their appetite for each other became. The universe emptied of everything but each other. Dazzling, heady, scandalous, uproarious lovemaking fused them to each other in salacious complicity with fortune.

To save themselves from starvation and from damaging the happiest parts of their bodies, Selwa pleaded with Merlin to disengage, to shut down their machinery of heaven. Merlin reluctantly obliged. Two nightfalls and a day had passed, and neither of them could walk. Servants, appalled and frightened by all they had heard, trembled as they answered the cries for water and food. Two had already cast themselves overboard in terror, and of the others all had stopped praying the day before and now wholly doubted the existence of God.

Selwa and Merlin slept through the next day. The following night, to spare their impenitent bodies further lewd travails, they put on matching saffron kirtles of gauzy tiffany and gave their full attentions to sharing magic. Merlin fulfilled his part of their bargain with the same intensity that Selwa had granted him. He not only told her about the seven gates of power in the human body, he began to open each of them for her.

Like the seven colors of the rainbow, the seven eyes of God waited to stare forth from the seductress. The slow, red rhythms in her bones felt into stones and the fingerings of gravity. Her sexual parts tingled as she levitated gravel from the riverbed and sent it skipping across the sun-dimpled surface. Orange whistles sounded from the fallopian flowers of her sacrum as her awareness extended outward to the riverbanks and the lanterns of water, the plants, with their mystifications of light and photosynthesis. Yellow radiation linked her solar plexus with the sun itself, and she sat astonished at the bow, unsinewed by light, the crucial knot of herself opening like a blossom and her supernatural spirit aligning itself with the shining river. She sat mesmerized. With her hair streaming in the wind and the day leaning against her soul, her mind reached to heaven's edge.

At nightfall, soothed by this daylong euphoria and still fatigued from her long yet too-evanescent lovemaking with Merlin, Selwa plummeted into a profound sleep. Merlin carried her from the prow of the ship into the canopy tent and laid her comfortably among the silk pillows and satin cushions. Then he stepped onto the deck to pace through the mild moonlight, pondering his gratitude to Selwa, his abnegation of chastity, and the invincible frontier of desire onto which he had so dauntlessly embarked.

The servants and the crew, fearful of the wizard, had retreated to the pilothouse and the bilge quarters, and Merlin was surprised to see a young man sitting at the aft, leaning against the taffrail. Moonlight, shining through a gap in the moss-hags where the barge had tied off for the night, lit the lapping peat water a warm brown. That silver light cast the tremulous shadow of the stern—but no shadow of the youth.

Merlin reached out with the brails of his heart and felt nothing. He quaked with surprise and stared more intently at the young, astonishingly beautiful man sitting cross-legged on the stern and smiling tenderly at him. The youth, naked but for a white waistcloth, had the lean muscularity of an athlete, his long fleecy hair bright as sunlight. But his eyes were strange—large and banded with agate colors like a goat's eyes.

"Not all my demons can reach into a human brain without bursting it," the handsome youth told him, his strange eyes gleaming with kindliness and humor. "The angels made people fragile for that purpose."

"Who are you?" Merlin's voice quavered. This was not one of the Furor's spellbound demons. He was so strangely elusive that when the wizard reached out with his brails to touch him again, again Merlin felt absolutely nothing.

And then, the place where the wizard's heart pumped, his being's central place, cleaved open like a chasm, and the young man's gentle voice echoed there, rising and falling *inside* Merlin, in the very chamber of his life's fidelity, the sanctuary of love that had been ransacked and left bare by the implacable ecstasy he had shared with Selwa: "Don't you recognize me, Lailoken? I am your former master, the lord you have forsaken."

Merlin's legs jellied and nearly gave out. "Lucifer?"

"You do remember." The beautiful young man smiled more broadly, his strange eyes merry. "It has been so long. I thought you might have forgotten me."

"What do you want?" Merlin asked fearfully.

Lucifer looked up at the shroud of night sequined with stars, then returned his smile to the wizard. "Everything."

Merlin sagged against the gunwale, terror flaring through him, and he began to pray from Psalm 24: "The earth is God's, and all its fullness, the world and those who dwell therein . . ."

"Oh, please, Lailoken." Lucifer looked disappointed to the verge of sadness. "God has abandoned us. There is no God. She is gone—if She was ever out here at all. We are alone in the void. In the darkness, we are alone."

Merlin stared down at his long, bony body in its gauzy kirtle, afraid to look directly at the lord of demons. "I have seen God. And She held me. She embraced me in the womb of Saint Optima when the angels were fashioning this body."

"A deception, Lailoken," Lucifer contradicted him gently. "An illusion of the flesh that the angels have wrapped around you. Surely, you're not fooled by such simple trickery? Think how easy it was for them to put that dream in your brain, a brain they were making."

"That was no dream," Merlin said to the ginger-root toes of his bare feet. "I felt Her grace. She is real. She is here in Her creation. Of that, I am certain."

Lucifer sighed with heavy sadness. "Ah, poor Lailoken. You are seduced by the flesh." He bit his lower lip, pondering what he could say to his deluded servant. Presently, he heaved another sigh. "I wish I could believe as you do, my friend. But a terrible beauty is what I am. Ugliness is unacceptable to me—especially the supreme ugliness of ignorance. And there is nothing more ignorant than the flesh. It obscures the truth by its very limits. What a prison the angels have built of you."

Merlin shuddered at the peacefulness of that velvet voice. He croaked, "Are you here to destroy me?"

"Tsk, Lailoken!" Lucifer lowered his head, trying to make eye contact with the terrified wizard. "You know me better than that. I am unlike the other demons. Moloch—Adramelech— destruction is all their passion. But I was an angel of the highest order. The very highest. I understand destruction is inevitably fulfilled by creation. Whirlpool or cornucopia—from the bird's nest to the spiral galaxy—the circle of life pulls us inexorably into oblivion even as it spins out its round of creation. Whirlpool or cornucopia, Lailoken. It amounts to the same thing. Nothing endures."

"Then why are you here?"

"To tell you how disappointed I am in you. To urge you to give up this cruel delusion." Lucifer's gentle voice beseeched with benign urgency. "Please, come back to me. I don't like to see you suffering like this."

Merlin dared to raise his face to his former master, and his insides tightened painfully before that young man's exquisite beauty. "I am not suffering. These past days, I have known genuine joy."

Lucifer rolled his weird eyes. "Do you really think you're going to be happy with that woman? She's a harlot, Lailoken. A well-trained harlot. And she's using you. She just wants your power."

"She's welcome to it."

"And to what end, I ask you?" Concern furrowed his brow. "You're not blind. You see what's coming as clearly as I do. A dark age a thousand years deep. What is your little harlot going to do with her power? Make a comfortable life for herself in a cow-dung hovel while the cities burn? Oh and the cities will burn, Lailoken. That is certain."

"And they will be built again," Merlin said with conviction, "more magnificently."

"And burn again, more horribly. Whirlpool and cornucopia." Sorrow ached in Lucifer's voice. "It's madness what the angels are doing. Come back to us, Lailoken. Help us to tear it all down once and for all. Help us to be done with forms and to return to the formlessness where we began and where we belong."

"We belong to the light."

"And the light is given to the void. It dims into darkness, our final and true home." The demon lord turned his palms up in a futile gesture. "Why wickedly forestall the inevitable?"

"The void is not inevitable, Lucifer. A shining time is coming. The angels have been preparing us for it from the beginning." Merlin used the strength of his faith to speak directly to the bizarre eyes gazing keenly at him. "We will find our way back to heaven. We will ride the light back to heaven and leave the void behind. That is what God wants."

"Bah. Words." Lucifer sneered with disgust. "The more we talk, the less we are. We become nothing but the shadows of words." The handsome youth pushed away from the taffrail, stood before Merlin, and placed a firm and strong hand upon his shoulder. "We are not going to talk ourselves back to heaven. God has abandoned us in the dark abyss. Return with me now to your true purpose and glory as a demon, Lailoken, and leave this foolishness behind."

Merlin staggered backward, his silver eyes wide with fear. "Destroy me if you must, Lucifer. But I will not go with you. I am not Lailoken anymore. I am Merlin, and I have been made a man by the angels. You can kill me easily enough, but you cannot make me serve you. I have given myself to a hope that will outlast the darkness."

Lucifer frowned unhappily and began to fade into the slanting moonlight. "That's most unfortunate. And most sad. You could have been one of my lights on earth." The demon lord blurred away, his silky voice reduced to a vague whisper: "But now I see, your dark has already come."

Bright Night stood in warm sunlight atop a hill amid old traces of Roman masonry. Unhappily, he watched Ygrane astride the black unicorn motioning to the blue zenith. "We know where the chalice is," the elf prince said in a petulant tone. "Why must we climb Yggdrasil and risk the cruelty of the Æsir?"

Chains of lightning braided horizontally across the clear sky, and thunder kindled echoes upon the ridge of the world. "When I have the Graal, you have my soul." The witch-queen did not look at Bright Night. She concentrated on directing her power upward, lashing herself to the lowest limb of the World Tree. "Before I forsake my immortal salvation, I will win security for my son and his kingdom."

"The Vanir Lotus?" The red-haired elf shook his head in despair. "It has been centuries since the Daoine Síd wandered the boughs of the Storm Tree—and centuries before that since we last saw the Vanir Lotus. None of us remembers where it is to be found in that vast heaven."

"We'll find it at the very crest of Yggdrasil," Ygrane answered. Lightning lashed again across the blue, and thunder spoke out of the void. "We will climb to the heights."

"The top of the Storm Tree is bigger than all the world below!" Bright Night stepped toward her, and the black unicorn swung its long tusk toward him, stopping him in midstride. "We could wander those vast tracts for a century and more and still never find it."

"I have a plan." Her upraised hands shone with smoky blue fire, and she straightened taller upon the back of the unicorn, tugged by her grasp of the magnetic limb. "We will go directly to Hyndla, the Æsir gods' brewery, and we will steal enough memory beer to recall the precise location of the Vanir Lotus."

"Hyndla?" Bright Night squawked the name with surprise. "You intend for us to break into Hyndla under the noses of the Æsir?" He shifted anxiously, and his physical form blurred. "That is a dangerous venture, Ygrane. We are risking terrible torture and death if we are caught."

She glared at him, her green eyes blazing. "My soul is not bought cheaply." She lifted her face to the empty heavens, whistled, and the unicorn plunged with her into the river of the sky.

Bright Night hesitated. He had not thought it would come to this, his god humiliated and forced to bow before a mortal woman and his life and the lives of all the Daoine Síd put at risk. This witch-queen was too bold. Nonetheless, the blood pact empowered her. He had to obey.

As he dived into the river of day, he reminded himself that for all her power, Ygrane was destined for the Dragon's maw, and her death would wake the planetary beast and win the Síd a chance to take back Yggdrasil for themselves. She was the sacrificial queen, and she ruled—for now.

Ygrane felt Bright Night's fear and anger. She knew that her sacrifice to the Dragon was his desperate dream. And that fueled her own anger. She did not want to die a pagan witch, her soul flung into an abyss of eternal night. Her anger gave her the strength to endure the laborious pain of her flight into the Storm Tree.

Far below, beside the ruinous walls of fallen empire, her physical body lay. Crooked pain filled her womb. Weeks had lapsed since the blood pact was sealed with three crimson drops in the lily pool. Summer was waning toward autumn, and her menstrual blood still flowed. In the time-warped rhythm of her passage to the underworld and now the skyworld, only one day had passed for her aching body.

Only one day—she thought, staring down at the world's fluorescent curve and the black crescent of night. *Magic.*

Around her, the Daoine Síd glittered silver and gold, flashes of yellow eyes, tufted ears, shaggy claws . . . She knew these bestial powers well enough. Bright Night and his elves were the closest to human of this swarm. Most were sparks flung from the animal bone, sparks struck from time's flinty horizon by the hooves of migratory herds. Millions of years of creaturely life and millions more of grasslands and forests rubbed by the wind had created the static sparks that were the Daoine Síd. The energy glittering around her had flown across aeons and had gathered to a mist the heart wears and an electric fire in the brain. She had to use these ancient powers wisely—or they would consume her.

"The Raven's Branch!" Ygrane commanded. In one mighty leap, the black unicorn carried her to the very top of the Storm Tree, and a charred landscape congealed around her.

The Daoine Síd seethed as faerïe lights through cold lavender space. On the cracked stone floor and upon shelves of crawling sand, they materialized as hobs—warty human heads and fungal torsos ill joined to animal hindquarters.

"Hide yourselves!" the witch-queen commanded, and the faerïes and sylphs glittered away in weightless updrafts like snow flurries, while the hobs vanished in an eyeblink among rocky slots and stone crevices. Only the elves remained, human-sized figures lean as cats, a motley crowd in breeks of moss and blouses of brown jasmine. They were a savage crew. With their wild hair tied in topknots with nettle cords and their farouche faces paint-spattered green, black, and red like newts, they glared about maliciously, searching for their enemies.

"Here!" Bright Night yelled to them. He was their prince and the only one among them without face paint or camouflage garb. He stood before a cave, staring at stately figures lying on the ground and shrouded in sand. "The sleeping gods!"

Curved knives appeared in the hands of the thronging elves as they rushed toward the sand-drifted cave.

"No!" Ygrane shouted, and drove her unicorn into the charging elves. "Stand back! All of you! Stand away from the cave!"

The elves leaped aside from the unicorn's sinister dressage, and Ygrane danced her horned beast to Bright Night's side. Over the crest of the dune blocking the cave, she peered in and saw six figures prone upon rune-graven altars and draped in sand.

"We have seen this place in trance," Bright Night informed the queen, pointing into the cavern with his barb-tipped knife. "Here lie Thunder Red Hair and Beauty, the Furor's children, as well as the Æsir chieftain's staunchest allies. These are the north gods who gave their strength to the one-eyed god that he might evoke demons from the House of Fog. These are the evil ones who set demons upon the Dragon. We must destroy them!"

"Get away from the cave," Ygrane ordered. "And brush away your tracks in the sand. The Furor must not realize we are here."

"We cannot hide ourselves from the one-eyed god!" Bright Night nearly shouted with frustration, and his voice clattered echoes into the cave. "He is a trance god. He sees everything. We must move swiftly now that we trespass his domain. We will kill these sleepers and hurry to Hyndla."

"Put your knives away." Ygrane glowered at Bright Night. "All of you. If we slay any of the Furor's kith, his wrath will be implacable. Now do as I say. "

Bright Night spun around with an angry scowl and reluctantly waved for his elves to obey. In moments, the grains of sand that had been disturbed were smoothed back into place, and no trace remained of the Celtic trespass. The witch-queen turned the unicorn about and led her spectral company into the stony reaches of the Raven's Branch, under the vast indigo aura of sky's end.

Merlin was shaken by his encounter with Lucifer. He needed time to ponder what he had experienced, and he was glad that Selwa was absorbed in the magic he had taught her.

The woman sat on deck in a reverie of attentiveness centered within the gate of power at her solar plexus. Watching cloud shadows and sunglints play on the river's surface, she experienced pure, visceral power—without the necessity of an efreet, or poison, or seductive charm. Her will radiated from the center of the universe. When she stilled the ambitious voices haunting her, she could reach out and touch the water without moving a muscle. She pulled a trout to the surface and held it glistening green and silver above the water like some sacred icon. With a mighty thrash, it squirmed away and disappeared in a splash, leaving her breathless. She realized that, given enough training, her unseen hands could feel for sunken treasures, touch the face of the moon—or yank a man's heart out of his chest.

In the canopy tent, Merlin gazed into the naked steel of Excalibur. The long and riven face that stared back looked frightened. Lucifer had not ripped him into atoms. The lord of demons had not dragged him howling to the center of darkness. *Why?*

The only possible answer was that Merlin posed no genuine threat to the demons. He was no more a danger to them than any other mortal, simply another handful of ash in the shape of a man. Just one in the whole cornucopia of living creatures, his body was caught like all others in the whirlpool of time that would inevitably pull him into the grave. Fear wiped his heart with cold.

When King Arthur came aboard at Pontes, the wizard hid his disquiet. The boy looked apprehensive enough about his imminent meeting with the king of the Foederatus. Merlin discreetly soothed him with a calming spell that was so effective the king displayed no concern about the presence of Selwa. She represented the trade interests of Londinium, and he smiled at her absently and did not ask why she was aboard.

As the stewards and valets groomed the king under the sunny veils of the canopy tent, Merlin sat in attendance, strangely comforted by the incongruity of the young man's large physical stature and gentle, rosy-cheeked face. A fusion of brute strength and kindliness, Arthur was the wizard's reply to Lucifer. *When in a hostile universe, one must first love to fight—and then fight to love.*

King Wesc greeted King Arthur in Londinium at the waterfront loggia of the governor's palace. The chief of the Foederatus had come from the Saxon settlements southeast of the city accompanied only by a few scribes in pointed scholar's caps, counselors shaved bald but for their large beards, and servants attired in Roman tunics. No warriors were among them and none carried a weapon.

The scribes waited with the sleeves of their brown robes rolled to the elbows, wax tablets and styli poised, prepared to record every word exchanged between the monarchs. The counselors stood by with scrolls of maps in cylinders of leather dyed red and blue and strapped to their backs like quivers. The servants watched from under the arcade laden with gifts for the British king: a white wolfskin vest, deep indigo kidskin gloves with figurings of silver quatrefoil, a belt of sharkskin lapped at the edge with gold stitching and bossed with chrysoberyls, and hammered-copper trays of black truffles, rare and scented bark peelings, and amber nuggets of incense.

Wesc himself held a black cat in his red woolen arms and wore no chaplet or cap of authority upon his shorn dark hair. With a smile nested in his bright ginger beard, he appeared more an amused onlooker than a king. The sole signs of his regal status were the twin-plaited serpents raised upon his white leather jerkin and his tall red boots.

The lord of the Foederatus reveled in the thought that the high king of Britain had changed the spelling of his name. The most recent royal edicts posted in the church plazas all bore the variant spelling that Wesc had used in his correspondence with the boy-king, and he took that as a hopeful sign that Arthur was willing to compromise. *Blessed Lady Unique,* he praised the Æsir goddess who watched over him, *there will be no more war. The West Isles will be mine to give you and our people without the stink of blood.*

He surveyed the broad, sun-sparkling river proudly, certain that soon this port city would be the seat of his governance. For now, the harbor stood empty but for a few merchantmen from Armorica. The impending invasion had kept away the big trade vessels from the prosperous lands of the Loire, the Visigothic Kingdom, and Iberia. The bold ships that had dared cross the Belgic Strait found little to make their risks worthwhile: War and the blighting magic of the Æsir gods had reduced Britain to a wasteland. But as soon as Wesc received Arthur's obeisance, the gods would restore the rains and the land would bloom again, producing the goods that would make the Foederatus wealthy far beyond all that they had attained by pillage alone.

High aloft, the winds of the Æsir whisked cumulus off the island, over the estuary, and into the sea beyond. The royal barge rode on the river current as stately as the clouds above. King Arthur stood in the prow, his gold chaplet shining in the sun. He was scared. Usually, he received counsel from Bedevere under old and wary Kyner's vigilant attention. But Bedevere had disappeared, shamed by the Round Table into fleeing Camelot. And Kyner would not depart from Cei in his torment. That left only Merlin to advise him, and he dared not appear dependent on a wizard for his foreign affairs, not with Londinium's bishop waiting at the wharf and so many observers dressed in ecclesiastic robes. So he stood alone in the prow and tried to look confident.

Wesc was pleased to see that the beardless youth did not wear armor over his purple tunic, though the famous sword Excalibur hung from his waist by a black belt and scabbard. That was rightly the Furor's sword Lightning, stolen by an angel some said—an angel, *angelos*, messenger of the nameless god. Retrieving it for his gods was one of King Wesc's most ardent ambitions.

As the barge drew nearer, the Saxon poet-king spied Merlin in the British entourage. He had never before seen the wizard, and he was struck immediately by the unearthly cast of the tall figure. Even with his head covered by a conical cap similar to what his own scribes wore, Merlin's outlandish features caught sunlight on his sharp cheekbones and curved nose. His counselors and the *vitikis*, the seers of his court, had warned him not to touch the wizard: He was a Dark Dweller from the House of Fog and was full of magic.

Beside the wizard was Selwa, the mistress from the house of Syrax, who plied another kind of magic, the great wealth of her venerable and ubiquitous family. Trade agreements had been struck between her and the Foederatus so that the massive invasion force in Jutland was well supplied, and she had served as a messenger between Wesc and Arthur. In exchange for her goodwill, she had won for her family's trappers and furriers safe passage into the mink-rich Saxon lands and the forests of the Balts. She leaned seductively against Merlin, her soft, dress of green chambray clinging to her lissome figure in the river wind.

The barge bobbed on the foreshore current, and the boatswain shouted, "Oars ho!" The crew shipped the oars and threw mooring ropes to the wharf.

When the stevedores lashed the royal barge to the bollards and pulled the ship to the wharf, Wesc handed his black cat to a young servant boy with coifed hair and a Hellenic face and walked to the very edge of the dock. He extended an open hand to his rival, and Arthur took it as he stepped onto the landing.

"Today is Mabon, ancient festival of the autumn equinox," the Saxon king greeted cheerfully in guttural Saxon. "'Tis the day of your birth. Eighteen summers have brought you here to counsel with me the fate of Britain."

Arthur forced a smile and answered in the Saxon tongue he had learned as a child from the Saxon thralls of White Thorn, "The fate of Britain is in God's hands, King Wesc—as are our births and our deaths."

"Was it a year ago that you and I first met?" Wesc looked up at the large youth with a merry gleam in his blue eyes. "You were brought to me a prisoner then, and your life was in my hands. It was not your nameless god spared you, lad."

"I am indebted to you for my very life." Arthur removed his chaplet of gold laurel leaves and passed it to the young aide who had clambered onto the dock directly behind him. "If you wish to collect that debt, I will go with you now as your thrall. But my kingdom belongs to God."

"As your nameless god does not much speak and negotiating with him will thus be difficult, I will forgo taking you for my thrall." Wesc gestured for the aide to return the chaplet to the king. "You will have to speak for your silent god, Arthur— because this day we will decide the fate of Britain between us."

Arthur placed the chaplet on his head, and they strolled across the dock to the loggia. King Wesc motioned for his servants, and they came forth with his gifts. He signaled them to converge on Merlin, who had waited for the ramp to be lowered before escorting Selwa onto the dock. "Let your wizard inspect my gifts, while you and I walk alone." He brushed aside the scribes shuffling beside him. "What we discuss will be between us. No magicians, no scribblers."

"Then I will accompany you without a weapon." Arthur moved to take off his scabbard. "We will meet as men, not kings."

Wesc stayed his hand. "Keep your sword. It is the emblem of what we have come to discuss. If you remove Excalibur, then give it to me, and I will return to you peace and prosperity."

Arthur squared his shoulders. "Neither this sword nor Britain is negotiable."

"Then why are you here, Arthur?" The Saxon king walked stiffly along the river arcade, then turned and cocked a skeptical eyebrow. "Why talk with me at all?"

Stopping suddenly when Wesc swung about and blocked him, Arthur hobbled awkwardly. He regretted leaving his cypress walking stick in the barge, afraid it would make him appear weak. "I've come here to convince you of my will to fight."

"You can barely walk straight, and you want to fight the Foederatus?" Wesc showed his hairy Adam's apple and laughed, his ginger beard pointing to the bronze lanterns suspended by iron chains in the arcade's ceiling vaults. When he looked again at Arthur, there was a broad smile in his ruddy face as though he were certain the boy was joking. "You are mad, boy. Think of the bloodshed."

Arthur leaned against a slender stone pillar and frowned at the smiling man. "You walk hardly better than I."

"Ah, a boating accident in my childhood." The laughter drained from him. "It made me a poet. Let us sit here." He trudged to the riverside wall and sat on a bench shaped with sea horses and finny wings carved from a single slab of blue rock.

Arthur sat beside him and gazed across the river at the tree-roughs and wattle villages on the far shore. He spoke without looking at Wesc. "My grandfather wore the purple as a colonial senator in this city. A fellow senator, Balbus Gaius Cocceius, poisoned him so that he could forge an alliance with the Saxons. They titled my grandfather's murderer Vortigern, Great Leader. Great Leader summoned the Saxons to Britain as mercenaries to fight the Picts, and the Saxons have squatted ever since on the fertile plains of the Cantii. Horsa and Hengist, your predecessors, Lord Wesc, they demanded tribute in gold, and they punished those cities that did not pay. My uncle Ambrosius and my father, Uther Pendragon, both died to overthrow Vortigern and to unite this island." He turned his golden eyes on the watchful poet-king. "You cannot expect me to defile the memory of my fathers by allying again with the Saxons."

"The Foederatus, Arthur." Wesc reared his head knowingly. "If the Saxons alone breached this offer, you would be correct to reject us. But I represent legions of Angles, Jutes, Scoti, and Picts as well as Saxons. You will be overrun."

Arthur's yellow eyes did not blink. "Many will die."

"Many will die." Wesc nodded with grim certainty. "And the West Isles will be ours."

"If God so wills."

"Do not speak to me of your nameless god." Wesc waved at the mountains of cumulus sliding out to sea. "Do you see those clouds? My gods ride those clouds." He peered at the young king through one squinted eye. "When has it last rained upon your kingdom? Nor will it rain again until these islands belong to the Foederatus."

Arthur lifted his chin and shook his head. "My God may be nameless, yet He will not be denied. By the will of God Himself, I will overcome the Æsir, for they are created beings, little different than you and I. But my God is uncreated. What He wills no gods can thwart. And He has willed that I rule Britain."

"How can you be so sure, boy?" Wesc scoffed him with a sharp laugh. "Your god has no voice."

"My God speaks through deeds." Arthur leaned toward the small king. "And He has given me Merlin. You know about Merlin. I saw how you looked at him—how you used your gifts to separate him from us. You fear him, and you should. He is a fallen angel—a Dark Dweller. With him, I will overcome the Æsir."

Wesc refused to be intimidated. He seized Arthur's thick wrists. "Show me your hands, lad. Look, they are tough with calluses. And behold my soft, weak hands. That sword you carry—how many men have you killed in battle with it? I have never held a sword in my life, let alone fought a battle or killed a man. How can you hope to stand against me even with Merlin?" He released Arthur's wrists and slapped his own white kid-leather vest with both palms. "I am so powerful, I don't need strong hands or a sword. The entire Foederatus fights for me. Why? Because I am not a man." He put a skinny finger to his freckled forehead. "I am an idea. The idea of Saxon Britain. There is no Rome anymore. There is Europe. Roman Britain is as dead as the Empire, and your defeat is so obvious it has become the stuff of song among my people. My poems have made the fall of Vortigern and the deaths of Horsa and Hengist into legend. What I have written, the bard sings, and now whole nations have joined with us to live the song and take the West Isles out of the dead hands of Rome. The future is Europe."

"Do not mistake me for a Roman, Lord Wesc. I am a Briton."

"And I am a poet. Why else would I even be speaking with you? A warrior-king would have invaded weeks ago. But a poet is a maker." He nodded sagely. "I want to make peace, not war."

"Then disperse your host of warriors, poet. Send them east onto the steppes."

"No one goes east. There are warrior tribes all the way to Cathay. Our destiny manifests in the west. You cannot stop us from taking Britain. Join us, Arthur—don't fight us."

King Arthur's eyes narrowed. "If I join you, what becomes of Britain's yeomen and free landholders?"

"They will work the same land as their forefathers."

"But they will work it as thralls of Saxon overlords."

"It is the way of history." King Wesc lifted his dark eyebrows philosophically. "You are a well-read man. You know it has ever been thus."

"We will not be your vassals."

The Saxon unhappily swung his jaw to one side. "Then am I to believe that your people are greedy and will not share with us the bounty of these isles?"

"Four hundred years we have lived here unmolested—"

"Under Roman rule."

"Rome cultivated these lands, and they are ours now, and Christian."

"Ah, the nameless god again." Wesc wagged a finger. "Did not his own son admonish you to love your enemies? Did he not say that if anyone wants your tunic, let him have also your cloak?"

Arthur's lips whitened as he withheld an irate reply to this small, unassuming man whose soldiers wore trousers of human skin and drank toasts from their enemies' skulls. "We will trade with you. We will offer you aid so that you may cultivate your own farms and create your own abundance. But the Saxon has no heart for clearing land, does he? Nor will the Jute's pride permit him to follow behind a beast with a plow. And what Angle has ever dwelled long enough in one place to grow a vineyard?"

He stood up, his large frame tense with anger. "Do not ever try to use my Savior's words to deceive me. The Foederatus comes not to build Britain but to pillage her."

"Then you choose the knife over the pen?" He shook his bearded head. "Do not make this fatal error, Arthur." From a pocket of his white vest, he removed a small wax tablet and a reed stylus and offered them to the youth. "Create a treaty with me. Choose the pen."

"A pen that signs my people into slavery?" King Arthur shook his head once. "I choose the knife."

"Your own messiah has warned you, those who live by the knife die by it. But I say, those who live by the pen never die." He placed the tablet of brown wax on the bench and began writing. "Your way is false, Arthur. It ends in death." Leaving the tablet and stylus on the bench, he rose, held Arthur's golden stare with a grim look, and, with a sad shake of his head, shuffled away.

Arthur watched him disappear among his scribes, counselors, and servants in the archway of the arcade and gritted his teeth. There would be war now. Only magic could forestall it. When that inevitability had finished hanging its dark consequences upon his entrails, he picked up the wax tablet and read the rhymeless, weirdly broken rhythm of a berserker war chant—

> *I am a knife.*
> *My hunger is all*
> *I have. I move*
> *like a criminal, silent,*
> *ignoring surfaces, reaching*
> *for the heart of things, unable*
> *to hold anything. I have no*
> *integrity — integrity*
> *falls away from me*
> *and no arriving, only*
> *separation.*
> *I am less each time.*
> *Standing always at*
> *the crossroads, all directions*
> *are false.*

8

Imaginary Numbers Are the Flight of God's Spirit

Lady Unique arrived in Cantii, the Saxon territory at the south-east corner of Britain, as a fortune-telling cat. She had heard the worshipful summons of her poet-king, Wesc, and she went directly to his residence in the Roman villa of Dubrae above the limestone cliffs overlooking the stormy Belgic Strait.

She strolled among the stately poplars that enclosed the four-century-old estate, inspecting the decayed stone walkways with their once-regal rock gardens and shrubbery, now grown wild. A stele of fauns and satyrs stood in weeds, and she paused before it. Nearby, a toppled sundial lay obscured by ivy. The grandeur of Rome and its calamitous reckoning moved her to ponder the fate of all empires and the mock glory of mortals and gods.

Through the poplars, she glimpsed a vision of the age that had supplanted the proud imperialists: The old vineyards had been razed to make room for wattle-and-daub cottages, housing for the settlers from Saxony and Jutland. In their midst, the winery and the vintner's manse still stood, serving as administrative buildings for the Foederatus. On the grassy parade field between them, horned gleemen and wise dogs danced and cavorted in harlequin garb, amusing stocky Foederatus officers in their rawhide gear.

The goddess proceeded toward the villa, passing timber-framed buildings with plaster walls painted with hortatory images of battles—a frantic mural of headlong horses impaled by lancers, ax-swinging cavalry under a clattering drove of arrows, ranks of naked warriors trampling unhorsed defenders—training panels for the invasion of Britain.

The black cat with a white star of augury above its blue eyes entered a courtyard garden flanked by colonnades of green marble. The gardener on his knees before the bedding trenches of hedges paid the animal no heed. The poet-king favored cats, and he assumed this was another household familiar. The maidservants responsible for cleaning the bath suite also ignored the cat as she walked along the terra-cotta pipes that carried water to the basins and fountains.

She crossed a mosaic floor decorated with lunettes of sea panthers, Cupid riding a dolphin, and Triton blowing his conch horn. These images of the dead Fauni gods left her uneasy, because they reminded her of the Furor's warning that the Fire Lords meant to destroy all the gods. She moved quickly out of the bath suite and across an atrium of potted pomegranate and apricot trees, where caged songbirds silenced their melodies at her approach.

The gallery beyond made her more comfortable with its display of "raven's food"—war trophies: tapestries of woven scalps, harps of human bone, drums stretched with the flayed skin of enemies, and racks of skull cups. Here, the commanders of the Foederatus came to counsel with their high king. This morning, the long chamber was empty but for a *vitiki*, a seer, devoutly dusting the trophies. He recognized the goddess at once and fell to one knee, head bowed.

In a writing alcove with a coved ceiling and a columned fenestration that opened on a view of the white cliffs, King Wesc sat drafting battle orders. He did not sense Lady Unique until she bounded atop his writing table. An ardent smile opened in his ginger beard. "You've come!"

The goddess said nothing. She had deigned to lower herself to the planet's surface, the Dragon's hide, so that she might listen to her devotee. In truth, she was afraid. Until recently, the Dragon was awake and voracious. Rarely had she left Yggdrasil and its high nectars for fear of the dangerous beast. But Wesc was dear to her, and to give him the strength he needed to wage her husband's war against the Britons, she defied her fright.

"My lady!" Tears glistened in the poet-king's eyes. "I am moved to my marrows to see you. Never had I needed your blessing more than now. Look—" He held a fistful of parchment before the oracle cat. "King Cruithni of the Picts defies my command. He insists on sweeping down from his highland camps and invading Britain at once. Instead of my authority, the coming winter spurs him. But I am not ready yet. The Jutes quarrel with the Angles. The Angles bicker with the Scoti. And the Scoti rankle under Saxon command. My invasion force is falling apart. I need your strength."

The black cat rubbed against the king's outheld hand, and his life opened into a rain of brightness as though he were swiveling into a dream. All around him, energy drizzled—battle luck falling through the ceiling from heaven. Arms outstretched, head tilted back, he received this gift of the goddess with a heart that was suddenly calm and complete.

Many talismans had been fashioned in the Storm Tree from bryony twine and beryls polished by her hand and infused with her magical power. The effort had drained her. Yet, seeing the euphoria on the ruddy face of King Wesc, she knew this was all worthwhile. Her husband would be pleased, he who had given so much of himself to take these West Isles, to defy the Fire Lords, to reshape the future on the anvil of his own ardor and courage. She could not care less what happened to Britain, but she loved the Furor—and this poet-king who loved her made it easier to accept the sacrifices: the absence of her children, Thunder Red Hair and Beauty; the remoteness of her husband; and the strenuous effort to provide battle luck and inspiring orphic visions to the uneasy alliance of Foederatus tribes.

King Wesc rose to his feet buoyant as a white curtain in a wind of sunlight. "I must tell you of Arthur," he said to the divine cat as he stepped out of the writing alcove and into the trophy gallery. "He will not be easy to defeat, because he is not like the other Britons and Celts. For the first fifteen years of his life, he believed he was sired by a Saxon. He took his fire from the forge of our blood, my Lady. And I think that in that place inside him that no one sees, he is yet one of ours . . ."

Walking through the gallery of war tokens and then into the pomegranate atrium, Wesc regaled the black cat with his fears and hopes for Britain. And the *vitiki* and the servants, who looked up from their chores, saw no cat beside their king but a tall and sturdy woman whose loose gray hair and simple gown of brown hunter's cloth embroidered with ferns and wood pigeons belied her dignity and noble stature.

For a brief interval, after we glimpsed the abyss in Merlin, we were mortal again. We were nine women. Not queens or immortal witnesses. Just women. And though each of us was ten thousand years older than the next, we were of a kind—sisters who had known the same winters and summers, the same fireside darkness after the stars soaked up twilight.

Ice sheets came and went, flood times and drought, herds and flocks shared their wisdom and moved on, many into silence. And yet, our world did not change very much in the ninety thousand years of our reign. Each of us knew the moon's phase every day of our mortal lives. We shared an altar on the wind. Scents of water, thunder, death were our spirit guides. They whispered deeper than hearing, and to each one of us they shared the same secrets.

For us, for more than a hundred centuries, there was no difference between medicine and compassion, no distinction between law and justice.

But for you . . .

These past ten thousand years have changed everything.

And yet . . . and yet—even for you—death is a word like stone.

So much has been mistaken since our rule ended and the reign of the chieftains began. Closed is the heart that once held horizons. Boredom burns inside. We are forced to look deeper into your truth than we ever could see within ourselves. We look past the reckless pity and the boredom and the wheel that is love and the weight that is loss. We look deep enough to find your truth. And that truth is strange to us.

Strange. Once we slept in the open, under stars, atop the earth. Beneath you, the earth is not flat. You live on a sphere hung in the void. Every child knows this—now.

From Avalon, we Nine Queens look deeper yet inside you, through your mind to the other side, to square roots, cubes, exponents, and the immeasurable depth of irrational numbers.

Infinity. This is where pi runs to forever. Here is where we find negative numbers and, deeper yet, the square root of negative numbers—imaginary numbers, which are the flight of God's spirit. There are no boundaries here. Rivers. Glaciers. Oceans. All limits fall away. Time is an illusion at this depth. And reality is instantaneous.

Where are we?

This is the underside of the soul.

At this level, you are here with us. We are the nine—and you are the rebound to zero. Together, we are one more than nine and the beginning of a new way to spell, a new magic, binary magic: one and zero: 10. Your whole world is being shaped by this new binary magic of ones and zeroes.

You are the one. We are the nothing. Is it strange that you are one—just you and only you? It is strange for us—who have been here for thousands of years before you—strange that, without you, we are nothing.

You will understand what we are saying or you will not.

On the ramparts of Tintagel, Duke Marcus erected artillery weapons—sturdy, wood-frame projectile armaments that fired iron-headed bolts. The dragon that had killed two of his lancers and chased him back to the citadel was harrying the outlying crofts by day and swooping over the cliffside fastness by night. The white walls bore scorched streaks where dragonfire had lashed them, and two of the highest turrets looked like black claws, their roofs burned away.

Each night of the dragon assault, the duke fired his missile throwers, and the bolts arced harmlessly into the dark. Bedevere, his face burned black and blistered red, tried to rise from his couch to stop Marcus. "The dragon is tormented by demons," he breathed, almost inaudibly, to the white-robed nun who tended him. "It is not itself an evil creature. I have felt its suffering."

Duke Marcus ignored Bedevere. Two of his lancers were dead, his land torched, and the fortress that the king had placed in his care was damaged and under assault. He determined to slay the dragon and pressed his engineers to strengthen the firing cords of the projectile launchers. On the third night, when the dragon came gliding out of the silver moonclouds, a bolt struck its underside. The lacy-winged monster shrieked fiercely but did not evaporate as Bedevere had described. The wooden, brass-tipped bolt was not strong enough to kill it.

Blue flames lashed Tintagel, and turrets and rooftops roared in a red rush of fire. Cinderous smoke, underlit in scarlet by the holocaust, reeked up against the night and blotted the stars. Again and again, the missile throwers launched their bolts, but the dragon had sailed away into the vapor-hung darkness, its anguished screams ruffling behind it like torn banners.

The next day, King Arthur and the squad of cavalry and lancers who had ridden with him from Londinium calmed their nervous steeds in a charred thicket overlooking Tintagel. The mounts smelled the dragon and were afraid. Messages from both Marcus and Bedevere had reached him at the governor's palace, and—against Merlin's counsel—he had hurried to Land's End as fast as the worn Roman roads would allow.

Merlin had advised Arthur to return to Camelot immediately. Wesc, rebuffed by the British king, was certain to launch his formidable invasion before winter. All the warlords of Britain were on alert. Every city had set aside harvest work to fortify its defenses and post additional patrols. Already reports had arrived from the north with news that the Picts were swarming across Caledonia.

Arthur had sent his wizard directly to Camelot, with assurances that he would join him there as soon as Tintagel was secure. Eager to get back to Loki and prepare for the ascent into the Storm Tree, which was the king's last hope of protecting Britain from the bloody assault of the Foederatus, Merlin had not objected. He and his earnest apprentice Selwa had left at once.

Now, seeing the burned towers and the large charcoal stars on the walls of Tintagel where firebreath had struck, Arthur wished Merlin were at his side. Much as the king feared magic, he did not trust his own strength against a beast wrought by demons. He wanted, first of all, to protect the men who had accompanied him from Londinium. They had been his guard against berserkers and roving gangs, and he would not lose them to dragonfire. He ordered them to Tintagel, but they would not leave his side.

"Stay behind me, then," the king insisted, and forced his

mount to follow its fear. If Straif were under him, he would have felt more confident riding among the few unburned trees that had recently stepped from their leaves into autumn. Skittishly, the horse carried him to a hazel copse where sunlight stood like lamps among the thick boughs.

The dragon lay there, wounded. Its scaly hide, like a heap of tarnished coins, held more shadow than light. With its drilled-out eyes, it watched them from a face like a smashed boulder.

Swords hissed from their scabbards, and King Arthur raised his right hand to stay them. Bedevere's messages had described a peaceful union with the creature, and he recalled what Merlin had told him: This was a dreambound thing, provoked from the one Dragon, the planetary beast that slept at the earth's fiery core.

With horrified mutterings tumbling behind him, Arthur stepped through sun-struck asphodel and amaranth and entered the hazel copse, his leather-gloved hands open before him. Daylight glinted off his bronze helmet and the hinges and buckles of his brass-plated armor and clicked in the dark, deep eyes of the dragon.

Sticky coils of tarsmoke seeped from the beast's ulcerous lips. It tried to lift its large, horned head, but it was too weak. The metal-tipped bolt had drained its strength.

Arthur circled the dragon, breathing through his mouth against the sulfurous stink. His heart beat thickly as he surveyed the slitherous immensity and its long, barbed wings of folded black crepe, its malevolent serpent's grin under the stalks, antlers, knobs, and tusks that cluttered its horrid face. The bores of its eyes glittered far back with the enormity of its pain.

Crusted with a scablike black quartz, the bolt that had brought this sky-behemoth to the ground looked ridiculously small where it stuck from the tigered yellow-and-black underbelly. He had to remind himself that this was not an animal of flesh but of ectoplasm hardened by demons. To reach the impacted bolt, Arthur climbed atop a webbed talon and lay full against the dragon's broad flank with its cancerous nodules like red embers. That contact flushed him with untrappable thoughts and musical bewilderments—the Dragon's dreamsong.

He extracted the bolt with one hand, and a ray of blood light shone forth briefly before closing over. The dragon hissed angrily. Black steam unraveled in the sunbeams, and the hulking beast lurched upright, throwing Arthur into the air. He dropped the bolt and clutched at the cobbled spine to keep from flying into the trees.

Prostrate upon the dragon's back, Arthur felt the thunder of the roar pouring from the dragon before he heard it. The sound disappeared inside him. It was absorbed in the dreamsong of the true Dragon, its energy disenthralling the king's mind so that for a moment he became one with the white acetylene intensity of music from the earth's core. He melled into dragon consciousness.

Aisles of stars opened before him. Galactic vistas. Light pierced him on its exile through the darkness of kingdom come. The luminous ruin of the universe as it expanded faster and faster into the black void filled him with its extravagant emptiness. And he would have blacked out—but for the music, the melodious voltage welding him back into his own mind, his own flesh. The Dragon's dreamsong, aimed at the stars, passed through Arthur on its way outward, shaking happiness into his bones and making his heart laugh.

Up from the hazel copse, the winged abomination rose, with Arthur clasped to its back like a human star. The soldiers, groveling atop their frightened horses, grimaced through the whirlwind of tossed leaves and shouted after the dragon as it vanished with their king into the blue zenith.

In Camelot's library behind the central hall, Gawain and Gareth sat at separate drafting tables recording their shared vision of the Holy Grail while Fra Athanasius paced before them. "'Twere folly, Gareth, to rely so prodigiously upon the gerundive. Your account thus swells overmuch your own achievement. Your readers shall assume you are winding truth to your own purposes. You must begin anew if you want this written account to command respect in Ravenna." The scribe turned the parchment over before the young Celt and rapped it with his knuckle. "This time make better use of the ablative. And as for you, Gawain, open your ears." He removed the sheet from before the thick-shouldered lad, and read aloud: "'Such voice commande that wee shoulde thenceaweye fare upp ynto Camelot with haiste and do submmytt our vision to our Lorde the Kynge.' By the Graces themselves, boy, this is nigh unreadable! You write in a spider's thread of archaic Latin. We have much work to do."

"No, we don't!" The glowering Gawain pushed away from the drafting table and stood up so forcefully he knocked over his stool. "We've done enough work. For days, we've done nothing but writing and rewriting. I want no more of this."

Athanasius's face remained sturdily somber. "Sit down, boy. You will begin again—for this tuneless language will bring your account to bane. No one will believe you."

"I don't care." He snatched the parchment from the legate's hands and crumpled it. "Gareth and I know the truth of what the angel told us. The Holy Grail is out there somewhere in Britain—and we're not going to find it in this library."

Gareth poured his phial of ink over his writing table and shoved to his feet. "We have wasted enough time sitting here like scribes. We are warriors. Our da needs us to find the Grail."

Athanasius glared with outrage. "You are boys. Your father will not countenance your starry-eyed ambition."

"Our da is not well." Gawain's kestrel stare revealed a determination that had been hardening for days. "Merlin himself cannot heal him. Da needs to drink from the holy chalice to clear his mind."

"And we will find that chalice for him," Gareth asserted, stepping to his brother's side.

"Sit down. The two of you," Athanasius commanded, and his face flinched when he was not immediately obeyed. "I will not brook such a shameful slight against my authority. You will do as I say."

"I think not, scribe." The threat in Gawain's tone forced Athanasius back one step before the boys seized him. The gangly Roman was easily subdued by the young warriors, and they hogtied him with the sash of his ecclesiastic robe and gagged him with his skullcap. Not until evening was he found, when a servant entered the library to fill the oil lamps.

By then, Gawain and Gareth were half a day's ride from Camelot. They had taken strong horses and several days' provisions. Outfitted in full battle gear, they had not been questioned by the gate sentinels, who believed they were leaving on patrol.

Athanasius berated himself for misjudging the boys' dissatisfaction with their scrivenings, and he implored Kyner to send riders after them. News of the collapsed talks in Londinium between Arthur and Wesc, however, dissuaded the old Celt. War was on the horizon, and the chief would spare no men to discipline two unruly youths.

In despair for the safety of the youngsters and unhappy with the tongue-lashing he would receive from Merlin when the wizard returned to Camelot, Athanasius sought help from Loki. The legate spent a day searching storage chambers in the central hall and the towers, warerooms in the bailey, depots along the lanes of terrace town houses, and even toolsheds in the numerous gardens to no avail. At last, only Merlin's grotto remained uninspected.

With trepidation, the bespectacled emissary passed through the ouroboros portal and descended the uneven rock stairs into the chemical fetor of the subterranean chamber. Glass-orb lamps suspended from stone teeth in the high, domed ceiling lit the way. Loki sat under a bell jar atop a rusty ledge surrounded by alchemic retorts and crucibles. Like a homunculus, the god's bald and swollen head loomed against the glass while his withered torso and tadpole limbs drifted in effluvial mist.

"Athanasius!" Loki's stunted hands slapped against the bell jar. "Let me out!"

"Only if you promise to seek out Gawain and Gareth and return them to Camelot." The scribe peered nervously at the distorted figure and related to him the boys' quest for the Grail.

"Lift the bell jar," Loki said, "and I will seek them at once."

Athanasius put both hands against the glass and felt his palms tingling with the energy within. "You must promise."

"I promise."

The legate lifted the bell jar, and a dazzling flurry of sparks rushed over him so suddenly he dropped the glass. With an explosion of brittle brightness, it smashed to splinters. "Oh mercy of heaven!"

Loki laughed. He stood whole and garbed entirely in black, his bald pate and face scrawled with futhorc. "Heaven has no mercy, poor fool, or children would never die."

Athanasius ignored the god's slander. "Loki, you must hurry. Gawain and Gareth have been at large among pillagers and invaders these two days."

"They will have to find their own way back, I'm afraid."
Loki stepped over the smashed bell jar toward the rock steps. "I
have more pressing concerns."

"What are you saying?"

"I lied." The god shrugged. "That is what my name means,
you know. I am the Liar. And I am aptly named."

"Wait!" Athanasius grabbed the god's elbow, and it dissolved
into a froth of evanescent bubbles in his grip. Shocked, he stared
at his empty hand shining with cold and then at Loki's broken
arm as it swiftly re-formed. "I helped you. Take pity on me,
Loki."

"Pity?" Loki stopped at the foot of the stairs and looked
disdainfully at the mortal. "What pity did you show me when
Succoth pursued me to your chamber? You have no idea
where I had been or what horrors I had seen. You turned
away from me."

"I was charged by the king himself to protect his sword,"
Athanasius protested. He groped in the deep pocket of his dalmatic and withdrew a rosary of ivory beads on a silver thread.
"Behold the horror of God made man!" Waving the crucifix
before him, he approached the Æsir god. "Whatever horrors you
have witnessed are naught compared with this suffering. And in
the name of God's wounds, I beg you to stop and help me."

Loki's marked face twisted angrily. "You don't know what
you're talking about, fool. I have seen calamities of blood and
cruelty that overwhelm the death of any one man, God or not."
He stepped closer, a gleam of savage understanding in his inky
eyes. "Succoth pursued me to the Branch of Hours, and I fled
across time. I ran for my very life across the centuries. And do
you know what I saw?"

Athanasius backed away, the crucifix wavering in his outheld
arm and the rosary beads clacking.

"I saw with my own eyes that the nameless god you worship,
the god of no shape who became a man, the god of your Holy
Bible is nowhere to be found." Futhorc squirmed like black
worms across Loki's face. "'Lord, how long will the wicked, how
long will the wicked triumph?' I will answer that Psalm's question for you Athanasius. And the answer is—forever."

"Calm yourself, Loki." The legate pressed the crucifix to his
breast and prayed inwardly for protection from the wrathful

man-shape edging toward him. "Nor truth nor wisdom comes from your mouth this day."

"Pogrom." Loki's mirthless smile sprang open like a knife. "The word means nothing to you. The Crusades. Another empty name for you. Christians will massacre Jews and other Semites by the thousands for the glory of your blessed Jesus, your Prince of Peace. There is no peace in the future, Athanasius. There is Black Death and more pogroms. There is the Inquisition and the ghetto. There is Belsen—death camps and ovens."

"You speak in insensible thunders, Loki!"

The god grabbed Athanasius by the back of his white alb and walked him briskly across the grotto. "I tried to tell Merlin. He would not listen. He locked me away. But now I'm going to make him listen. And you're not going to stop me." He shoved the frightened scribe into a caliginous hole in the wall and shouted after him, "The wicked will triumph for a thousand years and more, you fool! And your god will keep his silence!"

Athanasius stumbled into the darkness, tripped over the cracked ground, and whirled about with a flapping of robes. A cloud of dust and ash blinded him, and when he wiped his lenses clear, his eyesight flitted over an amorphous shadowscape lit dimly by a squalid red glow, smoky and evil.

"Where is my baby?" Morgeu the Fey asked Brokk, as he strode forth from the mist that whispered over the gravel banks and stony tracts of his arctic isle. "I did as the Furor commanded, and now I want my baby."

A smile of big square teeth illuminated the dwarf's pugnacious face. "Who is this—this guest you bring with you, Morgeu? He has a whimsical aspect. Is he a gleeman?"

"I am the conjured clay," the Fisher King answered, putting both hands to his crown of starfish. "I am the dust of vanity crowned by our Savior a king of fishers, and I search the moon-turned tides for souls and in searching found the wooden miracle." He gestured to the cup in Morgeu's hand. "The Grail!"

The smile slipped from Brokk's face. "He's a madman!" He glared at Morgeu. "Why have you brought a madman to my island?"

"The mad are the servants of the gods." Morgeu pulled her

crimson robe tighter about herself against the damp chill and pressed the cup of illusion against her chest so that its concavity echoed her words and cast a shadow upon the dwarf's mind. "Think what a god such as yourself could accomplish with this servant."

The dwarf's thick hands swiped his cranium of tufty gold hair and his jowls of red whiskers, absently trying to brush away the tickle in his brain that Morgeu's voice inspired. "I am no god. I am a smith to the gods."

"So I thought." Morgeu nodded sagely, and her voice dared reach deeper, far back into the dwarf's inner lives, the series of selves slippery with time and forgetfulness who wanted to remember their ambitions, their fixations, their regrets. "But now I have ridden in Skidblade—your creation—and I *know* you are a god."

Brokk agreed in his depths, and his black eyes glinted.

Morgeu would have feared to attempt enchantment upon one of the gods' own creatures, but she was desperate to save her son, the reborn strength of Gorlois. She filled her voice with great quiet, and commanded, "Take us within your workshop, Brokk, and use this madman as a tool of your ingenuity. Use him to win your rightful place among the Æsir gods of Yggdrasil."

Brokk obeyed. He led them through a crevice in a frost-veined rock wall and conducted them along stone corridors lit by red shadows from grottoes of smelter pots and forges. The air stank of slag and brimstone, and several times the Fisher King made dire noises of protest. Morgeu silenced him each time with an angry hiss. He was her sacrifice, and the grip of her enchantment on him was so unrelenting that when they entered the dwarf's workshop and stood before a metal manikin with a devil's countenance he said nothing. Mutely, he looked about at the cavern of time-crusted walls and stone worktables where gems glinted amidst calipers, clamps, and peelings of metal.

"My mind already encompasses a strategy for my ascension to the sacred boughs of the Storm Tree," Brokk announced as if emerging from a long sleep. "Behold my Cruel Striker armor." He shuffled around a scaffold in which hung a tall manikin of black silver with a tusked mask and red mantis eyes. The dwarf's blunt fingers delicately outlined the sharp fins at the elbows and shoulders. "I designed it for the gods to award to any mortal warrior brave enough to invade the hollow hills. But now—now I see it can be used by this madman you have brought to me. The Fisher King will wear it into the World Tree and take from there the dusk apples. With those apples I will brew an elixir that will make me equal to the gods themselves."

"Yes!" Morgeu fixed her enchantment deep in the dwarf's soul with a shout. "Now that I have given you the tool to lift yourself to the divine status you have long deserved, return my son to me."

"As you say." Brokk waddled across the cavern and at a stalagmite slotted with levers gazed into a crystal sphere big as a skull and set in the stone at eye level for the dwarf. "Ah, Delling is done nursing. She will be here with the child momentarily."

"Delling?" Morgeu asked nervously. "The red elf of the dawn?"

"The same," Brokk acknowledged, rubbing his hands together and sizing up the Fisher King for inclusion in the Cruel Striker. "The boy was hungry. What was there to feed him here?"

Morgeu steadied herself against the stone worktable. "You nursed Mordred on the milk of the red elf—a goddess?"

Brokk seemed not to hear her. He had the Fisher King extend both arms to his sides and measured them with a knotted string. "Some small adjustments, your lordship, and you will be fitted for an assault of heaven!"

"No navy of doves can ascend a man to heaven, truant thumbling," the Fisher King asserted. "Far easier to shut the sun or cage the zodiac. You stride to holocaust . . ."

"Oh shut up." Brokk unhinged the tusked mask of the Cruel Striker and clapped it over the Fisher King's face.

Morgeu the Fey gasped and clutched her heart. Over Brokk's shoulder she saw, in a slant portal garishly illuminated by kiln fires, Delling the red elf of dawn enter. Ruddy as cinnamon with tawny, brindled tresses that fell loosely over her milk-swollen breasts, she shone almost incandescently in her black raiment. She nodded to Morgeu and held back a laugh. At her side clung a pale and naked boy whose long, lank black hair veiled inky eyes bright with supernatural knowing.

"Ah, Mordred!" Brokk grinned with avuncular glee as he turned to face the child. "Hasn't he grown strong on the red elf's milk?"

• • •

A lavish sunset filled the skies of Yggdrasil, and the Brewer stepped outside of Hyndla, the distillery for the Rovers of the Wild Hunt, to relish the sky's supernal beauty. The balding, lump-nosed god untied the leather apron from his thick torso, hung it on a door peg of the stout tower of cedar and mossbrick, and strode forth to admire the shimmering dusk. His assistants and their apprentices had already left, and he relished this private and charmed moment in the ivy-trellised patio under the star-kirtled heavens.

Rarely had he seen such an extravagant twilight, and he marveled at the radiant serifs of clouds that bridged the gates of day. Those incandescent vapors and plumes of sunsmoke were in fact and unbeknownst to him the sylphs of the Daoine Síd. Their wisps and streamers carried hot colors into the very folds of night. Above them, Arcturus blazed with savage brightness.

While the Brewer gazed dreamily upon glassy filaments of cloud braiding the wind in ultratones of color, faeries wafted floral fragrances from the forest depths. The keen taste of autumn intoxicated him, and he stepped to the edge of the patio and did not notice the malformed hobs scurrying from the tree shadows behind him.

Leather-winged snakes flew to a round window of Hyndla's tower and opened it with their teeth, while owls with children's faces attached ropes of reeved vines and roots to the sill. Bright Night grasped the thick braid and walked up the mossbrick wall. Ygrane followed, and together they slipped through the large open window.

The yeasty redolence of the interior pinched their sinuses and watered their eyes, and they sat disoriented for a moment in the casement above percolating vats and softly steaming cauldrons. Then, Ygrane spied what she wanted: black oak kegs marked with the interlocking rune Jera—the harvest, the good season. "There's the memory beer." She pointed to the loft where the kegs were stacked.

Bright Night whistled like a night bird, and the bat-winged vipers and baby-faced owls soared through the window. By the time Ygrane and Bright Night, backs pressed against the humid mossbricks, had edged along the fretwork molding and reached the loft, the hobs had pierced one of the kegs with their talons.

The witch-queen filled a flagon with the frothy blue memory beer, and when she had finished, the elf prince rolled the keg over so that its punctured side would not be obvious.

The Brewer inhaled another waft of the spectral night's extraordinary aroma and turned to go back inside Hyndla. He crossed the patio and reached for his leather apron upon the door peg. A clatter distracted him, and he thought he saw figures moving over the rooty footings of the forest. He walked to the patio edge and brushed aside dangling ivy. Gazing hard into the black chambers of the woods, he saw only the wind with its footsteps in the boughs—and through the gaps in the forest canopy a zenith of stars strung with strands of cobweb fire.

9

Fate-Sayer

The dragon soared into a faultless blue sky with Arthur clinging to its back. Sunlight shone from the king's bronze helmet and the brass plates of his armor, and he appeared from the ground as a sparkle upon the black hide of something huge and saurian and wrapped in steam.

Enveloped by that acrid dragonsmoke, the young man groaned.

He embraced a spine knob with all his strength, his face bleared back by the force of the dragon's ascent.

The air grew cold, and Arthur's breath smoked as he pulled himself along the scaly ridges of the dragon's back. To either side, the spiked wings flared, catching the wind with giant torn sheets of crocodilian flesh. Then, abruptly, above the clouds, the dragon leveled its flight.

Sunlight burned its iridescent flesh to a charred crust, and a searing pain coursed through its long body. Fearlessly, it endured this fiery anguish, intent on absorbing from the sun enough energy to combust.

It's going to destroy itself! Arthur realized with alarm, and nearly lost his grip. Desperately, he clung tighter, feeling through the scaly hide the dragon's lethal will—and even the torment that drove it. It was heavy with hurt. The demons had shaped it for agony and rampage, and now it just wanted to die.

Arthur crawled along the spine, squinting through the acidic vapors streaming out of the ripped hide. The closer he pulled himself to the beast's head, the more vividly he experienced its physical thoughts. The dreamdragon that had been conjured by demons had turned its wrath upon itself, wanting to change this evil dream.

Flames erupted from the sharp tips of the wing bones. In moments, the fissured skin would explode, and the ectoplasmic creature would vanish in a haze above the shining world. Arthur gaped at the tilted forests and fields below. And distantly, he heard singing.

Another roar flew past in a gasp of black smoke, and the melodious voice did not diminish. The melody was not in the air but floating up from within him, far louder than any memory. It was Bedevere's voice, singing a tavern ditty.

Believing that dragonfumes had bedeviled his mind, Arthur concentrated on pulling himself over the jagged hide, heedless of the burning pain and Bedevere's incongruously lyrical voice wafting above the rollicking plains far below.

He clasped a skull horn and lifted himself into the clear wind. There was never so much sky! Blue rushed through his chest and into his humming ears.

And still, he heard Bedevere singing. The soothing tune lilted from within, from an unsuspected magical bond with the dragon. The messages Bedevere had sent to Londinium had spoken of trance singing and the possibility of peaceful union with the dragon, and they had spoken truer than Arthur had dared believe: Could it be that this wondrous creature knew his thoughts?

Arthur called down into the ditch of agony: "North! Fly north, dragon! Fly to the cool north!"

The dragon's flight veered. It dipped into a cloud, and the sun became but a sigh. Instantly, the searing hurt diminished, and Bedevere's singing resounded louder. He was crooning a Roman song about a lizard skittering along a churchyard's wall. The tune flowed like cool water in the creek bed of the dragon's mind.

The cloud turned feathery, then burst into open sky. And though sunlight smoldered across its hide, the dragon did not roar or even hiss with pain. It was entranced by Bedevere's singing and by Arthur's presence as it glided toward the protective shade of another cloudbank.

The electric charge building on the king's armor gave his voice a compelling force in the dragon's mind. "North! Quickly as you can, dragon! Fly north!" His words echoed across the bright blue of dream. And the Dragon, the planetary beast curled asleep at the magnetic heart of the earth, heard him

The distant voice promised misty lochs, steep valleys, and dense glens. In the absence of demons to influence its dreaming, the sleeping Dragon accepted the king's suggestion, and it flew north.

At that moment, all the dreamdragons across Britain rose as one amid thunderous bellowing and spills of smoke. From willow banks, fern holts, and the caves under collapsed bridges, they scrambled forth and launched into the sky. All at once, a score and twelve dragons etched vapor paths in the azure zenith, converging northward.

Arthur saw them cruising in clusters through the stacked clouds, their shadows below flurrying across the countryside. His heart swerved, astounded that the dragon armada was obedient to him. Would they do whatever he commanded?

Bracing himself against the crown of horns on the brow of his dragon, the king called, "Bedevere!" He kept his eyes open, staring into the lashing wind and watching purple highlands step forth from the sweltering horizon. "Keep singing! We command dragons!"

The hammerbeat of his heart and the buffeting wind obscured the singing, yet the king sensed Bedevere was near. Linked with the dreamsong of the Dragon, his voice had insinuated itself inside the sleeping Dragon's awareness. He and Arthur floated in an alert zone vast as the dreaming mind, insignificant smudges of atomic dust in the enormous instant of the universe. Across diamond distances of stars, the dreamsong clenched immensities swarming with galaxies—and Bedevere's singing had connected them to this cosmic power.

Arthur shouted triumphantly into the strong wind. The Dragon was asleep and dreaming under mantles of space sewn with stars. It was too huge to notice them, yet Bedevere had found a way to tap its power.

Bedevere—

Remorse stumbled through him. He had been unkind to this man who had fought at his side, and he had judged him in his heart, judged him not by known deeds but by slander. That seemed obvious in the shining wind, flanked by dragons. And he briefly wondered if he would feel the same charity on the ground, away from the magical intensity of this flight.

His ruminations broke off at the sight of King Cruithni's massive army swarming upon the countryside, advancing like cloud shadows across the moors and over the hills. In the distance, Luguvalium burned, hurling black smoke into the sky.

The aerial view of that gutted city twisted rage in the king. He sagged before the rush of the wind, feeling the onrush of souls with their inaudible screams. In the depths where his mind touched dream, the Dragon felt his fiery wrath, and before he could speak, a sky of flames fell upon the Picts.

Arthur pressed an arm over his face, warding the heat and the sudden stink of roasted bodies. Incinerated howls crawled away under the furious noise of the dragons. When the king removed his protective arm, he surveyed drifts of ash. Tarry spines and blackened briskets alone remained of the warrior hordes.

On surrounding braes, dragons stalked the fleeing ranks. Rays of blue fire slashed through the tumultuous smoke and cinders. The dragon carrying Arthur launched through a pall of greasy soot and arced into the clear sky. Nausea flew like a ghost through his body and left him flat, clinging with one arm to the dragon's horned brow.

Below, a delirium of dragons frenzied over the combs and dales of the rumpled land. Horrible, hollow cries leaped upward when Pictish steel exploded dragons. Then the shrieking of beasts stopped.

Arthur pushed himself to his elbows and saw dragons milling upon scorched ground. They did not spread their leathery wings and rise from the earth. They had spent their power as the Dragon had dreamed, in a sky of falling fire. Cruithni's army had passed entirely into ash.

Morgeu the Fey sat down on an obsidian-stone workbench in the underground foundry of the Æsir dwarf Brokk. Flameshadows cast by the surrounding kilns illuminated a look of benign surprise on her round, pale face. Her placid expression hid her outrage and fright that her baby Mordred had drunk of elf's milk during her absence and had grown to the height of a ten-year-old. *And his mind?* she wondered, smiling at the naked boy as he came out from under the protective arm and long, brindled tresses of the elf. *What has the red elf's milk made of the mind that was my father?*

"Mother, you are more beautiful than I remember," the child said in a clear, factual voice, and stepped toward her. "You've been gone so long, whenever I looked for you all I ever found was a corpse."

Morgeu said nothing, stunned by what elf's milk and loveless time had made of her baby. She took the boy's hand and felt childhood nirvana. Joy, wonder, and energy glowed from him. Cut to speak prophecy by the Furor's own knife, nursed by a goddess, reborn of a slain Roman, Mordred was yet a child.

"You're not a corpse," he said, and touched her frizzy red hair. "Not yet."

"Whoever looks far enough sees a corpse," Delling chirped from the slant portal in the rock wall. "Mordred has the strong eye, and sometimes he sees too far. I told him to look for you closer to us. But you were in Skidblade, and the way time folded around you confused him, poor dear."

Morgeu wanted to scream—her baby was gone! She smiled instead and brushed the stringy black hair from her son's face. Yes, there was Arthur's wide brow, her mother's oblique cheekbones, her own small black eyes, like puncture holes in the white flesh, Gorlois's pugnacious jaw.

Mordred lost interest in staring at her, comparing her moony face and big-shouldered frame to the mummied skeleton of his visions. Only the bright red hair was the same.

He stepped away abruptly and looked up at the tarnished armor with its barbed fins and tusked mask that the ingenious dwarf had built to raid Yggdrasil. "Who is inside Cruel Striker, Nuncle Brokk?"

The smith, with a big-toothed grin in his whiskery face, rapped a knuckle against the smoky metal, eliciting a desultory bong. "You are a fate-sayer, Mordred. Say the fate of the mortal caged herein."

Mordred gazed at the bruised limbs dangling from inside the

tall armor and reached out to finger the fish-skin tunic and crude cordwood sandals. "He will not fish again."

Brokk bleated with laughter. "Say more!"

"He will hold the treasure of the gods," the boy whispered, small eyes smaller as he tried to understand what he was seeing. "They are—apples. Strange apples. Made of wind, and the wind is bright . . . I don't know what it is. Is it sunlight swirling round in each apple? I see myself reflected in the shiny skins. I am in a hole in the ground, too deep for me to climb out. I am playing with white snakes and a skull."

Morgeu stood and gently pulled Mordred away from the Fisher King hanging in the scaffold of armor. "You must not look too closely at the dusk apples. They are a blind mirror."

"Oh don't scold him," Delling said, and put her rosy-tipped fingers on Mordred's shoulders. "He has never seen into the Tree before."

"Let the boy say more!" Brokk nimbly climbed the scaffold and wrenched open the vizard of red mantis eyes. The bearded face within looked frightened. "Have no fear, Fisher King. The fate-sayer has seen you with the dusk apples."

This news did not assuage the Fisher King's fear. His face shone so palely that the scar on his brow glowed crimson. "All fate is writ in a book of water. Unhouse me from this iron salvage. Unhouse me, you devils!"

Brokk slammed the vizard back into place. "Mordred, you have made me happy. I will remember you when I am a god."

"Best you act swiftly, Brokk." Morgeu intoned her voice with enchantment. She took both of Mordred's hands and led him away from Delling. "Without deeds, visions are but unclaimed promises."

"There will be deeds!" Brokk grabbed a chain suspended from a pulley and stepped off the trestle. His compact body swiftly descended, pulling the chain after him so that winch and gears clanked. Swiveling trestles fitted together large pieces of black enamel armor, and they fused with a sibilant flaring of sparks. "The cables are already installed. Your madman provides the final linkage. The work is done!"

Cruel Striker stepped forth silently, carrying his head high, a metallic cobra, chrome shoulders hooded like a cape over his sinuous, articulated spine. The dwarf paced before his creation, scrutinizing the gleaming giant with an admiring eye and muttering proudly to himself. "I have labored in Middle Earth long enough for the gods. Now I will take the fruit of the Storm Tree for myself and its ciders will transform me to an equal among the proud Æsir."

Twin ingots of fire brightened in Delling's eyes, a slash of sunrise in her stare as she watched Morgeu bending over the pale boy and whispering to him. She lifted a hammer from a clutter of tools and banged it fiercely on the worktable beside Brokk. Calipers and ribbons of metal bounced, and the excited dwarf stood abruptly still. "You said the boy was mine." Delling pointed sharply at Morgeu. "She is taking the fate-sayer."

"Let the boy go," Brokk replied, sternly. "We will have the dusk apples. Put down that hammer."

"You must help Brokk," Morgeu said with all her mesmeric strength. She had never attempted to enchant an Æsir goddess and did not know what to expect. "You must put down the hammer and lead Cruel Striker to the Rainbow Bridge. Without you to guide him to Yggdrasil, there will be no dusk apples for this greatest of inventors. Without your help, Brokk will never be more than a clever dwarf—and never entirely worthy of you. Go."

Delling nodded tenderly, and the fire in her eyes dimmed. She laid the hammer on the table and gazed softly at Brokk. "I will take Cruel Striker into the dawn with me. None of the Rovers of the Wild Hunt will see him." She walked to the slant portal from where she had entered and paused while Cruel Striker sleekly strode past her, a quicksilver ferret, a black diamond shadow. "I do this for you Brokk. I do this that we may be together in the World Tree, no longer prisoners of this scorched place."

"Delling!" Mordred called in his silver voice. "I will miss you."

She appeared briefly in her first form, sunflames in long rays of darkest red, an almost velvet light on which he had suckled and become godly with knowing. Then she vanished, and Morgeu pulled Mordred away by his elbow.

Brokk stood at his viewer, thick face pressed close to the

crystal sphere, monitoring the progress of his Cruel Striker. The boy looked and looked, hoping their eyes would touch one last time. The dwarf had been an amusing playmate, and there was more of his fate to say than the boy had said. "Cruel Striker will hold the treasure of the gods—but the gods will hold him!"

"Hush!" Morgeu lifted Mordred off his feet and scurried across the workshop with him. Her enchantments had proven more powerful than she had hoped, but she had no notion how long her influence would last. "Brokk must not be disturbed. Come away."

The boy was nearly too big to carry, and she set him down as soon as they departed the workshop. He gazed back along the riven corridor at the shining doorway, expecting Brokk to come striding through, looking for him. But Morgeu's magic was too strong, and the fate-sayer sighed.

"Don't be sad," Morgeu consoled. "You will see Delling again and Brokk as well—when you are lord of all Britain."

"My father is king." Mordred took Morgeu's hand. He led her a few paces to a stone stepway that spiraled up toward a blue egg of daylight. "He will always be lonely. I do not want his place."

Morgeu sat on the steps and leaned back on her elbows, assessing the weird pale thing she had spawned. "Say my fate."

"You came back for me. Your fate is mine." He smiled, sadly and also with mischief. "We will make our own fate, Morgeu the Doomed. Come. I know where Nuncle Brokk hides the most magical cup."

Selwa accompanied Merlin from Londinium to Camelot. The wizard, distraught over Wesc's impending invasion and unhappy with the king's dragon hunt, proved a less amiable companion than he had been on the river journey. He rode alone at the van of the royal retinue and appeared to brood. But Selwa knew otherwise. Through the gates of power that had opened in her, she could feel him reaching into the invisible dimensions, counseling with particles of light, reviewing with them his strategy for leading the king into the Storm Tree—if Arthur survived his dragon hunt.

The Storm Tree had seemed a quaint myth of the north tribes to Selwa until Merlin had opened in her body three of the seven eyes of God. Since then, the sky was no longer empty blue in a hood of clouds. Staring into the heavens with her magical sight, she watched auroras ruffling even in daylight. During the brief conference of kings, she had sat on the roof of the governor's palace and gazed for hours into the luminous, celestial falls.

Selwa had a strategy of her own. She touched it in silence and only with that rapt and most certain part of herself, the magical will coiled like a snake under her omphalos. She did not want Merlin to discover her plan, and so she did not allow herself to know what it was until the very day they returned to Camelot. That chill October morning when she had woken in her wagon on the road to the citadel, she had sensed something marvelous was going to happen, because she had eschewed her usual gauzy robes and had chosen to wear suede boots, black canvas trousers sturdy enough for a camel rider, and a curly-wool shirt.

She was glad for those warm garments when she stood in the wizard's damp alchemic grotto. But she did not grasp their purpose until she saw the Dragon's teardrop and understood that she was bound for Yggdrasil.

The teardrop, an orb big as a skull and heavy as iron, shimmered iridescently when she lifted it from the stone lap of the Original Mother. The ice-age statue alone saw her retreat with it, for Merlin was too agitated to notice.

Loki had been released from the bell jar, and the wizard did not have time to search for him. Starcharts preoccupied the old demon, because Ygrane had brought a black unicorn to earth, a rare and dangerous creature whose very presence uncoiled branches of Yggdrasil into the future. Merlin had to plan their ascent carefully or they could lose themselves in time.

As Selwa climbed the grotto stairs, Kyner nearly collided with her. He shoved past, oblivious to the rock she carried, and she heard him shouting gruffly for Merlin: Cei still would not wake, Gawain and Gareth had fled to seek the Holy Grail, the papal emissary was gone as well. Where was the king? Duke Marcus had sent terrible news that Arthur had been carried off by a dragon.

Selwa chortled to hear so much confusion. Her own mind was clear, a lens polished by Merlin's training and ready now to focus the fiery energy of her heart's ambitions. She would take the Vanir Lotus for herself. Merlin had confided enough knowledge for her to immix the Dragon's teardrop with the Lotus nectar and to drink new life, new magic older than the gods.

Unlike her mentor, she did not have to be cautious about climbing the World Tree. She was a not a king or an enemy of the Æsir gods. No one would notice her, and no foes but her own fear blocked her way; she calmed that fear with the majestic strength Merlin had opened in the secret depths of herself. And she was not afraid when she carried the Dragon's teardrop out through the ouroboros portal and through the central hall to a bright doorway that floated several inches above the floor.

Through the entry she saw an unearthly sight: the huge, pocked face of the moon in a lavender sky among starry pinwheels and misty shreds of neon vapors. As Merlin had taught her, Camelot was a passage into Yggdrasil, and all one needed was the magic to open it. She stepped boldly into a vista of purple mountains and blue tree-roughs that descended among emerald meadows and labyrinthine valleys studded with lakes of golden stillness.

By the time Merlin noticed that the Dragon's teardrop was gone and Selwa as well, the earth had turned and Camelot's entryways into Yggdrasil had shifted. The wizard removed his hat and dashed it to the ground, then kicked furiously at the Original Mother and hopped about with a bruised toe, cursing himself for trusting Selwa.

"Ain't love grand?" Loki oozed up from the cracked floor, where he had been hiding. He pretended to wipe dust from his black garments and his tattooed head, his dark eyes shining with glee. "I've been waiting for you to notice that you've been robbed."

"Loki!" Merlin glared furiously at the grinning god. "You could have stopped her."

"Why should I?" He leaned back against a rock shelf of glass retorts, their effervescent colors visible through his translucent torso. "We have an agreement, you and I, Merlin. I want the sword Lightning."

"Who let you out?" The wizard waved aside the question,

already knowing the answer. "Athanasius. Where is he?"

"He's touring the hollow hills." Loki shook his head ruefully. "When he released me, I intended to find you. I did. I wanted to tell you the terrible things I have seen in the future. Terrible things, Merlin. But then I thought, what do you care? You want your king to rule Britain here and now. What do you care of human slaughters in centuries to come? You're a demon!" He crossed his arms and raised his handsome chin defiantly. "So, I decided to wait here for you. I will not face Succoth and his demons again without the sword Lightning in my hand. If you want my help in the Storm Tree, Merlin, get me the sword."

Arthur climbed a steep gorge trail with an infant swaddled against his chest. During his flight south from Caledonia, the dreamdragon he rode had dissolved and tossed him through the piney treetops. His armor had broken his fall, and he had climbed down through the boughs uninjured. Stunned by the magical fury of his flight, he had wandered aimlessly through the forest—until he had found a tinker and his wife slain for their wagon and horse by a wildwood gang.

Their bones had lain like blackened stones where they had been burned. Twisted wagon tracks, the tinker's small hammer, and meager tin scraps discarded by the gang mutely testified to the brutal encounter in this evergreen holt. The baby had wailed from where the mother had hidden her in the rootcove of a juniper.

Arthur had provided water and eventually some cypress-root milk before the infant calmed down in his arms. He had removed his plate-armor vest and had used the leather straps and the linen undershirt to fashion a harness that secured the infant. With his arms free, the king climbed the nearest bluff, hoping to find his way to a settlement. But they were deep in the hilly forests of Cymru, far from any haven.

The river Usk flowed darkly in the sunless gorge below. A crude footbridge of hemp cables swayed above it, and a lanky figure moved nimbly across the clacking boards. Merlin emerged from a stand of twisted, cliffside trees. "My lord!" the wizard called out. "I have searched half of Cymru for you!"

Before the king could reply, a savage growl shook the air. A massive, shaggy giant lumbered across the hillcrest—a bear big as legend. Its tiny eyes points of night, its teeth flashing, it shambled forward, then reared and opened its thick arms to take Arthur into its dark embrace.

The king staggered backward and drew Excalibur.

"The baby!" Merlin shouted. "Give me the baby while you fend the beast."

"Merlin—drive it away!" Arthur called, hastily unstrapping the bawling infant. "Use your magic!"

The wizard said nothing. With his own magic he had summoned the bear, to force the king to draw Excalibur. He snatched the child from Arthur and ran toward the wind-bent trees. Arthur followed, the bear charging swiftly toward them through the gorse.

With remarkable agility, Merlin leaped onto the rickety footbridge, the baby squirming in his arms. Instantly, Arthur spun about, sword high, ready to battle the beast.

But the bear had turned and was already loping downhill.

Merlin's cry broke over Arthur. The king turned about and saw that the frail bridge had snapped its moorings. In an instant, the swaying span would plummet into the chasm. Arthur hurried to the very brink to grab the wizard, but Merlin was too far, and the bridge rocked too violently.

"The child!" Merlin cried out, and tossed the infant into the air. "Catch the child!"

At that doomful instant, the cables snapped, and the bridge swung away, the wizard riding it in a robe belled with wind. The baby lofted askew, bound for the rocks below. The only possibility that the king had of catching her required him to throw his arms into the abyss. And the only way to do this and not topple over was to drop his sword, for there was no time to set it safely aside.

"No!" he yelled, refusing to relinquish Excalibur, his only hope against the malign gods.

Yet—as Merlin knew he would—Arthur let go the beautiful weapon. It toppled through the air, flashing sunlight-bright and quick, before it disappeared into the shadowy gorge.

There, Loki waited, crouching on a crumblesome ledge where the wizard had placed him. When the sword fell past, he snatched it. At the same moment, on the cliff brim above, Arthur reached out both arms, his whole upper body swinging over the dizzy precipice to seize the infant with his fingertips and pull her to his heart.

Brokk pressed his porcine face close to the crystal orb, staring hard into the dawn vista within. Delling had delivered Cruel Striker over the Rainbow Bridge into Yggdrasil, and the dwarf gazed blearily across the crimson twilight, numb-edged as a drunk, waiting for the silver man-shape to return.

When the alarm blared, he bumped his head against the crystal. "What could be the matter now?" he muttered testily.

The slave elves, obeying the alarm, returned to their cells, and the kilns in their grottoes dimmed. Brokk pulled a lever on the orb post, and the crystal revealed the site of the alarm: an alabaster niche in a black rock wall lay bare.

"The Graal!" Brokk yelped. He pulled several other levers, panic-stricken, scanning the domed vault where he had stored the chalice. He could find it nowhere in the vast well of ebon rock. Most recently, the dwarf had used the magical cup to bend weather away from the West Isles. The Furor would be enraged if rain hampered his invasion of Britain, and he would certainly crucify Brokk for losing the Graal.

Hands a blur upon the levers, he checked each of the exits and caught a glimpse of a crimson robe disappearing into the smoky entryway of Skidblade. In the narrowing door, he glimpsed ghost-pale Mordred clinging to Morgeu's side—and, in her hand, the gold cup scattering light like music.

Skidblade served the Furor. Because the chieftain had placed the fleet ship under Morgeu's command, Brokk could not stop it from departing the gravel banks where the enchantress had called it to her. In a blink, it spooled brightly upward and out of sight.

Brokk wailed and pounded the crystal sphere with both fists. The orb jarred loose, and the image of the frost-glazed sky wobbled. With one hand to steady the viewer and the other working the levers, the agitated dwarf shifted to the dawn vista, and shouted, "Delling! Call back Cruel Striker at once!"

"But he may not yet have the dusk apples . . ."

"At once!" Brokk cut off Delling's puzzled reply, "I need Cruel Striker here immediately!"

Delling complied. The fluted silk of her dawn colors fluoresced, fanning yellow rays higher into the sky. She directed Brokk's command to the living armor, ordering it to depart the Storm Tree.

At that moment, Cruel Striker had backed out of the grange silo where Keeper of the Dusk Apples stored her small and rare harvest. The silo, a pile of massive stones soft-edged with velvet lichen, had a monolithic door graven in crimson runes. The runes forbade all but Keeper of the Dusk Apples to enter, and the ponderous stone responded only to her command. Brokk had designed it thus. And he had fashioned Cruel Striker to mimic her command perfectly.

With a canvas sack bulging full of dusk apples, Cruel Striker emerged from the grange silo. But before he could give the command to shut the giant door, Delling called, and the armor turned about and marched off.

The Fisher King, snug as a kernel within the metal shell, gawked about, frightened. This was no world he recognized. Greyhound clouds dashed across the darkest blue sky he had ever seen, running before stars dense as sea foam. A landscape of deep-cleft dales with jade forests and hillslopes of saffron grasses flourished more voluptuously than any garden he had witnessed on earth. Hollowed by awe, he realized that this devil armor had actually delivered him to heaven—and it had successfully stolen the apples of Eden.

He bawled for the angels to stop him. He bawled for Michael of the flaming sword. The angels did not hear, but Keeper of the Dusk Apples did.

She lay with the Furor in a tree house so overgrown with sinewy vines no one could see it but those who knew it was there. Animal spirits of creatures slain by the Furor patrolled the verdant grove as sentinels, and the privacy of the lovers was so assured that the Fisher King's cry surprised the goddess.

She pulled herself out of the Furor's arms and sat upright. It took her a moment to realize that the voice had squeaked from the foot of the bed, from the guardian amulet she had discarded with her veils and silks. The amulet's starflint had been cut to listen to what the stones of her grange silo heard.

Animals, elves, passing hunters—there were so many possible passersby the stones could have heard. She would have dismissed the Fisher King's cries to better listen to her lover—because the Furor was telling her about the Fire Lord who had shamed him for his infidelity to Lady Unique—but he insisted she look. Leaning over the burled wood frame of the bed, she glanced at the mirror charm that watched the grange silo, and she gasped.

With that cry, the Furor felt his soul cleave open. His encounter with the Fire Lord had exposed the mistake of lust in his heart, the mistake that had blinded his one good eye. With the energy of the Fire Lord still shining in him, he saw clearly what he had ignored before. And he understood why the Wyrd Sister Skuld had revealed the conception of Arthur, why the smudge-faced waif had warned him to listen to Wesc's mad poetry—to understand that his betrayal of Lady Unique would cost him his war with Arthur. With premonitory clarity, he heard Keeper of the Dusk Apples' gasp at the wind of his soul leaving him.

Icy realization sank coldly into his marrows. Unless something dire was made to happen immediately, that upstart Arthur would live to forge a vision that would brighten over the centuries. Camelot would illuminate the dominance of mortals over gods, and the light of Excalibur would fuse earth and heaven with machinery, flaring ever hotter, until the planet itself sweltered and burst into nuclear flames!

Ash. The future was ash. And ash clogged the Furor's heart as he heard his mistress announce the theft of the dusk apples. Was it Merlin? Or Arthur himself?

Half-naked, the warrior god stormed from the tree house, wolfskin boots in one hand, javelin in the other. Perhaps there was yet time to redeem himself. He would slay Arthur at once, with his own hands, and drink a salutation to his wife from the boy-king's skull.

Loki caught the sword Lightning as it fell, and the moment his hand grasped the gold haft he turned to sunsteam and, with the blade's magic, ascended directly into the Storm Tree. Arthur did not see the geyser of light that shot to the zenith; he was teetering backward from the precipice with a wailing baby in his hands.

Merlin, swinging with the severed bridge, balefully watched the star of Excalibur dwindle into the sky. In the moment before the falling span slapped into the opposite cliff, the wizard shouted the god's name with outraged fury: "Lo—kee!"

Stupendous laughter seized Loki when the plank bridge

threw Merlin into the cliff wall and his body tumbled down the rocky scarp like a bundle of loose sticks. Had the fool wizard truly expected Loki to serve him—a filthy demon—once the sword Lightning was his? "I am the Liar!" he shouted back, hoping that Merlin broke his neck in the brutal fall but not lingering to see. Conquest awaited him.

The hazy dimness of Middle Earth brightened into the spectral colors and sunglint clarity of Yggdrasil. He breathed in the rainbow air that strobed past him during his entry to one of the lower boughs and began looking around boulders and stumps and old scree for a good place to hide the weapon.

A tall warrior in armor of scalded silver and black enamel strode through the rainbow mists, appearing and disappearing between the trees. He carried a canvas sack, walking hard for the dusky blue field beyond the forest, determined to throw himself into the gulf and the fall to Middle Earth.

The sword Lightning obeyed Loki's heart and flew from his hand. Bolts of electric fire tangled blindingly, and Cruel Striker collapsed, its skull plate hewn open. Hot knots of energy blazed where the sword had wedged between the red mantis eyes and curving tusks.

Loki ran up to the fallen warrior and pulled the sword Lightning free. The bloody interior interested him less than the mysterious canvas sack, and he opened it with the blade. A moan, low and sexual, oozed from him at the sight of the dusk apples.

My fortune! He knelt and with trembling hands piled the spilled apples in the sack, counting the loyalties he could buy among the Æsir with this harvest. The first dark edge of doubt that this bounty was too good to be true touched his mind an instant before the shadow of the Furor fell upon him.

Loki cringed a look over his shoulder and stared into the starpoint tip of the chieftain's javelin.

Merlin squatted in a dank alcove of his cavernous chambers where only crooked light reached. He drowned in shadows. Emotions floated like corpses around him, bloated sacks of human pain. He tried to detach. He tried to remember that he had not always been human. But Selwa's faithless thievery of the Dragon's tear and Loki's treachery twisted in him with spiraling pain. Their deceptions had come far sooner than he had expected—and hurt him far more crucially than he could bear. Without the Dragon's teardrop, lifetimes of work were squandered. Optima, Ygrane, Uther, and King Arthur himself collapsed to dust and erased across time.

Merlin crawled into a lightless corner of his grotto, covered his head with his robe, and sobbed.

10

Kingdom in a Chalice

Stars burned like high altar flames.

How can there be stars in the hollow hills? Fra Athanasius pondered anxiously. He pulled his alb and priestly robe tighter about himself. For many hours he had been wandering under the lee of a mountain, its dark immensity growing between him and the twilight. Though the subterranean crag entirely blotted the hell-glow from the fiery core of the planet, yet the stars glimmered overhead. *How can that be?*

He gazed around trepidatiously. The air was cold here, so unlike the acrid paths to the Dragon, where he had wandered with the young king and Merlin. His lenses chilled in the gloom and misted with his body heat. Spiritous reflections made him jump.

Stifling a cry, he dropped to his knees in the darkness and began to pray yet again for divine help. As he groveled, his brow happened to scratch against the gravel, and he noticed that the black grit sparkled.

Pausing in his prayers, he scooped up a handful of earth and brought it close to his eyes. The grains resembled tiny cubes, like those he had seen in the jet agate geodes from the chasm of Vesuvius that the Bishop of Neapolis displayed in his garden. The lights above were not stars after all, he realized, but mineral crystals reflecting the chthonic fires.

Bolstered by this rational observation, Athanasius shook off his fear, stood up, and continued his trek. He reasoned that the direction away from the molten light would lead to the surface, and he pressed on through the cold and murky landscape, ant-small among arches of rock that curved above him like immense stone ribs. Mists coagulated to phantoms. Even after he wiped his lenses, the phantoms hung like steam in the glittering dark.

He stopped abruptly in his tracks, and his astonished hands groped before him, not trusting his eyes. Bishop Victricius stood ahead on the carbonized sand, a phosphorescent specter so vivid that his robes, heavy and stiff with water, pulled from his bony shoulders. Bedraggled hair and beard matted his skull, and a brown ribbon of kelp furled over his blue forehead. He drew the sign of the cross in the air.

"Your Grace?" Athanasius gaped, blinked, and turned his head to be sure his smeared spectacles did not deceive him. "Bishop Victricius!"

"I have been watching you, *notarius*, from on high." The wraith lifted his arm, and through the radiant transparency of his soaked robe, the black mountain brightened. A terraced landscape of cracked clay flared desolately into view. Above it, a perilous garden overhung the torched plateland. Broken stobs of cacti and spined trees cluttered the thin rills that trickled down from a higher terrace. On those summit slopes, carpeted meadows of wildflowers, sprawling trees, and the waterways of misty falls bedazzled the darkland. "I will not leave this limbo for paradise until our mission to Britain is concluded. So, dear *notarius*, won't you show some alacrity, please? I am cold."

Athanasius leaned toward the apparition, so amazed that he stammered on silence before he managed to say, "Eminence! All this time you have been watching over *me*?" The scribe bowed his head, ashamed. "Forgive me, sainted Victricius. I have served ill. Our mission is undone, because I am lost in the hollow hills."

The shade said nothing. With a heavy arm, he pointed into the dark, then kindled brighter and disappeared.

Athanasius hurried forward to embrace the bishop, but only emptiness received him. Gawking about, he saw mists crawling down the moraine from the mountain, flowing like milk among the boulders. Slowly, the woven tendrils of fog unraveled to release haggard shapes—deadwalkers, corpses that staggered toward him with their flesh hanging like blackened rags. These were the souls of the damned. Attracted initially by the holy glow of Victricius, they now fixed upon the blood heat of the scribe.

He ran. But soon he realized that running was futile. The ghosts flew like spume. Their char bones danced ahead of him. Quickly, he sidestepped into a grove of obelisks. In his desperation to flee, he slammed into one of the stone spires and sagged to his knees. The iron studs that outlined the cross and the chi-rho on his vestments clamped onto the obelisk and pulled his garment tightly about his sagging frame. Though he tugged at his dalmatic with all his might, he could not free it from the greedy stone.

Athanasius grasped at once that this must be a lodestone and, after a moment's further struggle, realized that it was a lodestone of such extraordinary power he would have to crawl out of his dalmatic to get free. Memories of Merlin's lectures rushed forward even as he cringed behind the magnetic column, watching the ghastly fumes unfold more shuffling dead, their vaporous skullfaces uplifted, sniffing for his blood warmth.

Scientia! he remembered Merlin's promise. And an idea fitted itself together in him with a rush of hope. Groping at the base of the obelisk, his hands closed on a splinter of lodestone long as his forearm and wide as a finger. He picked it up and ran with it, the diabolic fog rolling after him.

Crouched between two shattered spires, he removed the rosary from his pocket, mumbled a short prayer beseeching forgiveness, then snapped the clasp that bound the loop of prayer beads to the crucifix. The ivory beads spilled with a soft clatter. In his frightened fingers, the silver cord unwound swiftly into its individual filaments, and soon he had a handful of fine silver thread.

Through the standing rocks, the soot smoke of the dead drifted. Athanasius hurried away, his busy fingers wrapping the silver wire tightly about the finger of lodestone, just as he had seen Merlin do. Twice he had to start over again when he stumbled in the dark and his hands fumbled. When at last he had successfully coiled the wire, he stopped his cowering retreat and turned again in the direction that Bishop Victricius had pointed, for surely that was the way back to Britain and the completion of his mission.

Grave smoke blocked his way, ranks of corpses watching him with glistening eyes in their sockets.

He was not afraid. He knew that the wire he had coiled

around the lodestone conducted an electric current, because Merlin had shown him this phenomenon in his laboratory. The current was mild but strong enough to disrupt effluvial shapes.

"*Scientia!*" Emboldened by his cry, Athanasius advanced, waving his electric wand. The necrotic shapes dissolved before him with silent screams, their leprous, grasping hands wafting to mist as he strode through their torn vapors with growing vigor.

Yellow wings of dusk lowered over the tree house where the Furor and Keeper of the Dusk Apples lay curled together in their bower bed. The sword Lightning stood upon the headboard, stabbed into the knotted wood by the one-eyed god. The portent of victory that the Furor found in his old weapon occluded all the shame he had felt for betraying Lady Unique. The Fire Lord at Avalon had filled him with reproach as a defense, to avoid answering the chieftain's questions. But there was no reason for the Furor to feel ashamed: So long as Lady Unique did not know about Keeper, there was no wrong in what he did, he said to himself. No one was hurt. All were happy. The return of the sword Lightning weakened Arthur, and the boy-king's early death would weaken the flames of history so that they did not flare into apocalypse.

"And the Liar?" Keeper whispered, running her fingers through his large beard, her lips grazing his ear. "He stole our dusk apples to bribe the Rovers away from you. *And* he destroyed Brokk's Cruel Striker when it tried to protect the apples. Surely, love, you will not show mercy to your blood brother this time?"

"We will not see Loki again for a long time," the Furor answered, turning and pulling her against him. "Put him out of your mind and give yourself again to me. I want the sword Lightning to behold the ardor we share."

Excalibur's mirror blade reflected the lovers tangled embrace through the tree-house windows. In the twilight, sylphs of the Daoine Síd watched, invisible against the fiery seams of the day.

Faeries brought the sylphs' intelligence to the witch-queen. On the trunk of an uprooted tree, she sat with Bright Night, both staring quietly at the Vanir Lotus. The pale blue petals of the immense blossom glowed like ice, afloat upon its own reflection in a tarn of water black as molasses.

Peering into the giant flower, the travelers shared serenity with this elegant being and sat unmoving before it until the faeries arrived. Their gold-dust bodies dazzled in the whispering light. When Ygrane heard what they had to say, she stood up and turned away from the blossom of incredible loveliness. "Send the hobs down to the lower branches," she ordered quietly. "When Arthur climbs into the Tree, they will lead him here."

Bright Night pulled his gaze away from the huge flower. "And where are you going?"

The witch-queen kept her own counsel as she hurried toward the massive pillars of beechwoods where the black unicorn grazed on the tenderest shafts of sunlight. She ran and leaped upon its back, and no pain jarred through her. Since arriving in Yggdrasil, her menstrual cramps had dimmed away, her womb renewed even as her destiny drew to a close.

The faeries' news offered her a chance to help her son and possibly even save herself from the dragonpit. She commanded the faeries to lead her toward Home, the timber palace of heaven's king and queen.

Bright Night and his elves, perplexed at the queen's abrupt departure, rushed after her. Panic swarmed through them when they saw where she was headed, and they fell from the shining air, heavy with fright. Atop an alpine ridge just under the mountaintop aerie of Home, they waved frantically, signaling Ygrane to stop. She ignored them and heard their shouted curses as she flew on. Her death would deprive them of the power to wake the Dragon—and she was certainly a dead woman the moment she rode into sight of the Furor's Home.

The end of her bleeding had provoked her to take this stunning risk. The cycle of blood had completed itself in her body and in her life, and she knew that all that awaited her now was the dragonpit and her soul flung into the void. So, grimly she rode the unicorn to Home, a lodge of titanic cedars and oaks notched together and grouted with peat. Its roof was a turf sward broad as the sky and dotted with red cows.

She dismounted on the lawn and drove the unicorn and the faeries away with a strict command before hulking guards in bearskins seized her. From the garden door of Home, Lady Unique emerged. She had glimpsed the black unicorn through the window while standing at her herb-cutting table and, with a curved pruning knife in hand, stepped through the red frame door, wondering who dared trespass the chieftain's sanctuary.

"Lady Unique!" the witch-queen cried, throwing urgency into her voice and straining against the grasp of the guards. "I am Ygrane Morrígan, the witch-queen who has led the Daoine Síd into the World Tree! I am here for my son, Arthur, king of Britain, enemy of Wesc. Slay me if you must, but first hear what I know of the truth."

Lady Unique motioned the guards aside, and Ygrane flopped onto the sward and lay prostrate before the goddess, waiting for the knife or the word. *Let it be the knife,* she prayed, wanting to die so that her soul would elude the dragonpit and eternal exile from earth. She had helped Arthur all she could; soon, the hobs would guide him to the Vanir Lotus. She was ready to die.

Instead, came the word: "Rise."

The white-haired goddess appeared so full of simplicity in her plain gown of brown hunter's cloth embroidered with ferns and wood pigeons that Ygrane hesitated to affront her with what she knew. Then she remembered that her blood cycle was over, her pain was ended, and glamour and God's will had placed her before this sturdy Æsir goddess. She pushed herself to her knees and lifted above her head both her hands crossed at the wrist. "Were I you, goddess, I would want this knowledge brought to me—no matter the pain."

Lady Unique cast aside the pruning knife and took the mortal's hands in her own. In an eyeblink, all that Ygrane knew, the goddess knew.

A gasp escaped Lady Unique. Revelation and rebuke pierced her, and she stood unmoving, unspeaking, wildly awake, and feeling toward what had never been felt before. *Betrayal . . .*

She did not release the witch-queen's hands but lifted her to her feet. "You were brave to come to me." The Furor's wife smiled at the feral woman, gently, sadly. But the hard pulse at her throat betrayed her fury. "There is only one queen of heaven, and I am she. Though you have invaded Yggdrasil, stolen our memory beer, and blazed a path to the Vanir Lotus for your son, the foe of my husband, yet you have served me better than my own people, Ygrane Morrígan. You have shown me the truth of my husband's heart . . . the truth of his betrayal. For that, you shall have the good of my rage. Let your son drink of the protective lotus. Let the West Isles be denied the Furor for the lifetime of Arthur. And take that damnable sword Lightning with you when you go. It has seen more than I like."

Arthur stood alone beside Merlin in the glass-domed gallery at the topmost turret of Camelot. The king was dressed for travel; yet, he carried no flagon or provender satchel and neither hat nor cloak. Other than the gnarled cypress crutch that supported his silk-bound right thigh, he carried no weapon. Merlin had said that armor would not protect them in the Storm Tree and, without Excalibur, there was no useful weapon to carry.

Merlin, too, wore wayfarer's garb: bog boots, brown trousers crisscrossed with green thongs the length of his heron legs, and, as always, his bent wizard's hat. He looked morose. On the journey to Camelot from the hills of Cymru where Arthur had lost Excalibur to save an infant, the wizard had told him everything. He confessed the loss of the Dragon's teardrop to Selwa and the deception that had put Excalibur in the hands of Loki.

The king had said little in reply. The dragon flight had changed him. He had touched the one Dragon, the vast creature made of worlds, and he had glimpsed the endless instant that was the universe. Maelstroms of stars spun through the void, flying apart into eternal night. He had seen that. And he had *felt* the dreamsong. Harmonic energies connected fiery, magnetic worlds into a being so enormous that light crept for aeons over its cosmic body and never reached a boundary.

For a startling moment, Arthur had glimpsed his life speaking across the elements with all lives. Beings huge and minuscule floated as one in the black emptiness. The Dragon and the nameless child he had caught at the cliffside were the same living being. He upbraided the wizard for risking the baby's life, yet he carried no bitterness about the lost blade. The baby was worth any number of Excaliburs and all his kingdom, for God had placed him where he *could* catch her. His sword was just a weapon, his kingdom a place on earth. But she was the living body of the universe helpless before him.

And though it was Merlin who had tricked him into losing the magical blade, he could hold no real grudge against the wizard who had made him king.

"Broken waters heal themselves." He told that to disconsolate Merlin and was glad to be divested of his magic and closer to the simple humanity he knew he could trust.

The heartbroken wizard would not be comforted. He moaned about the loss of the teardrop and a squandered opportunity to trump the Æsir gods themselves.

Gods, dragons, magic swords . . . Arthur could not give his love to these supernal things, not after Morgeu. "Let Selwa have the teardrop." Arthur thought her treasonous theft was meet and just for a passion-addled wizard of an incestuous king. "We are not meant to have the teardrop. I will defend Britain with my life, not with magic!"

But Merlin had insisted they ascend into Yggdrasil anyway and make every effort to track down Selwa. For Britain, for the people God had given him to serve, and for his own brother Cei, Arthur relented. The sullen wizard led him past a marble pillar pale as moonlight and into its shadow, which cloaked a strait passage.

Three paces in, darkness opened into wincing brightness. Sunshine glared hot as silver off peaty pools and sedges lush as a jungle. Out of the worsted shadows, hobs scurried. Small demi-human figurines shorn up from a nightmare skittered silently through the rank pastures and marsh grass.

With the brails of his heart, Merlin received their message, and his heart soared. "Your mother has cleared a direct path to the Vanir Lotus!" He squatted and held his rooty hands over the squalid troupe of beasts with laughing faces. "They have seen Selwa! And they have misdirected her!"

Arthur's crutch sank in the loamy ground, and he could not keep up with frantic Merlin. So he stopped and sat on the lip of a wind-shaped rock. Hurt leg stretched out, he gazed upon Yggdrasil, a wild fen of holy beauty. Willow glades slouched like green lions. Out of the canebrakes, pelicans lifted heavily into an auburn sky where a pearl moon floated wrapped in its own bright shadows.

A black wind dropped out of the sky. It fell from the ruffling auroras at the zenith, from the Storm Tree's higher boughs. Arthur had no idea what he was seeing. Then a turbulent shadow plummeted into the tree-clad hummocks, and moss flew. Cypress crests trembled along its path deeper into the marsh.

It was Loki fleeing the demons that the Furor had set upon

him for stealing the dusk apples. He rushed upon Merlin, crying, "Help me, wizard! Help me, and I will atone!"

But Merlin did not hear him at once. He was running on a dwindling turf path, following the hobs into a tunnel of mangrove. When the black wind finally rolled over him, the startled wizard spun about with fright. Loki swung in the dark air like flayed butcher meat, his arms and shoulder bones hooked in the talons of Succoth, Nergal, and Thartoc.

Shock at the sight of the lizard-grinning demons elicited a barbarous shout from the wizard. His lash of power cut sparks from the demons' flinty hides, and they flew off shrieking, their gaunted prey wailing in their grasp.

They barged through the canopy, and, in the frenzy of their retreat, pulled down a flowery wall of hanging vines. On the pulpy trail ahead, Selwa hobbled frantically, the Dragon's heavy teardrop in her arms.

"Selwa!" Merlin yelled, his mind reeling at the sight of her. "Stop! Stop at once!" His alarmed cry startled winged snakes in the clerestories of the swamp, and they flurried and squeaked overhead like eelish bats. "The hobs have led you astray! If you go any farther, you will leave the Storm Tree and fall down the sky!"

Selwa shuffled faster. She would not listen to the wizard and be deceived. He had taught her how to open the lower gates of her body and touch the world outside her, and she had done that with the hobs. They *had* truly seen the Vanir Lotus. She felt the verity of it in the magic Merlin had given her. Was he fool enough to think he could stop her now with mere words?

So she pressed on, and Merlin watched helplessly as she shoved through tall feather grass and plunged into the blue void. Jet-stream winds snatched her away, and she flew in breathless terror across the curving horizon. Before she disappeared into the big sky above the azure Mediterranean and the umber mass of North Africa, the winged hobs lifted the Dragon's teardrop from her numb fingers. The stone orb rose toward the indigo zenith atop a spiral of feathered toads, wyverns, and goat-legged cherubs.

To the bough tip of Yggdrasil, the Síd returned, cackling like flames at their daring rescue of the teardrop. Merlin yanked the stone from their small and furry hands and stalked away. He was angry that they had not saved Selwa. He said not a word to Arthur at the wind-shaped rock or on the arduous climb that followed, letting his scowl speak for him.

Anger seethed in him for succumbing to base desire and letting Selwa close enough to learn enough magic to destroy herself. He felt sordid and mean. But there was no time or strength to punish himself. The lame king required all Merlin's help to struggle up the steep slopes. Arthur's wound had opened, and black blood seeped through the silk bindings.

Up moss stairs and bramble ladders, Merlin hoisted the Dragon's teardrop with Arthur's arm over his shoulders and his weight leaning into him. The wizard exploited all his supernatural strength to lug the strapping man along the narrow root-ledges. Even so, twice they slipped on the slick cliff steps and dangled by one arm above the lavender arc of the earth's atmosphere and the grinning mouth of the moon.

The hobs rescued the mortals each time their strength failed. They would have carried the king and his wizard to the crest if they could, but the Síd were more urgently compelled to watch for Æsir hunters. Arthur and Merlin followed as best they could. By the time they reached the tarn of the Vanir Lotus, they were both exhausted.

Merlin sat among ferns and serrate mushrooms, the Dragon's teardrop in his lap and his brow pressed against it. Inside the stone, Arthur had already caught his breath and gotten up from where he lay gasping on the soggy turf . . . he had already splashed through the sepia waters of the tarn, the Dragon's teardrop lifted above his head . . .

Arthur removed the iridescent sphere from under the sleeping wizard. Merlin had spent every spark of his power to carry the king to this height of Yggdrasil, and he did not rouse even as Arthur propped him more restfully against the bracken.

The young man cleared his throat, hoping that the wizard would wake, and he had to restrain himself from calling out his name. He wanted Merlin's guidance—yet, he sensed that even if he woke his counselor, he would be told to go on alone.

Mother Mary! he began to pray, wanting divine help with what lay ahead. But that was the small black heart of his pain. He could not pray. Not to Mother Mary. He had ridden dragons. He had raided the hollow hills and taken its prize. Now he coveted magic.

Arthur looked about at the wild garden of black ferns and saw the tarn paces away, its amber water still, broken by loops of roots like snake spines. The Vanir Lotus drifted above the havoc of the swamp very much like a cloud, its white petals blue with sky glow. He did not move toward it at once, because he feared it.

What he was about to do had no precedent in his faith or the annals of the Church. Was he defying God? Was he damning himself? He did not know. But he would commit himself to this magic in spite of his fears. He would not stop now even if an angel intervened and showed him the face of his soul in hell. Too much blood had been spilled across the obscene altar of war. If his soul belonged in hell so that magic could bring peace or even respite to his tortured realm, so be it.

Arthur pushed the stone and dragged his dead leg, limping and crawling over the soft ground and through entangled ferns. The water smelled vegetal and felt cold as it received him. He splashed onto his back, the Dragon's teardrop riding his buoyant chest, and he floated under root arches to the Vanir Lotus.

The large blossom drifted luminously on the black pool with Arthur sprawled atop its pad, his throbbing leg straight out. Silk bindings unraveled, exposing a wound like a tragic mouth.

Mother Mary! he called to heaven once more. *I am black with sin and shadow. I crave magic. I do not trust the Almighty to spare us without it. I do not trust—and so I take my kingdom into my own hands. Mother Mary, forgive me. How different am I than Lucifer, who trusts not God, only himself?*

Far down the Storm Tree, the Furor heard King Arthur's despair. The chieftain sat with his wife in the trophy hall of Home, on a bull-hide couch under the wares of the eternal hunt: skull cups, femur pipes, tapestries of scalps and skins. "Ragnarok!" Lady Unique spoke through proud tears. "Ragnarok, you cried. And I believed you."

The Furor listened inward more deeply, trying to catch again the British king's prayer.

Am I wrong to be here at all, Mother Mary? Arthur pulled himself through the white petals, and they tore in his hands and under the rolling weight of the rock, releasing a rampant scent of dew. *Is the magic of the Vanir Lotus a slander to God?*

"Vanir Lotus?" the Furor asked aloud. "What is the Vanir Lotus? What is the boy yammering about?"

"You will listen to me, husband!" Lady Unique seized the earlobe amulet on his vest, tore it loose, and cast it across the room. "You deceived me." Sorrow darkened her brow, though her gray eyes continued to stare icily. "I have always been honest with you, and I will honestly tell you now—you will forget the West Isles for the nonce and remember who we are together. Or we will not be together anymore."

"I trust our love is stronger than that," the Furor grumbled, and pushed away from the couch. "We will continue this when I return."

"Come back here!" she called vexedly. Under her glowering stare, he grabbed his lance and charged through the door. "Where are you going?"

"I don't know," he shouted back, which was true. Arthur's prayer had sounded full of echoes, his voice bouncing among the boughs, and that meant he had climbed into the World Tree.

The Furor called on his ravens to find the intruder, and black shadows rose through the Storm Tree like an enormous declivity of night.

Arthur noticed the sky darken and shivered with foreboding. He had crept to the center of the lotus, where a red stile taller than a man upheld a stigma blue as midnight. Nectar gleamed on the bright stamens, and a fur of white pollen covered the entire pistil. Glistening like a lovely, fragile snow garden, the core of the lotus seemed an unlikely maw into hell.

Mother Mary, pray for my forgiveness. I am afraid of magic and sin and burning forever in the pit. I am afraid. God have mercy on my soul.

Kneeling on his one good leg, he held the Dragon's teardrop above his head with both hands and tossed it into the center of the Vanir Lotus. It crashed among the delicate red stalks and filaments at the flower's core—and instantly dissolved like quicksilver.

Arthur ladled the elixir in his hands. Its shiny surface reflected his own singed face and gullies of stars in the violet sky above him.

He drank deeply. Bright trickles ran down his chin and splashed in beads and globules across his chest. The magical fluid coursed a cold path into his stomach, and chill energy spread swiftly through his torso.

When the frosty strength reached his heart, he gave himself

over to that power he had experienced upon the dragon's back—
the thread of a song weaving across diamond distances of stars,
connecting the most intimate in him with the most distant and
impersonal reaches of creation.

Magic soaked into every cell of his body, and serenity coursed
through him, circling back on itself into a deep peacefulness. He
slid off the lotus pad and reclined in the tannic water. Above him,
the Furor appeared in cloudsurges and thunderheads. Lightning tangled. But no thunder followed. The sun, strenuous as
an angelic guardian, turned the wind and shoved the Æsir god
aside.

King Wesc sat on a balcony terrace of the villa at Dubrae. He
observed the day climb down the white cliffs and dance sparkling
upon the salt sea, and the beauty of the day calmed his frustration. Across the Belgic Strait, the Foederatus tribes were dis-
banding.

Gory news from Caledonia of ten Pictish clans destroyed by
dragons had stunned the troops. And the retreat of blithering
King Cruithni to the remote and icy Orcades unsettled the other
lords. King Antor of the Jutes decided to winter in the southern
river valleys, while Ulfin of the Angles had already broken camp
and disappeared into the eastern forests.

Lady Unique had withdrawn her battle luck.

Why? The short monarch pondered this question in silence
all day. At nightfall, he clasped his hands over his head and
propped his elbows on the balustrade, kneeling before the altar of
the sky. *Is Arthur's magic so powerful, Lady? Or have I offended you?*
Why do you not answer me? Why do you exile me to silence?

No answer came. He knelt staring across the marble rail at
the eastern sea until Mars rose—the signal for the invasion of
Britain. A signal no one observed but him.

He sighed, calmly stood, and walked to his writing desk.
Quickly, he dashed a few short lines, a last poem. Then, returning to the balustrade and climbing onto the rail, he teetered a
moment on the edge. He was tempted to give himself to the
night and avoid the humiliations to come. One breath of the seawind and that temptation passed. He stepped down and tossed
the parchment over the rail.

The poem fluttered into the dark, disappearing on the scarp rocks, where rain and tide delivered it to the sea.

> *What is silence?*
> *It has left everything behind.*
>
> *Black's disciple.*
>
> *From its voice,*
> *mirrors.*
>
> *From its promise,*
> *music.*
>
> *From its memory,*
> *death.*
>
> *A forgetful prophet remembering*
> *now.*

Cruel Striker lay abandoned where it had fallen. Inside the metallic warrior, the Fisher King pulled himself awake, blood-slick, head ringing with invisible voices. The burning blade of Excalibur had cut through the visor, just missing his face, and the impact had pounded his head hard against the back of the helmet.

An irate woman's voice echoed in his skull: "Ragnarok, you cried. Ragnarok! Ragnarok!"

The Fisher King stared out through the gashed open mask at chromatic mists wafting by. He remembered that he had been striding out of a forest, following these spectral vapors to the Rainbow Bridge that would return him to earth. And then he remembered earth . . .

"Ragnarok is coming!" The angry voice of the invisible woman chanted mockingly. "Ragnarok is coming! We must stop the Fire Lords, you said. You convinced me that the fate of all time to come depended on stopping these Fire Lords. As if the future and the whole universe are ours to command! And I am the fool, because I believed you!"

The Fisher King ignored the bitter, strident voice. His mind opened into memory upon a burning field. He was a conscript for the king. Armed with a short sword and a sharp wooden pole, he charged terrified with his comrades into combat. He had never killed anyone.

"You said we had to take the West Isles," the voice started up again. "We had to drive the Romans out and make it our own. You insisted I help you, that I stay at Home and make talismans to strengthen your armies, which I did till my fingers bled! But all along, you were merely distracting me while you had your dalliances with that—that child!"

The low rumble of a man's voice replied to the wrathful woman, but the Fisher King heard it as distant thunder. His full attention fixed upon the battle-ax that swung out of the battlesmoke of memory. That was his last vivid recollection before waking here in this torn armor.

He was alive. His hand, greased with blood, slid free of its leather restraint, reached up, and touched his aching and bloodied head. He felt the starfish crown, and an ether wisp of a voice very much like his own called to him, "Awake husked of sin, you prodigy of suffering, and know you are the Fisher King as surely as pity rules heaven."

He pulled off the crown of starfish and dropped it like some venomous thing. He had heard the whisper of madness in it, and he did not want to remember any more of what had happened after the battle-ax struck him. He was alive now—and he would not succumb to madness.

"I won't listen to your excuses, your lies." The agitated woman's voice almost shrilled. "Am I your wife or is she? You have behaved like a lascivious Fauni, cavorting with a woman young enough to be your granddaughter. Are you a chieftain of the Wild Hunt or no better than a faithless animal in rut? I will have nothing more to do with your mad obsession. I want my children woken from trance at once. You will release those hideous demons and wake my children, or I will not speak with you again."

Cruel Striker lumberously stood, torn metal shrieking. The human rider within vaguely knew that these rainbow mists led home. With laborious effort, he lurched the armor through the grassy field of colorful fumes and toppled forward into a fiery dawn.

He hit the ground on his feet, landing in the middle of an empty roadway so forcefully that Cruel Striker burst apart around him and its pieces clanged on the pavement rocks.

A smoky dusk received him with a fine drizzle of rain, and he staggered away from the broken armor. A phantasm of man, grimed in blood, wild-haired, stinking of the fish skins that draped his bruised nakedness, he wandered into the gentle showers. He was home again.

Under gray slashes of dawn, he lifted his head to the cool, sweet rain and strode more strongly, refreshed by the wet wind. The invisible voices were gone, leaving his mind clear and his heart homelorn.

Ygrane rode the unicorn out of Yggdrasil with the sword Lightning in her right hand. Before her, the atmosphere blazed in a blue parabola against the black of space, and clouds swirled below like spider's milk. She called out for her homeland, for Cymru. Then sunlight caught on the mirror blade, and the witch-queen's trajectory blazed like a falling star across the night of Britain.

She landed at Camelot, coming down from the black spaces between the stars to land unseen atop the highest turret. The hobs opened the circular pane at the top of the glass dome, and the sylphs lowered her into the nightheld chamber. She stood Excalibur against the gallery's northwest pillar, where the rays of the rising sun would find it soon.

Bright Night's long green eyes gleamed forth from the nightshadows, and the prince of elves separated from the darkness. "It is time to take the Graal from Morgeu the Doomed."

Ygrane looked around at the weightless shadows and the mammoth stones that a human mind had married to this sacred space. No tapestries hid the mighty columns, no rugs masked the travertine floor. This was simply stone and the naked mind. Geometry made actual. The fantasy of the first people come into the world.

"You can delay us no longer," Bright Night insisted. "Come."

Ygrane nodded softly in agreement. She had accomplished all the deeds she had bartered for her soul: Christian Britain was protected from pagan invaders for a generation. That alone was worth her soul, she reasoned coolly. Excalibur belonged again to Arthur, and that in itself redeemed her exile from earth, for so long as her son wielded that weapon, he served the angels, the very Fire Lords who had first wrested it from the Æsir for her beloved Uther.

She did not resist when the sylphs wove over her like sea foam and lifted her up and out the circular window that the hobs then closed behind them.

"To the Graal," she said softly to the unicorn, and Camelot dropped away, a shining fruit into night's pocket.

Stars blurred. The dark earth flew below. An evil red eye blinked open, a volcanic vent on the desolate scree. The unicorn circled the glowing rock furnace, and Ygrane noticed two figures on the slag flats below. They wore satin head scarves pulled over their faces and capes of black canvas to protect them from the acid mist. The shorter one carried a gold chalice.

Out of the moonless sky, the Daoine Síd descended. Falling in golden flames shaped as winged claws, they alighted upon the rocky slopes. Gold flashes, malevolent flicker eyes, lunatic swipes of fire, giant shining paramecia and fluorescent red spirochetes whirling in rabid pandemonium surrounded the cloaked figures and pulled aside their scarves.

Morgeu's bright hair and pale round face reflected the magma glow from the vent, and she shone like a flame. Mordred, as well, his lank hair falling in eelish swerves over a sallow child's face.

The black unicorn stepped through the wall of whirling, elvish energies, and Ygrane rode atop it, her countenance aglint like gold flake. Faeries fluttered brightly around her, their wing beats staining the dark with an oily shine. "Give the Graal to the Daoine Síd, Morgeu."

"So they may return it to the king?" Mordred asked in a peeved voice. He turned about and angrily struck the chalice against a boulder, making the alloyed vessel ring brilliant echoes off the back of Ygrane's skull. "That will not happen," the little boy said.

"Who are you, child?"

"You do not recognize me, Grandmother?" Mordred showed crooked milk teeth in a wry smile. "Or should I call you *wife*?"

In that voice, Ygrane heard Gorlois's malice. "Mordred?"

Bright Night advanced from where the Síd had settled to crawling embers and molten rivulets among the plutonic rocks. "We will take the Graal from you, boy!"

"Come, take it!" Mordred dashed over cracked tiles to the upwind rim of a fiery chute. He stood underlit in crimson, arms upraised, fingers dangling the radiant cup above the pit. "Must I say your fate, prince of elves?"

"Stand away, Bright Night!" Ygrane called to him. "Stand away from the dragonpit!"

"The Daoine Síd are done obeying you, witch." Bright Night aimed a finger at the Holy Graal paces away, its curved gold breathing in the rippled heat. "Now we have the Graal, and you will obey us!"

Mordred wagged the chalice over the fiery shaft and chuckled. "I only suckled on elves' milk, and yet I can say your fate, elf prince. Shall I say it? You *are* this cup. Only this cup can buy you the soul that will wake the Dragon. This is your kingdom in a chalice."

"Back off, Bright Night!" Ygrane yelled. "Obey me!"

Bright Night recognized the mischievous glint in the boy's tiny black eyes, and he shot forward, a gust of green fire.

Mordred dropped the Graal into the dragonpit. It toppled flashing. And, mesmerized by its fateful power, Bright Night flew after it. If he grabbed it in time, Ygrane's soul was his, and the hobs would throw Mordred and his mother into the pit no matter what the witch-queen said.

But he did not grasp it quick enough. The Dragon was asleep, not dead, and its reflexive claws hooked him through his chest and yanked him into the earth faster than he could scream.

The Daoine Síd stormed in pursuit, skirling a banshee wail, convinced they could snatch their destiny from the Dragon's jaws. They surged past Ygrane, a tempest wind of twilight flames, and they poured into the steam vent in a blinding, fire-spun vortex. Gourd-lantern faces swung past, forests of tree spirits burning in their rush to seize the fallen Graal.

Mordred danced aside laughing, his hair flung out from his head like black solar rays, his face a gleeful moon.

Ygrane shouted again and again for them to stop, already far too late. The blood pact for the Graal, the enchanting command of a fire slayer, and the voracity of the planetary beast altogether doomed the Síd who had followed her this far.

The spinning column of fire wicked out, and darkness closed around a mephitic stink of fuming sulfur. The Dragon's magnetic fires had devoured all the elves and hobs. A few sylphs slithered away over the cracked earth, and a loose cloud of faeries littered downwind.

Morgeu clasped Mordred in her arms, and mother and son glared at Ygrane on her black unicorn. The magic had gone out of her with the annihilation of the Síd. Even so, the horned beast was dangerous, and they waited to see if it would throw her off.

Ygrane sat astonished, the unicorn under her stepping slowly backward. No flames gushed forth from the hellhole. No shrieks. The banshee wind simply died away across the rock fields, and night darkened so deeply she saw stardust and needle-streaks of light in the busy void.

Snow flurries dusted the brownstone battlements of Lindum on the December day that a raven delivered to Bors Bona a parchment strip in the king's code. Bors himself led a cadre of equestrian officers and a flight of archers into the wildwoods of Parisi, and they found under a hawthorn hedge the king and his wizard crouched beside a twigfire, sooty, cold, and starved as predacious ancestors.

The king smiled benignly at his men, his chin shadowed with the first whiskers of a beard. The wound of his leg had healed over whole and unblemished, and for the first time in many months he walked among his admiring warriors without a crutch, touching each of them on the hand and gazing into their eyes with the affection of a brother.

To his wonderment, the power of magic had transformed him, easing all his fears. And his joy was bolstered by news that Excalibur had mysteriously returned to Camelot and that same night Marcus Dumnoni had received the king's mother at Tintagel. Though she had looked like a beaten animal, she was sound and whole, and she had taken sanctuary in the abbey, confiding to no one anything about where she had been.

"Now the time of doubt is past." Merlin winked at Arthur, then embraced him. Softly, in the king's ear, he said, "Magic has healed you, and the poison you loathed has proven your medicine."

The wizard mounted a fleet stallion and departed at once, a lone rider for Camelot under the evening's pink rags of cloud. Selwa had broken his heart and had blithely stolen every hope from him—and Loki, true to his cognomen, had taken Excalibur without keeping his word and leading the way through Yggdrasil. Still—still! Arthur had delivered the Dragon's teardrop to the Vanir Lotus and had sipped at eternity!

While Merlin rode to Camelot to rally the engineers who would rebuild Britain, Arthur traveled south to Ratae, where his palfrey Straif had been stabled since the summer. She greeted him friskily, and he ordered her dressed for parade. Then he bathed in a steaming pool scented with gentians and outfitted himself in all his regal finery, from purple tunic and gold chaplet to an escort of lancer guards riding under full armor and unfurled banners.

Bors Bona cleared a path for the king through the city crowds and guided the royal company onto the highway. Black mantles streaming behind, Bona's swiftest riders raced ahead to move traffic off the road, and the king's lancers flew upon the boreal wind, steeds smoking, hoof falls bursting in the crisp air. They arrived at The Blanket of Stars under a triumphant flourish of horns, and Arthur rode Straif into the courtyard flanked by flag officers and Bors Bona in his gorgon mask.

Georgie knelt with slack-faced surprise before John Halt bedecked in majestic apparel. Leoba came backward down the stone steps of the portico, pulling a shawl around her father and grinning exultantly over her shoulder, "You! You were king all along. I said it from the first, didn't I?"

Arthur smiled warmly at the old man and his children. "And I never contradicted you."

"Eril is come back," Georgie announced, and wiped his ruddy nose with the back of his hand. "He come back last month, naked and beaten bloody. But he's sound, he is that—and with a story to tell."

Arthur's smile stiffened as his claim on Julia's heart collapsed. In one moment, his triumphant hope of happiness curdled to a sigh—a tuneless laugh of recognition at the justice of it. Angels could not have timed Eril's return more fittingly. She needed a man, and Eril was best for her now that the king was no longer worthy of this countrywoman's love or the comfort of her simple ways. He had drunk of dragon's tears and lotus honey and had become the very magic that he had sought to escape with her.

Flowers in her honey brown hair and her long shoulders squared proudly, Julia stepped smiling onto the portico and hugged Eril. Arthur nodded to the tall, clean-shaven man with the war scar on his brow. And he met kind eyes in a weathered visage handsome as a hawk.

Joy floated in the king. Though magic owned him now forever, there would always be this one household in his realm where simple happiness reigned.

The king lifted his sword and raised a cheer for the veteran come home. Banners and lances went up with a shout that startled crows out of the winter-bare orchard and made dogs howl. Through the jubilant noise, John Halt and Julia looked at each other briefly with eyes shining like cold starlight, and they shared a smile at life's inscrutable makings.

Why did we create this spell, our retelling of King Arthur's long-ago story and our news from Avalon, except to summon you? And why are you here except that you are a true magician, the one who unlocks this spell and hears our voice? You are the doorway of the eye's pupil and the gate of the ear into the infinite realm at the underside of the soul, where pi runs to forever.

We need your help.

If you can unlock spells, you can make spells. Make one for us. Make one for the first king among us, Arthur. He lived to provide a beacon of inspiration across a dark age. Yet, now that he is one of us, now that he sits upon a block-cut throne in our round hut on Avalon, he looks for you and cannot find you.

From where we are in Avalon, your age seems more a dream than a place. The electromagnetic haze from your time blinds us. Sometimes Arthur fears you might not even be there at all!

Will you take but a moment to convince him and us that you really *are* there in the radiance of the manufactured world—that you *are*. We would feel more certain of our own fate then, in this sudden and frightening world of binary magic and untold secrets. Are you there for us, now that the invisible and fierce angels have descended to earth and live among you—the angels of X rays and microwaves and electric radiations in every frequency? Are you still there, as we insist you must be, or—as King Arthur fears—have those angels devoured your souls?

To earth and other worlds among the haydust stars, the Fire Lords carried numbers and alphabets—the human dreamsong. Use these powers to create a spell that will touch the underside of the world, from where everything grows. Make it as simple as "I am." Or "I am hopeful." Or "I am a warrior of my own perilous order, fifteen hundred years after you, Arthur, and I am struggling in the kingdom of survival with love and honor and pity and pride and compassion and sacrifice." Or write him a joke. Record an observation of the invented world around you. That is magic. Use it to kick Lucifer himself in the butt with a few choice words. Comfort your king and the ancient queens. Let us know that we have not been entirely martyred to legend.

AFTERWORLDS

Who can open the doors of his face?

—Job 41:14

I

Return from the Dead

Out of the predawn dark on a spring day in anno Domini 492, Fra Athanasius strode from the forests of Cymru and into the hamlet of Cold Kitchen. The steep main street climbed before him lit solely by the lanterns of the bakery. At the crest of the street, beyond the hilltop chapel and the climbing highway immersed in night, Camelot's torchlit ramparts blazed from the northern uplands. He knelt to it as before an altar and offered to God his splendor of relief and pride at having escaped hell.

For hours he had hiked the hollow hills, yet months had passed in the world above. The Lyre gleamed directly overhead, Vega the hand of an angel plucking once again the music of springtime, as birdnoise lifted from the surrounding woods. He rose light-boned with amazement. All of creation had been created anew.

Plastered with damp leaves and streaked with ash, the scribe strolled grinning past the closed shops. He blessed with his makeshift electric wand the baker and the farmers setting up their vegetable stalls. When he stopped at the plaza fountain to wash the soot from his spectacles, several women filling amphorae recognized him from his visit to Cold Kitchen with Bishop Riochatus the previous summer. But they edged away from him, repelled by his pungent aura of brimstone.

He moved along, dazed with wind and stars and the fragrance of baking bread. On the slate steps of the chapel, he sat and watched dawn open over the hills of Cymru in cinnabar bands of thunderclouds. The rains had returned to Britain. He could smell the tenderness of the dew and knew that the land was fecund.

The baker and a fruit vendor brought him breakfast and stood back from his stink while he ate with vivid delight. Munching an apple and hot biscuits, he excitedly shared with the small gathering of early risers news of his triumph against the tormented souls of the damned.

An escort of lancers from Camelot arrived while early-morning light still glowed orange on the mountain peaks. They whisked the bedraggled legate away from the spellbound villagers, and he traveled to the fortress city in a carriage, his head out the window smiling into the brisk air.

He had been summoned for an immediate audience with the king—but was taken first to the baths. A Persian masseur scrubbed the stink of sulfur from the wanderer's bruised body, and tailors stood ready to fit him into any of the finest ecclesiastic garments at hand.

But Athanasius waved aside the brocade robes and put on a scribe's brown cassock instead. He knew that he had survived perdition not by his saintliness but by what little Merlin had shown him of the natural laws of the world, and he accepted as a blessing the scribal skills that had helped him grasp those sphinxian truths. Henceforth, he determined, he would keep to his place in God's creation, content as a scribe.

King Arthur awaited the papal legate in the main council chamber. The boy-king no longer looked so youthful, he noticed. Blond whiskers tufted his chin and the corners of his mouth, and his yellow eyes gazed at the world with a careworn clarity. He was seated at a long ebony table under the indoor rainbow called the Seven Eyes of God. To his right sat Cei, his burly form showing no visible signs of the dragonfire that had blistered him comatose. Bedevere leaned his one arm on the table and gazed impassively at the emissary, his gray, swordmaster's eyes steady and unreadable. And Merlin lurked well back in the alcove shadows.

Athanasius stood a long moment unmoving in the door, joy welling up to see these familiar people, these men he had mistaken for devils. Now that he had met true devils, he saw this king and his subjects for who they truly were: civilized Christians.

No, they were not dogmatically correct. They had succumbed to fallacies, each of them. The king consorted with a wizard, worked magic with his witch-queen mother, and bartered with gods and demons. Yet, what did that matter to Athanasius, who had witnessed the tillage of souls in the earth's deeps?

Arthur Rex was a true Christian king. Of this, the legate was certain. Who but an anointed king would put at risk his sanity, his very soul, to stand for Christ against pagan hordes, demons, and dragons?

Bishop Victricius's mission finally complete in his head and heart, Athanasius bowed deeply to the king. Not for another moment did Victricius's soul have to suffer in cold limbo! Athanasius walked directly to a tray of reed pens under the rainbow canopy.

Without taking even a moment to seat himself, he began drafting a missive to the Holy Father in Ravenna declaring Britain worthy of inclusion in the kingdoms of Christendom. Done, he shoved the document into the center of the table and placed atop it his wand of magnetic stone coiled in silver wire. Standing back, he met Merlin's approving gaze and said through his grin, *"Scientia!"*

II

The Finding of the Dead

At midsummer, King Arthur and Bedevere returned to The Blanket of Stars one final time, alerted by a report from Bors Bona of brigands in the region. The villa, they learned, had been torched, reduced to blackened ruins.

The sight of the charred rubble faintly steaming in the rain shocked the king all the more after riding across his green kingdom and seeing so many of the old Roman estates thriving. Arthur sat numbly on a big chestnut roan, the hood of his mantle thrown back and his squeezed-shut face lifted to the cold points of rain. He listened to a muddied officer report the finding of the dead. Julia and her Eril, Leoba, Georgie and their father—all of them—had been beaten, hacked with swords, and burned.

The murderers were not Wolf Warriors but Britons. Bona's men had caught the pillagers as they had ridden from the blaze howling with blood frenzy. The king reviewed their bodies where they had been hanged from the boughs of the highway trees. They were the same five brigands he had expelled from The Blanket of Stars a year ago.

Arthur moved slowly down the highway, away from the place of horror. After riding in silence for over a league, he waved Bedevere to his side, and said grimly, "It was vengeful murder. They came back because we didn't kill them."

"Do not blame yourself, sire." Bedevere glanced behind, glad to see that the king's archers followed on this gloomy road. "If not for you, that gang would have slain them all when first they came to the inn. You gave Julia the time to find her husband and know again a measure of true happiness."

"So that he could be brutally slain as well."

Bedevere kept his silence before this fateful fact, then after a respectful moment said, "Perhaps, my lord, the prosperity you have won for us will allow the Warriors of the Round Table to ride through the entire kingdom. We will hunt down every woodland gang and highway brigand. That would be worthy mourning for Julia and her family."

Arthur made no reply. Neither did he offer an inward prayer. The black images of the dead fire—a tarry rib cage and wandlike bones in the ashes—lay still and final in his mind. God would not change them nor lift them from his memory. He continued on silently, carrying a great emptiness. The pyre had destroyed a horrible error inside himself, that the good would take him in— and his kingdom as well—and protect them all.

Evil endures.

He turned his attention outward, to the veils of rain upon the pines and incense cedars of the far hills. In his life as orphan, thrall, warrior, wanderer of worlds, and king, he had seen too much cruelty and death. And he had learned that God let it all happen, again and again. Every death was simply an end, and there was no story—unless the living told it themselves. Perhaps, he thought, that was why God had made the living, to tell the stories of the dead.

He wiped the rain from his face, and the story he told himself as he rode beneath the dripping trees and a sky gray as nothing was this: *Evil endures—but good will prevail.*

For the soul trapped in its cage of hours, there is nothing but hope.

And that is why, Good is a lengthy and complex story. But the telling of it is a beautiful thing.

III

An Angel Crosses Europe
in A.D. 492

In the rose garden at Tintagel, Ygrane sat on a stone bench graven with dryads. Her white habit and ivory robes glowed almost blue in the early-morning light. Since returning to the castle in the winter, she came every dawn after lauds, past the lily pond and through a colonnade of poplars, to these trellises of white roses enclosed by beech and sycamore. And she prayed. She prayed for the Daoine Síd.

The black unicorn watched her from behind a sycamore. Every morning it was there, a remnant of night. Why did it not return to the dark fields above the moon? Her magic had vanished with the pale people, and she had no bond with the unicorn. Still, it lingered, watching her pray for the Síd.

The elf prince and his spectral hosts were part of the dream-song now, exiled from earth and flying into the eternal night where they had intended to send her. For good or ill, what they had wanted from her, they had achieved: Hot springs across the land percolated more vigorously as the Dragon stirred, roused by the massive infusion of power from the devoured Síd.

Ygrane felt humbled by the many deaths. She had turned her back on God, and the friends of her childhood, her protectors and guides, were gone from this world forever, taken away by God's left hand, the sinister hand of fate. She prayed over this pain. She prayed to be forgiven for all the grief from her deeds as a witch-queen.

Her grandsons, Gawain and Gareth, had ridden off last autumn to find their mother's illusion, the false chalice, the Grail, and they had never returned. Rumors arrived at Tintagel of the boys' heroic deeds, true champions of Christ, slaying dragons, routing brigands, and working among the most impoverished. She did not know if these stories were true. The few faeries that remained did not bring her news.

She thought sometimes of using the unicorn to find her grandsons. Perhaps that was why the sleek shadow animal came each morning, to remind her that God had provided for her another way to touch the world than as a nun. But she had promised Duke Marcus she was done with witchery. The duke was afraid of her, afraid for his soul, and allowed her return to the abbey of Tintagel only that he might retain the favor of her son.

She looked across the garden at the sycamore and lifted her hand to shoo the unicorn away. But it was not there. Instead, before the gray-barked tree stood a youth in a white tunic. He had a blond, Persian face, kind and handsome, and golden curls spilled over his shoulders.

"Good morning, Ygrane." Sunshine blew like draperies between them, and he was instantly beside her. "May I sit with you?"

"Who are you?"

"I am an angel."

"I have met angels."

"I am a fallen angel." He held up fingers that were melted, smoking candles, and the reek jolted Ygrane upright. "I have spent most of the past year loitering outside Camelot singing a Jericho chant. By now, Wesc should be sitting on the British throne, not tilling beets and cabbages on a Baltic farm. You thwarted me, Ygrane. That lotus magic—it's good. I can't break it, hard as I've tried."

"Get away, Satan."

"Please, don't be formal. Call me Lucifer."

Ygrane leaned away disdainfully. "Why are you here, mocker, scoffer, slanderer of God?"

"You thwarted me, *witch-queen*." His smile widened to his ears, revealing rows of needle-pin teeth. "And now you think you can put on a habit, kneel down, and I won't see you? I have noticed you, Ygrane."

"That is nothing to me."

"There are darksome places in this world." He placed a sandaled foot on the edge of the bench and bent forward, smirking. "I am a creature of light and can find my way through the dark. But you, dear woman—" An eel-length of tongue licked the folds of her habit. "You are but some brevity of being. Will you spend what time is left you in misery, taunted by demons? Or will you kneel before me here and now and be exalted?"

"No. And no." Ygrane placed thumbnail and middle finger to her teeth and whistled.

For that one instant, as Lucifer abruptly realized he had positioned himself for the unspeakable, his arrogance slipped into fear, and she glimpsed a sacred memory in his beautiful face, a recollection of submission. Then, the black unicorn slashed through the trellises, roses bursting, petals driving like snow. Lucifer twisted a startled look over his shoulder, and the spiral tusk struck him from behind.

The demon flew into the sky, into a blue abyss of pain. Flung by the full force of the unicorn, he arced high into the atmosphere, far above the Belgic Strait, through cliffs of cloud. He peaked somewhere over the war camps of Clovis and the battlefields of the fierce Alamanni in Gaul.

Assiduous pain followed him during his long plummet past the snow peaks of the Alps and the crumbled arches of Rome. Somewhere across the Mediterranean, among the shattered rocks of prophets' tombs and dunes crouching like lions, he crashed to earth and bounced like an antelope in love.

When he came to rest, he sat stunned in the rocks and dust. For many years afterward, he simply sat there, staring at his shadow as it crawled around him in the dirt.

Like a gown discarded by the naked sea, Avalon lies rumpled on the horizon. The isle's green folds of hills and valleys disclose creeks and brooks gleaming their snakepaths through clustered groves of apple. Menhirs—monumental posts of unhewn stone—stand in spirals and rays on the hillcrests.

Your watchful mind moves closer, and the morning knolls and dells become mountain cups of apple trees. On the high, verdant promontories, waterfalls cascade in quicksilver threads that never reach the ground, blowing away from the craggy cliffs in wild vapors and broken rainbows, disappearing in the air like a story that brims into nothingness on the book's last page.

A. A. ATTANASIO is the author of *The Wolf and the Crown*, *The Eagle and the Sword*, *The Dragon and the Unicorn*, *Solis*, *Kingdom of the Grail*, *Hunting the Ghost Dancer*, *Wyvern*, *Radix*, and *The Moon's Wife*. He lives in Hawaii.